the
TWO

BOOK TWO OF THE ALIGNMENT SERIES

the
TWO

KAY CAMDEN

THE TWO

Editing by Jennifer Wingard
Photography by Keith Lee Studios
Cover art by Damonza
Book interior design & typesetting by Bookery

ISBN-10: 0-9910044-2-6 (paperback)
ISBN-13: 978-0-9910044-2-3 (paperback)
ISBN-10: 0-9910044-3-4 (eBook)
ISBN-13: 978-0-9910044-3-0 (eBook)

For more information about Kay Camden go to kaycamden.com

the
ALIGNMENT
SERIES

CHAPTER 1

TREY

MY GRAVEL DRIVEWAY has never been a more welcome sight. There's too much road and not enough home between Virginia and Montana. Beside me, Liv looks as spent as I feel. We descend through the conifers, the mountain snug around us. River dashes from the woods and circles the car with a warning that's become far too common lately: we have a visitor.

I stop the car. "Someone's here."

"No…" Liv puts her face in her hands.

I glance at River again. She's not satisfied I understand her. After a pointed look in my direction, she hightails it toward the house, expecting me to follow. "Something's not right."

Christian's white Infiniti is parked out front, partially in the grass like he drove up fast.

"That's Christian's car. I probably shouldn't be relieved." I hope he lets me get some sleep before he breaks my nose. After what I said to him, what I did, I deserve it. Maybe Liv can talk to him. She's the one with all the common sense.

"He beat us here?" she says.

I compared him to his father. There's no worse insult in our world. "We stopped in Chicago."

"Be good." She lays her hand on mine. It's cool on my skin. Her eyes are a sleepy, faded blue. She's let her hair down. It puddles against her back, slightly messed from being in the car so long.

"I will." I'll just let him talk. Keep my own mouth shut. Tell him I was out of line, I was caught off guard, I thought he wasn't— "Shit."

"He'll understand."

"He drove his own car, which means he's going to stay awhile. Let's go in, I'm dead tired."

There's no sign of him inside so we go out back. He's at the far end of the porch. He turns when he sees us. Liv follows me out and closes the door behind us.

When he looks at me I get a jolt. I hardly recognize the guy I grew up with, my cousin who's more like a brother. His clothes are well-slept-in. Bloodshot eyes with dark circles. I'd swear he was drunk but he's standing too straight. Too rigid. I saw him a few days ago. This is not the same guy.

"Trey, god Trey. I can't..." He presses both palms against his eyes, digging in, as if to clear them.

"What?"

Instead of looking at me, he looks at Liv. Then pulls a gun from the back of his pants and aims straight at her.

"Trey, god, I have these compulsions, and I can't…I'm so sorry."

"Christian. You don't have to do this. Give it to me. I can help you." I'm too far away to get it from him, and he has the damn thing trained on her like he means it.

"No you can't. Fuck! You can't!"

I gauge the distance between us. Set my feet. If I go for him he could pull the trigger, but it looks like he's determined to pull it anyway. "Christian."

He pulls the trigger. It's going off again as I lunge, screaming Liv's name because she's my world and it's all about to end. I slam into Christian; my shoulder goes through the porch railing. There's a surge of magic around us, hot and fuzzy, sparking in my head, too powerful to be mine or his but maybe they've combined. I twist Christian's arm, forcing him down until he drops the gun. I kick it across the porch. He's apologizing like it's his life at stake, but there's no time to talk. One blow to the back of the head knocks him out cold, then I run to Liv and fall to my knees at her side.

The force of the bullets has spun her and thrown her back several feet to the porch floor. Her hair is splayed like a dark animal pelt on the decking. A dead thing. No—not dead. Can't be dead. Not my Liv.

I roll her limp body onto her back and brush her hair off her face. Check her pulse—it's there. Breathing is too, but faint. Blood runs from her nose. I unzip her jacket, searching for the bullet wounds. Forty-caliber rounds fired at close range, but where the hell are they? I jerk her jacket down below her shoulders, trying to breathe, trying not to think about how this is the second time I've had to do this because of *them*. The family who raised me. The family I need to destroy.

But there's no evidence she's been shot. No wounds, no blood, no torn fabric. I roll her to her side and yank her jacket off to find her back is clear too. I stop to take a breath and look at Christian, crumpled and unconscious. Did I hallucinate? No. I know what I saw. He aimed straight at her chest and fired. I was right here.

I reach for the button on Liv's jeans to check her legs, but something catches my eye. Three bullets glint in the low light, lying on the floor between Christian and Liv. I scoot over on my knees to pick one up. The smashed tip looks like it hit a concrete wall. This is impossible, but I know a lot of impossible things have happened lately.

Clothes rustle, and my head jerks toward Liv. She exhales. I return to her side.

"Liv?" I try to keep my voice level as I wipe blood from her nose with my sleeve. Time is running out. If she doesn't wake up soon, I know I'll lose it. And I'll take no responsibility for what I do.

With my hands flat on either side of her, I lean over her face, watching for any sign of assurance. Just give me something, anything to show she's okay. Time is almost out.

She exhales again. Her eyes flit back and forth under closed eyelids. I want to say her name but my body has turned cold and immobile.

Her eyelids flutter and open a crack. "Ow," she whispers.

"Tell me what hurts."

"My hand." She raises her balled fist to me as her eyelids squeeze closed.

"Your *hand*?" I take her fist but she has a white-knuckled grip on something. Prying up one finger at a time, I see scorched skin already blistering, as if she stuck her whole palm into a roaring fire. With her hand open, the object falls to the floor, and I pick it up. The amulet.

The metal is charred, the design barely visible. I stare at her open hand, at the burned outline of the amulet's design on her palm.

Liv gasps. "Is Christian okay?" She tries to get up, and I help her sit.

"He's fine. Nothing else hurts?"

"My head—bad headache." She wipes her nose with the back of her hand then notices the smeared blood on her skin. "But I think I'll live."

When I don't react, she gives me a reassuring smile that ignites an explosion of relief and leaves me weak. I pull her against me and bury my face in her hair.

"Trey, I can't breathe." Her voice is muffled against my chest. I release her and hold her out to look at her.

"How did you know?" I show her the amulet. She'd brought it with her but couldn't have known she'd need it. Coincidence, maybe? Destiny?

"I didn't. I guess I was still holding it." She shrugs. There's a scratch on her forehead. This is the last time her blood will run because of them. I swear it. She places her good hand on the floor. "Help me up."

I stand with her, settle her on her feet, and guide her to the sliding door.

"What about Christian?" Her sky-blue eyes fill with worry.

"I'll come back out for him once you're inside."

In the kitchen, she lowers herself into a chair while I wrap some ice in a towel. She takes it in her fist, and I dab the blood off her face.

"The bullets didn't hit me at all?" She tugs her shirt collar down to examine her chest.

"It's like you had a shield…" I can't believe it.

"I guess now's a good time to thank you for the amulet."

All I can do is stare at her. There are no words.

"My head." She cradles her face and lowers it to the table.

I sit to take another look at her palm. "Looks like a burn. Don't move." In the cabinet I find a jar of aloe vera, and I grab the gauze.

"I see the roles have reversed," she says into the table when I apply the aloe vera.

"This will never happen again." I knew better than to let my guard down. There's no comfort at home, no comfort anywhere. Christian's car being here isn't something I can blindly accept as a casual visit. It doesn't matter if he's like a brother to me; anyone can be compromised by them. I walked us straight into a trap. Never again. From now on, I can trust no one. Not Christian, not my mother, not even my twin sister. If the Moores can get to Christian they can get to anyone. The only person in the world I can trust now is Liv.

Once they find out she's pregnant with the baby destined to destroy them, they'll load every weapon they have.

With her hand bandaged, she lifts her head from the table and my mind vividly displays what would have happened if she hadn't had the amulet. If I'd never given her the amulet. If she hadn't found it in her purse at the exact moment she did. Right now, I'd be holding her dead body in my arms. How many people would I have to kill to avenge her? The entire world.

I lead her to the couch, help her lie down, and spread a blanket over her. "Stay," I say, and she nods and closes her eyes.

In the basement, I load two guns, stick one in the back of my pants and take the other to Liv. She tucks it between the couch cushions and closes her eyes again.

Christian is still in the same spot outside. His fingers I broke a few days ago jut at abnormal angles as if I just broke them all over again. Liv can set them when she feels better. If I try to do it now, I'll probably end up making them worse. I heave him up by the arm, get my shoulders under him. I carry him past Liv, down the hall, and into the bathtub. He doesn't flinch when I turn the cold water of the shower on full blast.

"Please tell me you're not going to torture him," Liv says when I settle onto the couch under her legs.

"I can't. Because I am." From her expression, I can tell she doesn't take me seriously. But I'm not kidding. He's in for a wild ride.

"You wouldn't."

"It's for his own good." And ours. If I don't purge whatever caused him to turn on us now, we'll never get him back.

She sighs. "Was I crazy to think we were coming home to peace and quiet?"

"We'll never have peace and quiet."

"I think I finally get that now."

My head hits the back of the couch, but I'm careful not to give in to the fuzziness of sleep closing in fast. After that long drive back to Montana, I expected to take it easy for a while. But I have a lot of work to do tonight. A doze is only going to make it harder.

"Are you sure you're okay?" I look back at Liv's face to better gauge her reaction, hoping she understands what I'm asking. I don't want to be one of those guys. Always freaking out about the safety of his unborn child.

"Yes, just fine. Both of us."

As usual, nothing gets by her. "I'm going to have to leave you alone for a while."

She rolls to her side and pulls the blanket to her chin. The contents of Christian's pockets on the coffee table catch my eye, and I almost laugh out loud. Phone, wallet, and car keys would've been soaked by now if he hadn't emptied them before Liv and I got home. He's always had all the good luck.

I return to the bathroom. Looks like I'll need something stronger than cold water for his wake-up call. I turn off the shower and feel for a pulse. Good, I didn't kill him.

In the basement, I select several books and flip through them in search of the strongest cleansing effect I can find. Christian's resilience while under their influence proves how much he can handle, and my effect has to be stronger than all of theirs. I finally come across a real nasty one. He'll hate me for this, but it has to be done.

With the two jars of compounds and my notes of the spoken spell, I go upstairs and find Liv sound asleep. In the bathroom, Christian still shows no sign of life. I wave the smaller jar I prepared under his nose. He coughs and twists away. His arms flail, his legs shuffle, and his eyes blink open. He starts to sit up.

"Oh no you don't. Open up." I press my palm against his forehead, holding his head against the wall. He squirms, so I dig my fingers into his forehead and hold the larger jar against his mouth. After he swallows it all, I hold my hand over his mouth, pull the notes out of my pocket with my free hand, and read the words aloud. When I release him, he jerks forward, gripping the side of the tub with his good hand.

"What the hell, you know this isn't my fault!"

I swallow my guilt. Finding a more humane way to get him clean will take time we don't have. He needs this poisonous magic out of him now. He should know I don't want to do it this way, even though I tried to kill him a few days ago. I need to stop trying to kill the people I love.

"This is the only way to get you back to normal. You know that."

"I don't know what you're talking about."

"You'll know soon." He's still under the influence of whatever they did to him. It's hard to determine how much he understands.

"Shit! What's up with the cold shower anyway?"

"All part of the fun."

"You going to help me up, or what?"

"Nope. You have to stay there for a few minutes."

"Dude, you have to fix my fingers. I swear to god—"

"Do I look like a doctor?" I'm sure I look more like a sadist right now.

"What about Liv? Isn't she a nurse?"

"You're not in the position to be asking her for any favors."

His eyes roll back into his head, and I catch him by the neck before his head smacks the tile wall. Finally. A conversation with him is the last thing I need right now.

Good thing Liv is still asleep so I don't have to answer any questions while I slip into my heavy coat and tug on a sock hat. I head back into the bathroom and throw Christian over my back as I did before. This is going to be a long night. He seems much heavier soaking wet.

Outside, the cold fall air taunts my guilt. I focus on my path and try to think of the best place to go. The sound of the river drowns my thoughts, and I follow it to the third curve then turn straight into the woods. He gains fifty pounds as the ground rises in elevation, and when I've had enough, I drop him to the ground to catch my breath.

The guilt returns, but I shove it away. Everything my mother taught us will save him from freezing or starving to death out here. He'll also be able to find his way back to the house. Soon he'll be awake and I'll be gone. He'll have to remember all of it himself. And when he does, he'll reconnect with the real Christian and recognize that Moore spell for the pollutant it is. He'll cast it out, and he'll be clean. Moore family tricks can't exist in a mind full of Bevan magic.

River and Liv's dog find me. I scratch River's ears and try to remember what we named Liv's dog. It was something really stupid. Tributary. That was it, in homage to River.

"Trib," I say aloud, and he looks at me. Trib it is.

It seems fitting they've buddied up. River needed a pack mate—she was too much of a loner. Just like me. It seems we both have a pack mate now. Remembering Liv alone in the house, I'm propelled to my feet. I throw Christian over my back again.

"Go back to the house and keep guard," I say to River, and they both run off, eager to help.

I wonder if Christian knows we aren't related by blood. I wonder how much he knows at all. He's probably as much in the dark as I was. As soon as he's better, I'll tell him everything. Arm him with as much knowledge as I can because the more he knows, the easier it will be for him to fight them. *If* he gets better, that is. If he doesn't, well, I don't know any other way to fix him. This rude reawakening is the only way he'll reconnect to reality, to the things my mother taught him. It's a sadistic method but it's all I've got in my limited time. How many of them would I have to kill to avenge *his* death? It'd never seem like enough.

Whether he lives or dies, they need to be brought to their end. I'll have to figure out how to keep Liv safe here by herself for a few days so I can return to Virginia and finish them off. There's too much risk taking her there again. The first time was a lesson I'm grateful for. I can't forget how much I have to lose now.

Fatigue hits me thirty minutes later, and I know if I don't stop now I'll never make it home. I drop Christian on the ground and turn around without looking back. Even I'm lost now, so I look to the sky, trying to make out some of the stars behind the clouds to find my bearings. If the clouds get any heavier, he won't have a fighting chance. By the time

I reach my curve of the river, my feet feel like they're dragging giant ruts in the earth with my weary tread.

Gunshots pop in the stillness just before a wave of adrenaline blasts through me. Damn them. I can't even leave for an hour without them going for her. I take off in a sprint, ripping off my sock hat so she can recognize me as I get near the house. I sprint around the property in a wide circle for the best sight, and as soon as the front yard comes into view I see the guy limping around the other side of the house.

He's already injured, probably from Liv's gunshots. I'll have to convince her to give up her aversion to killing them. Hearing me, he turns. I charge him. He dodges. I catch his shirt, spin him, grasp his shoulders with one arm and snap his neck with the other. He falls to the ground with a dull thud.

I roll him over with my foot to make sure he's dead. I'll have to dispose of the body later. Now, I need her. And then sleep.

CHAPTER 2

LIV

I OPEN THE DOOR for him and he walks into me, dissolving my impending words with his embrace. Something feels strange about him, a droop to his normally solid frame, so I push away to look at his face. It reminds me of the night on the bluffs he came into my mind and taught me all those things.

"What did you do?" This degree of fatigue is rare for him.

"Took a walk." He stoops to untie his boots.

As I watch him shrug out of his coat, my panic from waking up in an empty house rushes back to me. The intruder only magnified my fears—Trey overpowered,

Christian killed, and one man sent back to finish me off. "Where'd you go?"

"Took a long walk." As if that clears it all up.

"In the middle of the night?"

"I had to take Christian for a walk."

"Where is he?"

"He'll be back."

"What did you *do*?" I repeat, with new meaning.

"He's fine. Don't worry." He takes my hand, flips off the light, and drags me into the bedroom.

He fumbles out of his clothes. It's rare to see someone nodding off while upright. I need his definition of "fine" but if I smack him awake for questioning I doubt he'd even feel it.

"Don't ever do this again," I say, my words falling on deaf ears as he gathers me under the covers and kisses me, breathing in deeply. He's asleep before our lips part.

Nuzzling into his neck, I try not to think about Christian or the man who came for me tonight. Or all the other men who will be on their way to kill me in the coming days, months, possibly for the rest of my life. As I turn over within the circle of his arms, I glimpse the early light of morning through the window and fall asleep to the rhythm of his breath against my hair and the pulse of his heart against my back.

The angle of light coming through the window tells me it's late morning. My back feels sweaty from being pressed up against him all night. I slip out from under his heavy arms and kneel on the bed to look at him. I kiss his cheek and his lips and hop down just before his sleepwalking arm captures me.

I head outside to the flat field of clover past the farthest row of the garden where the cold frames sit closed. The ground is hard and dewy, and the trees stand tall all around me as if this small plot of land was simply scraped out of a thick pine forest. Although the river is close, I can't hear its babble. I wonder if it got cold enough to partially freeze overnight. The warmth of the sun cuts through the crisp morning air in stubborn determination, clinging to the last shred of summer. Seasons change hastily in Montana, something I heard that I now experience. And the change in temperature between day and night can be a bit jarring. With my muscles stretched and eager, I throw myself into a rigorous gymnastics routine, completing moves I haven't attempted in months. I shed layers of clothes as my muscles warm up and the day warms around me.

When the sun reaches its pinnacle in the sky, I take a seat on the ground for some deep breathing. An earsplitting whistle shatters my concentration. Shielding my eyes from the sun, I spot him on the deck. He's high up and too far away for me to see his expression, but I already know I'm in trouble. I gather my discarded clothes. His eyes are on me the entire way back to the house.

I climb the stairs and walk confidently into his accusatory glare, sliding my arms around him. His arms remain at his sides, stubborn and unwilling to return the affection. He must not know what all his great muscle tone can do to a woman.

"Are you trying to get yourself killed?"

"You smell so good."

"Don't change the subject." He grabs my shoulders, holding me away from him, but the irritated expression doesn't hold. Something's captured his interest. He brushes my bangs off my forehead and stares at a spot just above my eye.

"What?" I ask.

"That scratch from yesterday. It's gone."

I touch the spot above my eye, fingering for the evidence of a scab. Then I remember my burned and blistered palm, an injury that should've been painful under the impact of such a workout. Opening my palm reveals new pink skin. No trace of a burn, not even a scar. My eyes quickly meet his.

"It's in you now." His eyes brighten. "My immortality. It's inside you."

"With her?" If Trey transferred his immortality to our child as it was designed to be passed, then as long as she's inside me, my body must be immortal as well. "Bonus," I say, smiling up at him.

His face hardens. "Doesn't matter. You still have to be careful."

"Oh, please." I turn away.

"So you're reckless now, too?"

"Like you?" I laugh, remembering our conversation when I called him reckless. "Hopefully not."

"I'm going to have to make some rules. You can't just leave the house like this, flaunting yourself in front of them, oblivious to everything around you."

"Oblivious?"

"You didn't even notice me."

"If you'd been a threat, I'd have noticed."

"Would you have?"

I give him my weariest of sighs. If he's going to be like *this* now—

"You're pregnant."

"And immortal, apparently."

"There's a limitation to that. You can only heal if healing is possible."

"That never seemed to slow you down when you were immortal."

He looks away, exhaling hard. "We're talking about you. You're their target now. They're after something much more important from you than they were from me."

"You think they're not going to be after you anymore? Now they know they can kill you. With you gone, getting to me will be easier."

"I'm not arguing with you about this. Stay in the house. From now on."

And I'm not arguing with him either. He can make all the rules he wants. This is yet another temper tantrum, a clumsy grasp to find control when his world has been flipped. I'll just have to wait until he can settle in. Acclimate. Become rational. Okay maybe expecting rational is a bit much. "Are you going to tell me what you did to Christian?"

He gives me a long look then slides open the glass door and waves me inside.

"Just tell me so I don't have to worry."

He snorts. "If I tell you, you'll worry more." He leaves the room.

I stand at the back door, looking out across the land, wondering where Christian is and if he's okay. I doubt he knows these woods like Trey does. Maybe Trey took him to my house, to keep him away from me. On foot, so he wouldn't have easy access to a car. Unfortunately for Christian, I think the only thing to eat at my house is canned tomatoes. With no can opener.

"It's a cleansing effect." He steps back into the kitchen, toweling his head dry. "With a twist. I gave him something to purge his system. Then dropped him off in the middle of nowhere with nothing but the clothes on his back."

"My god, Trey, he was soaking wet. Why?"

"To help him reconnect with the Bevan side of him. The Moores have suppressed it somehow. It needs to become dominant again."

"How long are you going to wait before you go for him?"

"I won't need to." He can be so arrogant when he thinks he's right. "Now you'll understand why he's so pissed off when he gets back."

"You were right. You shouldn't have told me. What if he shows up when you're not around and tries to kill me again?"

"He won't try to kill you again." He looks out the window. "We need to do another mind sharing effect. I need to teach you my language."

Another mind share with him is tempting, but I doubt learning his language will do me any good. Yeah, his adoptive family will no longer be able to talk over my head, but our best strategy is to never encounter that family again. They'll kill us on sight. I do hope to see his mother again, and I'm sure I will. She's a Bevan, part of his real family.

She did shame him for not teaching me Irish. Maybe that's his motivation.

"Why does your mother call you by your middle name?" I ask.

He shrugs. "Never thought to ask her."

"Tara and your grandmother must call you that because your mother does. But Christian and Kate and all the Moores call you Trey. And you call yourself Trey."

"It's just easier. Imagine how often I'd have to spell Fearghus."

"She must call you Fearghus because it was your real father's name."

A silence drags out before he speaks. "Maybe."

"What was your real father's last name?"

His eyes shift to the back door behind me and glaze into that pensive look he gets when he falls into deep thought. "Tara didn't tell me," he answers after a few moments, still staring outside. "I'm going to unload the luggage from the Camaro. Pack some stuff you want to take to your house. We can take a load over."

"Shouldn't we stay here in case Christian—"

"Christian knows how to let himself in."

I watch the door close behind him and wonder what he's going to do if Christian doesn't come back. How long will he allow him to stay out there by himself before going after him? How will he even find him? The weather is unseasonably warm today, but what if it freezes tonight?

One thing I know for sure—we are not sleeping at my house tonight. We're staying here, to be here if Christian comes back. At least, I know I am. If he's going to be an arrogant ass he can sleep at my house by himself. He can't make me sleep there with him. Actually, he probably could, but I'm not going to let him know I know that.

The front door opens, and our luggage lands in the entryway. The spell packets in the gun bags have lost their fragrance. The spell has probably worn off. I need to ask him how his magic works, how any of his family's magic works. If all spells—including love spells—are as short-term as the one he created to hide our guns.

I unpack our overnight bags and start packing new bags to take to my house. How strange it is that I've moved around so much in the last few weeks, first to my new house, then here, then traveling to Virginia, Chicago, and finally on the road all the way back here to Montana. And no matter where I am, as long as I'm with Trey I'm home.

I'm compelled outside in search of him, with a foggy head and tunnel vision as if in a drunken stupor. Just thinking about him has me craving him with unexpected craze. I find him with the hose and a bucket of soap, drying off his new car.

"I have to get this fixed. It's a crime on a car like this," he says, squatting to examine the scrapes running along the side from when he drove the car into the woods to save my life.

Noticing my silence, he looks over his shoulder at me. I simply look back at him. I didn't come out here to talk. Now I know this love must be fabricated. It's too powerful, too controlling, like a pleasure gone wrong and consuming my every thought.

He drops the towel at my feet and grabs me. He's got it too. His lips are urgent against mine as if we haven't seen each other in months. I'm lost in a whirlwind of love for him, caught in a time warp, blind to my surroundings, until I feel the backs of my legs hit something that must be the foot of the bed, and my shirt lifts over my head, and his warm bare skin presses against mine. I fall back onto the bed and crawl backward on my elbows, his weight crawling with me, against me, until we settle into position and I'm lost all over again.

TREY

"I'M GOING TO fall asleep if we don't get up." Every muscle is paralyzed. I think I've become part of the mattress.

"Mmm." She sounds like she's already half-asleep herself.

Just as my awareness begins to drift away, she jabs me in the ribs. "Okay. Let's get up."

I clutch her fingers before she can withdraw, and she gasps.

"You have a real problem with going for people's fingers, don't you?"

"Keep them to yourself, then." The humor in my voice still surprises me. I don't know how I was able to survive in a bad mood for fifteen years. It's a good thing she showed up when she did.

She rests her finger along my cheek. "How did you get this scar?"

I chuckle. "Which one?" She has many to choose from. I'm a well-used voodoo doll.

"It looks like something cut you up here, then skipped a spot, then cut into your lip." She draws her proposed cut with her fingernail.

I turn my face away from her. "I got that a long time ago."

She gets out of bed and I roll to my side to watch her get dressed. I wonder what would have happened if we hadn't connected, if I hadn't fallen off the roof, if our alignment had never taken place. The alternatives aren't very appealing. We'd probably still hate each other. I'd have killed her. Or I'd have taken the lazy route and let them kill her.

My phone rings. Liv plucks it from my jeans pocket on the floor and tosses it to me. The display says "Tara."

"Hi," I answer.

"What's going on?" she demands.

From her tone I know exactly what she's referring to. It's amazing how well I can understand a woman I met only a few days ago just because she's my twin.

"Nothing."

"Don't patronize me. Mamó knows something's going on."

"Why'd you call me then?"

"You're infuriating. Let me talk to Liv."

It's probably not a good idea for her to talk to Liv about this. "Christian's here." It won't be easy to be vague with someone who can already tell what I'm thinking.

"Let me talk to him."

"He doesn't know who the hell you are."

"I'll make something up."

"Well, you can't. He's busy."

She stays quiet. I can almost hear her tapping her foot.

"He's being cleansed."

"With what?" Not just a question. An accusation.

"Skullcap, Lady's Slipper, Yellow Dock, and a hefty dose of *Amanita Muscaria*."

She laughs. "You're sick. How is he?"

"I'm sure he's fine. He's out in the woods somewhere, participating in a little survivalist lesson."

"Did you use the wording from the fifth text or the seventh?"

"The seventh."

"You're ruthless. And I know firsthand. Mamó used that on me once when I was sixteen."

"Did it work?"

"Oh, yes."

"I'm sure you deserved it," I say and mean it.

"Let's just say I was a rebellious teenager."

"Too bad I wasn't there to keep you in line"

"Are you kidding me? With your influence, I would've been worse."

She has something there. I owe a lot to my stepfather for keeping me on the right track when I was young. Maybe if Tara and I would've had each other growing up, we wouldn't have rebelled as strongly as we did. Our rebellion could've been a symptom of our separation. Martin Moore must really love my mother to have put up with me.

"Hello?" Tara says.

"I'm here."

"So, call me when he's back so I can tell Máthair to stop worrying."

"She knows too? Can't you women just keep your mouths shut?"

"Tell Liv I say hi." She hangs up.

"Tara says 'hi,'" I say to Liv and set my phone on the nightstand. I can tell she's dying to be filled in. I start putting on my clothes.

"What's the seventh text?" she asks.

"One of our family's ancient texts. Books of effects. Spells. You know this."

"What's all that stuff you said you gave him?"

"They cleanse the blood. The organs. Strengthen the mind." Her eyes bore into me. I can't keep anything from her. It grates against my soul. "And a strong dose of a hallucinogen. It's part of the magic," I explain, trying to downplay it so she doesn't hate me.

"So he's running around in the woods with no coat and no food, high as a kite."

"Yep." I can't control my laughter. If he doesn't come back, I'm going to feel rotten for laughing. But I know he'll come back. "He probably thinks every tree is Leatherface."

"You'll be responsible for killing your own brother."

I shrug. "Add him to the list. And he's not my brother."

"Yes he is. Let's just go find him now." She takes my forearm in both hands.

I look away, knowing how easy it is for her to play me. What a sucker I've become. This reminds me.

"Rules." I grasp her shoulders and push her down to the bed.

Her eyes narrow. "I hope you're kidding."

"Rule one. You can't leave the house by yourself."

"Or what?" She cocks her head.

I haven't thought of repercussions, but they aren't going to be necessary. "Rule two. You have to carry one of your Rugers at all times you're away from me."

"You're contradicting rule one. If I can't ever leave the house by myself—"

"The only time you'll be away from me is when you're at work. I'll drive you and pick you up at the door. Ruger, on you, at all times at work."

"Get real."

"Rule three. No strenuous exercise. Those back flips you were doing this morning? Out of the question."

"So you're a doctor now?"

"It's just common sense."

"It's a myth."

"Rule four. Stay out of Christian's way when he comes back. I'm not sure if we can trust him yet."

"How about this? I break all the rules at once and leave the house by myself, unarmed, on a long, strenuous hike to look for Christian." She stands, hands on hips, glaring up at me.

My jaw tenses. That familiar harshness in her voice touches the rage from that day she pushed me. We don't need any more holes in the walls. Somehow, she knows exactly what to say to incite me.

"Rule five. Shoot to kill. From now on, aim for the forehead or the chest, and nowhere else."

Her eyes blaze. "I am *not* you."

These words are like daggers, slitting holes in my control. My mind replays our conversation on the bluffs that night we did the mind sharing effect, when I feared I had turned her into a killer like me. Somehow, again, she managed to touch one of the hottest wires in my brain.

I realize I'm holding my breath. Before our stare turns into a standoff, she steps around me and out the doorway. I don't care if she's mad. This is just the way it has to be. She'll get used to it.

Outside, the cool air refreshes me and calms my blood. I rearrange the garage to make room for the Camaro, and by the time I'm done, the setting sun has sunk behind the mountain. This is the best time of day to go for a ride on the Ninja. With the helmet in my hand, I glance toward the house. Damn it, I can't leave her alone. The sound of the garage door sliding down startles the flock of rosy finches in a nearby tree, and as I watch them take flight, River's warning howl sounds across the yard.

Crap. This is getting so old. I'm setting up all my traps again. Tomorrow.

I jog to the house where the door opens for me and Liv hands me a gun. I hold her gaze to remind her what's expected of her now, and she glares back at me, her lips in a defiant, tight line.

"Behind you," she says.

I turn around to see a figure leap behind the rear of Christian's car. Maybe I should disarm this guy and have a talk with him. Does he not know who he's fighting? Is he stupid enough to think *he'll* be the hero, the one who finally gets me? And who's training them? It can't be my stepfather. He's skilled enough, but he's too old now, and it's not in him to do it. I've already killed the rest of the Moores capable of training them. It must be someone on the outside. Someone I don't know.

Tired of waiting, I fire at the ground around him to draw him out. I'm careful not to hit Christian's car. He's going to be mad enough; I don't need to give him any more reasons. A bullet grazes my arm just as I slip around the side of the house. I look down. Blood weeps through my shirt. Now I'm pissed.

As much as I'd love to take him down with my bare hands, it's a bad idea with my arm already wounded. I hate to admit it, but I can't afford to be reckless anymore. It isn't just me I'm protecting now. I move to the back of the house, climb to the roof, and crawl on my stomach to the peak. From here, I can see the top of a head looking out from around Christian's car. One shot and he's down.

I drag his body behind the garage to take care of later then go into the house. Liv sighs when she sees the blood running down my arm.

"Don't worry about it," I mumble, but she's already off the couch.

She joins me in the kitchen and forces me down in a chair. After bandaging my wound, she looks up at me. "I'm still mad at you."

"Suit yourself." I get up to start on dinner.

She sets the table, and my irritation soars as I realize how much it pains me to have her mad at me. This isn't the first time, and I doubt it will be the last.

River and Trib appear at the back door, so I get them each a piece of cheese from the fridge. Liv helps me prepare dinner, working alongside me in wordless harmony, carefully avoiding my eye. Seated at the table, I unfold the newspaper and skim it while eating. It all seems so familiar, yet from another lifetime. A glimpse of her expression tells me she's thinking the same thing.

Folding up the paper, I turn my attention to her. She refuses to look at me.

"If something happens to me—"

"No." Now her eyes cut through me.

"Leave immediately and go to Tara. Don't waste any time. Just leave my body here."

"Don't *ever* say that again."

"I won't need to. You know now."

Her mouth drops open. She must think I'm being controlling, but I'm just being logical, thinking of her protection. Why doesn't she understand that?

"Is this the kind of father you're going to be? Perhaps I made a mistake."

A sharp pain penetrates my core. I shove away from the table and stand. I have to get out of this room. I push my chair against the table and as it makes contact it falls backward, crashing to the floor. The door slams behind me as I descend into the basement.

With both palms pressed into my worktable, I bow my head and breathe. Thoughts fire in my brain, but nothing makes sense, so I turn it all off and load my barbell with weights. When I feel like I'm going to die after one more rep, I put all the weights away. The heavy bag taunts me from its spot in the corner, but I know I shouldn't. Two weeks ago, I'd be over there kicking its ass without a second thought. My new mortality weighs on me heavier than that barbell.

I turn off the light and climb the stairs to a clean and empty kitchen. I take off my shirt, throw it in the laundry room, and drink a glass of water. She's on the couch when I pass through the living room.

"I can't believe I said that," she says to my back just before I enter the hallway. There's an emotion in her voice I can't read.

I hesitate in the doorway as the words gnaw at my state of mind. Finding they can't penetrate, I continue to the bathroom and take a shower. On my way back through the living room later, she looks up from her book and I hesitate again, waiting for some useful words to form. She says nothing to help me. I pass her by and go into the basement.

Christian will need some protection when he goes back to Richmond, and it needs to be uncommon so they won't recognize it and can't counteract it. Losing myself in my books offers a much needed escape, and before I know it, it's past midnight. I leave the books propped open and go upstairs.

Pausing in the doorway to the bedroom, I wonder if I should sleep on the couch. Fuck it. I'm sick of sleeping on the couch. I slept on the couch every night before we got back from our trip. I strip off my clothes and get into bed. As soon as I'm under the covers, she rolls against me, still fast asleep. Even the power of my anger cannot extinguish my desire for her.

CHAPTER 4

LIV

MY EYES ADJUST to the dim light, and I sit up in bed underneath Trey's heavy arm. The blue letters of the clock read 5:34 a.m. It's too early to get up. As I lie back against the mattress, I hear it. Someone is in the house.

I roll off the bed and reach on top of the dresser for the handle of my dagger.

From the hall, light shines into the living room from the kitchen. Trey must have left the kitchen light on. I wait in the hall with my back against the wall, straining to listen. Feet shuffle in the kitchen so I dart into the living room, staying against the wall, out of the beam of light. I creep toward the doorway for a better look. The light flips off. A body comes at me through the doorway in the dark.

I'm on the ground on top of him, my dagger poised against his jugular.

"Damn it, Liv! Fuck!"

Christian. Before I can release him, I'm yanked upward and thrown behind Trey's hulking frame. My mind catches up to my ears as I hear him barge into the room after it already happened. All my focus must have been on Christian. Trey's anger with me is going to reach a new level. I probably only have seconds to live.

Trey backs me up to the light switch and we are all momentarily blinded as the light flips on. My eyes adjust to Christian, lying face down on the floor and making no attempt to get up.

"Are you crazy?" Trey roars, facing me, gripping my shoulders and jerking me once for emphasis.

I have nothing to say in my defense. Maybe I am crazy. Why didn't I wake him up?

"I—" I begin, with no end in mind.

"Don't answer." His irises are so green it's all I can think about. They're those funhouse eyes again, swirling me into the center of his pupil, muting my thoughts.

I avert my eyes. He wants me to fight him, but I won't take his bait. We'll talk when we've both settled down, when the real me is back. We should've talked yesterday; I have so many things on my mind I can't make sense of reality anymore.

Dull pain throbs in my shoulders when he releases me. He offers a hand to Christian and doubles over as Christian's fist lands hard in his stomach. Squinting, Trey raises a finger in the air to halt an onslaught. Christian takes one step back.

Trey straightens up. "That all you've got?"

Christian swings again, and Trey makes no effort to block the knuckles that land on his cheek. His head jerks to the side.

"Good thing you can't use your left." Trey catches another blow to the jaw.

I throw myself between them. "Christian! Enough!"

Trey maneuvers between me and Christian, forcing me to back away.

"Forget it. I'm done anyway." Christian flexes his right hand. His left hand hangs in an unnatural position with his broken fingers wrapped in a makeshift splint of torn fabric and sticks.

"I swear to sacred stone," Trey says in my direction. Somehow he's managed to get even more furious with me.

"Give it a rest, Trey," Christian says. "You've no right to be mad at anyone right now."

"Glad you made it back," Trey says, still glaring at me as if he's pondering what to do with me. "Record time."

"Fuck you, dude."

"Feel like your old self again?"

"If my old self wanted to kick your ass, then yes, I do." He sits on the couch and cradles his crippled left hand.

Aware I'm breaking one of Trey's rules, I sit on the coffee table, facing Christian.

Trey's voice returns to the one reserved for me alone. *"Go back to bed."*

"You go back to bed. I'm fixing his fingers."

"Yes. Thank *god.* Just let her do this and then you can kill her."

I unwrap the fabric and examine his fingers. Fractured and dislocated, just as I expected. But no cuts, so no risk of infection. He got off easy. "I'm going to have to straighten them back out again."

He grimaces. "Do it. Quickly before I change my mind."

It's a good thing we don't have neighbors. We should thank the damper of forest around this cabin because his cursing would surely wake up a whole neighborhood. I wouldn't be surprised if the cops show up, even as remote as this house is. It's a good thing it sits nestled between mountains instead of on top of one.

"Is it too early for a drink?" Trey asks Christian.

"Yes," I answer. "Ibuprofen, please."

Trey brings the whole bottle. I drop four in Christian's hand and Trey hands him a glass of water. I go in search of something to wrap his fingers properly. In the basement I find a thick cardboard box. I use one of Trey's many battle knives to cut off a section wide enough to support all his fingers then return to my spot on the coffee table.

"I don't know what you gave me, but that was the worst trip I've ever had in my life," Christian is saying to Trey.

"So how do I know you don't need another treatment?" Trey asks from the armchair.

"I don't. Trust me. I spoke to Buddha himself. And everything was all sunshine and rainbows until he turned into that guy from *Texas Chainsaw Massacre*..."

Trey bursts out laughing. "Leatherface? No fucking way."

"Yes fucking way. I think he killed me like five hundred times."

Trey leans forward, rests his forearms on his knees, and laughs harder. "How did I know it was going to be Leatherface—"

"You put that in my mind?!"

"I didn't need to. You're already obsessed."

Christian is the antidote to Trey's foul mood. As soon as Trey and I are alone again his temper will surely resurface. I'll have to take my time fixing Christian's fingers to extend Trey's good mood as long as I can.

Christian scoffs. "Obsessed. Right. More like severely traumatized. How old was I? Like, eight? And you were thirteen. A sick, sadistic thirteen. I couldn't sleep for months. I hope you rot in hell."

Trey's laughter rises to hysteria. I glance at him to take it all in. I've never heard him laugh like this. I wish Christian didn't live so far away so I could invite him to dinner whenever Trey was in one of his moods. Trey catches my eye and clears his throat, cutting himself off. So much for that.

"I didn't get to apologize to you," Christian says to me, his face suddenly somber. "I was out of my mind. There's nothing I can say—"

"You don't have to. I understand. Please." I place one hand on his knee.

He covers my hand with his good one and exhales while staring into my eyes. His blue eyes are bloodshot, and his tousled blond hair is caked with mud and tiny leaves.

"You need to take a bath." I grin at him. He's impossible not to like.

He scratches his stubble like it's been bothering him for days. "Will you help me?" His eyes sparkle.

I smile and look away, remembering what a shameless flirt he is. No wonder he's such a ladies' man in Richmond.

"What?" he says in Trey's direction, raising his free hand in the air.

Trey grunts.

Christian returns his eyes to me. "So that's a nice outfit you've got going there."

I look down. I'm wearing the tank top and underwear I went to bed in. "I could say the same for you."

Christian's wet, muddy clothes are torn and ripped in random places and hanging off his body like the outfit of a badly dressed scarecrow. Something soft slams into my back, and I reach behind me for the robe Trey threw at me.

"Aw, come on," Christian whines at Trey.

"You're starting to wear me out," Trey says.

"You're already worn out. What are you now, like, fifty? I'm much closer to her age."

"What happened after we left the estate?" Trey asks.

"Left? That's putting it lightly. They followed you. They came back without finding a trace. What'd you do?"

"Nothing," Trey mumbles.

"Nothing? Right. They would've found you."

"Nothing of importance."

Christian snickers. "You cheated." He turns his attention to me, and I pause my work to look up at him. "He cheated for you. That's impressive. He never cheats."

"I don't know what you're talking about." I'd love to know more, but it's not the time or place. I'll have to catch Christian alone, get his side of things. He'll tell me more than Trey ever will. When I catch Trey's deadly stare and find it directed at Christian instead of me, I know I'm right. There's a lot more to what happened that day. He only told me how he saved my life because I figured it out and asked directly. There's no way it could have kept the Moores from finding us. He had to have done something else, something

I don't know about. But I have no desire to press him now when he's in such a foul mood.

Christian laughs. "Tell me later," he says to Trey.

The heat still radiates off Trey's glare, but it seems to have no effect on Christian.

"Anyway," Christian says, "they came back empty-handed. Your dad got into it with one of our cousins, and then Seanmháthair came down and shut everybody up. End of story."

"Seanmháthair came down?"

Christian snorts. "Yep. Serious business. Leave it to one of your outbursts to bring Seanmháthair down."

Trey mumbles something in Irish and Christian snickers.

"Who's Seanmháthair?" I ask Christian.

"Grandmother. The last time she left her room was when—" He looks at Trey, decides to shut up.

I pull back to look at my work—all four fingers wrapped against the cardboard. "You'll be fully healed in six weeks." I stand.

"*Six weeks*?" He bites his fist and fakes a sob.

"Ice and elevate and take it easy."

"You are the best." He has the brightest smile. It's almost hard to look away.

Trey clears his throat. "Your luggage in your car?"

Christian stands to find his keys, and they go outside together. I start the coffee in the kitchen, make an ice pack for Christian, and stare out the window, trying to come up with words to say to Trey when we find ourselves alone again. I hear them come back inside, the shower turning on. Footsteps approach, and I turn toward the doorway as

Trey appears. We stare at one another for a few moments until I get the urge to speak.

"I—"

"Don't." He takes his phone off the table and dials. "Hi. He's back. He's fine." He pauses. "Nothing." He pauses again, turning away from me. "*Nothing.* I'm hanging up."

He called Tara to tell her Christian is back. I take three mugs out of the cabinet. She must have heard something in his voice; she knew something else was up. My phone rings from my purse on the counter.

"Don't answer that," he says in a voice not worth questioning. I wonder how long he's going to be like this. I wonder how long I'll be able to refrain from kicking his ass.

I answer my phone. "Your brother's throwing a fit."

He opens the refrigerator. I tell Tara we're all fine and not to worry—I've wrangled two-year-olds who refuse medical treatment and junkies in the ER rabid for a fix. A grown man throwing a tantrum is nothing. I go to the bedroom to get dressed. On my way out, I run into Christian in the hall, and he seizes me in a hard yet warm hug.

"I mean it. I am so, so sorry," he says in my ear.

"You don't need to apologize," I say into his chest, wishing Trey would walk by so he'd see me breaking one of those precious rules.

"How did you not die? That was point-blank range."

I shrug. "Magic."

"No shit. I knew that guy was useful for something. It takes forty-five years for him to finally become handy to have around." He turns on that smile again.

"But he's physically thirty," I remind him.

"And mentally fourteen. It's impossible to shower with this, by the way." He holds up his bandaged hand.

"Put a plastic bag over it next time."

"Aw, I thought you were going to offer to bathe me."

He follows me into the kitchen where I get another dirty look from Trey to remind me I'm breaking one of his rules. He should know that rule is out now. He can trust Christian. If he can't trust him now, he never can.

We all sit at the table, and Trey points his fork at Christian. "Out with it. All of it."

Christian groans. "Can't I eat first? I've been eating grass and ants for two days."

"Don't lie. There aren't any ants out there."

"Okay then, grass. Just grass. I'm trying to look somewhat tough in front of the lady. Care to cut me some slack?"

"Eat and talk," Trey says.

Christian takes a few big bites and swallows. "Kate wants you back."

Trey makes a choking sound. "She's lost it."

I get a sharp tug of jealousy—a feeling as new to me as this new world I'm a part of now. This was my fear before we went to Richmond, and I was prepared to fight for him. I still am.

"She's always been crazy. You should know that. Isn't that why you liked her?" Christian says.

"She thinks if you get Liv out of the picture I'll come running back to her? I'll come back all right, for her and a few others."

"Good luck with that. There's this new guy at the house—a Moore, a cousin of ours from the Midwest you might remember. He's a real dick and surprise, surprise,

Kate's all over him. Sorry, man," he adds, catching Trey's expression. "She wasn't like that when you lived there. Just now. Well, just since you left."

I stare down into my food, feeling like this is a conversation in which I shouldn't be involved.

"Which cousin?" Trey asks.

"Dillon Moore."

I stand up fast, rigid. My blood has gone cold. I look at Christian, try to rehear what he just said.

"He was there when you were last week. He came with her when she moved back. I guess you didn't have the pleasure of seeing him," Christian continues.

"Sure didn't." Trey looks up at me, furrowing his brow. "Doubt I'd recognize him."

He reaches for my chair which has shot a few feet behind me, and I pick up my mug and go over to the sink so he can't see my face. He was there. He was there when I was there.

"I know the baby's his. She thinks she has me convinced it's mine, but I swear I haven't been with her in years. I don't even remember being with her before Aaron was born, but that's not saying much because I was living in outer space at that time. I wouldn't have known it if I'd slept with the queen of England. Although, that would be awesome." He raises an eyebrow and nods, amused at a conversation that's left me sick.

"Yeah, you were pretty messed up there for a while. I thought you were on drugs or something." Trey takes a long drink of coffee.

My mind can only process their conversation. Everything else is on hold. I need to know more.

"Well shit, man. Next time I'm acting like a crackhead, could you maybe send me to rehab or something?"

"Sorry. I was kind of out of it too."

"Yeah. An understatement. So, I guess I was on drugs but not of my own free will. I honestly have no idea what they had me on. I'll admit to Aaron. But this new baby? No way." Christian lays his fork on the table. "Trey, I swear to you. I've never seen Kate as anything but your wife. I would never—"

"She's not my wife."

"Unfortunately, she is. Sucks for you. But seriously. To me, she was yours. Even after you left. I never would have, ever—"

"I get it," Trey snaps.

Christian sighs and picks up his fork. "You know the messed up part? Every time I came here to visit you, they programmed me to forget Aaron was mine. Forget all about him. And forget Kate was alive. And then I'd return home and remember. But picking up the phone and calling you once I remembered never occurred to me."

"Then why did you come here a few weeks ago to tell me they were alive?"

"I have no idea." Christian shakes his head. "It's like, all of a sudden, I knew everything."

"Were you cleansed?"

Christian thinks for a moment. "I don't know."

"You had to have been."

"Yeah, but who'd do that? Your mom? She'd have done it years ago if she was going to do it."

"Maybe the programming wore off."

"That abruptly? I don't buy it."

How can I return them to the subject without giving anything up?

"I'm giving you something before you go back. So they can't use you anymore. It'll take some time to prepare. How long are you staying?"

"As long as you'll have me." Christian looks over at me and winks. I turn away from him and dump my coffee into the sink. The drain gawks at me. I'm going to be sick.

"Good. Then you can help me. Let me take a quick shower first," Trey says, getting up. He stops in the doorway and turns around. "Did you know Aaron was yours when I thought he was mine?"

Christian makes a sound of disgust at the back of his throat. "No. She sprung it on me when he was already a year old."

"And you trusted her?"

"Not until I got a DNA test. I missed the first year of his life because of that b—" He glances at me. "Bad woman."

Trey nods, like everything now makes sense. Nothing makes sense. It's gone from crazy to impossible. He leaves the room.

Now is my chance. I have to know. It's probably one huge coincidence, and once I verify that, I can relax and forget all about it. Christian sips his coffee, lost in his thoughts, and I wait until I hear the shower turn on then rush into the bedroom and dig through my stuff to find the bag I packed of my most sacred, personal things. Ripping it open, I search frantically. My time is limited. There. This is it.

"Christian," I say when I reach the kitchen, desperate, and he looks up at me, confused by my tone.

I flip the photo album open and thrust it toward him.

He stares at the photo. Confusion turns to awe, and his head snaps back to me. "You've got to be fucking kidding me."

"That's my wedding photo," I whisper, about to throw up.

"Yeah, I see that. That's also Dillon Moore." He snatches the album and flips through each page, the awe on his face only becoming more pronounced. "Fuck me to death," he murmurs, and I jump to the sound of the shower turning off.

I cram the album inside my purse.

"You *have* to tell him." He stands in front of me.

"How?" I whisper, staring up at him.

"How do you tell him or how is this possible?"

His question is too complicated. I can't speak.

"If you don't tell him, I will." A threat. A warning.

"No." I grab his arm.

"Okay then, you have to tell him. Trust me. I've known him a lot longer than you have."

I back into the counter and grip it with both hands.

"The longer you wait, the worse it will be," he says.

I close my eyes. My head spins.

"Liv, snap out of it. He's coming."

CHAPTER 5

TREY

"WAS SHE LIVING at the house the whole time?" I ask when I return to the kitchen.

It takes a long moment for Christian to look at me. "No. She was living near downtown Richmond. In the Fan. They bought her one of those Queen Annes for half a mil."

"Did my mother know she was alive?"

"Hell no. You know they don't tell her anything."

"Did my father know?"

He takes his sweet time thinking it over. "I'm trying to remember if there's any reason to think he did. It's hard to say. But you can't base anything on what I know. They could've told me the sky is green, and I'd probably have believed it."

"Sit down."

A guarded look passes between Christian and Liv. They must have been talking about me while I was gone. He takes his seat, and I drag my chair away from the table and sit. Liv begins cleaning up our plates.

"We aren't related," I say to Christian. I don't know any easier way to do this.

He doesn't look convinced.

"I learned some things after I left there the other day. A lot of things."

"How?"

"I can't tell you that. But it's a valid source."

"Why can't you tell me?" He doesn't seem offended. Curious, yes. But he must understand I can't trust him with something like that.

"For their protection."

"Okay, so we aren't related. What does that mean?"

"It means I'm not your cousin. Martin Moore is not my father."

"No shit." He leans forward to rest his forearms on the table.

"None of this goes home with you. I have to trust you." I could easily ensure that, but I'm not going to dope him up any more. They've done that to him his whole adult life. I won't do it.

"I'll swear a blood oath. But you know what they can do. They can get it out of me."

"They won't have any reason to think you know any-thing. And with what I'm sending home with you, they won't be able to touch you."

"Messed up," he says, leaning back.

"That's not all. The prophecy? The one we know? It's just their spin. To my real family, my heir is a savior. Leading them, us, out from under the Moores. The Moores kid-napped me, and my mother, when I was two weeks old."

"You're full of it."

"Think about it. It makes sense. I'm a threat to them. They wanted me under their control."

He turns away, staring into the air at nothing in par-ticular. "That would explain why you've always been such a pain in the ass. Wow. What else?" He turns back to me animatedly, as if he's onto something.

"Liv is pregnant." It still thrills me to say it.

Liv spins away from the sink, looking a little pissed. She didn't expect me to tell him so soon. But there's no way around it.

"Congratulations…" Christian says to her, his eyes as wide as hers.

"The Alignment? Us." I gesture between Liv and me.

He turns back to me. "So you lost it."

"The effect? Yeah, I'm now thirty and some days."

"Bummer for you."

"Not really. Life was getting boring. Fifteen years of being the same age gets old fast." I still feel Liv's gaze on me. I guess pissing each other off is going to be a common theme now.

"Well, it's going to take a long time for that black eye to go away."

"Thanks for that, by the way. You got me good."

He chuckles. "Am I still tripping? Maybe I never came back. I'm still in the woods, waiting for Leatherface."

I finally glance over at Liv. She looks like she needs to say something, so I stare at her, daring her to. She's pushed me so far beyond the line I can't believe she'd attempt to push me further.

"*My* family put the effect on me," I say, returning my attention to Christian. "To ensure this." I gesture toward Liv again.

"This is insane."

"And you know why they love using you like they do? You're part Bevan. You had too much of my mother's influence. They may not know the specifics, but they know. My mother raised you as a Bevan. Remember all that stuff she taught us? That wasn't all Moore magic. Most of it was Bevan."

He slaps the table. "She would say, 'This is classified *Fearghus Christian only.*'"

"Yes, she *would* say that." I never realized my mother was such a badass.

"How can she live there, knowing…?"

"She loves my father—stepfather—apparently." I still don't comprehend it myself.

"Sick." He rubs his face with both hands like he's trying to scrub something off. "They are pure evil. And I'm one of them."

"By blood, not by choice. You're on our team. They killed my real father, trying to prevent all this."

Christian stares at me, speechless. I didn't think that was possible with his perpetually overactive mouth.

"For hundreds of years, they've been massacring my people. And they continue to, to this day. As long as Bevans exist, their power is threatened."

"I always thought it was weird you weren't named Moore." For some reason Christian looks abruptly at Liv.

"I never thought about it." And I don't understand why I didn't. Maybe I knew subconsciously my name was correct. Or I never questioned it because I never felt like one of them to begin with.

"How the hell did you find all this out?" he asks.

"It doesn't matter. But like I said, the source is valid. When you go back to Richmond, I need you to be my eyes and ears with anything that concerns my mother. I need to make sure she's safe."

"You know I will. She's a mother to me, too, you know."

"Do you have any idea who's training all these guys who are coming here?"

"No idea. Could be that new guy, Dillon." Another look at Liv.

"We need to find out more about him."

Christian shifts in his chair. Glass shatters on the floor at Liv's feet.

"I'm sorry," she whispers, frozen in place, her hand still holding an invisible glass. It seems very unlike her.

"Don't move. It's all around you." I get the broom from the back of the basement door.

"I'll do it." She takes the broom from me while making an attempt at eye contact that I ignore.

When I return to my seat, it feels like I missed something. "What were we talking about?"

"So is that all you learned? I mean, it's enough, but is there anything else?" Christian asks.

"One more thing. Kate's baby, the one she's carrying, is to the Moores what my baby is to the Bevans. Two leaders born to destroy the other, determining which family lives and which is destroyed."

"How did I not even know *that*?" He slams his fist on the table. "God, that pisses me off. And what's their purpose for trying to make me think he's mine?"

"He?" I unconsciously meet Liv's eyes.

"Yeah, he. She's having a boy."

My future little girl is going to have to battle a man? The odds are already against her. I can't allow that. What kind of person would I be to send my little girl off to war? Against a man? I know Liv could stand against a group of men, but somehow that's different.

All of a sudden I don't feel like talking anymore. With the floor swept, Liv dumps the dustpan in the trashcan and leaves the room without a look in my direction. I also need to get the hell out of this room. "I want to show you something."

He follows me out to the garage and I jerk open the door.

"You bastard. Camaro ZL1? Don't you ever get tired of black?" he asks.

I hand him the key.

"Did you sell the ZX-14?"

"Nope, still have it." I cock my head toward the Ninja in the corner of the garage.

"*Two* toys? Looks like someone hit their mid-life crisis. Jeez, what did you do?" He leans down for a closer look at the body damage.

"A little off-roading. I'll get it fixed."

"Off-roading? On purpose?"

I nod. He gets in the driver's seat. The engine roars alive, and he lowers the window. "You coming with?"

I look toward the front door of the house. I can't leave her alone.

"Come on, she'll be okay for ten minutes. Did you forget what she did to me this morning?"

"Ten minutes," I say and slam the passenger door behind me. "And go easy. I just washed it."

"Okay, Gramps." He floors it out of the garage and digs ruts in the gravel all the way up my steep driveway.

"You owe me a new set of tires," I say after he hits the main road and leaves a trail of rubber.

"Just breaking it in for you. Man, this sure beats the hell out of my Infiniti."

"Anything beats the hell out of your Infiniti."

"Yeah, the ladies like it though. Something you aren't very familiar with, so you can just take my word for it."

I choke on my laughter.

"So, you and Liv? You're in it for good?"

I don't answer.

"Even though you want to kill her right now?"

"What makes you think that?"

"Don't make me laugh. You should be thankful, you know. You're with a woman who can take down an intruder and you don't even need to wake up."

"In her condition?"

"Condition? God, you worry way too much. Are you sure your body isn't making up for lost time and you're actually like eighty?"

"Turn around. We need to get back."

He makes a U-turn, leaving more rubber on the pavement. I could get on the road to Virginia tomorrow, leave Christian here with her. Together they could fight off three men, maybe more. I can't remember the highest number of guys they've ever sent at once but I'm sure it's never been more than three. We descend back down the driveway, pull the car into the garage and go in the house. Inside the door, I hear Liv talking on the phone.

"Who are you talking to?"

She spins around in alarm. "She called again. I couldn't ignore her." The bleakness of her voice sounds out of place.

"Tara?" I ask but already know.

"Give her a break, Trey," Christian says behind me.

I snatch the phone out of her hand. "What do you want?"

"What's up your ass? I was talking to Liv."

"About what?"

"My period."

"God." I hand the phone back to Liv.

"I know," Liv says into the phone as I watch her. She needs to hang up now. Instead, she faces me squarely and says to Tara, "Maybe I will take you up on your offer of the room. Moving back to Chicago sounds pretty good right now."

I'm about to grab her phone again when Christian shoves me aside.

"Let's go downstairs. You're being a dick." Christian yanks open the basement door. "It's really, really unnecessary," he says when we reach the bottom of the stairs.

"What?"

"Your attitude."

I know she's just trying to get to me. She can't leave. She wouldn't. And if she did, it would be my fault. I'm doing it again—attacking someone I love—and I can't stop. How do I stop? "Are you going to help me with the effect or what?"

Rolling his eyes to the ceiling, he joins me, and we go through all the books I left propped open from last night. His knowledge of the Moores from the last fifteen years is crucial—they're doing things now I never would've guessed. We throw out all but two of my ideas then raid the bookshelves to look for more options.

Liv brings us lunch, and Christian kisses her cheek but I remain buried in my book until she turns around, trudging back up the stairs. The vision of her dispirited posture almost breaks me. She almost died. I've been given a second chance, and if I ruin things with her, I'll have lost it. I won't get another.

Hours later, when the door opens again, Christian closes his book and hollers up to her. "We're coming up!"

I follow him up the stairs and eat dinner in silence, only partially listening to their conversation. Finishing before them, I clean up, and as soon as Liv finishes she leaves the room.

"How long are you going to do this?" Christian asks.

"Do what?"

"Don't be an idiot."

I pour two glasses of scotch and down mine in one gulp. He takes a drink from his.

"You're still drinking this crap?" He takes another drink.

I fill my glass again, and he finishes his and returns it to the counter. I refill it. We move into the living room. No one's talking but we both have a lot on our minds. I hear Liv come out of the bathroom, go straight into the bedroom, and close the door behind her. Christian gives me a look, and I let out a long, irritated sigh. Sometimes he can be such a nag.

"Now would be a good time to have a TV. You are so fucked in the head."

"There's never anything good on," I say.

"The game?"

I hold up the newspaper.

"Holy crap." He rests his head against the back of the couch and laughs.

My eyelids drop a few times before I force myself off the couch and take our glasses to the kitchen.

"Do you need blankets?" I ask just before my eyes settle on a stack of blankets and a pillow Liv must have already left out for him.

He gives me the thumbs up, so I head to the bathroom then the bedroom. She's sitting on the end of the bed, with her elbows on her knees and her chin on her fists as if she's been in this position for hours. When she sees me, she stands. "I was just about to go get—"

"What? I'll get it for you." No pain I have ever felt compares to the pain I feel now.

"A glass of water."

I leave the room and fill a glass in the kitchen. Christian's loud snoring proves he's already sound asleep.

After closing the bedroom door behind me, I hand her the water and look down at her as she drinks. When she lowers the glass, I take it from her and set it on the dresser. Again, she looks like she needs to say something. I watch her and wait.

"I was mad at *you*," she says.

"So?"

"You turned it around. You're mad at me now. How did you turn it around?"

This didn't occur to me. She *was* mad at me, and I was unaffected. But, then she said what she said.

"What you said. You said—"

"I didn't mean that. I told you that. It was an accident. I don't know why I said it. I take it back."

"You can't take it back."

"Yes I can!" Her eyes reflect with a threat of tears.

If she cries, it will rip me in half.

"Erase it," she says. "It wasn't me. I don't even think that. That thought is not mine."

Somehow, her words sink in. Her lips take me captive. Her soft skin calls be touched. Catching myself, I look away, but not before my eyes run down her body, betraying me. Forgiveness hungrily consumes every other thought in my mind, making room for a pain so intense it can only be eased by taking her in my arms. An infatuation so wild I can't be expected to deny it.

"It's the most wonderful thing that's ever happened to me," she says. "I couldn't think of anything else I'd want more."

I touch her cheek and lean toward her, kissing her slowly, fighting hard to keep command over my desire. It just wouldn't be fair to ask that of her after treating her like crap all day. I'm a sick person. I do this over and over and I never learn. To the one person I can't live without.

I unwillingly break away and turn off the light. I drop my jeans to the floor, pull off my shirt, and get under the covers. "Are you coming?"

She walks to her side of the bed and sits. Is she not tired? What could she want?

"Trey…" She sighs. "There's something…"

I hook my arm around her waist and tug her toward me. She yields, dropping to her pillow, facing away from me. I pull her closer.

"I'm sorry," I say, not because I need her to forgive me, but because I am. The next time I'm angry I need to remember this, how it feels to be a scumbag. Seeming harmless enough, I kiss her shoulder and up her neck, hesitating on the back of her neck. Her fragrance smothers me. All thoughts are now surely gone. Except for one.

She turns to face me in my arms, and it's just enough to set me off. It's not my fault—it's all her. She's responsible for this one. And it has never been so good.

LIV

Dreams of dillon wake me in the night. I turn over, expecting tousled blond hair, the favorite Yankees T-shirt he'd always wear to bed in our drafty old Chicago house. But the man next to me is shirtless. With broader shoulders. Dark hair clipped short. I sit up, lean against an old wooden headboard that should be upholstered leather. I look around the spartan tiny room, four of which could fit in my old bedroom I shared with Dillon.

I'm stuck between worlds, and the dead quiet of the night only magnifies the surreal. I'd put Dillon behind me. It seemed the only way to move on—bury his memory like we buried our baby girl. Now that baby girl is back, alive inside me. She's wanted and welcome, but Dillon, her original father, is not. He was wrong for her and he's wrong for me. He should be merely a stranger to me, a distant relative of Trey's I'd be unlikely to meet. But he's my husband, the man who abandoned me when I most needed him. The man I'm trying to forget.

When I stand, my legs are weak, and a tremble starts in my belly and spreads to my limbs—a shiver without the cold. I find slippers and a robe and sneak past Christian on the couch, with that blond, tousled bed head so much like Dillon's I'm surprised I never noticed before. Cousins by blood, but how close? It doesn't matter. I fill a glass of water in the kitchen and stand at the sliding back door, looking outside across Trey's moonlit garden. My insomnia had been cured until now. Pills I'd been dependent on too long unceremoniously flushed down the toilet. Addiction doesn't matter when it's the only thing that provides peace. But I'm sure I'm getting ahead of myself. I'm awake now because I was unable to tell Trey about Dillon. I have to tell him soon, and I'm nervous. That's all. Once I tell him, everything will be fine. Dillon will be behind me again, and I'll be able to sleep.

I dump the water and open the cabinet by the sink, standing on tiptoe to see all the way to the back. I'm not sure what I'm looking for until I hear Trey's words. *It's habit forming.* His herbal tea. I don't know if it's the ingredients or the magic but it makes everything right until you come down and want more. I hope the stuff's gone because the last go nearly killed me. Tomorrow I'll tell him if there's any left in the house, get rid of it. I don't need the temptation. Neither does he.

Back in bed, I lie awake, trying to breathe down the trembling, and watch the sun light the window as the wall between my worlds rebuilds with me solidly on one side.

When morning has reached full force and he turns over and opens his eyes, I say, "That was my first time."

"For what?" He closes his eyes again, rests a hand on my belly.

"Make-up sex."

"Is that what that was?"

"Yes. I've never had it before." When he doesn't offer a reply, I ask, "Have you?"

"Oh, yeah." He sounds a little sarcastic.

"Really?"

"Kate and I fought like hell."

"How often?"

He rolls to his back and opens his eyes at the ceiling. "All the time. I always thought she picked fights."

"For the make-up sex?" I laugh, trying to get a grip of my overwhelming jealousy. If I could admit the feeling belongs to me, maybe I'd get over it. But there are too many things I need to admit. Things I need to get over.

"Maybe. Who knows. Who cares."

"We never fought," I say solemnly. How am I ever going to find the nerve to tell him? If hours of preparation aren't going to help me, I'm just going to have to blurt it out. But how can I knowingly ruin this pleasant morning when yesterday was so rotten? I could change the subject and postpone it again. Spend another sleepless night trying to work out the words.

"You and that prick you were married to—are married to—never fought? Hard to believe." It's a statement to mark the end of the conversation. This is the perfect chance, and I'm losing it.

"Trey…"

He rolls to face me. I place my hands on his cheeks and stare into his eyes one last time before he loses it. Before hell breaks loose.

"I have to tell you something."

The seriousness of my voice causes him to start to sit up.

"No," I say. "Stay here, please." He'll do more damage if he's upright.

"What?" He props himself on one elbow.

It's too late now. I have to say it. The process has already started. Would it be better to do it with Christian in the room?

"Spit it out," he says.

"My husband is Dillon Moore." My body goes numb, like it knows I can't show any emotion. I need to remain blank until the bomb's debris has settled. Then we can talk. I can explain, tell him I'm stuck between them, that I never got to say goodbye, I never had closure. And I can ask him how his family's spells work, determine if our love is fabricated. Temporary. Not real.

He's sitting on the edge of the bed, gripping the mattress. I reach for his arm. "Wait. Please wait."

His arm is defined by every individual tensed muscle. "Coincidence." A slow, thorough pronunciation of each syllable, like he's trying to talk himself out of it—the instinctive, blind reaction I know too well. There's a monster inside him, thrashing around, and he's trying to rein it in.

"No." Honesty is the only way. Rip it off, like a band-aid. "I showed Christian a picture. He said it's him. Please. Look at me."

He remains in position, a wild animal poised to attack. "I'll kill him."

It chills me to the bone, for reasons I can't voice right now. It would be fuel on an inferno. "You can't."

"He is *mine.*"

"It's not—" I fumble for the right words. "He doesn't deserve that."

"I know *exactly* what he deserves."

"Talk to Christian first. He knows him, too."

"He said he's an asshole!" He finally looks at me.

"No, he didn't." I must remain calm. I try to remember Christian's exact words.

"Wait." He turns away to stare straight ahead, narrowing his eyes. "How long ago was it?"

"How long ago was what?" There's a ripple through my numbness, like I've overlooked something that's about to make me wish I'd postponed this. It's too fast. I needed to think on it more. I'm about to be brought into the light, the secret I must keep from Trey exposed.

"How long ago did he leave you?"

"About seven months." The words are clumsy on their exit from my mouth.

"How pregnant is Kate?"

I remain silent. This idea chips away at the happiness still so new to me. That happiness is now in the forefront of my emotion, taking the brunt of the attack.

"He cheated on you," he says. It rings in my ears, deafening.

"The baby might not be his," I hear a voice answer, but it sounds too far away to be mine.

He watches my face as I claw the dirt walls, struggling against the downward force of being yanked back into the dark pit I lived in for so long in my other life. The corner of the sheet dabs my tears before I'm enclosed in the comfort of his arms.

He helps me to my feet, to the bathroom, and turns on the shower. I undress and step in, and he steps in behind me. We take turns in the stream, an orchestrated routine that occupies my mind. We don't talk—there's nothing to say. When the shower turns off, I miss the noise of the water.

He hands me a towel. I dry off and follow him to the bedroom to get dressed. We make the bed together and go past a sleeping Christian to the kitchen. A mug of coffee materializes in front of me on the table and I take it in my hands. It's warm. I've never been so cold.

"Drink it," he says, and I realize I've been holding it for a while.

Two plates of food appear on the table, and Trey sits across from me.

"You have to eat."

I pick up my fork, chew, and swallow. Christian places a plate of food on the table and drops into the chair between us. The silence is painful but unavoidable. Trey takes his empty plate to the sink, and Christian stares at me until I meet his eyes.

"Did you tell him?" he mouths, and I nod. He turns to Trey. "So you know?"

"Yes," Trey says.

"And you're fucking taking it out on *her*?"

"No, I'm not fucking taking it out on her. She just found out that he fucking cheated on her."

Christian looks at me, holding my gaze with the softness of an apology. "How?" He turns back to Trey.

"Timeframe," Trey says. "Kate's been pregnant longer than they've been separated."

"Are you sure the baby is his?" I ask, startled by the sound of my own voice.

Christian shrugs. "As sure as I can be. But…"

"But what?" Trey asks.

"He's been coming around her house in the Fan a lot longer than that. And she and he have always…" The rest of the sentence is written all over his face.

My fork falls onto my plate. "He's not a bad person. He wouldn't do this. None of this is true." It all comes out in a rush.

Trey and Christian exchange a look.

"Is he a bad person?" Trey asks Christian.

Christian throws his hands in the air. "I'm not—"

Trey drops his fist on the kitchen faucet to shut the water off. "*Is* he a bad person?"

Christian looks at me again, like he's to blame for this. He turns back to Trey. "He is seriously fucked up."

"No," I say, "he's not."

"Yes." Christian lowers his head to meet the level of my eyes. "He is."

They both stare at me. How can I make them understand? They don't know him like I did. He made some mistakes. We've all made mistakes. Why is he being judged so harshly?

"You still love him," Trey says to me, like it's an indisputable fact.

I open my mouth to speak but nothing comes out.

"She does," Christian says to Trey, as if I'm not in the room.

"No," I say. That's not the right way to describe it. "I still…care about him. No. I feel for him."

Christian stands next to Trey and crosses his arms on his chest. They watch me like riot police guarding the perimeter of an event about to get out of hand. There's a reasonable way to explain this—it was perfectly reasonable in my head. But the words I worked out last night are cruelly eluding me.

"Fine. Maybe I do still love him." I bury my face in my hands and drop my head to the table.

The static in my mind disguises their murmured discussion. I don't care what they're saying anyway. They'll never understand, and it's not my job to make them understand. They can think whatever they want.

"Liv." Trey sits in the chair next to me.

My head clears. I raise up to look at him.

"Christian and I are pretty sure he put an effect on you."

"Why?" I choke.

"To trick you into loving him. And he wasn't decent enough to remove it when he left you. You still think you love him."

"He wouldn't do that."

"And you continue defending him."

"You don't understand." How can I make him see?

"This is what they do. He's one of them. There's a reason they did this to you. There's a lot more to all of this, and we'll figure it out."

"I found it." Christian surfaces from the basement holding an open book which he hands to Trey.

Trey sets it on the table and skims the page. Upon reaching the bottom, he looks up at me. "Tonight we'll remove it. Your mind will be free."

I shake my head.

"If he didn't do it, my reversal won't change anything. So indulge me." His smile is a beacon of light, a reminder of why I love him. "Get your stuff. I'll drive you to work."

He's waits for me by the front door. When I join him, he holds my coat out for me. He turns me around and pulls a sock hat onto my head.

"I'm going to kiss you." He doesn't wait for my response.

The warmth of his lips defrosts a portion of the cold that's invaded me, and when he withdraws, I cling to him. I want to take him back to bed with me and stay there all day. I want to be held by someone who truly loves me, to be reminded how that feels. I'd done my best to bury my feelings for Dillon, and now they're back as strong as ever and tainted with the worst poison: infidelity. I was a fool—satisfied with knowing so little about the man I married, questioning nothing. It's a realization that digs deep.

My emotional cold is no match for the temperature outside. He's already warmed up the Camaro.

"I'll pick you up at five. Call me if you want me earlier. I'll be home all day. I have nothing going on for work for a while."

Everyone at the clinic is pleased to have me back, probably more because I ease their workload than anything else. All the nurses seem overly jovial, almost giddy, and the lights are too bright. It's my own sleep deprivation, and the crash of reality onto the surreal. Once my eyes adjust and I'm fixed again in the normal world, the giddy voices return to a natural level and my routine clears away the haunting of the night. Even the revelation of my cheating husband gets a new perspective—the best thing he could've done was give me a reason not to love him anymore.

When I clock out at the front desk, Rachel spins around in her chair. "Go see Shawn. He wouldn't stop asking when you'd be back."

She points her pen down the hall, and when I look, he's at the far end with his empty dolly, writing on a clipboard. He looks up. Smiles big. He swivels the dolly and wheels it toward me. "There she is!" He picks me up off the floor in the familiar bear hug.

"Shawn, I missed you."

"Not as much as I missed you."

Trey will kill me if I don't make our relationship clear to Shawn like I promised I would. Actually, he won't kill me. He'll kill Shawn. Slowly and painfully.

"Trey and I are together now." Fast—another ripped off band-aid.

"Not my business." Shawn is clearly unaffected.

I forgot how persistent he is. "You and I are friends, like I've said all along. I like you. As a friend."

"You two don't have to be exclusive," he says.

"Yes, we do. We are. Exclusive."

"I don't see a ring on your finger."

I can't tell him he'll probably never see a ring on my finger due to Trey and I both being married to other people who probably have little intention of going along with divorce. "I don't have a lot of friends, so it's a very high honor. You should take it. It's all you're gonna get."

His smile falls away. "You know what I don't like?"

The change in his mood has me a bit anxious to hear the answer.

"That guy has a new scar every time I see his face. There aren't enough places in Black River to find trouble like that. He must go looking for it."

I'm unable to answer.

"And guys like that often like to beat up on women."

"Shawn, you *really* don't have to worry about me." Although no one's near enough to be listening, the space around us presses on me to move our conversation along. "Come on, walk me out."

He launches into a story about how he once startled Dr. Wu with a late delivery, one that has me cracking up due to what I assume is a bit of exaggeration. I'll take it though. I need it. I almost want to hug him again.

Trey's truck idles outside.

"Your chariot awaits," Shawn says. "I don't know what you see in him. Why is it the best women always go for the assholes?"

"I'll see you tomorrow, Shawn." I take a deep breath to calm my laughter before leaving the building

"Funny guy," Trey says when I get in.

"He is."

"Did you tell him to back off?"

"I told him we're friends. I think you need to back off."

He snorts. I don't have to be in his mind to know he's going over all the different ways he could kill him.

"You picked up the truck from the airport?"

"Had to use Christian for something. I can't just let him lounge around all day like he does at home."

Dinner is already prepared and waiting for us when we get to Trey's house.

"Did you cook?" I ask Christian when we enter the kitchen.

He guiltily closes the lid on the pot as Trey starts laughing. "You kidding? This spoiled little rich kid couldn't cook to save his life. And he can't even wait for us before raiding my food."

Christian sneers. "*Imeacht gan teacht ort.*"

I don't need to know Irish to know an insult when I hear one.

"Well then, you can just eat my ass," Trey says.

Judging from the amount of insults being thrown around, I can tell they must have had a good time together today.

"I'm still in shock, that's all. Every time I visited before it was like eating at a Russian prison. Unseasoned beans for every meal and bargain brand coffee. Had I known all it would take is a little female company to get you to cook me actual food I'd have brought you a whole busload."

Trey hands me a jar containing an ashy substance. "Took us all day to prepare this. It was trickier than usual since you're pregnant, but all the ingredients have been approved." His special look for me tells me he had to call Tara for her approval. "Do you want it in a capsule or in a tea?"

"Capsule," I say. "I've had too much of your teas."

Christian, already seated at the table with his dinner, slaps the table. "No shit! He got you with the Black Horehound, Damiana, Lemon Balm, Skullcap…what else is in it? I can't even remember."

"He never told me what was in it."

"My own secret ingredients," Trey says, making a plate for me and a plate for himself.

"Your own secret ingredients are the shit I want. You're going to have to make us some of that tonight." Christian rubs his hands together.

"You're still on lockdown, my friend," Trey says.

"Bastard," Christian mutters.

I take my seat at the table and Trey sets a glass of water and two capsules in front of me.

"Take them first." He stands over me.

I swallow them both. "What's going to happen?"

"You'll go to sleep for a few hours and wake up with Dillon fucking Moore out of your head."

I jump to my feet. "No."

I don't want him gone. Why didn't he tell me this before I took the capsules? I'm at the sink, staring into the drain, shoving my finger far down my throat. Trey hauls me back to my seat at the table.

"Are you kidding me?" He holds my shoulders against the chair.

"He got her good," Christian says without looking up.

I grip Trey's forearms. "I don't want this."

"You can't see you're still under his power. You don't know what you want."

"You're going to take him away from me all over again!"

"The only thing I'm taking away is his control over you. You'll still have your memories. Just relax. Eat your dinner."

He releases me and I'm on my feet again, dashing for the sink. He catches me around the waist. I twist away, get a firm hold on the countertop to pull myself toward it. He catches me again by the waist and pins my arms behind me.

"Am I going to have to tie her up?" he asks Christian.

"She has to eat something or she's going to get sick."

"Yes," Trey says, turning to me. "You'll get sick if you don't get something else in your stomach."

He forces me back down in the chair and loads my fork with food. He aims the fork for my mouth. "Open."

If I refuse to eat, he's going to have to allow me to purge the capsules from my stomach. He won't let me get sick.

"Open your mouth."

My lips lock together under their own will.

"Please." His soft plea carries so much more power than a rough demand. He must know it goes straight to my heart, to the place that houses my darkest thoughts. Where I'm weakest, where his tenderness overwhelms me. "Trust me."

With tears spilling down my cheeks, I open my mouth, and he feeds me forkful after forkful until I collapse under a grief that shakes me to pieces, each sob more painful than the last. Christian brings him a rope, and Trey ties my wrists to the chair. I struggle against the ropes, barely hearing the words Trey recites from the paper he holds, then I see Christian clamp a hand on Trey's shoulder.

"You have to leave her. It won't work unless you leave her."

"I know!" Trey roars. He takes my face in his hands and kisses me before leaving me all alone in my own worst nightmare. My recurring hell of abandonment, once repeating over and over in memory, fires up again with the full might of reality.

CHAPTER 7

TREY

"HE'LL PAY FOR this," I say to Christian when we're in the living room far enough away from her.

"She'll be asleep in five minutes."

"Keep an ear out for her. I'm going outside." I won't stand around and listen to her suffer like this.

The force of the wind hits me as soon as I step outside. Heavy gusts rip through the trees, bending them in ripples like the air has become sentient and enraged. I jump into the back of my truck and throw the two bales of hay to the ground. River and Trib join me from the woods, play-fighting against my leg as I haul their new insulation. I don't know where Trib took cover before Liv came along, but River's shelter is big enough for two.

After filling the shelter with the hay, I brush myself off and stand in the driveway, staring at the house. Someone needs to be punished for this. I'll gladly take a substitute for Dillon Moore right now. Where are they when I need them? Not that he'd be off the hook. I want to feel him squirm. I need to see the picture Liv showed Christian so I have a face to use when I picture myself cutting his throat. I can't leave until Liv is herself again but damn, I need to get on the road to Virginia now more than ever.

She has to be asleep by now. I crack open the front door, listening for any sign of her. The doorknob jerks out of my hand, and Christian gestures me inside.

"Wuss," he says.

"Fuck you."

"She just stopped, but I haven't gone in there yet."

I rush into the kitchen to untie her. Her wrists are chafed red from the struggling. It's a good thing we're separated by half a country, or Dillon's throat would be in my hands right now. I carry her to the couch and draw a blanket over her.

Christian wanders into the room and takes a seat in the chair. "Another great opportunity to watch some TV. Want a drink?"

"Hell yes."

"What do you have besides scotch? Any beer?"

I shake my head.

"I'll make a beer run. Anything else you want?"

"Dillon Moore's head under my boot. Where's that picture she showed you?"

"In her purse, the last time I saw it."

I follow Christian and find her purse in the entryway as Christian closes the front door behind him. There's a photo album inside. I study the words on the cover.

Dillon & Liv

Forever

Forever. Think again, asshole.

I open the cover to reveal an informal shot of Liv, carefree and beautiful in a strapless wedding gown. She's smiling wider than I've ever seen her smile and cocking her head toward a blond guy who's holding her hand. I could rip his arm right off his body. Her petite frame looks like a child next to him. A heavyweight. Probably six-three. About two thirty-five. This must be what she looks like next to me. But there's one big difference. I can tell by the evil in his eyes that he's a Moore. I'm not a patient person. I'll never last, waiting until the day I put a much overdue end to his sorry life.

I flip photo after photo, my head burning hotter with each turned page. I've never seen her look so happy, and I hate him for it. This is not merely jealousy. This is a call for payback, a score that needs to be settled. And I know as soon as we find an explanation for this coincidence, the price of his head will be even higher. If that's at all possible.

An empty page. One of the photos is missing. This must be why they ransacked her house. They needed proof she's here, to ensure their assassins were targeting the right woman. This missing photo was probably taken straight to Dillon himself, for his verification.

Christian almost runs into me as he comes through the front door carrying two paper bags. "Jeez, have you been standing there this whole time?"

With one last glance at the photo on the first page, I tuck the album back in her purse and follow him into the kitchen.

He drops the bags on the table, his coat on a chair. "I've been gone at least thirty minutes. You have a serious problem." He gauges my expression and decides to shut the hell up. "Check it out. That liquor store on Main—awesome, as usual. Double Dragon, Brunehaut Amber, Guinness Extra Stout, and Samuel Smith's of course." He unloads the bags.

"Why do all you fucking Moores look the same? Inbreed-ing?"

The pack of Samuel Smith's freezes in the air, and he looks at me hard. Guess that hit a nerve. I take a Double Dragon, open it, and chug it.

He eyes me. "Maybe I didn't buy enough."

"This stuff is weak." I hold it up to look at the label. "What is this, Welsh?"

"Weak? Should be perfect for you then, sweetie."

He throws his hands in the air when he sees my answer-ing glare. I open two more bottles and take them into the living room with me.

"Know anything about the blonde waitress from the rest-aurant next to that liquor store?" he asks when he joins me.

"Kristen?"

He gives a burst of a laugh. "Guess you do. I thought you avoided women. Up until Liv, I mean."

"I did."

"She seemed to know you." He drops into the chair.

"That's her problem."

He exhales, stretching his legs out. "I'm taking her out tomorrow night."

"Poor thing."

"Hey, remember that time we went out with those two sisters—"

"No. You're getting on my nerves."

"I wouldn't have to make small talk if you had something around here to entertain me."

I ignore him. Finish my beer and pick up the next. Rest my head on the back of the couch. Close my eyes.

"That waitress said I have a strange accent. Do I have a strange accent?"

"No."

"All the times I've been here, no one's ever said that before."

I shrug, still staring at the backs of my eyelids.

"People must be intimidated by my good looks." Smug. On purpose.

A laugh erupts from me.

"Okay, your conversation sucks, and I have some energy to burn. I'm going to go hit your weight set."

"Knock yourself out." Hopefully he will, and I'll get some peace and quiet.

I hear him open another beer in the kitchen and then tromp down the basement stairs. With a hand on Liv's calf, I sink into the couch, allowing my sleepy mind to drift into rest.

Jerking awake, I hear a muffled radio playing Metallica in the basement. Liv's got the big eyes of a wild animal, staring at me from the other end of the couch.

"You're awake." A breath loosens tension I didn't realize I had.

She grasps the couch behind her, pulls her knees up and pushes away from me with her feet, still staring at me with those unusual eyes.

"Liv."

Her eyes dart wildly around the room then back to my face. "How do you know my name." It's not a question. It's a demand.

"What?" Dread smolders inside me.

I reach for her, and she launches herself backward, over the arm of the couch. Lands on her feet. Before I can stand, she snatches my phone off the coffee table and dashes to the fireplace, yanking the poker off the hearth.

"What are you doing?" I struggle to keep my voice level. Something went wrong. Very wrong.

"Who are you!" Again, not a question.

"You know me. You're disoriented. Come sit down." I take a step toward her.

"Don't move," she hisses. She lifts my phone, presses three numbers, and I'm on top of her before she can press SEND. The fireplace poker catches me in the ribs as I grapple with her contorting body. All the training I gave her is backfiring on me in a way I never would've predicted. I manage to jerk the fireplace poker away from her and throw it under the couch.

"What the fuck!" Christian bursts into the room.

I need to subdue her gently, without hurting her or the baby. I see an opportunity to throw her to the ground but hesitate, knowing it'd be too rough. She takes advantage of my hesitation and twists away from me. I catch her ankle. She spins on one foot to face me as I keep my hold on her leg.

"Stop struggling! You're pregnant!"

She jumps on her free leg, smashes it into my jaw. I release her leg so she can land without falling, and Christian catches her from behind, pinning her arms behind her. She slams her head back into his face, but he keeps his hold.

"On the ground!" I yell, and he and I lower her to the floor as she sinks her teeth into my forearm.

Once she's down, I get on top of her. Hold her wrists against the floor, use my body weight to keep her down.

"Rope," I say to Christian.

We bind her hands and feet then lift her to the couch. Her chest heaves, and I sit next to her, hands on my knees, bowing my head to catch my breath.

"What the hell?" Christian's as out of breath as me.

I look up at him and laugh. "She got you good."

"Fuck yeah, she got me good." He wipes his bloody nose with the back of his hand. He rotates his bandaged hand, checking the bandages.

I lift my shirt to reveal a huge bloody gash in my side from the fireplace poker.

"She busted your jaw, too," Christian reminds me. "What happened?"

"She doesn't know me." I look down at my arm where she bit me.

"You don't remember Trey?" Christian asks her.

She meets his eyes with a cold gaze. No answer.

"Do you remember me? Christian?"

Same cold gaze. Still no answer.

Christian turns to me. "We fucked up."

I go into the kitchen to think. Blood trickles down my side, so I strip off my shirt, wad it up, and hold it against my wound while staring out the back door. I'm at a loss. I have no idea how to reverse this.

Christian brings the text we used from the basement, drops it on the kitchen table, and sits down, leaning over it on his elbows. "Chill out, man. I'll figure this out. It's got to be something simple."

I should call Tara. She approved the ingredients for use on a pregnant woman. This is her fault too.

Liv is still sitting rigidly in her spot on the couch, and I feel her defiant eyes on me while I search for my phone that must have gotten lost in the struggle. "911" is still on the display when I find it. I clear it out and call Tara. As I wait for her to answer, I sit in the chair across the room from Liv and keep pressure on my wound. We stare at each other, both refusing to break eye contact.

"What now?" Tara answers.

"Something went wrong."

"What do you mean?" I can almost see her smile fade.

"The ingredients you approved. It messed her up. She doesn't remember me."

"What?!"

"She's out of her mind."

"Okay. What did you use them for?"

"Fourth text. Number twenty-seven."

"Which one is that? Hold on," she says.

I hear her rummaging around, then she's mumbling to herself, flipping pages. I wait while she reads it, still staring into Liv's wild eyes. If she wasn't restrained, she'd be tearing my face off right now. I flip my wad of shirt to the clean side and maintain pressure against the gash. I have a normal body now. Too bad I don't remember what normal is.

"Okay," Tara says finally. "First of all, you didn't tell me what you were using that stuff for. The ingredients are fine. But this? No way."

"What do you mean?"

"Relax. What I mean is, whenever you go messing with love, you have to be careful."

"I'm not messing with love. I'm messing with control. His control, over her."

"And her *love* for *him*," she says. "It's part of that. Temporary, yes, but still part of it."

"So?"

"This one is temperamental. You have to use it on someone who's alone. Did you leave her alone?"

"Yes, I know that. I left her alone." That kind of reminder is not something I need right now. I need a solution. A recipe and the wording to fix this. Bring Dillon Moore back, as long as I get Liv back too.

"Hmm. Well then, I don't know."

The window wants me to drive my fist through it. I rap my knuckles against my forehead instead.

"Wait." Her voice drops with the sound of sudden understanding.

"What?"

"She wasn't alone. Your baby was with her."

It's like hitting the ground from a ten-foot fall. How could I have overlooked that? I was so determined to get him out of her mind that I wasn't thinking of anything else. I didn't think it through.

"So what does that mean?"

"It's always so complicated with pregnant women," she mutters.

"What do I do?" My voice sounds hoarse. The guilt that was rooted into my brain for fifteen years was nothing compared to this. If I lose her—

"I'll find out. Sit tight. I'll call you back." She hangs up.

I test the waters by walking toward Liv. Her gaze becomes more deadly and my guilt becomes more vicious with each step I take. I'm her enemy now, some stranger. I'm the guy that day who trashed her car. She probably doesn't even remember that. If I tried anything right now to make her remember, she'd only end up hurting herself in her struggle against me.

"I've got someone on it," I say to Christian's back when I return to the kitchen.

"I'm about halfway there. We need to separate what we did and then remove it. I know how to separate it, but I haven't yet found how to remove it."

"We made a huge mistake." I take a seat next to him as he looks up from the book. "She wasn't alone. The baby."

His face drops. "Fuck me."

"Yeah." I look away.

"Then this might not even work." He gestures to his notes.

I slump in the chair, disgusted. It's an unforgivable oversight. I lift my shirt wad to check my bleeding. Christian pushes away from the table, throws me a beer from the fridge, opens one for himself. We drink together in stunned silence until my phone rings on the table.

"Hi," I answer.

"You have to go into her mind. No damage was done. She just lost some clarity. It'll all return with time, but I'm sure you don't have time to wait."

"I don't."

"Okay then, do a mind share. Don't be aggressive. Remind her of all the things that happened recently. No big deal." I can sense her grin over the phone.

"Are you sure?"

"One hundred percent."

"And it's safe for her and the baby?"

"Yep."

"I owe you."

"I know, I'm keeping track, so don't worry."

I hang up and look at Christian. "Easy. I go into her mind and remind her of everything."

He releases a chest full of breath. "We didn't erase her memory?"

"No. She's just out of it. It'll come back, but a mind share will speed it up."

He points to my phone. "Who was that?"

I hesitate. If the Moores find out about Tara, they'll dispatch men to kill her without a second thought. Whatever I send home with Christian will have to be some powerful stuff.

"My twin sister."

"My ass."

"I swear on the elements."

"Hmm. Well, since we aren't related, is she hot?"

"That's creepy, man."

"Yeah, it kind of is." He follows me into the basement.

I stop at the bottom of the steps and he just about runs into me. "We can't leave her up there by herself."

"Let's bring her down here then." He heads back up the stairs.

I stare after him, knowing there isn't any other option. We enter the living room and catch her just in time. With one hand loose from the ropes, she's quickly untying her ankles. Christian leaps for her feet and fastens the ropes as I tie her wrists.

"Listen to me." I kneel in front of her, holding her hands in mine. "You're disoriented, and you've forgotten some things. That's our fault. We're going to fix you. You'll have to trust me." *Again*, I want to add. Since I failed her the first time.

Her eyes burn into me but she makes no other response. I carry her downstairs to a stool and untie her ankles. To my surprise, she doesn't struggle. I want to untie her wrists, but she's too dangerous with the training I gave her.

Luckily, I kept the jar of the binding agent Liv and I used the first time we did a mind share. That's one less thing we'll have to prepare.

"You make mine and I'll make hers," I say to Christian, referring to the tablets we'll need to switch our consciousness to the necessary state for the process to work.

"You don't trust me to make hers? Screw you."

"Okay, you make hers."

"Well, you shouldn't trust me. I don't remember this."

"Shocking." I glance at Liv. She seems to have lost some of her hatred. She watches us curiously, and I wonder what she's thinking. If she doesn't remember anything I've told her, anything she's experienced since meeting me, my basement must look like some psycho's lair—a wall of guns and knives, shelves of dried herbs and old books, a workbench holding a well-used chemistry set. The perfect place to be cooking up some kind of illegal drugs. And here she is, held hostage by the two of us. She doesn't remember sitting on that stool not long ago, watching me measure ingredients, join them over flame, cut the final product into a perfect, dissolvable cube.

Yet she's retained her fighting skills. She remembers our combat training but she doesn't remember me. Tara's right. Love is a complicated thing.

After I refresh Christian's memory, he starts on my tablet and promises to take care of Liv if it kills me. We work quickly, and when we finish, I copy the wording out of the text. We head up the stairs, me walking Liv up by the arm.

"I'm just going to take her to bed," I say to Christian. It's late as hell, and I'm tired. She must be too. This way, when we're done, we can just stay asleep.

"Oh, she's going to love that right now."

She eyes me warily. I drag her to the bedroom, sit her down on the bed, and close the door.

"Will you behave if I untie you?"

Her expression answers with a firm no.

I exhale and sit next to her. "See all this stuff in here? This is all your stuff."

Recognition flashes across her face. I yank a drawer out of the dresser and hold it before her.

"All your clothes. Folded. By you yourself." I put the drawer back and open the closet door. "My clothes. Because we're living together."

"Then why don't I know you?"

Her voice is a breath of pure oxygen after I've been suffocating for an eternity.

"Because someone put a spell on you, and in trying to remove it, Christian and I made a mistake. So now we have to fix it. I'm going to untie you, and you're going to trust me. Okay?"

She gives a slight nod, and I go for the ropes on her wrists. Her eyes are on me like she's dying to say something. Instead, she points to my fireplace poker wound.

"Yeah. Thanks for that."

Then I see what she's thinking. I need medical attention. Nurse Liv is always on the job.

"You don't need to worry—" I stop when I realize she's right. I do need to worry about infection now. And if she's concerned about me, she's probably not going to make a break for it when I go across the hall for the bandages and ointment. Unless that concern is fake, and she's hoping I'm a sucker.

She must remember what a sucker I am when it comes to her.

I go to the bathroom for the bandages and she doesn't move a muscle. The concern must be real. She's a nurse though—it's her job to be concerned about the health of strangers. I dab on some ointment, find the biggest bandage in the box, and tape it on myself. I'm not going to make her bandage some psycho kidnapper. Although, not long ago I was exactly that. "Happy?"

She takes my arm and turns it, bite mark up. Gives it a good look. I'm not bandaging up a damn human bite wound. She must read something from my body language because she doesn't push it.

I pick up her tablet. Hold it in front of her lips. She opens her mouth.

CHAPTER 8

LIV

T HE TABLET BEGINS to dissolve on my tongue, and he places another tablet on his tongue and returns his eyes to me.

"Hold out your palms."

I comply, knowing if this really is a dream, I'll wake up unharmed. But it all seems so real, and I can't shake the incessant feeling I knew this man in another lifetime. I may not know his name, but there's a deep region of my brain that approves of him—and approves of me going along with this ritual.

He smears a drop of a brown, gluey substance on each of my palms then does the same to his. My defense mechanism has been subdued for now, but I can still feel it laboring inside me, analyzing the room, seeking the quickest escape, the closest weapons. If I've been kidnapped and taken hostage, I certainly couldn't have asked for two better looking captors. And both walking around shirtless. This has to be a dream. Either that, or I'm stuck on the set of a soap opera.

"Hold up your palms, facing me."

My hands do as they're told. I have no idea why I'm going along with this aside from how right it feels. But I know if he so much as makes one inappropriate move—

The electric touch of his skin against mine sends a charge through me as he places his palms against mine, intertwining our fingers. I open my mouth to speak, but my words evaporate when his smile fills my whole world. The room around me blurs, dissolving with each syllable of a strange language flowing from his lips toward me in a river of sound.

Now I know I'm dreaming. Soon I can wake up and go to work and this will all be forgotten. I'm in the middle of a lively outside market. People swarm around me carrying baskets of vegetables, watermelons on their shoulders, babies on their hips. I stop in front of a display of ripe, luscious tomatoes. Hunger seizes me. How unusual. I've never felt hunger in a dream before.

I pick up a tomato and hold it in front of me. The skin is like silk, and my mouth waters. A person steps up next to me, casting a shadow over my wonderful tomato. Annoyed, I look up, into the most handsome green eyes I've ever seen. They're the color of a juniper bush, a color that reminds me of home.

"On me," he says, handing the vendor a dollar bill.

I'm unable to look away. This is the same man from earlier in my dream, but now he's different. He leans down, holding my forearm, and takes a bite out of my tomato. Juice runs down my arm, and I watch his lips as he chews and swallows.

"Trey," I say abruptly.

"Yes!" He's clearly thrilled. "Would you like to go to the beach?"

I remember being on the beach once. He accepts my silence as agreement, and, taking my hand, he leads me to the edge of the market where we step onto white sand and walk toward the sea.

My tomato is gone. I stop and turn. So is the market. I look up at him for an explanation, and he takes my wrist and holds it up to show me a delicate bracelet of shiny white shells.

"Remember?" he asks, those green eyes now eager.

I nod. He gave me this. Two times. I'm not sure why he gave me this two times, but I know it doesn't matter.

"Can I kiss you?" Seeing my uncertainty, he drops my hand, and we begin to walk together down the beach.

"I don't know where to begin," he says. "I'm skipping all the bad stuff. That can come back on its own."

"You are so handsome." I can't help myself. Dark hair, a pleasantly weathered face. Instead of ruining his looks, his scars enhance them. Like a gouge in a mahogany desk, it's the contrast of the gouge that causes a person to notice the beauty of the wood.

"We definitely need to do this more often."

"How do I know you?" His hair used to be longer, long enough to fall onto his forehead. But now it's buzzed short. I'm not sure how I know that.

"Just walk with me. When we come out of this, you'll remember everything."

I'm overcome with weighted confidence in his statement. Not trust of someone else's sentiment, but genuine confidence coming from inside me as if that statement was my own raw thought. What quickly follows is a satisfaction, also inside me, but not mine—until it is mine.

"Stop overthinking it," he says. "Just relax."

Overthinking what? I want to ask, but the question is snatched away before I can voice it.

"Relax," he says.

I look at him. The few things I know about him are trivial, insignificant. Randomly selected frames in a film. The whole they make up is still a mystery. I should ask him how I met him to jog my memory, but it seems like a breach of trust. I trust him now? I think I do, but I'm not sure why. And with it recognized, it's all I seem to need. We walk together, and I lose myself in the rhythm of the tide, my hand warm inside his.

When I notice the sea has swallowed the last bit of sun, he collapses to his knees, dropping my hand. I kneel beside him. He looks at me, his eyes dim, exhausted.

"Trey." My Trey.

"Yes." The word is a surrender, an exhale, a much awaited finality.

"*Tá mé i ngrá leat,*" I say.

"Now that's what I like to hear." He falls to his back on the sand.

I lie against him, and he wraps his arm around me. The tide kisses our bare feet, soothing us both into a gentle sleep. Just before I drift away, I remember how we came to be the two people aligned by the stars. The ancient spell that orchestrated the event. And my fear that love built by magic will fade or be broken as easily as it conquered us, and this bliss I've found will be dead.

I don't remember these are thoughts I'd prefer to hide from Trey until it's too late and they've already been thought.

The alarm clock shrieks, and I slap it off, leaving a brown glob on the snooze button. I settle back into the circle of Trey's arms and stare at my palms. He was in my mind again, to help me remember what I forgot. It was bad enough to fear the spell wearing off. Now I know I'm not only capable of forgetting I love him, I could forget him entirely.

He exhales, turning to his back.

"Are you awake?" I whisper.

He doesn't answer. I remember how exhausted he was the first time we did this. I wipe my palms on the sheet then wipe his palms and jerk the sheet off the bed to the floor. Knowing I should let him sleep, I slide to the edge of the bed but he snares me, pulling me back against him.

"I have to get up for work," I whisper. I hope what I just learned doesn't sound in my voice.

"No," he says against the back of my neck. It gives me chills, quickens the beat of my heart.

"I *have* to. Go back to sleep. You need to rest."

He's quiet a moment then says, "*Cén t-am é?*"

I glance at the clock. "*Tá sé deich nóiméad tar éis a seacht.*" My hands fly to my mouth.

"Beautiful."

He taught me his language. It feels so natural, like I've known it my whole life. It's unfair to be attached to someone in so many ways—love, a child, two common languages—when now I know how easily our bond could be severed.

"I'm going to be late." I struggle against his iron arms.

"Come get me when you're ready to go. I'll drive you."

"I can drive." I slip out of bed.

After my shower, I dress quietly in the bedroom against the sound of his deep breathing then go to the kitchen. Christian is already up, sipping a cup of coffee at the table in his boxers with a mess of disheveled hair.

"Glad to have you back," he says around a tooth-paste-commercial smile. "You're lucky you didn't break my nose. I have a date tonight."

"I held back. For some reason I didn't want to hurt you as much as him." I jerk my thumb toward the bedroom. It'd be a joke if it didn't make me feel so sick.

He laughs. "Wish it was that way all the time. Usually I'm the one getting railed on. At least, that's how it's been lately."

I pour us each a bowl of Cheerios, cut up a banana, and bring it all to the table.

"Wow. Great service here. I could get used to this."

"Don't be silly. You are used to it at home."

"True." He takes a mouthful.

"So, I guess he's going to be out cold all day?" I already know the answer from past experience.

"Yeah, I'll let him sleep it off. Old age is catching up to him."

"How old are you? Five years younger than Trey?"

"Yep. I'm twenty-five."

I chuckle. "Five years younger than the age he *should* be. So you're forty. You don't look forty."

"And you don't look—how old are you again?"

"Thirty-two." I know he's pretending to know just so I'll tell him.

"Trey, the cradle robber."

"I thought you said he was mentally fourteen."

"Yeah." He looks into his cereal as if it just turned sour. After a moment, he gives me a contemplative look. A how-much-should-I-tell-her look. It doesn't last long. "That's a joke, but there's a sick truth to it, too. Something happened to Trey when he was fifteen and he was never the same. He didn't have a normal childhood. Neither of us did."

I lay down my spoon. I've seen the broken man who lives inside the tough exterior. I can imagine the innocent child he once was. Some of those memories live inside me now, remnants of a mind share that wandered from his mind to mine without his knowledge.

"He'll kill me if I tell you."

"I can handle him."

"I know you can." He drums his fingers on the table while looking at me hard. "I feel like you need to know. My family started fearing Trey when he was fifteen. And when my family fears someone…well, they usually respond with violence."

"What happened?"

"Did Trey tell you how hard his father trained him? His stepfather, I mean. Martin. My uncle."

"He trained him to be a fighter."

"Right. He trained us both, but it was always all about Trey. Knowing the truth now, I can't understand why they'd do that." He rubs his forehead. "Guess they figured he'd never betray them. Never know."

I nod. My coffee warms me. The room has gotten so cold.

"So, my father is a real prick. And I don't say that lovingly. He kicked my ass so many times when I was a kid it all started blurring together. I hung out with Trey and his mom as much as possible so I wouldn't have to be around him. I didn't have a mother. She died when I was a baby."

It's a rare thing to meet another person with a dead parent. As a child, I used to pretend my dead parents were simply lost. That they'd left me with someone and gone to run errands and gotten lost in the city. That any day, they'd show up, breathless and weary from walking, and take me from the children's home to our real home. It was easier than admitting they were dead. "I heard about that."

"At some point, my dad started getting in on Trey's training with my uncle. When my uncle wasn't around, my dad would really give it to Trey. He told us he was trying to make him stronger, but really he was just using him as a punching bag. This went on for *years*. A defenseless kid, you know?"

Fighting tears, I say, "Sick."

"Totally sick. But when Trey was fifteen, he'd finally had enough. By then he was good. Really good. He could hold his own against adults twice his size. And one day, he just snapped. He gave it right back to my dad. Almost killed him. I had to pull him off—he wouldn't have stopped. And from that day on, everyone had it out for him. They already treated him like a piece of shit. But it got so much worse."

"Did Martin or Sloane ever know?"

"I don't know. When you're young, you just don't notice what goes on with the adults."

"How could they expect him not to defend himself?"

He drains his coffee and gets up for more. "Trey did a little more than defend himself that day. It proved just how much he'd been holding back, how dangerous he was. It scared them. I'll admit it even scared me."

Those memories are in Trey's head somewhere, and it's a lottery whether they'll accidentally transfer to me. If taking them would erase them from his mind, I might consider the burden to free some weight from him. It just doesn't work that way. It's yet another thing I should talk to him about, but I'd have to admit to him the unplanned transfer of those memories happened in the first place. "Yes, I can see how it would."

"That's why he's such an ass sometimes. Me? I was used to the abuse. I just take it and move on. He's different. He harbors it, obsesses about it, lets it eat him alive."

And then comes to a breaking point and takes it out on the nearest wall. Or person's face. "That's why he drinks so much."

"Probably. It calms him down. But he's also just got that personality. He gets so intense about things. He's got a one-track mind. What a freak." His laugh tries to lighten the mood. "But at least now you know why."

I take our empty bowls to the sink. How could I feel so overprotective of a man who could snap me in two? A man who has killed so many people he's lost count? A man who walks into a brutal fight head on, reveling in the challenge? If the bout of amnesia hadn't happened I might be better prepared to hear these things. Love this intense needs time to settle in or it manifests like a mental illness. Everything's happening too fast.

He raises both arms to stretch his back. "Sorry to ruin your morning."

"Don't either of you ever wear any clothes?"

"Nope." He toasts the air with his mug.

Christian's the one I could ask about the spell, but I can't find the nerve. It feels wrong. "Thanks for telling me. I think I understand him a little better now."

"None of us will ever fully understand him." He pauses thoughtfully. "I don't think he understands himself. He just charges ahead and won't back off. He's like a pit bull."

"I've thought those exact same words."

"He's always been like that to a degree. But that day he snapped, it's like something was tripped in his brain, like his competitiveness was turned up to the max. He's been like that ever since. And it's not like he has to win. He just has to exhaust whatever's in him at the time."

"Like the last time you were here, when he tore up his knuckles on his heavy bag."

"Exactly. Classic Trey moment."

"He doesn't know when to stop."

"His stopping point is just so much beyond a normal person's. Like I said. Freak." He grins.

I start packing myself a lunch, and Christian leans against the counter next to me.

"What are you going to do all day?" I ask.

"I'll figure something out. And I have that date tonight. Don't be jealous. You're still my number one."

My laughter recharges me after such a depressing conversation. This is why I love Christian. "Can you move here?"

"Why?" He looks surprised.

"You're good to have around. You're a mood stabilizer for him."

He looks away to stare out the back door. "I considered moving with him years ago. When he first left, when he thought Kate was dead. He was messed up." He pauses, watching something play out in his mind. "It was bad."

"He needs you."

"Nah, he's good now. He has you. You have no idea what he used to be like. I barely recognized him when I came to visit a few weeks ago, when you were here. Even with the news I brought, I couldn't believe how happy he was."

"He was raging out of control!"

"But he was happy. I could see it, for the first time in fifteen years." He shakes his head, disgusted. "And what was always so funny to me is that Kate treated him like shit. And he took it. He was so much better off without her, but he couldn't see that. It's just another example of how obsessed the dude gets. Loyal to the end and beyond. To someone who never deserved it. Hopefully he's over that."

I know he means nothing by it, but the idea is already in me and hasn't yet been squashed. She could still have hold of him. A part of him could still love her. Just like—

Holy shit. Dillon. The weight is gone.

"Just don't ever betray him." Christian continues his train of thought. "His loyalty is strong, but betray him, and you're a goner. You won't even see him coming."

"It worked," I say.

Christian appraises me over the rim of his mug.

"It's gone. I'm not bound to him anymore."

"Heck yeah." He sets down his mug and raises his good hand for a high five.

My hand meets his and holds on tightly. "I had no idea—"

I had no idea I was a slave.

"Of course you didn't. That's part of the trick."

I stare at him, speechless. This is going to take some time for me to process.

He lowers my hand and releases it. "So, your last name used to be Moore."

I nod.

"And you're still legally married? That means you and I are related. Cousins…somehow…"

Which means Trey and I are related. He was adopted in, and I married in. I know he doesn't talk as if he's part of that family anymore, but this is damn complicated.

"When you found out my family's name, didn't that tip you off?"

"I just thought it was a coincidence." That's the conclusion I arrived at, after a near freak-out on the plane. Moore is not an uncommon name. It was Trey's mother having the same name as my daughter that gave the coincidence its fangs. Their name *is* an uncommon name.

He scoffs. "There's no such thing as coincidence when my family is involved. But I'm glad it worked. I'll give you the satisfaction of telling him."

I pick up my keys.

"I'll drive you," Christian says. "Let him sleep. Just let me throw on some clothes." He returns a few minutes later in rumpled jeans, a coat, and a sock hat, but still no shirt. Leaning down to pull on shoes over his bare feet, he looks up at me. "Hey, do I have a strange accent?"

"Not to me. Why?"

"Someone told me that yesterday."

"You should have an accent. Your family's from Richmond."

"We haven't always lived in Richmond." He takes a Glock off the top of the refrigerator and I lead him outside.

"How'd you know he doesn't want me to drive by myself to work?" I ask once we're seated inside his Infiniti.

"Because I know him." He hands me the gun.

The car's luxurious engine purrs alive, followed by the heavy thumping of industrial techno. He must have a trunk full of speakers. Leaning forward against his seat belt, he pumps his shoulders to the beat until we get to the road, then he lowers the volume.

"You like electronica?" he asks in a fake German accent.

"It's not bad."

"It's way better than that aggressive hardcore rock Trey listens to." Hearing no response, he looks over at me. "Don't tell me you like it, too."

"He never listens to music. Not around me, at least." I should try harder to preserve this light conversation but with all our earlier talk, too much unfinished business has me anxious to talk some of it out. Understand it. Expel it.

"That's right—I forgot. He gave up music. Hard to torture yourself when—"

"What if Trey still does have feelings for Kate?"

"Honestly? Well, I do know she fights dirty. You know that now. She's manipulative, cunning, and pure evil."

"Why does she suddenly want him back? It's been so long. Yeah, they're still married but she left *him*, and let him think she was dead for fifteen years. And it sounds like she's moved on."

"Probably because you have him."

"Great." I stare out the window. I don't know how she couldn't still have feelings for him. I still have feelings for Dillon, even though I know what he did to me. Even though the crippling weight of losing him is gone. We shared things. We had good times. Good memories. Some things you just can't fake.

"She probably wants to take back what she thinks is rightfully hers. But to answer your question, I think you'd know. Trey isn't capable of hiding his feelings. And like I told you, once you betray him like she did, it's over. So don't worry."

He sounds a lot more confident about it than I feel, even though I know he's right.

"She will keep trying, though. She thinks she can play him like she used to. She thought he was stupid. She still thinks he's stupid."

"Trey?"

"Yeah, I know. She can't see any depth to people because she's too obsessed with herself."

I'd love to explain to her that devotion, and love, can blind a person to trickery. That a person can appear to be stupid, when really they've just surrendered to your games. That no one can cut a situation down to its stark reality like Trey. He can blast through bullshit easier than anyone I've met. And if for some reason he was fooled by her it wasn't because of a shortcoming in IQ. It was because of an attribute. His loyalty. His protectiveness. His love. The person lacking smarts is the one who couldn't recognize it, the one who'd give him up.

He stops in front of the clinic. "Do I have to walk you inside?"

I'm not sure if he's joking or actually determined to cover for Trey one hundred percent. "He just drops me off here. I guess I won't see you tonight?"

"Hopefully not. I seriously need to get laid."

"Good luck with that." I leave the gun in my seat as I get out of the car.

He catches my hand. "I'm glad you're free from him now. He was going to kill you, you know."

"He wouldn't have killed me." It's just a reaction. My knowledge of Dillon Moore means nothing. I can't trust anything I know about him.

"Yes, he would have. He followed you and Trey that day when you left the estate. He knew you weren't dead, and he was going to finish you off. He wanted to kill you in front of him." The set of his jaw and flash of fury in his eyes gives me pause. For once, he looks like he could be Trey's brother.

"Don't tell Trey," I say. It's all I can manage.

"Too late. I already have."

I'm not sure what my face looks like, but it's bad enough for him to kiss my hand.

"Next time listen to me when I tell you someone's a bad person," he says when he releases me.

I close the door of the car and walk inside. What if Dillon had found us that day? Trey couldn't have saved me and fought him at the same time. I don't know how he managed to evade him, but whatever he did saved both of our lives.

Glancing at the clock in the lobby, I take a deep breath. One minute into my shift and I'm already sick with longing for him.

CHAPTER 9

TREY

SOMETHING SNAPS ME in the face and I open my eyes.

"Dude, get up. You have to pick up Liv."

I roll over, and he snaps me in the back of the head with his tie.

"Can you stop?" I sit up.

"Don't make her wait." He flips his collar up and fastens his tie around his neck. Clean-shaven, styled hair, and a five hundred dollar shirt and tie. He must have a date.

"I'm up. Resume playing dress-up."

His laughter follows him out of the room.

I throw on my clothes and rub my hair down. As I'm putting on a coat and hat, Christian steps into the entryway sliding into a fitted khaki jacket.

"Aren't you cute," I say.

"Are you in love with me or something? I'm sorry, but you're just not my type." He feels his pocket for his keys and opens the door. "I'll see you in the morning."

"Good luck with that."

He gives me a funny look, closes the door behind him.

A few minutes later, I catch up to him in my Camaro and go around him, inches from his rear bumper. He plasters his middle finger against his window without looking in my direction as I pass him by, so I cut him off on my re-entry into the lane before leaving him in my dust.

I just about run off the road when I think of it: Liv's only easy for them to get to because she's at my house. I could stash her at a hotel anywhere between here and Virginia and they'd never find her in time. Christian could come with me. We could kill them all together. His dad could be the grand finale.

It's a perfect plan neither of them are going to like. They'll just have to learn to.

When I get to the clinic, Liv seems to be running late. Each time the door opens, it's not her. I pull the Camaro out of gear and set the parking brake, trying not to think of reasons why she could be hung up because none of the reasons I come up with are nice. No one's ever had a reason to call me optimistic. Hell, how do I know Christian dropped her off here this morning? Maybe he's still compromised, and he killed her and threw her body in the river. I readjust myself in my seat. Each increment of the

Camaro's clock heckles me. How long should I wait before I go inside for her?

The front door of the clinic opens and she appears, doubled over in laughter, followed by Shawn who seems to be in the middle of an animated joke. I watch until he leans down to hug her, then my feet hit the pavement and the car door slams behind me.

Liv looks up, surprised before her face falls. I reach for Shawn's hand and he takes my handshake. There's no reason to be impolite before I kick his teeth in.

"I don't have a problem with you and Liv being friends, but I do have a problem with you putting your hands on her."

I see Liv's mouth drop open out of the corner of my eye, but my focus remains on Shawn. It's strange facing someone near my height; I can look him straight in the eye.

He lets out a hearty laugh. "If I can't give her a friendly hug, then that's your problem, man, not mine."

"I can quickly make it your problem."

"I doubt that."

My palms tingle. I struggle against the need to shut him down permanently. Does he ever stop smiling?

"I'll drive *myself* home." Liv pushes past me and walks around the car to the driver's side.

"I'm not warning you again." I wait, daring him to respond. It's all I need. He drops his smile. His gaze shifts to Liv. He's thinking the same thing: not in front of her. I want to tell him I can make it too fast for her to see, but I don't. The words would be wasted. He'll have to be shown. I remove Liv from the driver's seat and walk her to the passenger side. Shut the door behind her. Give him one last look. *Next time.*

I take my seat. Arms crossed tightly over her chest, she hasn't yet buckled up. I reach across her for her seat belt, and she doesn't look at me or move when I fasten it in place. When I reach for the gearshift, she looks at me.

"You are *out of control*."

The fury in her eyes hits me like a chemical explosion, and I grasp the back of her neck and kiss her hard. She shoves me away, turning her whole body away from me. "So now you're marking your territory?"

"I missed you." I step on the gas and we pull away.

"Right. Is that what you call it when your testosterone is raging out of control?"

A laugh escapes my mouth. She's so cute when she's angry. As soon as I get her in the house, she's not going to be angry any more.

She plucks her phone from her purse, stares at its display, and takes a deep breath. "You know what I want to do right now?"

"What?" I can think of a few things I want to do right now.

"I want to call Shawn, apologize for your behavior, and then offer to take him out to dinner to make it up to him."

"You wouldn't do that." There's tension in my jaw from the vision of that idea playing out in my mind.

"No, I'm not going to. Because all it would do is incense you, and then it'd be two days of the silent treatment when all I want to do is be with you after a horrible experience of forgetting who you are. After finally being freed."

"Freed?" My relief, my triumph, waits impatiently for release.

"Yes. But I'm not talking about that yet. I don't want it ruined. I'm going to calm down, and then we're going to talk about what just happened, like adults."

"What just happened?" I try to think back, but all I can think about is the taste of her lips, the feel of her skin against mine.

"You *know* what just happened. You embarrassed me at work, you insulted my friend, you acted like a complete jerk!"

"That had to be done. It was overdue."

"Trey, I swear to god." She stares out the window for a few minutes. She finally clears her throat. "I'm driving myself to work from now on. You have too much control over me, and it's not healthy."

"Control?" That hits a nerve. "I'm protecting you."

"Yes, but you're also controlling me. If I can't walk out of work sharing a joke with a friend without you storming over to pick a fight—"

"I wasn't picking a fight. He was picking a fight." Was she not there?

"I don't know what world you're living in. You—"

"He should know better than to touch you."

"You'd let Christian hug me."

"Totally different."

"Okay we're just going to go in circles, so forget it. But if you can't promise you'll stay in the car, then I'm driving myself."

"I'm not good with ultimatums." I almost want to agree just so she'll be content. I can't be without her tonight.

She remains quiet, obviously waiting for me to give her my word. She knows it's too risky for her to go alone every day. We reach the house, pull into the garage, and get out of the car. Inside, we shed our coats, then she looks up at me. "So?"

I raise my eyebrows.

She points at me. "Do you promise?"

"Don't make me promise. What if I need to get out of the car to help an old woman with her groceries?"

"At the clinic?" There's a smile in her eyes. She's tightened her mouth as if all that's left of her anger has settled there.

I touch the spot just under her bottom lip, like there's a button there to disarm it. I trace down her chin, down her neck, down her chest, where she catches it with a grip only I could have taught her. "Promise."

"I'll try."

She sighs heavily. "Can we eat dinner?"

I take her hand and lead her into the kitchen. "What do you want?"

"Nothing's ready?"

"Not today. You're getting spoiled."

"How late did you sleep?"

"All fucking day."

"Because now that Christian's here, every sentence must have the F word."

"All darn day," I correct.

"When the two of you get together, you just make each other worse. I feel like I'm living in a frat house."

"No more cursing around the lady. Got it."

She slides her arms around me. The pressure on my ribs sends a weakness through me, a blip of nausea more alive in mind than body. I have to catch myself from stumbling backward, pull it together like I'm eating the floor in the ring, about to be declared TKO in a fight I wasn't sober enough to enter. Power to the arms first, get them under me. Bite down on the mouthguard and shove. Next, legs. A quick glance at the ref to make sure he's keeping the guy off me. If there is a ref. A missing moment then I'm on my feet, empowered to full strength, ready to kill. Remembering this time, I can't kill. This is just playtime.

Then I'm back in the room with Liv against me instead of the body of my opponent. All that was years ago. Now's not the time for that shit to come back.

"I'm starving." Her cheek is against my chest.

Shawn, Dillon, dinner all come rushing back. And the inches of Liv's body in contact with my own. It's too much. It's not enough. "I don't have cooking on the mind."

She shifts a little. Her grip is gentle but the pressure on my ribs is like a vice. I peel off her arms.

"How about some oatmeal then?"

"Done." I get the oatmeal and a pot and put it on the stove. When I turn around, she's letting her hair down from her ponytail. "You shouldn't do that."

"Please. Everything I do isn't for you."

"Yes it is." I pick her up and set her on the counter facing me. I hold the backs of her calves tight against my hips.

"I can't believe it." She crosses her legs and binds them behind me. "How…severe it was. I was enslaved. That's the only way I can describe it."

"Why didn't you tell me?" If I'd known she was under his control, I could've purged it so much sooner.

"I didn't know. I just thought it was grief. That it was normal to be completely lost without him. Now I realize I never loved him in the first place. *I never loved him.*" She covers her mouth as if this is the first time she's realized it. "And all those times he'd go out of town. He told me he was visiting his brother in New York. I can't believe it."

When I hear my teeth grinding together, I take a deep breath and willfully relax my jaw. She needs to stop talking about him.

"He isn't all bad, you know. It probably wasn't his idea to do that to me."

She pauses for me to respond, but I have nothing to say. I don't care if he's Mother Teresa. I'm still going to rip out his throat.

"Don't look at me like that. I want you to let it go. I was happy. He treated me well. He served me meals in bed for two days after my dog died."

"He probably killed your dog."

She squints, focusing past my shoulder. Opens her mouth. Closes it. I reach behind me to uncross her legs and free myself, but she catches my arms.

"You need to know he didn't do anything bad to me. I had a perfect life until the end. It only got bad at the end."

"It's over. I'm sorry we didn't get it right the first time. It was a stupid mistake," I say in an effort to take her mind off him.

"I'm sorry about your jaw." She strokes my face where I know it's bruised deep.

"Don't forget about this." I lift my shirt to reveal the gash in my ribs from the fireplace poker. "And this." I show her the bite mark on my arm. "Who taught you to bite?"

"Wow." She laughs. "I'm an animal."

I turn off the burner and dish up two bowls. We sit across from one another in our usual seats. After a few bites, she looks up at me like she wants me to say something, and I wonder if she asked a question I didn't hear. "What?"

"Christian told me about your childhood."

I don't answer. I'm not sure how much he told her.

"Don't be mad at him. I made him tell me."

"After last night, I'm sure you could get anything out of him." It's probably a good idea to steer the conversation away from any topics that might put a damper on tonight.

"It really…bothers me." She seems to search for the right words. "It—"

"Christian blows things out of proportion. He's too sensitive."

"No, I don't think so." She's shaking her head.

When I don't respond, she changes direction. "Why were you so rude to your stepfather when we were there?"

I try to remember the conversation, but it all blurs together. The only vivid memory of that day is my hands, covered in Liv's blood.

"It sounds like he loves you, that he was a good father to you, in a very difficult situation. Why were you rude to him?"

Words rush to me, and I release them before they burrow down, buried forever. "He always sides with my uncle. With all of them. And I can't respect that."

She moves her spoon around, thinking for a moment. "Maybe he's afraid of your uncle."

"My father's afraid of no one. Can we not talk about this?" My voice rises louder than I mean it to, and I close my eyes in reaction to a storm building, blurring my vision, clouding my mind.

I open my eyes to a line of tears on each of her cheeks. There's no end to this. They are making her cry? I won't allow them to make her cry.

She wipes her cheeks with her sleeve and goes back to her oatmeal as I envision snapping the neck of every last one of them. I shove away from the table, pour myself a glass of scotch, and take a long drink, staring out the window over the sink. No matter what I do, no matter where I go, I can never escape them. They always find some way to infiltrate my life. If it's not them directly, it's the part of them inside me. A festering hate, a revenge unfulfilled and building each day into something impossible to pay. I can only kill each of them once.

I finish the glass and refill it.

"I wish you wouldn't drink so much."

"It doesn't hurt me." I take another drink. She doesn't need to worry about me.

She stands. "I ruined your mood. I'm so sorry I brought all that up." Her eyes are liquid and reflective. On the verge of overflowing.

I look away, shaking my head, disgusted. She has no reason to be sorry. I should be sorry, for bringing her into all of this. *They* should be sorry—they *will* be sorry. "Doesn't matter if you bring it up. It's always there."

I'm shocked by my clarity of mind. My candor. I sit at the table, and she watches me a moment then sits on my lap, straddling me. She studies my face, and I set my drink on the table so my hands are free to hold her. She shoves the glass to the other end of the table.

"Let's not talk anymore tonight." There's a playful curl to her lip. Her eyes are deep blue, magnified by those tears waiting in reserve.

As I open my mouth to ask her what she'd like to do instead, she puts her hand over my mouth.

"Starting now."

I like this idea.

She takes my face in her hands, and I release the breath I'd been unconsciously holding. My shoulders relax, relieved of tension I didn't notice until now. Her eyes hover on the bruise on my jaw, then her arms go around my neck, her lips against mine. All my unleashed pain, all my torment, drowns in the calm wave of serenity that flows from her into me.

CHAPTER 10

LIV

WE SIT UP simultaneously to River's warning howl in the night. Trey rolls out of bed and pulls on his jeans. I reach for my pants.

"You're staying here." He pulls a shirt over his head.

"I'll stay inside. I'll back you up." He can't keep me from helping. I want to tell him how I worry he'll get knocked out again, his energy will reverse, our love will be turned off like it was so easily turned on. Like a switch. But now's not the time.

Hurrying through the living room past a soundly sleeping Christian and down the basement stairs, I hear the front door close behind Trey and quickly locate a small rifle. I shove some ammunition in my pocket and take the stairs two at a time and go out the front door.

The clear night sky illuminates the yard, but I see no sign of Trey or any intruders. I take another step onto the front porch, raise the rifle and wait. The pine forest is at rest. Stars blink above. I wonder where River is, if she's followed Trey or if she's gone back to patrol. Branches snap in the woods and I swing my aim toward the sound. The frigid air makes every tiny noise sound like it's directly next to me.

A scuffle breaks out in the woods, but I can't see anything from the porch. My pulse pounds in my ears; I breathe to steady it. I can't see who's winning. The scene in front of me is stationary, asleep. If it weren't for the sounds coming from beyond the first line of trees I'd think this was any other night. What if Trey is down? Adrenaline walks my feet off the porch and along the side of the house in the shadow of the eave.

The combat in the woods abruptly stops, but I'm blind to the victor. As the silence presses down on me, I wait, trusting Trey could never be beaten. He's never been beaten. Why would tonight be any different?

Through the sights, I see him emerge from the woods. I lower my rifle.

"You were supposed to stay inside," he says as soon as he's within earshot.

"I can't—"

He jerks the rifle out of my hands and holds my gaze, mad enough to turn my own gun on me. I reach out to the torn collar of his shirt and he yanks me inside the door with him. His roughness with me is expected but futile.

I'll never cower inside when he's outside fighting for his life. He's the one who trained me. He should know this.

"Liv, I swear—"

I shush him and point to Christian on the couch. He glowers at me for another drawn out moment then heads for the kitchen, where I know he's going to have some wounds to bandage. He goes straight to the sink.

"I guess Christian didn't get lucky after all," I say behind him.

"A shame." His attention remains on washing mud off his hands until he turns to me and sighs. "Liv—"

I stretch his torn collar aside. The wound is a slice, not a stab. I can suture it. I point to the chair and he removes his shirt and sits.

"Why do they always get you with a knife? Why don't they bring a gun and just shoot you when you step out the front door?"

"He had a gun. I took it away from him." He leans forward to extract a gun from the back of his pants.

I drag a chair to face him and use his wadded shirt to apply pressure to his wound. It was me they wanted shot when I stepped out the door. "Why was Christian sent to kill me? How'd they know I'd survive that arrow?"

He gives me that look—the measuring one most people follow with a white lie. Trey doesn't lie, even when he wants to protect me from something I'm better off not knowing. Maybe I shouldn't have asked.

"Kate sent him. She knew I could heal you."

"How'd she know?"

"Because I could heal her."

I drop my eyes and focus on the pressure on his wound. It would be a lot easier to accept if I hadn't met her.

"Are you jealous?" He's grinning now, and it only makes me feel sicker.

If I believed he hated her it would be different. Real love isn't that easy to turn off. Love mixed with grief is even harder. Although he now knows he had no reason for the grief, the whole thing is a complicated mess that was supposed to be resolved during our visit to Richmond. Here we are, back in Black River, with things between Trey and his wife still unresolved.

I start to clean his wound. When I turn to find a suture needle, I catch a glimpse of his face. His eyes have gone hard again.

"What am I going to have to do to get you to stay in the house?"

"I'll never hide inside when you're out there. We're a team. You seem to have forgotten that."

"You'll help me best by staying out of danger. The immortality is making you feel invincible. You have to recover your fear of death, your sense of self-preservation."

"No more talking while I do this." I start the first stitch.

"I'm done anyway. You know." The look in his eyes is so harsh I'm tempted to tell him off. But if we start fighting now, it will be two overtired people yelling at each other about a subject that doesn't need discussion. He's controlling. I get it. Doesn't mean he can control me. No amount of arguing is going to convince him of that.

He remains silent. I can't decide if the disgusted look is the remainder of his demands or a result of having a wound sutured with no anesthetic. When I'm finished, he takes my hand and flips off the light. On my way through the living room, I take Christian's ankles and turn him straight against the couch. He must have come home, sat down, and fallen right asleep. I remove his already loosened tie from his neck, unbutton his top two shirt buttons, take off his shoes, and throw a blanket over him.

Inside the bedroom, Trey's sitting on the bed, gripping the edge of the mattress, head bowed. I walk into him, and he wraps his arms around my legs and hugs me hard. He looks up at me, that dimple in his forehead, a pleading look in his eyes. "I can't be without you. I'll self-destruct. Is that what you want?"

I wipe a smudge of dirt off his cheek with my sleeve. "Nothing can hurt me."

"Those bullets from Christian's gun would've killed you. Blown your heart to pieces. The immortality couldn't have repaired that."

"You have mud in your hair."

He exhales hard.

"I can't help you at all?"

"You can help me from inside the house."

"There aren't any good vantage points from inside the house."

"You'll just have to make do."

"If they want us both dead, why don't they just blow up the house?"

He falls back onto the bed, and I lean on my elbow next to him.

"Too messy. It's just not their style."

"Not their style?" These people surely have some twisted set of values.

"That's just how arrogant they are. And they created me. Their time and money—I'm too valuable to them to destroy."

"So Kate thought—"

"It doesn't matter what Kate thought."

"Kate thought if I was dead, you'd take her back."

He closes his eyes. Sighs. "Kate thinks a lot of things."

"Would you take her back?" I ask softly.

His eyes fly open, suddenly fierce. "Do you need me to answer that?"

"You have no feelings for her at all?"

He sits up fast. "The only feelings I have for Kate…" He looks at me. Leaves rustle against the house outside. "We need to go to bed."

I don't move. He can't leave a sentence like that unfinished.

"It'll give me great pleasure to kill her myself," he says.

"You wouldn't kill her."

"I plan to kill her."

That plan requires a return visit to Richmond, which I can't allow. The last time almost killed me. The next time will kill him. "We aren't going back—"

"No *we* aren't. I am. You'll stay somewhere they can't find you."

"Trey—"

"I don't care how well you fight, how good your aim is. It's not worth it. I can't live without you." That rule-making voice has returned. He's the parent, I'm a child.

I never asked to be paired with such a controlling asshole.

That unfamiliar heat stirs inside me. It's his anger, not mine. A side effect of our first mind share. I take a steady breath, searching for somewhere to stuff the emotion that's all wrong in my head. The reaction it's tied to is not mine, and I don't want it invoked. I'm not a skilled handler. Neither is he.

He's still watching me like he expects some response.

"Is that you talking, or something else?" I ask.

"What else would it be?"

"Pollux and Mars." I stop there. I've gone too far.

His face has gone blank. His eyes shift away. "Pollux and Mars," he mutters. Two of the four bodies that aligned our minds, triggered the spell that made us fall in love.

In the space between us, a wall has gone up, built with bricks of my doubt.

I wake in the kitchen, my hand on the cabinet where Trey keeps his herbs. There's a rush of air behind me.

"Liv."

I turn around. It takes a moment for the room to slow its spin. I become aware of the tremble in my body, the shaking in my hands. Please, don't let him see.

"Why are you up?"

I shrug because if I answer, the pang in my chest will turn into a sob I'll be unable to restrain. I'm so lost.

He jerks his head toward the bedroom. I follow him there. We toss and turn together in bed until I end up in his arms and I'm found again, my doubt on hold, our wall temporarily raised.

"*Déjà vu*," I say to Christian who's sitting at the table with a mug of coffee. In his boxers. "Now, I know you had clothes on when you went to sleep last night."

"Yeah, but now this bastard likes to keep the heat cranked. I'm used to freezing my ass off when I'm here. Now I roast. What's with that?"

"All in your mind." Trey says.

"No, you just aren't into torturing yourself anymore now that she's here. Decent cooking, heat…"

"That right, Freud?"

"Hey, what happened to your bruise?" Christian asks.

Trey's hand moves to his jaw, and I walk over to him and pull his hand down so I can see. "It's healed."

"Looks like you need to invest in a better pregnancy test. Thank god for that. I was starting to worry about Junior Trey being inflicted on the world."

I trace his jaw where the bruise darkened his skin yesterday. What if something happened? What if she's gone? I can't live through another loss. It will kill me.

"I was wondering about that." Trey looks at his arm where my bite mark should be. Now there's only a slight bruise where each tooth sunk in.

"About what?"

"Looks like it goes both ways. Now you can heal me," he says.

"That's not—"

"It must be pretty potent. But it could work. It did work."

I stare up at him, shaking my head. If I can heal him like he could heal me before, then I won't have to worry about him getting killed. As long as he's careful not to take any lethal bullets, as long as I'm always with him, he and I can both be considered immortal. Just like it was before.

"Am I missing something?" Christian has turned all the way around in his chair, watching us like we're in on something he's not.

Trey clears his throat. "It's private."

"Private? You kidding me?"

"He doesn't know?" I ask Trey.

"Well, I guess he does now." He cracks an egg into the skillet.

"Any day." Christian widens his eyes at us.

"She healed me with sex."

Christian looks to me for verification, but it's Trey who speaks again. "When I was immortal, I could heal her with sex. Now, she's immortal. And apparently it works both ways."

Christian releases a surprised laugh. "How is she immortal?"

"Because it passed from me to her." Trey takes a step toward Christian. "You're privy to a lot of inside information now."

"And?"

"And I'm just reminding you." Trey stares him down before returning to the stove.

Christian raises one eyebrow at me. "So, say if someone had some broken fingers…"

Trey laughs. "Over my dead body."

"Don't be selfish, man. It wouldn't mean anything. Totally platonic. Kind of practical, actually. What do you think?" He stretches his arm out to me, ready to shake on it.

I know he's not being serious, but it's hard not to envision all the people I could help. Is there even a limit to this? Can it cure disease?

Trey says, "Are you going to turn the man down politely, or should I?"

"Does it have to be intercourse? If it's in my body, it's in my bloodstream. Is there another way to transfer it?"

"What, like inject him with your blood or something? That's disgusting."

"Yes, but what if it worked?"

"Yeah, what if it did work? I'd be free of this." Christian holds up his bandaged hand. "Although I'd prefer the original method, if I have a say in the matter."

"And just think of all the people I could help. There's this little girl who comes to the clinic for dialysis. What if I could help her?" I ask as I set the table.

Trey brings the eggs, cereal, and milk and we all sit.

"Can't happen. Our magic has rules like everything else, and if you don't follow them—"

"What harm could come with helping a little girl?"

"The effect wasn't intended for that."

"How do you know? Maybe it should be."

"Trust me. I know firsthand. Overuse and misuse get you some bad repercussions."

I look at Christian, who drops an exaggerated sigh. "He's right."

"It's designed to keep our child safe. To do that, it protects you and me. That's it."

I frown at him. I shouldn't—that's a very good use for it. She's going to need all the protection she can get. But what a shame to have this power and not be able to spread it. I see one person after another at work who could benefit from a shot of my immortality. I've got a secret cure for all sickness and disease and I have to watch people suffer?

"What a total tease," Christian whines.

I point at Trey. "But you used it on me without knowing—"

"I didn't care."

"But what if—"

"Change the subject." His eyes burn into me.

"Uh-oh." Christian does a low whistle.

I shouldn't push it. This sharing of immortality is too perfect a system. Our togetherness keeps all three of us safe. It's been timed to transfer to the one who needs it most, the one in most danger. First it was Trey. Now it lives in me. When she's born, it will be hers. Until then, I can give Trey regular doses, to keep him safe so he can protect us, so he's around to train her to be the warrior she must become. This intricate plan was designed especially for us and set in motion by a force more powerful than I could ever imagine.

"Liv," Trey says.

I look into his perfect eyes. What brought us together may be a magic trick, but what we have is real. It has to be.

"You okay?"

I stab an egg and put it into my mouth.

"So no luck last night, I take it?" Trey asks Christian.

"Yeah, can you believe it? She kicked me out. Everything was going great, and then suddenly she's all, 'Can we do this again sometime?' and before I know it, I'm out on the porch."

"Smart woman."

"It'll never work out though."

"Why not?" I ask.

"*Kristen* and *Christian*? Come on," Christian says.

"That's the only reason? Isn't that a little superficial?" I wonder what Trey meant about repercussions. Without knowing the rules, I'd never know if he broke one, and I doubt he'd tell me on his own.

Trey snorts. "And finally you understand my sick-minded cousin. Friend. Whatever. What are you?"

"Brother," Christian says. "We were raised by the same woman. You will always be my brother."

"Just my luck," Trey mutters, but I can tell he's pleased.

These two have more love for each other than they'd ever admit.

CHAPTER 11

TREY

After dropping Liv off at work, I pull onto the road and stomp the pedal just to feel the speed. My vigor has returned so unexpectedly I didn't recognize it. It's taken on a new twist now—it's almost more satisfying, more valuable, now that I know it comes from her.

As I park the Camaro in the garage, I see the Ninja. It's been too long. I'm careful not to spray gravel as I pull away. I wouldn't want to nick Christian's darling Infiniti with a stray rock. I know all the best twists in these roads, and soon I'm testing the rules of physics like I'm immortal again. Probably stupid. But this bike is stupid. We're the perfect team for taunting death.

Christian meets me at the front door when I get home. He opens his palm for the key. "My turn."

"I'm not so sure I want a cripple riding my bike. Key's in the ignition."

He gives me the finger and goes past me out the door.

I take Liv's amulet on its new enclosure out of my pocket and set it on her spot at the kitchen table. Now she can wear it at all times.

Dialing Tara's number, I walk to the back door to watch the wind blow the trees outside.

She answers before it has a chance to ring. "I had my hand on the phone to call you."

"I have some news," I say as the same words in her voice echo in my ear, followed by her maniacal laughter.

Before she can speak again, I say, "You first."

"Martin told Máthair that they have one more group of guys trained, and if they don't succeed, they aren't sending any more." Like me, Tara gets right to business.

"Can we trust that?" They've fed me lies my whole life.

"He doesn't tell her a lot of things, but of the things he does tell her, they're the truth."

"Notice he said they aren't sending any more. Not they aren't training any more. So they could be training an army."

"You took the words right out of my mouth. What's your news?"

"Dillon Moore's brother is in New York."

"New York. Okay, what else?"

"That's it."

She chuckles. "That's all you got from Liv? Didn't you ask her—"

"I'll get more." It's pointless anyway. It's not going to change anything.

"How is she?" Worry floods her voice.

"Good. It worked. The cleansing, too."

"Is she okay knowing what he did?"

"She seems to be. She's glad to be free."

"I bet. Okay, I'll look up some people I know in New York."

"Did you talk to Máthair about Dillon?" I swallow the revulsion I feel saying his name for the second time.

"She had no idea about the connection to Liv. She'll find out more." Picking up on my silence, she adds, "You promised you wouldn't do anything rash."

"Just a few harmless fantasies."

"Your fantasies are never harmless." A child's voice calls in the background. "Winifred's up. I'll call you later." She hangs up.

When Christian returns, I make him come into the basement to help me work on the formula for his protection. We can't come up with anything strong enough, so I pull more books from my shelves and stack them in front of us. I open one and shove another in front of him. He's high from the ride and won't stop talking about whatever senseless shit comes to mind. I stop listening and skim pages until something he says breaks my concentration.

"What?" I look up at him.

"I knew you weren't paying attention. Listen. Kate's on a rampage. I wasn't going to tell you, but I can't keep it to myself anymore."

I look away. "Try harder."

He ignores me. "Before I left, she threw a huge fit in the house about how they should've known about Liv and killed her a long time ago. I've never seen her so—"

"Why are you telling me this?" If he doesn't have a good reason for bringing her up, I'm going to make him wish he hadn't.

"Shut the fuck up and listen. Kate woke up, demanding to talk to me. That's probably when she programmed me to come here. But she also told me she's not giving up on you, and she's going to do whatever it takes to get you back."

I place my palms on the table and bow my head, breathing deeply in an attempt to purge the fury building forces inside me. "I should've killed her when I was there. Why didn't I kill her?" I ask the table, popping it with my fist.

"You'd never kill a pregnant woman. You may be a sick bastard but you're not that sick."

"Yes I am."

"Do I need to cuff you to a chair or something? There's more, and you're not going to like it."

"Go." I stare at him.

"Seriously. I don't want to make Hulk mad."

"Too late."

He sighs, obviously buying time for me to relax. I sit on a stool to appease him. He drags a stool over and sits.

"I overheard my dad and Dillon and several more of them talking on my way out that day. I was…out of my mind, so focused on getting here. I can't believe I heard it at all. Things are coming back to me, things I heard, things I knew about but didn't—"

"What?" If he doesn't stop blabbing and get to the point I'm going to take him outside and beat it out of him. Shit. I'll beat it out of him right here.

"They set it all up. They sent Dillon to find Liv years ago, to put that spell on her, to keep her married and happy, hoping to keep her from finding you. They knew about her. That she was the one."

I get up; Christian shoves me back down.

"And for some reason, it didn't work. So Dillon gave up the mission and came back to be with Kate," he says.

"Mission?" A mission to toy with Liv's life for their own gain. To use her, as they've used me.

"That's how they see it. You know how they are."

I start to stand again, and as he grabs my shoulders I throw his arms away from me.

"Trey, if you freak out nothing gets solved."

"There's an easy way to solve all of this."

"Yeah, but they're two thousand miles away."

They've been tracking her since she was a baby, just like they did to me. They must be responsible for her being an orphan; it's likely they killed her entire family.

"Why didn't they just kill her?" I ask.

Christian shrugs. "Who the hell knows. But you know they've got a reason. Maybe it'll come to me tomorrow." He gives me an obnoxious smile.

He shuts up long enough for me to get a few chests full of air and find some calm before I tear my whole basement apart.

"Why didn't they just kill you?" he asks, suddenly serious again.

"Because it pleased them too much to know they could use me as a weapon against my own people. Did you tell her any of this?"

"No, but she's worried you're still hard for Kate. I told her you're not, and not to worry." He hesitates as if he needs my confirmation.

"I need you to promise me something. Make it a blood oath. If anything happens to me, promise you'll protect Liv with your life."

I pick up a knife from the table, slice my palm, and hand the knife to him. He slices his palm the same and we grasp hands.

"*Ceangailte go brách*," we chant, to seal the deal.

"You know I would anyway," he says. "Great. Now both my hands are useless. Thanks a lot, asshole."

I slap him hard on the back, and we head upstairs. He opens the fridge and gazes inside as if more bored than hungry. "You stock the stupidest food—"

"What exactly *did* you tell her?"

His face falls. "Just what you should've told her yourself."

I wait, knowing he'll cave.

He slams the refrigerator door closed. "That you fucked my dad up, and from then on they all treated you like shit."

"Great move."

"Now she understands why you're such a pain in the ass all the time."

"You're going to help me take some stuff to her house."

He squints at me. "What does that have to do with—"

"We're moving there."

"Why is it that whenever I come for a visit you always find some menial labor for me to do?"

"It's good for your spoiled little butt. Don't you ever get sick of being a useless punk?"

"Never." He drops into a kitchen chair, stretches his legs out in front of him, and fastens his hands behind his head. "Care to get me a drink?"

"*Bailigh as.*"

He tsks at me. "No respect."

"Come on. We've got three hours."

We load my truck but drive separately in case Kristen calls and 'finally gives in to her carnal desires.' He follows and parks behind me in her driveway. My stone circle still surrounds Liv's house, and Christian gives it a casual look before stepping wide over the line of marked stones. I shouldn't admit I'm relieved he made it across without the magic being disrupted by an enemy force. I need to learn to trust the guy again.

"It could also mean your spell is shit. Don't look so at ease," he says over his shoulder.

River and Trib gallop out of the woods. They took the shortcut here—through the woods, over the footbridge that crosses the Black River, and up the side of the mountain Liv's house is perched on. Her cabin is surrounded by open air and backs to a view of the Rockies north of us. It's a stationary target easily visible from three sides, but it's only vulnerable from two. One is a complete drop off into the river. The other is a slope so steep you'd need a rope to hike it. And the stones mark territory. I'll know if they're crossed by a foe.

He returns from propping the front door open and I drop the tailgate.

"You're not going to back up closer to the house? We can redo the stones."

I ignore him. It's a good effect. I don't want to redo it.

"Then just drive over it. It'll be fine."

I hand him a box. He groans. We unload the truck into the front room then take a tour.

"I can see why you want to move here now," Christian says, looking up at the cathedral ceiling with the skylight I replaced after one of their men broke it out in an effort to ambush us.

"The main reason is two bedrooms."

"You mean I can have my *own room*?" He gives me a wide-eyed child's look of excitement.

I ignore him. "Come with me back to Virginia."

His back stiffens, all amusement leaving his face. "Why?"

"I have a lot of people to kill and I could use your help."

He shakes his head.

"I'll drop Liv in a hotel on the way so she's safe."

He's still shaking his head.

"We owe ourselves. They have it coming."

"Do you have any idea how many of them there are now?"

"Doesn't matter."

"My son lives there now. Your mother."

"We get them out beforehand. It'll be easy."

He's shaking his head again. I didn't expect this conversation to be a test of his loyalty but now it's starting to look like that. Maybe he is still under their influence.

"You go back there, with me or alone, you die. It's a dumbass move, and if you'd think for a second you'd see that. You're lucky you made it out the last time. You're lucky Liv didn't die."

He's got me there. But I won't make that mistake a second time. For years, my plan was to go in firing but

I when I finally made it back there, I had my new conscience with me in the form of a woman named Liv. My plan changed. Manners, talking, compromise—all ineffective. She won't be with me this time. No conscience, no mistakes. And nothing to lose. I kick open the door and start firing. Easy.

"Let's check out the basement," he says.

The basement is huge, empty, and clean. I walk the perimeter, checking for leaks. As it turns out, it is also dry.

"We should finish it," he says, standing next to me in the middle of the open space.

"We?"

"Yeah. It's going to cut into my social life but anything for you, bro."

He helped me build my garage and countless other things. It would be like old times. Work has been slow for me. It'd be nice to have something to do. "You still know how to swing a hammer?"

"I do kind of owe you for trying to kill your girlfriend."

"It's going to be hell getting drywall down those steps, but that's the worst of it. We'll begin tomorrow." I start back up the stairs.

"What? I didn't mean tomorrow. I'm still getting some R and R after being cleansed of a nasty spell—"

"I have to pick her up." I glance at the clock. "I'll see you back at the house?"

He checks his phone. "Guess so."

When I return home with Liv, Christian is dozing on the couch. She drops her bag at the door and heads straight for him as I take off my coat. She sits next to him and picks up his bandaged hand, examining it closely. He opens his eyes.

"I worried about your fingers all day. You could've dislocated them again when you had to subdue me the other day."

"One night with me and you won't have to worry about them anymore."

I glare at him from the doorway.

"Yes, but then Trey would kill us both."

"That's okay. At least I'd die happy." I know he's tacked on a huge grin without even seeing his face.

I retreat to the kitchen before my fist keeps an appointment with his mouth. They join me later, Christian's bandaged hand half-unwrapped. Liv hangs the amulet around her neck and looks up at me, but her eyes dart straight to Christian reaching for a glass.

"What did you do to your other hand?" she says.

He nods toward me. "Another one of his great ideas."

"We're going to finish the basement," I say.

Her face lights up. "You are?"

Christian snickers at her reaction. "Well at least *someone* is getting laid tonight."

"It'll be easy. I have the time off, and I'll have him here to put to a good use for once in his life."

She goes to the sink, and Christian takes the opportunity to throw a sharp look my way. He wants me to tell Liv her marriage was set up by my family. I give it right back to him, but he won't look away. Liv leaves the room.

"Are you going to tell her?" As if I need him to give a voice to the look he just threw at me.

"I got it the first time," I say.

Liv returns with fresh bandages for Christian's hand, and I stand and pour myself a scotch. All of a sudden, her body is wedged between me and the countertop.

"Don't," she says. "You don't need it."

"It's not a matter of needing it." I smile at her.

She twirls against me and takes the glass out of my hand, which has become rigid from the sensation of her body twisting against the pressure of mine. She pours the contents of the glass back into the bottle, puts the bottle in the cabinet. When I turn around, she's already bent over Christian's fingers, but he's staring at me, eyes wide, eyebrows raised as high as they go.

"Fuckin' A." He laughs a high-pitched laugh.

Liv looks up at him harshly.

I clear my throat. "No more F word in front of the lady. It's a new rule."

"What the fuck am I supposed to say instead?"

"Be creative. We've been accused of running a frat house."

"What's wrong with that?"

"Nothing at all if you're nineteen years old," Liv says to him.

"I'm ageless, baby." He gives her a toothy smile then yelps when she corrects the position of his hand.

"Stop talking," she says. "Pay attention and stop moving."

I go downstairs to work out. I'm unfocused and weak until Dillon Moore's face pops into my mind. The heavy bag pays for his crimes. Boxing turns into kickboxing then I move on to my weight set. Back upstairs, I pass Liv and Christian on the couch having some kind of animated girlfriend conversation and take a hot shower.

She's in the bedroom when I get out, sitting on the bed with a book open on her crossed legs. I close the door behind me and dry off, wishing there was a way I didn't have to tell her. She frowns when she sees my face.

"It's going to be hard for me not to say the F word."

"More bad news?" She's visibly expecting the worst.

"Christian remembered something today. Things are coming back to him."

She closes her book, keeping her eyes on mine.

"Your marriage to him was a setup. They arranged it all, to keep you away from me. They knew about you."

She looks down at her hands. "I thought it might be something like that."

"They used you, just like they used me. For their own gain."

"They didn't win." She raises her defiant eyes. "And they will never win."

I hurl my bath towel to the floor. Instead of releasing energy, it boosts it, makes me want to pick it back up and throw it through the wall. I clutch the edge of the dresser, bow over it, tensed and wanting to kill. Someone, anyone. I just need a volunteer. Or not.

"This bothers you more than it does me," she says softly from her spot on the bed.

"How can it not bother you?" I shout, spinning back toward her.

"Because nothing can keep us apart." Her smile strikes me in the head. Bursts. Flows downward, filling me with a potent tranquilizer. It feels like ecstasy.

I fall onto the bed on my back next to her, and she leans over me, her hair falling against my bare shoulder.

"*Mo ghrá thú,*" she says.

"Show off."

She plants a gentle kiss on my bottom lip. I take her face in my hands.

"You heal me in so many ways," I say before I can quell the words.

CHAPTER 12

LIV

T REY'S STARING AT his palm when I wake. On it is the same mark Christian has on his, only Trey's is sealed like a week-old wound.

"You too?"

He lowers his hand and looks at me, ignoring my question.

"What is this, some kind of sick blood ritual?"

"Yep." He waits, his unbroken gaze daring me to respond.

"I can't leave the two of you alone."

He rolls, squashing me in his arms. I break free and lead him to the kitchen. "Do you think he'll be joining us?" I hesitate, my hand aimed for a third mug.

On cue, Christian appears in the doorway.

"Guys…" He's holding his bare left hand up in the air.

"You took all the bandages off? Why?" I rush to his side. His fingers are straight, all the bruises gone.

"I don't remember doing it."

"Flex your fingers," I say, and he does.

"Would now be an appropriate time for the F word?" His eyes are as wide as mine must be.

"Flex them again." After witnessing the same effortless movement, I turn toward Trey for an explanation.

Trey is engrossed with his own palm just as he was this morning. Only now, it must have something new on it—I don't think I've ever seen the man look so amazed.

"Oh, hell no." Christian checks his own palm.

I snatch Christian's hand. Yesterday's gash has healed into a clean pink line just like Trey's. Christian yanks it back from me and frantically wipes it on his flannel pants as Trey bursts out laughing.

"Sick, dude. Sick!" Christian yells.

"You asked for it." Trey turns away to hide his amusement, giving one more lingering glance to his own palm.

"I asked for it from *her*! Not from your sick ass!"

If they did some kind of blood ritual to heal Christian's fingers, then Trey wouldn't be so impressed by the outcome. He'd have expected it. So I don't understand what's going on here. I step around Trey so I can see his face. "Is that why you did it?"

"No, fu—god no," Christian answers for him. He drops into a chair, sulking.

"But his blood must've still been potent from me," I say. "It healed you."

"*Please* don't talk about it," Christian says as I sit down next to him and palpate each newly healed finger, watching his face for signs of pain.

Trey sets three plates on the table and takes his seat. He leans toward Christian and whispers, "Was it good for you?"

Christian looks at him, stunned and speechless for the first time since I've known him.

"What?" Trey widens his eyes, feigning innocence.

"You did it on purpose so I'd stop talking about sleeping with her." Christian's voice has slowed. He's much too still. It's unlike him.

"No, I didn't." Trey takes a big drink of his orange juice.

"Yes, you did. You can't control your jealously. You knew it would fix my hand."

"No, I didn't." Trey's voice lowers. He sets his glass down much too hard.

"Liar." Christian leans toward him with both fists on the table.

Trey stands. Christian stands to meet him.

"Say it again."

"*Bréagadóir*," Christian says.

Trey shoves him hard against the sink, and Christian pushes off, ramming Trey back against the wall with his shoulder. Trey's chair crashes to its side as the whole room vibrates under the impact.

"Stop it!" My voice gets lost in the commotion.

Trey shoves Christian even harder against the sink, rocking the kitchen with another blow.

Christian swings, and as Trey blocks it Christian swings his left. Trey takes it in the jaw but lands a fist in Christian's ribs. As Christian falls back against the sink, I throw myself between them for the second time in a week.

I plant my palms on Trey's heaving chest and shove, but he won't budge.

"You are grown men! Stop it!"

Trey's hostile eyes stare over my head, watching Christian for his next move.

Christian laughs behind me. "I told you he was mentally fourteen."

Trey allows me to push him back to his fallen chair.

"And apparently so are you," I say to Christian.

He shrugs, takes his seat, and resumes eating his breakfast. Trey picks up his chair and follows suit.

"Man, I'm going to have the worst bruise." Christian fakes a cough and holds his ribs.

Trey doesn't look up from his plate. "Next time I'm breaking them."

"*Diúl mo bhod.*"

"I hope you're joking," I say to Trey. If I'm the only one here with a brain, we're doomed.

"Is it safe to leave the two of you alone together?" I ask before I get out of Trey's car at the clinic.

"We've survived this long without you playing referee."

I kiss his rough cheek. "Behave," I say before closing the car door.

At the end of my shift, I convince Shawn not to walk me outside again. Yeah, Trey's supposed to behave but I can't trust him. It's like reconditioning a victim of abuse. A little at a time. And I don't want the beginning of a three-day weekend spoiled by his primitive impulses.

"So I see you survived," I say when I get in Trey's truck. "Did Christian?"

"I'd say yes, but he'll tell you a different story."

"And why's that?" Oh, I am so going to kill them both. After what I witnessed this morning, it's obvious the problem isn't solely Trey, as hard as that is to believe.

"He's not used to the work. We got a lot of framing done today. I need to pick up some beer to keep him compliant."

Okay, so no need to murder them—yet. "I have the day off tomorrow."

He grabs my hand. "Bonus. You can help us work at your house."

"You have something in your hair." I brush off his velvet-soft hair.

"Sawdust." He rubs his head.

The liquor store is in the heart of downtown, which consists of a few short blocks of buildings nestled tightly like one long wall on both sides of the street. Each shop has wide windows and a second floor that overhangs the first, creating a covered front walk just like the towns in old western movies. Erase the cars and neon signs, and two cowboys having a shoot-out would feel right at home. We angle-park in front of the liquor store and go inside. The owner nods to Trey and Trey nods back. He loads me up with two six-packs of beer and takes a third in his hand. I follow him two aisles over to the hard liquor where he browses until I realize he's picking out something for himself.

"Don't you have some at home?" I begin, unsure what to say. I don't want to badger him but he's drinking like he's still invincible and alone. He has someone who cares about him now. Who counts on him. Who loves him. He's mortal. That kind of alcohol consumption leads to hospital stays.

"I don't have this at home." He picks up a bottle.

"I just—"

"Don't be a nag." He softens it with the charming smile that only surfaces when we're alone together.

"Good choice," the owner says when Trey sets the bottle on the counter. "Did you see we got this in? When I opened the crate, I thought of you." He slides another bottle of hard liquor on the counter in front of Trey.

"I'll take that too." Trey pulls out his wallet.

Outside, a woman rushes out of the restaurant next door and Trey stops to let her walk in front of us. Surprised, she holds his eye a moment before continuing on ahead of us. As soon as she's out of earshot, he elbows me. "Christian's girlfriend."

"She's gorgeous." I watch her back as she walks down the sidewalk to her car.

"That's usually how he likes 'em."

"Does she know you?"

"Probably."

"How?"

"Everybody knows me." He lifts the bags into the bed of the truck and opens my door for me.

"And why is that?"

"I get around." He closes my door then gets in on the other side. "Chinese?"

"Sounds delicious."

He orders so much food it looks like we're having a party. While it's being made, we go next door to a small-town grocer for ice cream. He absentmindedly picks up the first carton and hands it to me.

I frown at him. "Plain vanilla?"

"It's for Christian. It's the only flavor he likes."

We browse, unable to decide between chocolate fudge brownie and caramel swirl until Trey reaches far back in the case to find a hidden carton of cookie dough ice cream. I look up at Trey, wondering if he remembers that night as vividly as I do.

"Don't." One look—that's all it takes to remind him.

We're locked in place. That night was pure magic, the beginning of the same feeling that's gripping us now. We're magnetic, inseparable, brought together by a love of unnatural might. It's a universe of sensation compressed, bundled, planted inside two human bodies. And now, it's infected with my doubt. Once voiced, it's become a contagion. Untreated, it's spreading, claiming cells, invading the bloodstream.

He breaks my gaze, lowers his eyes. He's caught it; he's a carrier now. I should ask him directly, bring it out in the open. Will the spell that brought us together last? The question itself is shaming proof of my doubt, and I can't bear to face it.

A freezer door slams nearby, and the noise of the busy store crashes around me. He leads me to the checkout and out the door. Our food waits on the counter for us when we return to the Chinese restaurant. He sets all the food on the seat between us in the truck and starts the ignition. I feel like I'm a mile away from him.

Christian is flat out on his back on the couch when we return to the house.

"What the hell took you so long? I was about to start eating my own arm." He takes the bags of food away from me and inhales deeply. "Oh my god, marry me."

"It was his idea." I nod toward Trey.

Christian opens a beer and hands it to me. I shake my head, pointing to my belly. We eat then pig out on ice cream. Their discarded bottles stand on the counter like an army.

"We should go for a walk," I blurt out.

"Yeah, right. I'm supposed to be on vacation and this asshole has me working my ass off all day. Now you want to hike the mountains. Screw the both of you."

Trey stands to look out the back door. "It's a clear night. We'll have good visibility."

"Let's go!" I must be on a food high.

"You two are made for each other." Christian heads for the couch.

Trey and I bundle up and leave through the front door. Halfway across the yard, he decides to go back for a gun. I follow him inside and holster my Ruger then we go back out into the crisp night air.

"I love when it's cold and clear like this. You can see the arm of the Milky Way." He stops walking. "Can you find Orion?"

I search the sky. I try to remember what he said the night he taught me how to find Orion. "I'm no good at this."

"You're making it too hard. Look, right there."

I follow his gaze and see it. "Trey?"

He doesn't answer. He must be remembering the look that passed between us in the freezer section, but I won't bring that up. Not on this night.

"What are the rules?"

His weighted silence tells me more than a voiced reply. He watches the sky, and I become aware of my tiny footprints on this planet and the universe looming over us. It's so clear, and so close, I can almost touch it.

"I just think I should know since—"

"There's a bunch of texts in the basement. Study up."

He starts walking. He's a few paces away before I realize I'm staring at the house. The lit windows leave a haze of warmth through the trees. It's a comfort to see it sitting there, waiting for us. It was a prison to me when I first arrived here. It's safety now. It's home.

He takes me on a new route that follows a deep ravine, gradually dropping us in elevation. The towering evergreens glide by us to mark our progress which would otherwise be unnoticeable under the multi-layered panorama of stars.

When the ground slopes upward, he pauses to let me go in front of him, and we climb for a long time until I see a large object looming in the distance. As we reach it, the moonlight reflects off the glistening ice which once tumbled down as a waterfall on a huge rock formation jutting violently out of the earth. It's as if the running water froze in place, preserving the roll of the water as it plunged down each level of rock.

"The grand finale." He steps up on the lower part of the formation and takes a seat facing me.

I walk into him, between his legs. For once, his eyes are on my level. "This is nice."

"*Tá tú go hálainn*," he breathes.

"Do you always switch languages when you're being sweet?"

He leans toward me. I move back, just out of his reach. Picking up on my tease, a playful grin breaks through the intensity of his expression. No one ever gets a glimpse of this secret sweetness inside him but me.

"I will tackle you to the ground."

"Oh, a threat?" I raise an eyebrow.

He tenses. Turns toward the woods. As he jumps down and yanks my body between him and the rock, I notice it too. The air has changed.

He scans the trees around us like a stalking predator. Branches snap in the distance—something coming toward us. I prepare to run, but Trey holds my arm.

"It's River," he whispers.

She bursts out of the trees, circling us, visibly distressed. Low growls turn into whines like she's trying hard not to bark.

"We're surrounded. At least ten of them."

My adrenaline surges, and I take a deep, calming breath. He opens his coat to draw his gun.

"No." He catches my hand on my coat's zipper as I go for my Ruger. "Go home. Get out of here, now." He spins me around and shoves me hard in the back.

"I'm not leaving you."

"Now!"

He pushes me so hard I have to break into a run to keep from falling. My legs run on their own, back in the direction we came, the downward slope causing me to run faster to keep up with gravity. When the ground slopes back up, I stop, leaning on my knees to catch my breath.

Gunshots shatter the stillness, jump-starting my brain. I don't know my way back. I couldn't go home if I tried. I spin in a circle, trying to get my bearings, but I end up confusing my sense of direction even more.

Another gunshot. I run toward it. At least I made an effort to go home. He can't be too mad at me. I know I could make a much better effort, but it's not going to happen. I can't leave him out here alone, fighting a battle that's as much mine as it is his.

I spot a figure ahead of me aiming a rifle at something farther ahead. I hasten my stride. Just as the stranger hears me and begins to turn around, I leap on his back, digging my fingers into his trachea. My momentum knocks him flat on his stomach with me still holding on. As my knees slam into the ground, he grabs at my legs but it's too late. Oxygen deprivation has already taken hold. His movements slow, grow still. I hold on, reciting the reasons in my head: *self-defense, Trey, our baby.*

I take his rifle, sling it over my back, and sprint away from him. His pockets must be full of ammo I could use, but I forget it. I can't touch him. I just can't.

Reaching the spot, I circle around to the top of the rock formation. From here, I can see them closing in—a glint of a blade, a creeping shadow, a moving tree branch. This is not a fair fight. It's an army against one. I try to remember how many gunshots I heard, but I know it doesn't matter. Trey didn't bring any extra ammunition. Just one gun, probably not fully loaded. And I'm not even sure if it was him shooting, so it's impossible to know how many shots he has left.

He must have relocated from the rock to the cover of the woods. A gunshot. A body falls. He's given up his position, so he's probably on the move. I lower myself to the ground and crawl toward the edge. I check the rifle. Three rounds are all I have. Each one has to count. Lying on my belly with the rifle aimed, I know I could start picking them off now, but with too many left, they'd figure it out quickly and come after me. If I make any noise at all, Trey will think I'm one of them. And then he will be after me, too.

CHAPTER 13

TREY

MY SENSES TELL me they're closing in, but I can't be certain until I have a visual. Thank god they weren't close enough to see her leave. They must think I'm out here alone. It's possible another group was dispatched to the house, but River will make it there in time to warn Christian. And to warn Liv, if she's made it that far already. She's fast on her feet, faster than anyone would expect.

A shadow catches my eye. I take a running start and lunge, catching him with my shoulder buried in his ribs. He recovers his stance and goes for my gun, but I'm faster. His knuckles crack as the gun comes down on them, then I snap his wrist, snap his arm, and snap his neck. Three down.

I discard my coat and gloves, stick my gun in the back of my pants. This method is more fun. And a lot more covert.

Two come at me at once, and my body reacts to each movement without giving me the opportunity to think. I catch an elbow with my face and a knee with my ribs, but it only fuels my game. Ducking three times for three swings, I wait and then swing back twice, knocking them down one after the other. One of them struggles to get up. I land knee-first on his neck, my fist slamming into his temple. Five down.

I run back to the foot of the rock to change my position. Bullets ricochet on the rock inches from me, so I turn and run up the other side and meet one of them head on. He misses me twice then goes for my knee. The blow knocks me down and I roll as two of them emerge from the other side of the rock. The original one goes for my throat just as I draw my gun, jab it into his stomach and fire twice. What a waste of a bullet. One would have done it.

Spinning on my back on the ground, I aim between my knees at the other two and a bullet catches me in the arm. I fire, but they've already scattered, so I leap to my feet and run back down the slope and into the trees. A body drops out of a tree directly on top of me, knocking me face first to the ground. I grab the wire just before it digs into my neck. Lean away, duck underneath it. He drops the wire and pulls a knife. We separate.

I steady myself, run, and jump, settling my knees onto his shoulders as the blade comes down on my chest. I twist his head until it gives, and as we both go down I knock the knife away with my forearm. How many is that? I've already lost count.

Spitting a mouthful of blood, I catch motion to my left. A sixth sense sends me running back to the base of the rock formation. I hug the side of the rock and hike uphill as three more convene on the spot I just left. Reaching for my gun leaves me empty-handed. I must've dropped it. Crap. That was one of my SIGs. Pain takes hold of my arm and my knee, but I push it away, shaking my head, clearing my mind.

Part of me wants to charge them head on and finish this so I can go home to Liv. But I know I'm more wounded than I think, and without my gun I have a major disadvantage. Crouching next to the rock, I wait.

All three of them disappear into the trees. They must be circling. They're going to try to take me all at once. Bullets hit the ground at my feet, so I move back to the base of the rock and two of them are instantly on top of me. I think I've been shot again but I have no time to think. They must've saved their best guys for last. Three blows to the face, and I see stars. Ducking, I charge a set of knees and feel another body crash on top of me, rolling me over, knocking all my breath out.

A gunshot echoes across the ravine, and I see sky where there was a body attached to the fist pounding my face. Another gunshot sounds, and the body on top of me goes limp, turning into dead weight. I shove it off and drag myself by my elbows to the rock, press my back against it to help me stand. I'm not even completely upright when one of them charges me from the trees. This is the end. Christian better hold true to his oath. I slide back down to the ground.

No. It's not the end. I have to stay alive. For Liv. For our daughter. To protect them. My legs push me up, and my arms push me off the rock, but before I make contact he's blown backward, landing sprawled on his back. I fall to my hands and knees, spitting blood, shaking my head, fighting the darkness, waiting. Is that the last one? I should've kept better count. My joints give, and I collapse and roll to my back. The night sky has never looked so beautiful. There are so many layers, so many dimensions of stars. I can feel the rotation of the Earth, of the whole solar system. It feels so good to close my eyes.

It must be human nature to imagine pain in death. Some kind of self-preservation. There is no pain. No pain worse than the combined pain of my life. The pain of disappointment. Of failure.

"Trey!"

I've dreamed about her before, but it's never been like this. I can smell her. I can feel the warmth of her breath on my cheek.

"Trey! Please!"

She looks upset. I try to reach for her, but my arms are pinned to the ground.

"You have to spit. Your mouth is full of blood."

My head turns to the side. I spit. She was right. How did I not know I had that much blood in my mouth? I gag and spit again. She takes off her hat and dabs my face. My head turns back toward her, and for a moment everything goes black.

"Wake up! You can't go to sleep!"

Something slides under me, drags me across the ground and up against the rock, its cold surface a shock on my back. I can smell her again. And I can see her.

"Trey, I can't carry you back. I have to go get Christian."

"No." I have a wet sponge in my throat. I choke on it. I'm drowning.

"Tell River to take me home. Trey!"

Something hot and slimy touches my hand. River is here? She ran away, before all of this.

"Tell River to take me home. She won't listen to me."

"Take Liv home," I say through the sponge. It's slippery and metallic.

"Here's my Ruger, and there's a rifle next to you."

"No." I won't take her Ruger. She needs it.

"Where's your coat?"

"My coat?" I feel like I should know, but I don't.

"Promise me you won't go to sleep."

I gag again, and she turns my head. I spit. "I'll try."

Then she's gone. I never got a kiss. She teased me before, and I never got it. We were interrupted. I lean my head back. The surface is cold. Hard. Rainbows of blasting colors flash before my eyes. It would be so easy to go to sleep. But I can't, for her.

My head drops forward, and I force my eyelids open. Glowing eyes stare back at me, then they're gone. I sense a commotion around me, but I can't see anything past the rainbows. A spectrum of a million colors. Layer upon layer. Overlapping. Blue undulating into purple. Into green. Pumping with the slow pulse in my ears. And the snow. Huge snowflakes, swirling downward against a backdrop of vivid color.

The howl of a coyote shatters the silence and I cover my ears to prevent the sound from entering my head. Nothing else will fit in my head. It's too full already. Sure is nice of them to join me though, now that it's all over.

Another coyote yips and howls, and my head falls back, shattering all the rainbows with an explosion of white. Pure white, so bright, I'm blind. Even though I was blind before. I wish she'd taken off my boots before she left. My feet are so hot they could be on fire. And my legs. Also on fire. My head is full of too much white, and the rest of my body is on fire.

"Trey."

Something cool touches my face, then it's gone.

"Again," I plead.

"You have to help us. We have to get you up."

It's her voice. Finally. Now I can sleep.

"Trey!"

A different voice. I open my eyes, but I can't see.

"Pick him up on this side. I think these ribs are broken."

The smoldering fire becomes an inferno as I'm heaved upward.

"You're too short. You're making it harder. Just let me do it."

A grisly moan escapes past the wet sponge. I'm heaved again.

"Can you put your feet down, just a little?"

I don't have feet anymore. By now, they must be charred stumps.

"Yes, like that."

"Are you fireproof?" I ask. He must be. The fire isn't catching him at all.

"He's out of his mind," he says.

"He is?" I ask.

"Christian, hurry!" she says. Her voice is the only sound I want in my head. No matter how full it is in here. No matter how painful it is. There is always room for her.

I am falling. Oh, wait, no I'm not. But this is better. I feel the air on my charred feet and legs. And cool water, on my face. I have died. This is heaven. And all the white goes black.

Brightness activates a jackhammer in my head, and I reach up to keep my head from exploding.

"Don't move," she whispers, taking my arms and gently forcing them back down.

I try to close my eyes, but they are already closed. My eyelids are not enough to keep the brightness out of my pupils.

"We're going to lift you up for a second. Are you ready?"

She doesn't wait for my answer. Arms go around my neck, pillows cram behind my shoulders, and a gut-wrenching groan tears from my lungs.

"We're done. Relax."

My head swells with sound. A thick, percussive, fuzzy hum. It deafens me. It is my world. It is all I know.

The hum fades. Awareness fills me. Every muscle jerks and jumps, out of control. My teeth chatter. My body will not relax until the cool, soft skin of her hands touches my cheeks.

"Will you bring more blankets? He's still freezing cold."

No blankets. Is she crazy? I will burn.

"Can you drink? You need to drink."

It just doesn't seem worth the effort.

"Please?"

I'm going to have to do it. I'm unable to say no to her. I'm surprised the water is warm. Most people drink cold water. But it tastes so good. I lean forward for more but stop when the action breaks me in half.

"Here." She gives me more. "That's all you can have. You're going to be okay." She places a hand on my forehead.

"It's too bright." It's pointless to keep closing my eyes. They are already closed.

Something soft wraps around my forehead, and my eyes bathe in the darkness.

"Yes," I whisper.

"What are you going to do?" His voice is farther away than hers.

"Nothing. I can't do anything. You know that."

"It would work. It worked on me."

"No," she whispers. I wish she'd get closer. I want to feel her again.

"To hell with it. We'll deal with the repercussions."

"No. He wouldn't want that. He'll be fine. Once he's fine enough…" Her voice fades.

His voice rises. "Do you not fucking see him?!"

"Christian, please. Don't make it worse." She makes a choking sound. Then a hard exhale. Her lips touch my hand.

"This is the goriest shit I've ever seen!"

"Shh."

"Those fuckers come here like it's personal. Like they know him. They don't fucking know him!"

My hand settles to the bed. I reach, but it's too late. She's shifted away from me.

A muffled voice. "God, I wish I had been out there." The click of the doorknob.

I begin to fall. It never ends.

"Trey?"

"Mmm?" is all I can manage. I don't think I'm awake.

"Christian made you something. You need to drink it."

I gag. It tastes awful.

"Drink," she demands. So I do.

Cold settles on my eye. Then on my opposite cheek.

"It's just ice. Be still."

"Liv?" I ask, but she's not here.

Wasn't she just here? I open my eyes, but they're covered, so I reach up and pull a towel away. My eyes water, squinting in the light, but as they adjust I notice the room is actually dark. The only visible light escapes around the heavy curtains on the window. Pushing away several blankets, I brace my hands on the mattress to lift myself just as the door opens, casting light in from the hall.

"Don't you dare." She's carrying a tray. She sets it on the dresser and sits next to me. "It's so good to see your eyes again."

I try to sit up to see her better, but it's impossible. I turn my head toward her and attempt a smile. "How bad is it?"

"Not bad." She smiles back, but a tear runs down each cheek. She wipes them away. "You lost a lot of blood. Your ribs are broken. Your knee was dislocated, but Christian and I fixed it while you were out."

"That's it?" I'm wearing someone else's face. My lips must be swollen. They don't want to move.

"I can't believe they didn't break your nose." She reaches, then she seems to think better of it and withdraws her hand. "That's the major stuff. Two bullet wounds. I couldn't find the bullets. We can try again later. And so many lacerations. I used up all the suture sewing them up." Her breath sucks in sharply, and she gives in to her tears, bowing her head into my chest.

"Please don't." My physical pain pales in comparison to the pain I feel seeing her cry.

"It was so hard to watch," she says after a moment, looking up, her pretty face in agony. "I couldn't get a clear shot. I knew that changing my position would waste too much time. And the whole time, I had to wait. And watch." She bows her head again, shaking with sobs.

I try to wrap my arms around her but she stops me, curbing her tears. "You should rest. Do you feel like eating?"

I nod, and she stands. "Can I open the drapes?"

"Slowly."

My head booms as my eyes adjust, but it's manageable. She sits down next to me with a bowl of oatmeal. I reach, and she shakes her head.

"I get to feed you."

I roll my eyes.

"Just let me. It's my fault this happened. It'll make me feel better."

"It's not your fault." Disgust sours my stomach. This is my fault.

"Yes it is. I wanted to go for a walk. It was my idea."

"They would've found us here."

"Yes, but it would've been much easier. We'd have had cover. And Christian could've helped. Open your mouth."

Swallowing is a challenge but I somehow survive each time the spoon hits my tongue. Watching her face makes it easier. When the bowl is empty, I'm rewarded with water. Water has never tasted so good.

"We need to watch for symptoms of frostbite. You—"

"You didn't listen to me." My voice isn't as reprimanding as I want it to be.

From the look on her face, I can tell she knew this conversation was inevitable.

She sighs. "Yes, I did listen. I left. I don't know how far I got when I realized I didn't know the way home. I wasn't paying attention on the way out there. But yes, I left. And then I came back."

"You shot the last two? Three?"

She thinks for a moment. "I think it was three."

"Awesome shooting with the Ruger."

"It wasn't the Ruger. It was a rifle."

"You didn't have a rifle."

She massages her temples. "I pillaged it from a dead body."

I get out half a laugh before my body seizes with pain. She holds the extra pillow against my side as if she's holding my ribcage together.

"I didn't kill anyone who had a rifle." Or did I?

She looks down. "I did."

"Impressive. I missed the gunshots." How could I have missed the gunshots? I guess they all weren't aimed for me.

"There weren't any gunshots."

"Bare hands? I don't believe it. How?"

"I crushed his trachea."

Sharp pain tears through me again as I react.

"Don't," she adds. "I don't want to think about it. Please. I don't even know why I told you. But laughing is good. It will help prevent pneumonia. Splint your ribs with this pillow and take some deep breaths now and then."

I try to put away the smile but it refuses.

"Trey…"

"Better him than you," I say to make her feel better. "Or me."

"Can I brush your teeth?"

"Am I in any position to refuse?"

She leaves the room and returns with my toothbrush, toothpaste, and Christian.

"Darn it," he says when he sees me. "I thought I finally had her all to myself." He crosses his arms and leans against the wall. His beaming smile carefully hides his worry. I know him too well not to see it.

"Yeah, where were you when we needed you? Dozing on the couch?"

"Pretty much. You know, you had those broken ribs coming to you. Next time you'll think twice about threatening me."

Liv sticks the toothbrush in my mouth, preventing my response.

"So how many were there?" Christian asks.

"Ten, I think," Liv answers for me.

"How many did you get?" he asks Liv.

"Four. And I'm not talking about it, so drop it now."

"He only got two more than you? Old man's losing his game."

"He wasn't armed most of the time. Will you drop it?" She gives him a cold look, then she turns back to me. "River's freaking out. She won't leave the back door. Can I let her in so she can see you're alive?"

She removes the toothbrush and holds a cup so I can spit. My spit is brownish red.

"She probably won't come in."

Liv leaves the room. Seconds later, the tick of dog claws on wooden floors comes toward me, and River trots into the room in a frenzy. I lower my hand so she can lick it. She sniffs all around the room then rests both front paws and chin next to me on the bed.

"She's filthy. I think she's been rolling in deer shit."

"Come on," Liv says, but River doesn't budge.

"Go outside," I tell her, and she goes out the door.

Liv follows her to let her out.

Christian looks like he wants to say something.

"What?"

"Can we shoot you up with Liv's blood?" It comes out in a rush.

"No." The force of my voice wanes, but not because it lacks certainty. I should probably stop talking. I'm wearing myself out.

"Why not? You know it would work. She'll agree, if you do."

"You know why. And, it's disgusting."

"*You* are disgusted by blood? That's bullshit."

I close my eyes, hoping he'll get the hint that I am not arguing about this.

"Seriously, dude. Have you seen yourself? It's not pretty."

Liv returns with crackers, another bowl of oatmeal, and a bottle of pills under her chin. She walks around to the other side of the bed and sits cross-legged next to me. She gives me pills, more water.

"Why are you being so agreeable?" She takes the glass away and picks up a cracker.

I don't answer. I just hold her gaze.

"Sick." Christian leaves the room.

"What day is it?" I ask.

"Friday. Almost dinnertime."

"You stayed home from work?"

"No, I was off today, remember?" She studies my face.

Right. That's why we took the walk. We'd stuffed ourselves full of junk food then had taken a late walk because we knew she had the day off. "So I've been out…"

"About eighteen hours." There should be a gripping bestseller printed on my face for the way she's looking at me.

"Not bad," I say just before she puts a spoonful of oatmeal in my mouth.

I manage to get two bites down before I involuntarily gag, sending a shockwave of torture from the epicenter of my chest to my extremities. Somehow, I keep the food down, but it's not without a struggle.

"Okay, no more food." She sets the plate on the dresser and returns to me to dab my face with a wet cloth. "Can you drink water?" She holds the glass away from me, like I can't be trusted with it.

I nod, and she moves the glass to my lips.

"What day is it?" I ask.

"You just asked me that. You don't remember?"

I think back. I don't remember.

"You have a concussion." She stands and hands me an empty plastic container with a lid.

"Empty your bladder. I'm going to take this food back to the kitchen." She closes the door behind her.

I follow orders, glad she mentioned it because everything else must have been masking the agony that is my full bladder. How is it possible she anticipates my needs before I do myself?

After a gentle knock, the door opens and she comes in and sits next to me like she did before. "Christian went to get a pizza for dinner. He's crazy worried about you. I wish I had a tranquilizer. He's driving me nuts."

"Just get him drunk," I say and wish I hadn't. I'm definitely overdoing it with the talking.

"Do you remember what we had for dinner yesterday?"

I squint at her. Why would she ask that?

"Do you?" She seems unusually eager for me to respond to such a random question.

"Chinese. Why?"

"Do you remember what you wanted to do today?"

"Work on your basement. What's with the third degree?"

"No reason." She fixes the pillows that slipped down behind me, and I relax against them. Yet again, I didn't realize I was uncomfortable. I close my eyes and feel her dabbing ointment all over my face, my neck, my chest, and my arms. If the amount of time it takes is any indication of how much damage I have, I'm screwed up big time. The bed shifts then shifts again, and she leans over and rubs my lips with something that smells like her. I open my eyes.

"It's my Chapstick. I couldn't find anything else for your lips."

Finished with me, she applies the Chapstick to her own lips, rubs them together, and smiles. If only I could lean toward her, breathe her in, pull her against me. But she leans toward me instead, and without touching me anywhere else, she gives me the lightest, most delicate of kisses that leaves my body begging for more, even in its pathetic condition.

"More," I whisper when she withdraws.

She leans in again, planting delicate kiss after delicate kiss until every molecule of my body hums with delight. Who needs pain reliever in pill form, when you can have this?

She pulls away. "We have to wait until you're a little better."

Powerless to complain, I have been weakened in a new and perfect way, and I yield to it, sinking into the bed, becoming a puddle of skin and bone.

CHAPTER 14

LIV

ICLOSE THE BEDROOM door and walk numbly to the kitchen. Christian takes one look at me and wraps his arms around me. His comfort dooms me, acknowledges the burn in my heart, the coiled sickness in my stomach I've been dismissing until now. He holds me together as everything explodes and I cry against his chest.

When I'm able to form the words, I pull away. "How could they do this to him?"

"A drop in the bucket compared to everything else." I've never heard his voice so glum.

"His brain could be swelling right now."

He wipes my face with the bottom half of his shirt. "There's a lot of room for expansion. He has a pea brain." He gives a strained grin. "Think T-Rex. Big mean body, little brain."

"I've never seen anyone so badly beaten. Not in all my years in the ER. All my years as a nurse."

He gives a weak shrug. His anger has fled, to where I'm not sure. I want to find it so he can have it back, and I won't feel so helpless and alone.

"He should be dead." My voice cracks.

"Don't worry." He pulls me hard against him again. "He's hard to kill."

"What would I have done if you weren't here?"

"You would've figured something out." Gleaning my next question from the look on my face, he adds, "I can't stay here. My home's in Richmond. There are things there I can't be without."

"Aaron." I state the obvious reason, knowing he won't easily admit to missing his son. "I can't believe you have a teenager. What's he like?" It's also hard not to be curious.

"More like me than his mother, thank god. But he does have a mean streak he gets from her. And an impulsiveness that's probably just his age. But you already know about that firsthand. Arrow through the chest. Remember?"

"No hard feelings. I understand his position. He didn't know I was aiming for Trey, not you."

"Yeah, who would've expected you to be aiming for Trey?"

"I didn't exactly have time to call it out."

I wonder what Christian has taught him. It's none of my business, but I can't hold it back. "Does he know any Bevan magic?"

"No." His eyes harden, defensive.

"*You* do." I don't mean to sound so accusing. It's hard to know if Aaron got the good Moore blood or the bad Moore blood. It seems Christian is the only one who got the good stuff.

"I know what's mine to share and what's mine not to share."

"Sloane is his…?"

"Grandmother. But she did just meet him, you know. She hasn't seen him since Kate left. Back when everyone thought he was Trey's. What a mess."

"Sloane doesn't hold it against you. She told me that."

"Yeah, but it's damn awkward. If the whole Kate, Trey, me thing hadn't happened and I'd just hooked up with some random woman, it would be a completely different thing. I can't blame Aunt Sloane." He drops his gaze. "She's done more for me than she ever should have."

"I should go check on him." I tiptoe into the bedroom.

His position is the same except his head has rolled to the side, tensing his neck at an unnatural angle. I straighten his head. A trickle of blood runs from his nose and down his cheek to a puddle on the pillow. No big deal. Noses bleed, all the time. And a lot. The glass wall that normally keeps my emotions in check when caring for patients is somehow missing when the patient is someone I love. Not that I'd have it any other way. I tuck a towel under his cheek and decide to clean his face later when he's awake. I don't want to risk disturbing him. He needs as much sleep as possible.

His shivering has stopped. Pulse and temperature are good, so I remove some of the extra blankets. I straighten the sheet and steal one last look at his face, bruised practically beyond recognition. I'll have to give him a bath in the morning.

Christian comes up the basement stairs when I return to the kitchen. "Check it out!" He holds out an old wooden chess set like it's a bucket of gold.

"Just let me make a couple phone calls."

"Hurry up." He heads toward the living room.

I dial Shawn's number before I have a chance to talk myself out of it. He answers on the second ring.

"Liv! Two phone calls in one day!"

"I'm going to take you up on what I called about before." I hate doing this, but I have no other option. Even if I knew where to order this stuff online I doubt I could get overnight delivery here. And I left my computer in Chicago, which is a good place for it since my house doesn't have internet service and neither does Trey's. "Only if it won't get you in trouble."

"I can swing it as a change order. No big deal. Are you at home?"

"I'll meet you somewhere. Not the clinic."

"How about my place?" Playful, yet hopeful.

"The sporting goods store parking lot. Can you be there in ten minutes?"

"I'll be there."

It's going to be hard coming up with a way to repay him for this favor. A way that won't make Trey want to kill me. I doubt I could even bake the poor guy some cookies. I put on my coat and grab my purse.

The chess board is assembled and waiting in the living room, along with a visibly impatient Christian.

"I have to go somewhere. I'll be back in twenty minutes." I turn before he can argue.

I'm halfway to the garage when he catches up to me.

"Do you want me to die?" He looks a little more pissed off than I thought he'd be. Okay, a lot more pissed off. "You leave, he kills me. It's that simple."

"Please, Christian. Twenty minutes."

"For what? Just tell me and I'll go."

"I have to go myself."

He throws a glance toward the house. Drums his fingers on his legs. "Fine. Twenty minutes. If you're not back in twenty minutes—"

"I will be."

I drive away before he changes his mind.

"This covert stuff has me all hot and bothered," Shawn says when I get out of my car next to his work van in the parking lot. "Will you tell me what this is for, or is it confidential?"

"Confidential."

"Of course." He sighs and opens the van's door. "I think I have an idea. I told you that guy is trouble. Did he mangle somebody or something?"

I thank him, pay him, and get in my car before he can hand the money back. Cold spreads inside my stomach. It could be a mistake mixing Shawn into this.

I make it through the front door of the house one minute before my deadline. But not at Trey's—at mine.

And the time limit isn't enough to stop me from tearing through each room like I'm in a race to find a prize. I don't know what it is, but once I see it, I'll know. I have no time for this, and Christian's going to kill me. If I could just figure out what the hell it is I need, I could go straight to it.

Five minutes later, I'm no closer to knowing what it is. I lock the door and sprint to the car. On the drive to Trey's, I try to grasp what just came over me. Rushing to my house on a whim to get something, and I have no idea what it is? The urge is deep and a little frantic, much like how it felt to be addicted to sleeping pills. It can't be that. I've been off them too long. Withdrawal doesn't just return out of the blue like this.

Christian meets me at the door, beer bottle in hand. "Do you know how late you are?"

"I know. I'm sorry. I had to—"

"I don't care what you had to do. You say twenty minutes, you come back in twenty minutes. So not cool."

"I just need to get some stuff out of my trunk, then I'm in for the night."

"I'll get it." He hands me his beer and snatches my keys.

There's no easy way to walk on gravel in bare feet and he proves it by his little dance all the way to the car and back. It may as well be hot coals. I open the door when he makes it back to the porch. The anger has already left his face.

"You made a late night run for *medical supplies*? I had all that time to come up with all these ideas… I guess I should have known." His laugh echoes through the house, and I shush him.

"Sorry," he mouths, taking his beer from me. "Ready for a game of strip chess?"

"*Right.*" I take the stuff into the kitchen. "Since when did it turn into strip chess?"

"My boredom multiplied while you were gone. So now we have to do something more entertaining to combat it."

My phone rings. Christian shakes his head at me, slowly, the look in his eyes mimicking a crazed mental patient. It's Tara. I answer. She's relieved by Trey's progress. I say goodbye before she starts crying and gets me going again too. With her on the phone I'd feel like an imposter crying over her brother when I'm not sure how I can love him.

Christian retrieves another beer from the refrigerator. "Ready now?" The expectation on his face is childlike and adorable.

"I'm all yours."

"Now don't get me too excited." He throws his arm around my shoulders and walks me into the other room.

We take opposite ends of the couch with the chess board between us. I try to remember the names of the pieces. "You're going to have to refresh my memory. I haven't played this in years."

"I'll explain as we play. You first."

I cross my legs underneath me and make my first move.

"So how did Trey end up with such a straight-edge? You go out late for some secret excursion, and come back with medical supplies? Why didn't you just tell me? I could've gone."

"I'm not a straight-edge."

"Well, maybe not completely. You do, at times, walk around in your underwear when guests are present—"

"That was the middle of the night. I had no idea you were here."

"And you kill people. So that counts for something." He gasps as I take his queen.

I point at him. "Your fault for bringing her out so soon."

"Aw, crap. Game is over."

"You can't win without your queen?"

"Can I say the F word?"

"No."

"Then no. Plain old no. I can't."

"Try. You may surprise yourself." I smile at his boyish sulk, wondering how it's at all possible that he and Trey were raised together. They couldn't be more different.

He stares down at the board, creasing his brow, and I imagine the wheels turning in his head. He takes a drink of his beer without looking away from the board. After all this thought, a great series of moves must be forming. I need a strategy of my own. Before I can develop a plan, he slams his beer bottle onto the coffee table and laughs. "I got nothin'."

I stifle a giggle. "Just move." He's got a talent for making me laugh, even with Trey recovering from a near-fatal beating in the other room. And my battle of emotions from everything else.

He makes a move and throws his hands up in a 'whatever.'

"You and Trey are so different. I don't see how you could've grown up together."

His eyes dart toward the bedroom where Trey sleeps. "He used to be more like me. He changed when he left the house."

"How was he more like you?"

"He was more fun." He flashes a grin. "He's always been the way he is. But before he left the house there was a microscopic part of him that was…I don't know. Can't think of the word. Fun. Carefree. Despite it all."

"He can be fun."

"Yeah, he's a lot better now that you're here. His old self is slowly coming back. There were times I'd visit and he wouldn't say more than a few words the whole time I was here. I learned to understand him through his grunts."

His smile conveys a joke to soften it all, but I know he's telling it how it was. I had a glimpse of it when I first came here. It's hard to remember the Trey I knew then. He was a different person to me. He was a different person altogether.

From the distant look in Christian's eyes, I can tell he's remembering too. He rubs the back of his head and snickers under his breath.

"What are you thinking about?" My insatiable appetite for any knowledge about Trey's life before me has figured out how easily Christian will talk.

His grin widens. "You don't want to know."

"Now you have to tell me."

He takes a long drink then returns his attention to me. "Before Trey got married, we used to fly to random cities over the weekends just to see how many clubs and bars we could get thrown out of in one night. It was a running challenge. Each new city, the number had to be higher. It was ridiculous. But god, was it fun."

"Get thrown out how?" I wouldn't know how to get thrown out of a bar even if I wanted to.

"Just being idiots. Messing with people. Picking fights."

"Doesn't sound like my idea of fun."

"One time, there was this guy. He was huge, a real heavyweight—super heavyweight. Trey's not a small guy either but he was leaner back then. I kept daring him to start something with the guy. I was an idiot." He laughs, seeming to enjoy the memory a little too much. "Trey refused at first, but after a while he got so sick of me talking about it that he just got up, tapped the guy on the shoulder, and knocked him out cold. It was unbelievable."

"Why would he do that?" The image shocks me. I know how impulsive Trey is, but I've never seen him take it out on an innocent person.

"Exactly. We were idiots. And then the guy's buddies attacked us, and of course we got thrown out. So it was just stupid shit like that."

He laughs again and presses both elbows backwards, stretching his shoulders. I'm thankful I didn't know either of them back then. I doubt I would have liked them.

"Don't ever challenge him to do anything you don't really want him to do. He will *always* do it." He takes his beer off the table and takes a drink.

"How old were you?"

"In our twenties. I may have been nineteen. But this went on for years."

"So that was even before Trey was immortal."

"Yep. I don't know who we thought we were. But I wouldn't take back those times for anything."

So this proves my theory that Trey has always been reckless. It wasn't the immortality that made him that way; it was already in him. I know he's well aware of it—he admitted it when I confronted him about driving like a fool on his motorcycle. He acts like it's a joke, and I wonder why that is. Maybe it's not a joke anymore now that he's back to being human.

"Check," I say.

"You said you forgot how to play."

"Oh, come on, you're not even trying." This is a change for me. I'm used to being around someone who's ridiculously competitive.

He cocks his head. "Are you sure I didn't let you win?"

"Okay then let's go again." I return the pieces to the board.

"How can you stand living here? What do you guys do all day?"

"Work," I say condescendingly. "Some people have to work."

He scoffs. "He doesn't have to work. He just does, so he doesn't feel like a louse. And so he can get away with calling other people spoiled."

"Well *I* have to work."

"No you don't. You've got a sugar daddy now."

"He doesn't have their money. He left. And he was never one of them to begin with."

He lowers his gaze to the board. "You should ask him about that. So what do you do for fun around here?"

I didn't move to this town for fun. I moved to find peace. Guess you could say it backfired. "Go for walks?"

"That doesn't sound like a very safe hobby lately."

"There are a couple good restaurants in town."

"Been to all of them. Many, many times."

"I don't know then. I guess we just sit around." I look down at the board as he puts me in checkmate. "I knew you were bluffing before."

"No, I just got lucky this time."

"What about the girl you went out with the other day? Kristen? Why not go somewhere with her?"

"Yes… Kristen…" He drums his fingers on his chin. "I should call her."

"You should."

"But I'm stuck here until the prince returns to his former glory. He'd kill me if I left you alone while he was still out of commission."

"You should still call her."

If I'd run back to the house that night Trey would be dead. We'd have waited for him to return. We'd have gone searching. We'd have found him lying there on the cold ground in that puddle of blood I dragged him out of. And here I'd be, back in a pit of mourning, left to raise our child alone. It would be a death sentence for her. Without Trey, she'll never learn how to survive them.

Christian sighs. "Not again." He moves the chess board to the coffee table and wraps his arm around me.

"You didn't see it." I wipe my eyes with my sleeve. "You weren't watching, completely helpless. If he hadn't come back into that clearing…" He could so quickly be gone to me. How could I live without him?

"I know you won't agree, but I'm seeing this as a good thing now. You don't know what he was planning. His ass stuck in bed is the best thing for him right now."

"Christian, he could have died."

"And if he wasn't stuck in bed, he'd be on the road to Virginia walking into his own execution. He's got it planned. He asked me to go. Said he'd hide you in some hotel room on the way. And I didn't know what to say to him so guess what comes to my mind. 'Hey, let's fix up the basement.'

Anything to keep him busy here. Just my luck he'd agree and screw up my vacation."

"He can't go back there. You can't let him." I cover my mouth. My god, he's crazy.

Christian hugs me tighter. He takes a breath to speak but hesitates when his eyes catch the chain around my neck. He pulls the amulet out from under my shirt by the chain.

"He gave you this to wear? Shit, you don't need me at all then."

CHAPTER 15

TREY

Awake, suffering in a world of pain and unable to move, and needing to pee like nothing else, I stare at the ceiling and wait. She's curled up on the bed beside me, seemingly keeping enough distance so she doesn't touch me by accident. And she'll be asleep for another hour, maybe two. How bad would it hurt to get up? A lot worse than the ache of a full bladder.

I close my eyes and attempt to settle down, hoping to doze off and pass the time faster. My eyes open after less than a minute. This is when I miss being immortal. It could sure numb the pain of broken ribs right about now.

As if hearing my thoughts, she turns over in bed and opens her eyes. "Are you up?" she whispers.

"No. I'm sleeping with my eyes open."

"Smartass." Her lips seem lazy, not quite awake yet. "How do you feel?"

"I can't answer that without use of the F word."

"Pain reliever must have worn off. Let me get you some more." She closes her eyes as if to steady herself then gets out of bed.

"Can I take a leak first? I'm dying."

"Where'd you put that container?" She looks around the room before going into the bathroom to retrieve it. "How long have you had to go? Why didn't you wake me up?"

"I'm not going to wake you up." My helplessness is enough of an irritation without being reminded of it.

"Next time, you *better* wake me up."

She leaves. Returns a few minutes later with a fresh glass of water. Puts some pills from the bottle on the dresser in my mouth and holds the glass to my lips.

"I'm going to need more than that," I say.

She gives me more pills and another drink.

"You're good. How much am I paying you?" I just want to see her smile. It relieves me more than the pills ever will.

She sits next to me. Watches me. "Anything else? Can I fix your pillows?"

"Go back to sleep." I close my eyes with the hope she'll think that's what I want to do myself.

She lies next to me and pulls the covers up to her chin. I'd accept another broken rib to be able to hold her right now. The clock increments one minute at a time for an hour and a half before she stirs again.

"Still sleeping with your eyes open?" She stretches her whole body under the covers—god, I'd love to do that. "Were you awake that whole time?"

"Afraid so. I was hoping you'd talk in your sleep to entertain me."

"Are you still in pain?"

"Me? No." I scoff.

"You can't take any more pain reliever yet. Can you breathe okay? Take a deep breath."

I do, and it hurts like hell.

"One more."

I do again, ready to black out from the pain. But she seems satisfied.

"There are a few small lacerations I still need to suture. And you need a bath. Are you hungry?"

"I could eat."

She slides out of bed into my flannel robe. I hear her moving around in the bathroom, then her footsteps take her down the hall away from me. I stare at the ceiling thinking about all the things I wish I could be doing. Christian and I should be working on her basement right now.

"I hope you don't mind oatmeal again," she says when she returns and sits down on the bed next to me. "And this." She holds a mug of Christian's elixir to my lips. I take it all in one gulp.

"You're such a good patient." She sets the mug on the nightstand.

"I'm just partial to you. The night-shift nurse leaves me in bed all night with a full bladder."

"She does? I'll report it." Her voice is serious, but the corners of her mouth turn up, contrasting with her somber eyes. She's trying hard to hold it together for me.

I decide to let her feed me again because I know it makes her happy. The simple act of swallowing demands all my concentration anyway. Christian wanders in to check on me, and I give him the thumbs up. From the look of him, he just woke up.

He leans against the wall. "So, what's the plan for today? Lay around in bed like a slob all day?"

"No," Liv answers since I have my mouth full. "You're going to help me give him a bath."

"You've got to be kidding."

"We can do it right here."

I swallow a mouthful. "Don't do it for me, man, do it for her. She has to sleep next to me."

"She can sleep next to me instead." He gives her an evil grin.

Liv pretends not to notice and fills my mouth with a spoonful to keep me quiet. "Now, you have to tell me if you feel short of breath or if you feel dizzy, okay?"

I nod, watching her.

"Will you get me his toothbrush?" she asks Christian, and he leaves the room.

"I'm pretty sure they aren't broken through. Just non-displaced rib fractures. So they'll heal on their own. As soon as you feel well enough…just tell me when you're ready. For me."

"How about right now?"

She puts the last spoonful in my mouth. I hold her eye as Christian walks back into the room and hands her my toothbrush and toothpaste.

"Oh, god. Are you two having a moment?"

"Help me give him a bath." Liv squirts my toothbrush with toothpaste and waits for me to open my mouth.

He leaves the room. A minute later the shower turns on.

She finishes my teeth then offers me a glass to spit and another glass for a drink of water. My spit is still red. I wonder how much of my own blood I've digested.

I watch her get dressed, her offer from before becoming more appealing. I know it's just my imagination, but it's like every move she makes is a show just for me. She gathers her hair into a ponytail. "Oh! You need to call your sister."

I should've known Tara would know by now.

"Don't look at me like that. She called me. She knew something was wrong before I had a chance to call her."

"Of course she did," I say under my breath.

"She's worried, Trey."

"When did she call?"

"A hundred times yesterday."

She leaves the room and returns with my phone, dialing Tara for me.

"Fearghus?" Tara answers.

"Yes, I'm alive."

"I had an epiphany. I think every nightmare I've ever had can be blamed on you."

"Is that right?"

"I had a horrible nightmare Thursday night about being stranded in a snowstorm, but everything was on fire—"

"Stop. I can't laugh."

"Why would you laugh? It was awful. I was searching the house for something to put out the fire, and I found you, in the basement, consumed in flames."

A laugh rips through my body and I gasp, suffocating, every abused muscle tensing to absorb the agony created by it. Liv rushes to press the pillow against my side. I take a few of the deepest breaths I can manage then look for the phone, which is no longer in my hand. Liv finds it on the floor and hands it to me. She's about to cry.

"Next time I tell you to stop, stop," I say into the phone.

"Are you okay?" she gasps.

"I was until you fucked me up." She knows I'm teasing. "Continue what you were saying, but skip ahead a little."

"Okay…so I woke up and wondered if there was a reason for it. The more I thought about it, the more I had myself convinced something bad happened. You didn't answer your phone. And by the time I called Liv, I had totally freaked myself out. For good reason."

"Yeah, a pretty good reason."

"I'm glad though. I hate being wrong."

"Would've been nice for you to have been wrong about this one."

"So it got me thinking. Every time I had a nightmare, I could probably blame it on you doing something stupid."

"Very possible. I do a lot of stupid things."

"So when is she going to heal you?" she asks abruptly.

"That's none of your business."

She exhales into the phone. "Don't be a prude."

"How do you know about that?"

"Liv told me."

"Of course she did." I narrow my eyes at Liv, who returns the sweetest, most innocent smile. "You women talk way too damn much."

"It was the only thing she could say to keep me from flying out there and taking you to the hospital myself. Plus, you told Christian, so it's only fair."

"You know about that, too. Great."

"I know everything. Get over it. And be nice to her, she's barely holding on. She's probably being brave to your face but she's about to lose it."

Now it's my turn to exhale into the phone. "I know. I'm not an idiot. Are we done?"

"You have to call me when you're back to your old self. Just so I can stop worrying about broken rib fragments migrating into your lungs. Liv told me some scary stuff. She has a right to be worried."

I overdo my sarcasm. "I'll call you the minute we're finished."

She laughs. "I expect nothing less."

I hang up the phone and hand it to Liv who's busy straightening up the mess in the room.

She sits on the bed next to me and runs her fingertips down my face, across my cheekbones and jaw, over my lips. "Can I shave your face?"

"No."

"Is it too sore? I'll be very gentle."

"I'm growing a beard."

"No you're not!" A light shines in her eyes, finally breaking up the sadness.

I run my finger along her lips. She closes her eyes. I let my finger fall, down her chin, cutting a line down the middle of her chest, and as it reaches her navel she nabs it, halting its progress as she opens her eyes.

"I think you need to change your clothes again."

She absentmindedly licks her lips. "Why, you don't like what I'm wearing?" Feigned innocence. Pretending to miss the motivation behind my request.

"I like it just fine. You can put the same thing back on."

She releases my hand. It goes to her knee and runs up the inside of her thigh, where she catches it again.

"Lock the door," I say.

"We can't."

"Yes we can."

"You can't even sit up on your own."

"I don't need to sit up."

She looks away. I'm wearing her down.

"But you would. You wouldn't be able to control yourself."

"It'd be worth it."

She looks sharply back at me, worry clouding her expression. "No, it wouldn't."

"I'll let you do all the work."

She stares at me for a drawn out moment. "Tomorrow."

"Now."

"Tonight." She's willing to compromise.

"Now." I'm not.

She bites her lip and turns her head away again. The curled tip of her ponytail drags across her shoulder and drops down in front of her collar bone. If only my lips could be that tip of her ponytail. The pounding of my heart echoes in my ears. I've never wanted her so badly. And here I am, lying helpless, incapacitated, unable to take her in my arms and convince her to give in to me the easy way.

She looks back at me, sucking on her bottom lip.

"*Is mian liom thú*," I say.

She drops her eyes. "Don't."

"Please. I'm asking nicely."

She looks up at me and shakes her head.

"*Tá mé ag iarraidh craiceann a bhualadh leat*," I say.

She gasps through a shocked smile. "Stop!" The shower turns off, and she looks toward the doorway. "Tonight, when he's asleep. Not while he's just in the other room. It's weird."

I exhale and close my eyes. "You just like having the upper hand."

"I do have the upper hand." She drags the words out like she's realizing it for the first time.

"Tell him to go take the Ninja out for a few hours."

"A few hours?" She raises her eyebrows.

"Okay, thirty minutes."

"No, a few hours." She flexes that upper hand. "I'm going to make you beg." These words, coupled with her sly smile, set me on fire.

"You already have."

"Oh, that was nothing." She leans toward me, pauses her lips inches from mine.

My pounding heart, my breath, freeze in anticipation. I'm dangling over a cliff, poised to jump, waiting for a push. My tired arms stir, and she holds them against the bed at the wrists.

"Don't. If you move, you get nothing."

Her eyes reach into me so deeply I feel my will slip in the most perfect way. Captured, enslaved, by her. I'm no longer in control here, and what she might find in me if she looks too closely sends a wave of panic through me. But I'm too far gone to care.

I relax my arms. Time stops as she leans closer, removing the small gap of air between our lips. She presses her lips softly against mine, holding them there, savoring the sensation, turning my body into a concentrated mass of red hot desire.

Kissing her back is an ecstasy I've known before, but the memory of it can never do it justice. I know how good it is, but it's never as good as it is *right now*. In the moment of it.

As she pulls away, I lean forward through the pain, off the pillows, unwilling to allow the air to create a space between our lips. She leans farther away, and I fall back against the pillows.

"See what I mean? You can't control yourself." She holds her voice under tight control. Her desire is running rampant as well.

"All worth it," I gasp, trying to catch my breath as my body punishes me for pushing it too far.

"Tonight." She stands. "I'm not getting any closer to you until I've washed all their blood out of your hair and out from under your fingernails."

"Oh, now I see. You have to clean me up before you have your way with me."

"It's as good an excuse as any." She leaves the room.

She returns with an armful of towels which she spreads in a thick layer over her side of the bed after loosening the sheet and flipping it over me. She leaves again and returns with a very bored-looking Christian. He stands on the bed above me with his feet on either side of my hips, grasping the sheet above my shoulders. She takes hold of the sheet at my feet.

On the count of three they heave me on top of the towels. It takes every ounce of strength to hold back a scream.

"Are you okay?" She leans down into my face, the tip of her ponytail falling against her cheek.

"Fuck." My jaw won't unclench.

"Hey!" Christian says. "I don't abide that language."

"Don't go too far away," Liv says to him. "We need to do this again once I'm done."

I probably shouldn't tell her it will kill me.

She follows him out of the room. I hear their voices travel toward the kitchen and lose myself in a black fog of pain.

"Are you asleep?" she whispers. I'm not sure how long she's been back.

"No," I whisper back to mock her. I think she's right, though. I must have been out cold.

"Since when do you have such a continuing sense of humor?" She lifts my head and rolls a pillow underneath my neck. Under my head she places a shallow pan of water.

"Since I've been stuck in a bed for two days with nothing else to entertain me." I may sound bitter, but anyone in my situation would.

"It hasn't even been two days." She lathers up my hair. Her subtle touch gives me chills.

She rinses my hair then reaches for a towel. After removing the pan, she dries my hair, and I watch her face as she works. She's thinking about something.

"Do you need more pain reliever? I think you can have some by now."

I open my mouth. Pills, a swig of water. She positions the pan of soapy water next to me on the bed and lowers my hand into it.

"You'll tell me if I'm hurting you, right? You're not going to be macho?" She scrubs my fingernails with a toothbrush.

"Is that Christian's toothbrush?"

She laughs. "What is with you lately?"

I close my eyes, savoring her touch as she works on both hands. I know it's all I'm going to get of her for a while. She moves onto my face, neck, shoulders, and arms, lathering me up and then rinsing me with a wet towel. She washes my chest to my waist and skips everything between my waist and my knees.

"You missed a spot," I say as she starts washing my feet.

"Do you want me to? I will if you want. I just don't want to get you too excited." I can hear her smile in the sound of her words.

"You sure didn't mind getting me excited earlier."

"I don't know what you're talking about. Do you want fresh boxers?"

She doesn't wait for my answer. I hear her retrieve a clean pair then she throws the sheet over me, slides mine off, clean ones on.

"Wow. You must do this often."

"Actually, I do." She steps back to admire her work. "How do you feel?"

"Excited."

"Where's your deodorant? I don't want all my work to go to waste."

I hear her footsteps take her into the bathroom, then farther away. She comes back in the room with a tray full of food and my deodorant.

"Do you think you could stomach some noodle soup?"

"God, yes."

She applies my deodorant while I pretend the upward motion of my arms doesn't feel like medieval torture. I rest and try to breathe. Death might have been a better outcome for me—I'll need to remember that the next time I get my ass handed to me this bad. She makes up the other side of the bed with clean sheets.

Christian storms into the room. "Let's get this over with, I have a lunch date. Come on, come on." He rubs his hands together.

"Did you call Kristen?" Liv asks without looking at him.

"Sure did."

A lunch date. This means he's going to be out of the house.

Liv makes Christian help me sit up while she wraps a bandage around my ribcage so many times I feel my eyes roll back in my head. The next thing I know I'm lying back against the pillows.

Christian stands on the bed as he did before, and I try to relax this time without tensing any muscles as they move me back to my side of the bed. More steady breathing, more proof I should've just let them kill me.

"Now we have to get this dirty sheet out from under him." Liv tugs it gently.

When it finally comes out it's stained dark with blood. Christian helps her replace the pillows behind me so I can sit up then he's out the door.

"Lunch." She takes the bowl from the dresser and sits next to me with her legs crossed. She offers me a spoonful, takes one herself.

I place a hand on her knee. "We have the house to ourselves."

"What do you want to do?" Too innocent. She loves to play with me.

"You."

She tries to curb her smile but it gets away from her. Something is on the tip of her tongue, and I decide to wait for it rather than drag it out of her. We finish the soup, and she sets the empty bowl on the dresser then makes up the other half of the bed.

She holds a glass of water for me. "Drink."

I drink, and she drinks. She hovers at the foot of the bed, staring at me with a faraway look as if debating something in her head. After a moment, she takes the tray from the dresser and leaves the room. I close my eyes and try to relax. Her footsteps return.

"His car is gone." She stands in the doorway. "You should take a nap." She takes a few steps into the room and ends up at the foot of the bed again.

"I'm not tired."

I watch her face as her composure begins to fail. Her eyelids lower, focusing on me. Her lips part. Her breathing changes, and mine changes in response. My skin comes alive in a yearning so desperate for the touch of hers. Our eye contact becomes magnetic, a force of such power it almost takes tangible form, drawing me toward her and her toward me until she looks down, breaking the binding connection of our gaze.

"You have to promise me." She raises her eyes again to meet mine. "That you won't move off those pillows. You won't sit up. You'll stay there. The whole time."

"I'll try."

"No. You have to promise. Say 'I promise.'"

She's playing dirty. She knows I won't readily say those words. She waits, and I imagine what I'd do right now if I was able to get up from this bed. If this day was just another day, and I wasn't a crippled mess, I'd drag her into bed with me. Slide my hands up her bare back. Lift her thigh over my hip and roll on top of her. I'd stare into her eyes, waiting, teasing her, until her resistance breaks and she takes command, pulling herself toward me, her lips against mine. I'd kiss her back, pin her against the bed as I take the control away from her once again.

"I promise." The words spill from my mouth without permission, but I don't regret them. I'll promise her anything. The control is all hers today; I willingly release it to her.

She wets her lips, watching me, still trying to talk herself out of it. Her fear of hurting me weighs on her. She takes a deep breath, and I watch her chest rise and fall, marking the beginning of her acceptance. She steps out of her shoes. A teasing smile spreads from my face to hers, and as she smiles back, she rolls her eyes at my victory.

She moves to her side of the bed. Slides her pants down and steps out of them without breaking my gaze. Her shirt goes over her head. Time slows down as she puts her palms on the bed, then her knees. She crawls to me, kneels, places one hand on my other side so she can lean over me without us touching.

"You have no shame," I say, drowning in the depth of her blue eyes.

She smiles as she watches my lips speak the words. Her bangs catch on her eyelashes, and she brushes them to the side.

"You really are going to make me beg."

She nods slowly.

I would've never considered myself the begging type. But in my unfortunate position, she leaves me no other option.

LIV

I LEAN BACK, AWAY from his warmth, to look into his eyes. He doesn't need to speak; his thoughts are written all over his face. He reaches for me for the first time and I allow it, knowing how difficult it was for him to keep his promise. If it had been up to him, he would've strained all his injuries beyond the point of easy healing. But he held back, for me, simply because I asked him to.

He takes my face in his hands and holds my head, forcing my undivided attention. "Thank you," he whispers.

"Take a nap." I swing my leg over him and slide off the bed and into my clothes.

"When do I get my next dose?" His voice already sounds half-asleep.

"I'm going to remove some pillows so you can lie down more. Count of three."

I count then tug two pillows from behind him. He winces but I pretend not to see it. I draw the sheet and quilt over him. He's drifting asleep before I leave the room.

It's strange to be in the house alone, with Trey sleeping soundly and no Christian to keep me entertained. How have I not noticed the barn we're living in? Displaced furniture, clutter, dirty dishes in unexpected places—being consumed with worry for Trey has given me temporary blindness.

There's a clarity now that I know the healing process has been started. A fog has lifted. I take a deep breath and close my eyes. Everything's going to be okay. We'll get through this, as we've gotten through everything else. I tie back my hair and declare war on the mess in the house.

Christian is lost without a maid to pick up after him. His luggage is sprawled open, surrounded by an explosion of clothes. Unsure what's clean or dirty, I take it all to the laundry room. His bedding seems clean enough, so I fold it into a neat stack on the couch. All the dishes go to the kitchen which is another disaster. I take a last walk through the living room, replacing furniture and clearing clutter. It takes several trips just to clear all the empty beer bottles. Christian must be used to all this mess just disappearing as soon as he turns his back.

The lull of washing dishes gives way to the images I can't seem to dispel. In my head is the most violent movie one could imagine, with slow motion gore and graphic close-ups. Only instead of a Hollywood action hero, the leading man is my Trey.

It's the ending I don't want to see. Right before he picked himself up to face the last one, he gave in. I'll gladly watch every blow to his face, every strike to his body, over and over if I never have to see his surrender again. I don't know what went through his mind to make him get up that final time. He must have been running on instinct and reflex alone.

To see Trey admit defeat and accept death, even for that brief moment before he was back on his feet, sends a pulse through me every time I remember. When the sting of the memory fades, what's left is a sadness beyond words. And a sharp, cold fear.

I'm on my hands and knees wiping the floor when I hear the door open. It sends a jolt through me but I know it must be Christian. If not, I'll have to choke someone with a dirty rag. He comes straight into the kitchen and opens the refrigerator.

"Back so soon?" I ask.

"She is such a…tease." A censored word for my sake. He closes the refrigerator.

"You're a pig." I stand to face him. "Women aren't just for sex, you know."

"They aren't? I guess you're right. They're also for cleaning." He smiles, obnoxiously chewing a piece of gum.

It's not a very safe comment after I just cleaned up his sty in the living room. I'm tempted to dump all the junk back in there and order him to clean it up himself.

He seizes me in a warm hug. "You know I'm only joking." He releases me with a kiss on the cheek. He still looks as good as he did when he left. A white Oxford shirt under a sweater vest, khaki pants, hair parted on the side and combed to perfection. His sleeves rolled up to the elbow are the only difference from this morning.

"Aren't you ever in a bad mood?"

"That's Trey's specialty. Why would I bother when he's so good at it?"

"You can't go back to Virginia and leave me alone with him."

"Oh, please. You love his bad moods. You're a sucker for them."

"So you did have a date?" Since Trey didn't pitch a fit when Christian left, I knew they must be up to something. Trey would only let him leave me alone and without backup if Trey was getting something out of the deal.

"Yeah, just lunch. Why?"

"I thought it was an excuse for you to leave the house."

"Oh, so he could get laid? No, I wouldn't do him that favor. I like to see that bastard squirm. It's payback for a lifetime of his crap." He hesitates. A flash of that panicked worry he wore when we first got Trey back to the house crosses his face before he forces it down with a grin. "So did you do it?"

I cock my head at him and exhale wearily. Why is my sex life everyone's business lately?

"All right." He raises his hand for a high five.

I duck underneath it and rinse my rag in the sink. He leaves the room. I look up, right at Trey's herb cabinet. I forgot to tell Trey to get rid of that herbal tea and here I am again, drawn toward it like an addict. Fighting it would be much easier without the temptation. But maybe he already got rid of it.

I open the cabinet and peek in. My vision tightens into a tunnel. I shift around the jars, unsure if I'd recognize the ingredients.

"Hey."

I turn around. Christian's raised eyebrows tell me I must have a guilty expression on my face.

"You looking for something?"

"Just making sure it's gone, that's all." The sickness I feel saying those words proves it's a lie. I have a history of addiction. First it was zolpidem. Probably still is. Now, Trey's habit-forming herbal tea.

He closes the cabinet for me. "It's powerful stuff. Probably not safe for pregnancy. If he knows it has a hold on you—"

"It doesn't. I mean, not anymore." If I can quit zolpidem as fast as I did, I can quit anything. Even if I don't know exactly what I'm quitting. Somehow, that makes it easier. "Tell me something. Why is Trey so opposed to making promises?"

He sucks air in through his teeth. "Can't go there. Sorry. I do have boundaries."

I cross my arms and turn to face him. He'll give it up.

"You're going to have to ask him that one. Next question."

"Why is he so sensitive about being called a liar?"

The room fills with his exuberant laughter. "Are you referring to our little shoving match? You know, I don't know why that sets him off. It always has."

"You used it on purpose, knowing it would set him off?" This shouldn't surprise me.

He thinks for a moment. "Not really. It just worked out that way. Well, maybe I did. But he *was* lying—wasn't he? What was he lying about? I don't even remember."

"Me neither."

"He has a lot of triggers. I'm sure you know some that I don't. They can be very effective if used wisely."

"His jealousy. A male friend of mine sets him off every time."

"He kind of has a good reason for that."

"I am *not* Kate. He can trust me." It's something that bothers me more than it should but not because of Trey's own issues. Because of mine. And that nagging feeling I can't seem to purge: our bond was created by outside forces, not by us, and it won't last. I could ask Christian about that damn spell right now, if only I could get the words out.

"He does trust you. It's just baggage. He never lets anything go. You know that, right?"

I don't think Christian will ever know how much good he does. How he's helped me understand things about Trey that I may have never understood. And to be a loving brother to Trey, his whole life, when he otherwise would've been alone in that awful house.

"Trey wouldn't be the person he is without you," I say.

He gives me a puzzled look.

"I mean that in a good way," I add, realizing it could also be a huge insult.

"Ah, he'd be fine." He opens the refrigerator and takes a beer.

I catch his arm. "Do you know how many empty bottles I just cleared from the other room? Put it back."

His surprise is almost comical. I suppress a laugh. I don't want him to think this is a joke, especially since to him, everything is a joke. A few social drinks every once in a while aren't going to hurt anyone but these two practically have an IV feed. I've seen what alcoholism does to the body in far too many patients. I'm not going to watch it happen to two people I care about.

"That's not going to work on me." His face is frozen in shock, like he's witnessing a great atrocity.

"You two are alcoholics and you don't even see it. And it's too early to start drinking. Put it back!"

I take hold of the bottom of the bottle and elbow him hard in the ribs. The bottle falls into my hand, and I return it to the refrigerator and close the door. If he can save me from my addiction, I can save him from his.

"F word a million times over." His crazed, rigid stare goes beyond me and hits the wall somewhere behind me. "This is wrong in so many ways."

"That I'm disrupting the bachelor pad? Not my problem."

"No F word and now no drinking. I can't live like this."

"I didn't say no drinking. Just…be reasonable."

"A beer right now is completely reasonable to me."

I block the refrigerator with my body. "Okay, then be reasonable according to what I think is reasonable."

He eyes me hard. It might be intimidating to someone who doesn't know him like I do.

"Do you mind if I do your laundry?"

"Do you have to ask?"

I go into the laundry room and start a load, reading each garment label so I don't ruin all his expensive clothes.

Although, he probably wouldn't care. He'd just buy new ones.

When I leave the laundry room, he's standing beside the open refrigerator chugging a beer. Laughter falls out of my mouth. Maybe it shouldn't be funny but he's like a child cramming his mouth full of candy as soon as you turn your back.

He swallows. "Hey, just because little Fearghus is whipped doesn't mean I have to be."

"If I find that discarded anywhere but the trash can—"

He shushes me. It's so clipped, and so unlike him, it actually shuts me up. I follow him into the living room where we sit down on the couch together.

"Oh," he says. "I told Kristen you and Trey will come out with us for dinner next time."

"A double date? *Right.*"

"He'll agree." He takes a drink. "A couple more days and he'll be out of bed. Don't you think?"

"How would I know?"

"You're the professional."

"I don't usually deal with immortals."

He drains his beer. "But," he says, crossing his legs on the coffee table, "she's probably just using me to get to him. Wouldn't be the first time."

"And I'm sure it's worked the other way too."

"True." His attention moves to my hands. "You're shaking."

That's when I notice. My night shakes, now visiting in the daytime. I stand, to draw his attention away. "Too much coffee. I'm going to check on him."

Trey opens his eyes when I enter the room. He stretches, the best he can with limited mobility. I sit on the edge of the bed next to him, folding my arms against me so he doesn't notice them shaking. "I didn't mean to wake you up."

"You didn't. I was dozing."

I offer him a drink of water and he drinks the entire glass.

"I think your face is already looking better." I lean in to examine it closer. The bruises have lightened, and the wounds seem to have a layer of smoother skin. "You have a bullet lodged in your arm, so close to the surface I can see it."

He groans, rubbing his head with both hands. "Just leave it."

"I can get it easily. I think you're strong enough now." I leave the room for my boxes of supplies.

"Can I please eat first?" he asks when I return.

I pause and look at him. "Will you stay this sweet? After you're better?"

"No." He grins.

I remove a pair of long-handled forceps from their packaging and catch his discerning eye.

"You went shopping?"

I put on my gloves. I pick up the forceps and climb on top of the bed to sit next to him. The wound on his arm faces me, and I press against his skin until I feel the bullet. "I have anesthetic now. Not that it will help much at this point…"

"Don't bother. Save it for when we really need it."

I give him a look. His idea of 'really need it' might differ from mine.

"Just do it. Get it out so I can eat."

When I finally extract it, I hold it up in front of Trey, who gives me the blankest of stares. Digging foreign objects out of human flesh probably shouldn't be so rewarding. Patients rarely share in my joy but usually they're either in agonizing pain or doped up beyond words. I do a whip stitch to make it quick. He sinks a little into the bed when I'm done.

"What do you want to eat?"

"Anything."

I force Christian to help me prepare a meal, and together we carry it into the bedroom. Christian drags in a chair for himself, and I take a spot on the bed next to Trey. "Christian signed us up for a double date with him and Kristen."

"No."

"Too late. I've already committed," Christian says. "Do I have to remind you that you broke my fingers?"

"Do I have to remind you that you banged my wife?"

"You may have something there." Christian goes for his sandwich.

These two are something else. The same issues that cause them to want to kill each other one day are a harmless joke on another. Not enough time has passed to heal wrongs like these, but maybe these two have found a shortcut. After a life of practice, it's probably become easy.

Trey drips soup on his chest and I dab it off. It's nice, how this awful situation has forced us to slow down. Spend real time with each other. Form the beginning of something that's real, something I can trust.

"Your Camaro's in the shop. Do you want a new stock exhaust or something even more obnoxious?" Christian says.

"You feeling guilty about snoozing on the couch while I was out there getting my ass kicked?"

They start talking about the repairs to the car and I eat, trying to stay with them while being dragged away by a force I don't recognize. The lines tethering me to this room are being snipped and I can't see what's below me, what I'll fall into. It's an uncertainty that should terrify me, but I can't shake the feeling there's something down there I've forgotten. Something I need.

"Liv."

I look at Christian. The room settles into place around me.

"Your boy is bleeding over there."

I get up to wash my hands. I return and inject Trey's arm with anesthetic. As tough as he thinks he is, the wounds are already sore from removing the bullets and it's stupid not to use anesthetic when it's sitting right here next to me.

After I fix Trey up, Christian helps me gather our mess and take it to the kitchen. We clean up together until Christian's phone rings. From his inflection, it must be Aaron. He moves into the living room to talk, and I head back to Trey.

"I want to know something." I climb on the bed and settle next to him. "Don't get mad."

"Can you save it for later? I'd rather not ruin my food high."

"Why don't you like making promises?" I ask before I talk myself out of it. Before he talks me out of it.

His expression hardens, and he looks away. "Everything always returns to this."

"To what?"

He runs a rough hand over his stubbly face and looks away again. His reluctance to tell me fuels my fear of the worst. Maybe it's a bad time to prod him but I have to know. It's one of many things I have to know. I have to start somewhere.

He sighs and looks at the ceiling. "Kate asked me to promise her that we'd never be apart. And I did. That night she was gone, kidnapped and murdered. Or so I thought. For fifteen years." He lowers his head and looks at me.

It has to be a coincidence. She'd have no reason to set it up like that, and then leave with the infant he thought was his. Surely she knew the devastating lie his family would feed him. What benefit would it be to her?

"My guard was down because I believed they didn't care—" His eyes have gone distant. With a hard exhale, he returns his focus to me. "Broken promise or enormous mind fuck? You decide. But I don't make promises."

Christian's raised voice carries in to us. He must not be talking to his son anymore. Trey wraps a hand over his eyes, grasping hard at both temples. I go in to Christian to make sure everything's okay.

When he notices me, he points to the phone then does the circular this-person-is-crazy motion next to his ear. It must be Kate. Our favorite topic of conversation.

"You're not staying. I told you that. If Aaron wants to live there it has nothing to do with you." I can hear her voice from his phone. I start to leave, but Christian motions me over and pats the seat next to him. "It's not his house either, he's a distant relative." He must be referring to Dillon. He laughs. "You know what will happen if you try to do that."

Back inside the bedroom, I close the door to muffle Christian's voice. I can't listen to him talk about Dillon.

"What's got him going?" Trey asks.

"I don't know. He was talking to Aaron earlier." I'm not mentioning Kate.

He starts to speak but changes his mind.

I kneel next to him on the bed. "I'm going to miss this, you being my captive entertainment."

He snorts.

"You should break your ribs more often."

He doesn't answer. The silence weighs on me.

"I'm sorry I ruined your mood," I say.

He looks at me. His eyes are full of too many things for him to voice, too many for me to decipher.

"Can I make it up to you?"

He leans his head against the headboard and exhales hard. Captive is exactly what he must feel. I should try to get him up to move around. A walk around the bed and back to get his muscles working, his blood flowing. His fingers start tapping on the mattress and I cover his hand with mine to relax them. He looks at me. There's a dimple in his forehead, a sorrow in his eyes. His lips part just as the door opens.

"Oh, god, I should knock," Christian says, distracted, dropping into the chair.

"Who was that on the phone?" Trey says.

"Aaron. Then Kate." Christian's eyes catch mine, then he looks back at Trey. "Do you realize you and Dillon switched women? Isn't that kind of…messed up?"

Trey doesn't answer.

"I told her to get the hell out of my house and take Dillon with her. She thinks she has more right to be there than me. And she's not going to divorce you. Sorry, man."

"Doesn't matter."

"It matters to her. She thinks your marriage is still valid."

"It won't matter to her when she's dead."

Christian snickers. "Is that your grand plan? Just kill her?"

"Yep." Trey settles into the pillows with a satisfied sneer. "And him. I'll take my time on him. I'll do her quick. She doesn't deserve any more of my time. She's taken enough of it."

Christian sighs. "Trey, you can't kill my kid's mother."

Trey looks up as if this is the first time this idea has occurred to him. His earlier disgust returns to his expression but somehow it's worse. He covers his face and growls into his hands.

I share a glance with Christian.

"Just break her fingers," Christian offers.

Trey lowers his hands and leans his head against the headboard, staring at the ceiling. "Go take the Ninja for a ride." He looks pointedly at Christian.

Christian stands. "Actually, I'm going on a beer run. And I'll drop by and see Kristen at work. I'll take my time."

He leaves the room, and Trey and I wait in silence until the front door opens and closes.

His face is still hard when he finally looks at me. "Do your thing."

I know how to take a hint.

CHAPTER 17

TREY

T HE ROOM IS dark. She's missing from the bed. I strain to hear evidence of her in the house and pick up a muffled conversation followed by her bright laughter. Christian must be home. I turn to look at the clock—almost midnight. She'll be coming back to me soon. I drift back into sleep, relishing the memory of her teasing smile, the smell of her hair, the sensation of her skin against mine.

My eyes open gazing straight into hers.

She gives me the biggest smile. "You turned over in your sleep. That's great progress. How do you feel?"

I turn slightly and stretch, testing my body. Pain shoots through me in small isolated bursts instead of the familiar all-encompassing, crippling agony.

"Better." I return a smile.

"How does an omelet sound?"

"I'll take two."

I can practically smell when the eggs hit the skillet even though I'm on the opposite side of the house. My stomach is ready to play catch-up. Maybe I should have ordered three.

She warns me to eat slowly but it's damn near impossible. It's like I've been fasting for a week. I wash it down with my glass of orange juice and hers, then she leaves with the dirty dishes to get me some coffee. It's probably going to wind me up and make me need to piss too much when I'm stuck in bed but I'm far from caring.

"Christian will have to be your nurse tomorrow." She hands me a muffin that's swelling out of its wrapper. It might just have a halo around it.

"Not sure that's a good idea. He'll kill me. He can't even take care of himself."

"He brought these muffins. And he can iron. He's in there ironing right now."

"Of course he can iron. Looking good is that important."

"He can't pick up after himself but he can iron?"

"It's one of the things he was forced to learn when staying with me. There's no one here to do it for him. Leaving the house in a wrinkled shirt is that scary to him."

"Trey?"

She only says my name like that before some god-awful question. Some game-changing news.

"We don't have to name her Sloane," she says softly, but it hits me like a slap. "I mean, if you don't want to. Just because that was her name before."

"Of course we do. That's her name." I don't understand why she doesn't know this.

"But that was her name when I was…with him. When she was his. I know she's the same child but she might not look the same and—"

"She was never his. She was yours. And now she's ours."

"But…"

"You told me you picked that name. Not him. It's her name. And my mother's name. It's not a coincidence they have the same name."

She looks down at her hands. In this motion, I see another trace of that thing she's been doing. A slight withdrawal. She's done it enough now I have to admit I'm seeing it. Each time, it's an added inch of distance, too small for me to notice but she's gotten that part wrong. I notice. She looks back up at me. "Sloane Bevan. Just like your mother."

Pride erupts within me. If she grows to be as strong as my mother, she will hold the world in her hand.

She goes to refill my coffee mug and returns with a few books and a chess board.

"I'm spending the day in here with you." She straightens the covers next to me and sits.

"Why's he ironing? Does he think he's going somewhere?"

She shrugs. "I didn't ask. But he does have some serious cabin fever."

"Too bad. He has to stay."

"Why? He left twice yesterday and you didn't mind. You *told* him to leave the second time."

I give her a look. I have my reasons.

"So our safety takes a back seat to your libido."

"*Our* libido." I poke her in the forehead. "And I resent that. I am a dying man, and you are my medicine."

"Dying? Hardly. You'd heal without me. It would just take longer."

"Knock, knock," Christian says as he opens the door. "I'll be back in a few hours."

"You can't go anywhere." I look away from him.

"My ass I can't. That wasn't the case yesterday."

I don't answer him. Liv slides a chess piece on the board, so I advance my pawn.

"Have a good time," Liv says to him.

"Are you armed?" I say before he steps away.

He gives me the here-we-go-again look. "I have a whole stash under the seat of my car."

"Useless."

"All your guns are too big to conceal under my clothes."

"Dress appropriately." I catch Liv's amused grin.

"I don't want her finding a gun on me in a moment of passion."

"It could help your image. Women love danger and mystery. Right?" I hand the conversation to Liv. I'm not arguing with him about something he knows damn well.

"Yes, because women are so cliché and predictable," she answers.

With her hair slightly messed from hanging out in bed with me, it reminds me of how she looked the morning after the night she became mine.

"Hey, loverboy, consider it another favor." He walks out of view. "I'll bring home some lunch," he hollers just before the front door closes.

We play in pleasant silence. When more pieces clutter the bed than the board, she lies down on her side, propping her head up with her elbow. "Your turn," she says, looking up at me.

It's all too much. In these last weeks, my sorry, perpetually alone self got a woman, a baby, a new family, a bitter war—and my mortality. A guy can get used to being unbeatable. Returning to a fragile mass of slow-to-heal skin and breakable bones? Not so easy to get used to.

"What is it?" She goes to her knees, leans toward me on her palms. Worry creases her forehead.

"I think we're at a stalemate," I say to distract her. I'm already disgusted by my ongoing state of helplessness. Her concern only amplifies it.

She studies the board. "I think you're right. Do you want to play again?"

I shrug.

"What?" She creases her forehead again. "What are you thinking?"

I can't keep it back. "What kind of father would I be to send my daughter into this?" My ribs cave, forcing me to gasp for breath.

"Trey, don't." She takes my face in her hands.

I snatch her wrists to pull her hands away. Her eyes cloud with hurt, and I buckle under another onslaught of pain.

"You need to stop this. Right now." Her voice is strong but I know it's a front. She's only being strong for me.

"Am I wrong?" I don't mean for my voice to sound so vicious. I know I shouldn't be taking this out on her.

"You don't know what the future holds. It could all blow over."

"Is that what you're banking on? That's stupid and you know it."

Her lips tighten, and she looks away. After a long silence, she says, "We can only do our best."

"Our best," I pause for breath. "Would be to move to Mexico and distance ourselves from this whole thing." Especially after I kill all of them at the Virginia estate. Moores will be crawling out of holes all over North America and Europe to take turns torturing me before they put my head on a stick. "Shit, they'd find us in Mexico. Australia."

"We couldn't do that."

"We can do whatever the hell we want."

"We have a responsibility."

"Did you agree to take on this responsibility? I know I didn't. Our daughter's life is not up for grabs, to fight a war she has nothing to do with."

"She has everything to do with it. This is her family, counting on her."

"Maybe they picked the wrong people to count on."

"No." Her voice rises. "They picked the right people. The only people. You were prepared for this. Excited, even, on our drive home from Chicago. What happened?"

I don't answer her because I know she's right. I was ready for this. Their defeat finally felt so possible I could taste it. The map to my revenge was placed in my hands and I fell into line, headed to battle, without contemplating the reality of a process that involves my precious daughter. The flesh and blood of the woman I would die for a million times over.

"I don't know what happened." I close my eyes. Exhaustion like this is new to me and it pisses me off.

"You just need to get out of this bed. Being stuck in here is making everything worse. Things will be better once you're up and about."

"Why couldn't it be me?"

"You—instead of her?"

I don't answer.

"Because you aren't the right one. They didn't go to all this trouble without knowing exactly what they were doing."

I release all the air from my chest, sinking into the pillows. She leans over me, placing her palms on either side of me on the bed.

"You know you're too hot-headed to carry out anything that requires any amount of patience. Remember what happened last time? You can't even listen to a simple request from your mother."

The proximity of her lips to mine douses me with a burst of serotonin, and for a moment I forget everything in the world but her. But then it happens again—a shield over her expression, a quick look away. That slight withdrawal. One more inch I'm not supposed to notice.

"Will you let me shave your face?" She runs a finger down my cheek.

In moments like this she's impossible to turn down. She knows exactly how to play me. Needing no further encouragement, she hops off the bed and leaves the room.

"Have you ever done this before?" I ask when she returns with her hands full of the necessary equipment.

"A million times. Okay, maybe not a million." She slides a towel under my head and shoulders.

"Just hold a mirror and I'll do it."

"Do you have a mirror I could hold? Didn't think so." She dips a washcloth in a bowl of warm water and places it across my face. "Just pretend I'm a barber. What should we talk about? Sports?"

"You don't know anything about sports."

"I can improvise. So, did you see the game?" It's an obvious stab in the dark.

"Nope, missed it. I did hear about Fedorov versus Williams, though." Let's see where she goes with this.

"Hmm. Yeah. It was amazing."

"Amazing? Not quite the word. I would say badass."

"Badass." She nods along mock-knowingly.

"Yeah, Williams is just out to prove. He's too full of himself. He doesn't respect the sport."

"You *have* to respect the sport." She lathers me with shaving cream and runs the razor down the far edge of my cheek.

I wait, leaving her with the floor.

She takes a risk. "When the ball went over the line—"

"Ball? There's no ball."

"There isn't? Okay, so we aren't talking about tennis?"

Laughter may be the best medicine, but not for fractured ribs. "No," I say when I recover. "Try again."

"Okay. When..." She hesitates, rinsing the razor in the water. "What sport doesn't involve a ball? They all do!"

"Not all." She's not getting any hints out of me.

"Okay, no ball. Golf! Oh wait, that has a ball." She pauses. "Okay I have it. When Williams stepped out of bounds..."

"Williams barely had time to do anything before the match was over."

"Yeah, it was a quick match, wasn't it?"

"That's how it is with Fedorov. He waits for his moment, and then bam. Over."

"Bam." She nods, trying hard not to laugh.

"Even a busted nose can't stop that guy. He's an animal."

"A busted nose? Okay then, I guess we aren't talking about fencing."

"Fencing?" I squeeze both fists as I try to curb a laugh rising in my gut. "Of all things, you think fencing?"

"What else doesn't involve a ball? Archery?"

"You can't get a busted nose in archery either."

"Oh!" She starts on my other cheek. "Wrestling. No, boxing. It's definitely boxing."

"Close."

"Not wrestling either?"

"Nope." I try not to smile and impede her work.

"Do you want a moustache?" She hovers over my upper lip with a huge smile on her face.

"Mixed martial arts." I ignore her more recent question.

"Ah, I should've known you'd follow that. So will you be mad if I leave this?" she asks, referring again to my upper lip.

"You're the one who has to look at me."

She shaves it all then rinses the razor. She goes to the bathroom, returns to place another warm, wet cloth across my face.

"I'm going to stay in bed for the rest of my life."

She applies more of her Chapstick to my lips. "Can I paint your nails?"

"Try it. We'll see how well that goes over."

"Unfortunately, I don't have any—"

"Tell me everything you know about Dillon Moore."

Her face falls. She removes all the towels and gets off the bed. "You know I know nothing about the real Dillon Moore." She avoids my gaze.

"Tell me what you know."

"Why? What's the point? It's only going to enrage you. You need to relax so you can heal."

"I need to know what we're going up against."

"We're not going up against him." She busies herself arranging the shaving stuff on the dresser when we both know it goes back in the bathroom. She still won't look at me. "And why are you doing this? It'll be years before we have to think about this at all."

"We're going up against his son. I already know everything about Kate. You'll forget what you know about him with time. So you need to tell me now."

She sits on the edge of the bed. Finally meets my gaze. "His son may be nothing like him."

"His son will be trained, like I was. His son will be just like me."

She looks down in sudden understanding. With such a clear comparison, now she must finally grasp the reason behind my concern.

"Me, without my mother's influence," I add. "Without Bevan DNA. Moore through and through. Pure evil. Trained as a killer."

"You don't know that," she says to her hands in her lap.

I enunciate each word. "Tell me what you know about Dillon Moore."

"He was a loving husband!" she shouts. "He was funny, successful, sweet, charming! And he had a complete secret life I knew nothing about!" She pushes off the bed and walks over to the window.

"What are his skills? Does he own any guns? Is he athletic?"

She turns to face me. "I don't know." Her words are the coldest I've ever heard from her. "He ran every morning. He went to the gym a few times a week. He went out of town a lot. He told me it was for business."

"What kind of business?"

"Demolition. He was an engineer. He specialized in demolition."

"How did you meet him?"

"He came into work one day. I was working in the ER. He came straight up to me and asked me out."

"Why was he there? Was he a patient?"

"He told me he was visiting a friend."

"Lie number one. That easy." Fueled by my anger, the words are already out by the time I realize they sound insensitive. Like they were directed at her, as an accusation, as if she should have known better.

"You don't need to rub it in," she says, visibly affected by those words I shouldn't have said.

"I didn't…" I begin. And then I run into a brick wall.

"His favorite food was lasagna, he liked old Western movies, and he liked making love in the shower. There. Are you happy?"

I hear the sound of my teeth clamping down and feel it radiate in my jaw. Her eyes tear me to shreds. I know she's being vindictive, but it doesn't matter. The image has planted itself in my mind, pulling the pin out of the grenade in my head.

Her expression softens, and her eyes stare far away. "He proposed to me on the shore of Lake Michigan. He wanted to have a baby right away. When she was born, he said it was the happiest day of his life. He held my hand at her funeral. And five days later, he was gone."

His son will never know him. I will kill him before his son enters this world. I want to feel him squirm in my grasp. I want to witness the last breath leave his body. I want to watch his blood run, surging one last time as his heart beats its final beat.

"Did you have to bring this up?" Her eyes are wet but no longer sad. Her voice is cold again, a weapon, as if her pain's been turned back onto me. "It serves no purpose but to torment us both. You like to wallow in grief. Not me. So knock yourself out." She snatches the towels, bucket, shaving cream, and razor, and storms out of the room, slamming the door, leaving an abrupt silence behind her.

Both fists slam into the headboard behind me. I press my palms against my temples to control the explosions going off in succession, a battlefield I'm unable to join. I can only lie here while a war tears through me until my mind is kind enough to shut it off. To go numb.

CHAPTER 18

LIV

CRYING NOW WOULD be angry tears and Trey's not getting that out of me. I splash cold water from the bathroom sink on my face. My crazed eyes stare back at me in the mirror. I can't lose my temper like this. There's room for only one violent temper in this house, and his makes mine look like a mockery. I'll gladly leave the role to him.

But I won't be apologizing anytime soon. He pushes people to satisfy his needs with no consideration for their feelings. He's used to this. He's always gotten away with it. Who's going to complain—to him? The few who have probably didn't live long enough to comprehend their mistake and weren't around to repeat it. He'll have to learn it doesn't work that way with me. I'm not going to answer angry questions that shove me into places I don't want to be until he can learn to lose the anger, tone down the judgment, and ask with some degree of sympathy.

Yes it was all a setup, a fabricated life. Knowing this does not repair the heartbreak. My memories don't contain the lies—they're a real part of me. They still carry the same weight. My love for Dillon has been removed from my current state of mind, from my understanding of the past, but it's still mixed into those memories. Nothing can erase the desperation I felt those days waiting for him to come home, waiting for him to call, waiting for him to save me from that empty house, those sleepless nights, that cold bed. From the image of our baby's coffin I couldn't stop seeing.

Where's Christian when I need him? I drag myself into the kitchen. River and Trib peer at me through the sliding glass door. I open it. "Do you want to come in?"

Trib jumps backward as if panicked at the idea of being enclosed inside. Birds screech to one another across the yard. River leans to one side, peeking past me into the house. I step aside so she can get a better look. She's probably wondering if Trey's up and about. "He's still in bed. And not in the best mood. You should come back—"

She barks. It's so forceful and direct it sends a chill through me. A bird lands in the pine next to the house, sends another call across the yard. Trib returns to River's side. They seem to have the birds in a frenzy. I retrieve a piece of cheese for each of them, hand both outside, and slide the door closed. They both drop the cheese and look at me.

Maybe they do want in. I go for the door. They bark in unison, so loudly I jump.

The entire panel of glass shatters around me in an explosion of sparkling, refracted light. I hit the ground on my belly before all the glass has a chance to settle on the floor.

Glass crunches under me as I crawl into the living room and roll into a sitting position against the wall. Christian bursts through the front door, dropping his bags. He seizes me by the forearms.

"What was that?!" The fierceness in his eyes morphs him into a stranger.

"The sliding glass door just blew out."

He reaches behind his back for a gun but comes up empty-handed. "Shit! I hate it when that asshole is right. I need a gun. Where's a gun?"

I crawl over to the fireplace, snatch a nine millimeter off the mantel, and drop back to the floor. He holds up his hand, and I toss it to him.

"You can't go out there," I say.

"What, and wait for them to come in here? I'll be right back. Get yourself a gun and guard both doors."

He's out the door before I can answer. I scan the room but see no other weapons. I can't risk going in the basement and leaving Trey unprotected. Staying below the windows, I head toward the bedroom. He's out cold. I grab a Glock off the nightstand. If he wasn't snoring I'd think he was dead. He's woken from lesser noises while asleep—how did the exploding glass not wake him? No amount of pain would keep him in bed after a noise like that.

Gunshots sound from far away and I rush to the front window. Cold wind tears through the house. I reposition so I have a view of the kitchen to make sure we have no visitors coming through the back. It's wide open now. If their goal was to break and enter, the break has already been done. I remember the skylight at my house and aim at the broken door. The enter isn't going to go over so well. The front door opens, and I turn to cover it.

"It's me," Christian calls, out of breath. "Damn it to hell. This is not in my job description."

He strips off his jacket and yanks the shirttails out of his pants. Panting, he places his hand against the wall and bows his head.

"I caught him fleeing along the river." He's still out of breath. "He won't be coming back. Got him in the arm then the back of the head. His weapon is on the porch. Let's eat."

He picks up the bags of food he dropped on his first entry into the house, and I follow him into the kitchen.

He stops a few steps inside the doorway. "*Holy earth.* Were you in here when it blew?"

I nod.

"You almost got sniped. The prince is not going to be happy. I'm surprised he's not out here right now, jamming his fist through the glass of the other side."

"He's asleep. He didn't wake up."

"You kidding me?" He raises his eyebrows.

I shake my head and begin to sweep up the glass.

"You sure he's not dead?" He takes an urgent step toward the doorway.

"I just checked on him." My voice cracks. I clear my throat.

"Hey." He takes my arm. "Everything's fine. They only do stuff like this once. It won't happen again for a long time. Don't freak out."

"Easy for you to say."

"You're bleeding." He bends my elbow out.

"It must be from the glass." I check the other elbow and find more blood. I move to the sink to rinse the wounds. Wind pushes into the room, knocking more shards out of the empty door frame.

He toes loose glass out of the frame. "I'm sure he's got plywood in the garage. I'll check after we eat."

He swipes the tabletop with his arm to clear the glass and unloads the food. I get both of our coats from the front closet and join him at the table.

He puts on his coat. "You're not going to wake him up and eat with him?"

"No."

He appraises me while sucking the straw to his jumbo soft drink.

"He needs to sleep. He's in a bad mood," I offer.

"You two had a fight." He gives me a playful grin. The chilly breeze ruffles his hair. "What about?"

"Just Trey being Trey."

"Don't I know it."

They couldn't have timed this attack better. The bullet missed me, but it went straight through the core of my morale. Trey set the target with his onslaught earlier. He's right. How are we going to live like this? Australia sounds pretty good right about now. He's going to be impossible to shut down once he wakes up and sees what happened.

"Maybe we shouldn't tell him," I say.

Christian looks up at me.

I point to the missing door. "About that."

He swallows a mouthful. "You know that's a bad idea. Why keep it from him?"

"I don't know. He was on a rampage earlier. This is just going to make him worse."

"He can't get any worse. Plus, it's impossible to fix before he's up and about. We might have to order a new door. Unless you want to buy us some time and go in there and give him a few good punches in the ribs. And then swear yourself celibate."

I exhale out a building laugh. He always has to take a serious matter and turn it into a joke, and I just don't feel like laughing right now. "We could tell him it broke."

"He's not that gullible. And I'm not going to get caught in another lie with him."

"Fine. But don't tell him today."

"You're playing with fire, my dear."

"I can handle it." And we need a new subject. I can't think about Trey and his difficult personality. How I'm considering lying to him rather than deal with his anger. That my bond to him is not something I chose. That he's right—we didn't agree to this responsibility. We didn't agree to any of this. "Tell me about your date."

He focuses on something behind me. "Another reason you have no choice but to tell him. Looks like the door took your bullet." He gets up and sticks his finger through the hole in the door to the basement stairs. "God, what caliber is that?"

I swallow a lump in my throat. It must have missed me by a hair. I gawk at the enormous hole that could be in my skull. I didn't agree to any of this but maybe that's irrelevant. If I must live with this danger to have my daughter back, I'll take it. That *is* my choice. Knowing the danger she'll have in her life, it's a rotten, selfish one.

Christian squeezes my shoulders on his way back to his seat. "You should take Trey shopping for some curtains."

"I think we need a new door first."

He chuckles, wolfs down the rest of his food, and slurps the last bit of liquid out of his drink. "I'll get that plywood before we freeze to death."

When his footsteps return on the porch I get up to help him. He leans two sheets of plywood against the house and hands me the drill from the back of his pants and the gun from the front. He unloads his pockets full of screws into my open hands.

"Okay, you hold, and I'll screw."

I look at him, expecting a joke.

"What? Get your mind out of the gutter, woman."

He hands me the larger piece of plywood, and I hold it against the opening. Once a few screws are holding it in place, I move aside to give him more room.

He stands back to look at his work. "I forgot to get a saw." He eyes the doorway to the living room. "And how is this not waking him up? Are you sure he's alive?"

"I'll go check on him again." I drop my handful of screws onto the table.

"I'll get a saw." He follows me through the doorway and goes out the front door in his T-shirt, gun in hand.

A panic tightens my stomach when I see Trey's body in the exact position as before. I go straight for his pulse. It's normal. I lean over him, wishing I could check his brain activity because there's no way he couldn't have heard the glass blowing out, Christian's raised voice, the drill. He's frowning in his sleep. Clenching his jaw. If he keeps grinding his teeth like this he won't have any left. I smooth the wrinkle between his eyebrows with my thumb but it returns. I apply light pressure on both sides of his jaw to relax the tension. His breath seems tight for sleep, but I'm not about to wake him up to tell him he needs to relax.

Fighting with him is a grievous offense. I could've been dead in there. Withholding my apology is even worse—either one of us could be dead tomorrow. I won't let him bait me into a fight again. Maybe we don't have control over our destiny, but we do control our behavior. The urge to apologize to him right now overtakes me so I lean to kiss his smooth cheek. The touch should wake him. He should be alert and ready to choke an intruder right now. He doesn't move.

His blood must be saturated with my immortality. All this sleep will have him healed in record time. I'll have no choice but to tell him about the sniper and I'll have no way to keep him from charging straight to Virginia.

I catch Christian coming in the house with a circular saw and a roll of insulation. "You need to use that saw outside. We shouldn't wake him up."

"I can't believe he's sleeping through this. Did you drug him?"

Outside, the saw screams in the silence, getting even louder when the blade makes contact with the wood.

When the saw shuts off, Christian looks at me. "Sorry. Couldn't be avoided. There's no way in hell I was going to manually saw that whole thing."

The cut is a little crooked, but the plywood does its job, and Christian tucks insulation in the gap along the other pane of glass as I sweep the floor for the second time.

I put Trey's now cold lunch in the refrigerator, and Christian catches the door before it closes and reaches for a beer.

"No mouthing off after what I just did for you." He opens the bottle and takes a long drink.

I wouldn't mind a beer myself. Or a gulp out of Trey's liquor. I take off my coat. "Please take those off before you go anywhere else." I gesture toward his sawdust-covered pants.

He rips off his belt, strips off the pants, and hands them to me. No sense of privacy, no shame, but I'm not sure I expected it. I'm the housemother of a frat house. I take the pants and his discarded shirt into the laundry room. After starting a load, I find him in the living room, still in his undershirt and boxers, with his feet on the coffee table and his beer in his hand.

"What a fucked-up couple of weeks. Sorry," he adds, catching himself a little too late.

"I have to agree. Fucked up." I sit on the couch next to him.

He chokes on a mouthful of beer. Wiping the back of his hand across his mouth, he looks at me, eyes wide, smile on the verge of exploding. "Can I kiss you?"

"What if I said yes?" I lean my head back and close my eyes.

"Oh my god, don't tempt me. Yet another way to ensure death by Trey."

"You're not even attracted to me, so shut up," I say to the backs of my eyelids.

"My ass. You are hot."

"Don't lie. I know what kind of women you're attracted to. I saw Kristen."

"Yeah, she's hot too. I like variety. I don't discriminate."

Remembering Kate's statuesque, exotic beauty, I can't hold my tongue. "And Kate." I open my eyes at the ceiling.

"You're not going to get me to admit to her. I refuse."

"You can't deny she's beautiful. She's a supermodel."

"I'm not admitting or denying anything about Kate. My relationship with her was completely out of my control."

I hug my legs against my chest. He sets his empty bottle on the coffee table and stretches his arms out across the back of the couch. He should enter a beer drinking contest. I don't know how he chugs them so fast.

"I'll tell you one thing. He's lucky he doesn't have a kid with her. He owes me a huge favor for that one. Have a kid with a woman, and you can never get too far away. Unless you're a shit father, I guess."

"Once Aaron's grown it will be easier."

"True. Maybe I can convince him to move to New York with me."

"You'd leave the estate?"

He thinks a moment. "If she stays, then yes, I'd leave."

"But that estate is your inheritance. You can't just give it up to her."

He rubs his face. "I know, I know, don't get me started thinking about it. The whole thing blows."

"And Trey's mother. You can't leave her there."

"I'm not going anywhere anytime soon." His head drops in a heavy nod, assuring me of her safety, and closing the subject at the same time.

"But *he* is. As soon as he sees that door—"

"We just need to keep him busy. Clog the toilet. Break another window. Ask him to build you a nursery for the baby. A busy Trey, an irritated Trey, is a happy Trey."

"You have to take care of him tomorrow. I have to go to work."

"Aw, you've got to be kidding me. Can't we hire a nurse?"

"All you have to do is bring him food and water. And pain reliever if he needs it."

"I'll just bring him a bottle of scotch first thing in the morning. That will take care of all of it." He nods, smiling like it's the cleverest of ideas.

"He told me you'd kill him. I think he was right."

"He said I'd kill him? Wow, I'm hurt."

We both freeze at the sound of the bedroom door jerking open and footsteps coming toward us. Trey appears in the hall, his eyes on me. I want to demand what he's doing out of bed, but the words catch in my throat. There's a hopeless fury in his eyes, a lost restraint. His thin layer of discipline is missing as he advances toward me.

He crouches down in front of me. Grabs my shoulders. Studies my face. Christian speaks, clipped and harsh, but I don't understand the words. Trey's fingers dig in; I twist until he lets go. He touches my cheekbone. The fury has softened but in its place is something that doesn't fit the moment—a look of relief so desperate it goes through my heart. The same look he gave me the morning I woke up alive after taking an arrow through the chest.

Christian stands up beside us. Trey yanks me off the couch by the arm and pulls me toward the hall. I shoot a look over my shoulder at Christian: I've got this. He's my monster to deal with. I handled him alone before Christian came and I'll have to handle him alone after he leaves.

Trey and I face each other in the bedroom. He kicks the door closed. There are too many things to say, and they've created a clog on their way to my mouth.

Get the hell back in bed.

I'm so sorry.

Someone just tried to snipe me.

I love you.

None of those are going to work now but we can't stand here and stare at each other forever. "Trey—"

He surges forward and kisses me. It throws me off balance but he's caught me and I'm against him, pressed too hard against ribs that still need to heal but he doesn't seem to care. I cling to him. Tears scatter down my cheeks but I don't break away. It's all too much, but this is all I need. He's all I need. All the danger and complication is worth it for this moment in time.

He leans back to look at me that same way, like I've been rebuilt from ash, materialized from the dead. He touches my tears. I nudge his hand away. He sees sadness but it's more than that. It's relief. Salvation. Hope. Love. As real as it feels yet all a consequence of one spell that repowers itself every time we're together again. I'm defenseless against something so abysmal, something that speaks to everything inside me.

Real love built from magic? Or just magic? Magic potent enough to fool through and through.

His lips return to mine and dive down my cheek, down my neck, and I know he wants more than I should be willing to give him. We just fought, he's healing, I almost just got shot in the head. We need to talk. Common sense flees in these moments with him and I couldn't be more grateful. We must make the most of every moment. We could so quickly both be dead.

"I will never fight with you, ever again."

He pulls away to look at me. There's a resigned sadness to his face. "Don't say that. It's an impossible vow to keep."

"I don't ever want to fight with you again."

He tugs my shirt up, pulls it off. "Agreed."

Then he's against me again, sliding his hands down my back. He nuzzles my neck, pausing there, breathing in. I tilt my face so he'll kiss me, and he does, gentle, slow, unlike any kiss he's ever given. Like this could be the last time, and he wants to remember it.

A pang hits me and I break away. It's too much a mirror of my own thoughts. If we agree how easily we could die, it makes it too real. I sit on the bed. He goes weakly to his knees, his arms around me, his head in my lap. That heady smell of his skin, his hair, I'm drowning in it. And this tenderness he's never shown during sex—instead of throwing me off, it makes me want him more.

I lie back and wiggle further onto the bed. He moves along with me. Strips off my pants. Kisses a path from my navel to my ear. That's when I grab his head and make him kiss me hard. Just once, because it's familiar. It's the Trey I know. Not the one who's finally admitted he can die.

But he doesn't speed up. He takes his time and so do I. And when we're done, he won't let go of me.

"How's your pain?" I run my fingers down the bruised side of his body.

"Almost non-existent. Even after that. I feel like a million bucks."

"Only a million?"

"Don't take it personally. I'm very hard to please." A shadow of some caged emotion crosses his face too quickly to recognize. "I thought you were dead."

"Why would you—"

"I had a vivid dream. A noise woke me up, and I ran into the kitchen to find you lying in a puddle of blood and shattered glass. Dead from a gunshot wound to the head."

"A dream?" I start to sit up, but he takes hold of my face to hold me in place.

"It was so real. Then I woke up a second time, and I got up to find you. Alive. I couldn't believe it. That's how real it was."

"Trey," I choke, and he kisses me.

I roll to my back, trying to make sense of this, groping for the words to explain. The moment twists like a wrinkle in my consciousness, a surreal dark panic, like *this* is the dream. I really am dead. I'm in Trey's head, alive in memory, a projection of his imagination. I dig my nails into my palms—but the sensation of pain could also be fabricated by Trey's mind. A muffled radio turns off somewhere in the house, bringing my attention to it for the first time.

"Something happened," I say to the ceiling. "Your dream. It almost happened."

He props up on one elbow. "What almost happened?"

"I was in the kitchen. The back door blew out. I crawled into the living room. Christian came home, and then left again. He found someone."

He takes his time with this. His posture remains relaxed but his breathing has changed enough for me to know it's a front. "Who did he find?"

"A sniper." I turn toward him.

He sucks air through his teeth. The breath holds longer than humanly possible. He lets it out, so slowly it's barely noticeable.

"The bullet went through the basement door." I relinquish it all. The burden is too much.

He swings his legs off the bed and yanks on the first shirt he finds.

"Trey, please." I throw myself into my clothes. "Get back in bed. Don't push it. You need another day." I catch his shirt as he passes me. The seam rips and I let go, afraid to strain his injuries.

"Stop for just a second!" I yell, following him into the living room.

He collides with a sweaty, shirtless Christian. "Whoa," Christian barks, appearing to understand the situation immediately. "You need to slow down."

"Where's the body?"

Christian holds up a hand. "I'm not telling you shit until you calm the fuck down."

Trey shoulders past him into the kitchen. "Are you kidding me?" he says under his breath as he catches sight of the boarded-up door panel.

He walks farther into the kitchen, and I stop in the doorway. He swivels to face the basement door.

"Fifty caliber." He turns his fierce eyes on me. "They're shooting fifty-caliber bullets into this house. At you."

I shrug. Maybe it's the wrong reaction but what the hell am I going to say? None of this is my doing. I'm a pawn in this game. I've done nothing to these people but fallen in love with their most hated. He reaches for me. I cringe against his healing ribs but he's as solid as ever.

"We have to leave," he says against my hair. "Mexico, Canada, Australia—we have to leave now. Buy ourselves some time to find somewhere they can't find us."

I remain silent, knowing whatever I say will be useless. He knows as well as I do these people are magic. They'll find us anywhere. Perhaps we can hide but it won't come of hasty decisions. We need to think this through, which will be impossible until he's calmed down.

"I'd like to take a shower," Christian says behind me. "But I can't until I know you're not going to go ape-shit."

Trey releases me but doesn't answer him.

"Let's go in the other room." I pull Trey by the arm. He's gone introspective and yielding, and I take full advantage.

"Oh," Christian says when I push Trey onto the couch. "Some frantic woman left a message on my phone, trying to get in touch with you. Said her name was Tara?"

"When?"

"When I was down there working out."

"Don't move," I say to Trey, standing to get his phone. I read the display. "She called you, too. Five times." I dial her and hand the phone to him.

CHAPTER 19

TREY

I TAKE THE PHONE from Liv. Tara picks up on the first ring.

"Fearghus." Her voice sounds grave. Broken.

"Tara." I can't keep the roughness out of it. I should've waited until I cooled down before calling her back.

"Are you okay?"

I don't answer. I can't make sense of her tone of voice.

"Are you there?" she asks.

"I'm here. What's going on?"

"I need to know what's going on there first."

"Nothing. We're sitting here."

"Who?"

"The three of us."

"Liv?" Again with that broken voice.

"She'd be one of the three. What the hell's wrong with you?"

"Liv is okay?"

"Yes, Liv is okay." An awareness surges over me. It teeters on the edge of total recognition.

"Oh my god," she gushes. "Give me a minute to stop freaking out."

"You saw it too. You saw her death." Tara wasn't here to wake up and find Liv alive. She only saw what I saw in the dream.

"Mamó had a vision. Liv was killed by a bullet in the kitchen."

"Glass everywhere. Puddle of blood. She was shot in the head. But it didn't happen."

"Then how did you see it?" She does sound frantic. Christian wasn't lying.

"I dreamed it. I thought it was real. And then I woke up and she was fine."

Her breath sucks in over the phone. "You saw Mamó's vision in my mind. No—my mind sent Mamó's vision to your mind."

"What?" I rub the center of my forehead. She's giving me a headache.

"Well I don't know who was projecting and who was receiving but somehow, your mind got hold of Mamó's vision when she described it to me. You saw what was in my mind."

I lean forward, resting my arms on my knees and closing my eyes. This is insanity. "Mamó had a vision, described it to you, and somehow, it got inside my head?"

"Yes. While you were sleeping."

I exhale and lean back. "Okay, so what. Who cares? It didn't happen anyway. This is stupid."

"Fearghus, Mamó's visions are never wrong."

"Apparently they are. It missed her. It shattered the glass door then went through the basement door. The sniper missed."

She's silent so long I'm forced to speak again.

"She's fine."

"You're telling me there was a bullet, and there was broken glass, but the bullet missed her?"

"That's what I said."

The sound of a chair being pulled across a wooden floor filters through the phone. I imagine her sitting down at her table, staring ahead, stricken and stiff. "Do you not see what's happening here? It should've killed her. He shouldn't have missed. Mamó's vision was right. But somehow, some-thing else is at work. Something protecting her."

"Are you telling me she should've died?"

"Yes, she should've died. Something has changed the outcome, for our benefit. Something is keeping her alive."

I turn to Liv, losing myself in her eyes. She should be dead. I should've never woken up that second time. I should be living a nightmare, right now. Startled by my expres-sion, Liv takes my hand.

"This is actually happening," Tara says, "and it's more powerful than any of us ever imagined."

I don't answer. I need time to mull this over.

"I have to go. I have to call Máthair and tell her Liv is alive," she says.

"You can't call her. Every incoming call to that house is monitored. You'll be giving yourself up to them."

"It's too late," she says in a voice so bleak it doesn't sound like hers. "I called her already. I had to get Christian's number."

"Why would you do that?!"

"I thought Liv was dead! You wouldn't answer your phone! I had to talk to you before you did something stupid!"

"You gave yourself up." And I'm too far away. Helpless.

"It'll be fine. We spoke in code. They won't know who I am."

"They'll figure it out. And then you are dead." I swallow a sick violence rising inside me. "Do *not* call that house again."

"Someone has to tell her Liv is okay!"

"I will."

"Do it now. I'm not kidding. Right now."

"Okay." I look at Christian. It's a good thing he was probably under two hundred pounds when Tara originally called. This is complicated enough to me.

"I'm calling back in ten minutes to make sure. You better answer your phone."

"Okay." I hang up.

I turn to Liv. Her neck is bare. "You aren't wearing the amulet."

She reaches up, searching for the chain missing from her neck. "I must've forgotten to put it back on."

The amulet didn't save her this time. It was something else entirely.

"It should be on you at all times. You should never take it off."

"I had to. It's on the nightstand," she adds, reminding me why she took it off and placing part of the blame on me.

It's my fault. I should've remembered to fasten it back on her. Our intimacy is as much a danger to us as it is a safeguard. It puts me too much at ease, lowers my guard, dulls my vigilance. Her body can heal me, can keep me alive to protect her, but it also subdues me and opens the barrier to allow the danger inside in the first place.

"What's the number at the house?" I ask Christian.

"Maybe I should call." He's being cautious. Probably a good idea. "Your mom, right? I'll hand over to you once she's on the phone and I know she's alone."

He dials and waits for the other end to answer. "It's Christian. Is Sloane in her room? Yes, thanks."

While he waits, I grapple with the words I can use that will get my news across without giving anything away to someone listening in on the line.

"It's me," he says, nodding to me. "Are you busy? Is it a bad time?" He pauses. "You don't have important company? No gentleman callers?" His voice fills with natural humor. He could always make my mother laugh. "Okay, hold on a sec." He hands me the phone.

"Fearghus?" she asks before I speak. The pain and defeat in her voice strikes me under my defenses. It takes a moment to get a grasp on what I need to say.

"I am having a great day."

"A great day," she repeats, waiting for more. I can almost sense her grip on the phone.

"Yeah. My horoscope told me I should be having a bad day. It's never wrong. But today? Way off."

"I'm so happy to hear that." She sounds far away.

"I think you'll have good dreams tonight." She and Tara meet in their dreams. I need to make sure she knows Tara's in the know as well.

"That's so sweet of you to say. I think you're right."

"I'm sorry I didn't say goodbye," I add, referring to my last visit.

"Don't be silly."

"I've been told I can't listen to a simple request from my mother."

She laughs. "That's no news to me. I wouldn't recognize you otherwise."

Her laughter satisfies me. "I'll talk to you soon."

"*Tá grá agam duit*." She hangs up.

I hand the phone back to Christian.

"Awesome," he says. "I was so sure you'd screw that up."

I give him a weary look.

"What? You aren't exactly known for your way with words."

Liv places her hand on my knee. I'm not sure what she sees on my face that causes her eyes to fill.

"So Tara is your sister." Christian looks proud of his delayed observation. "And you have some kind of psychic connection."

"Yep." I wonder how many of my dreams and nightmares can be attributed to Tara. And vice versa. Our whole lives. I wouldn't wish my shit on anyone much less my own sister.

My phone buzzes in my hand. God, she's impatient.

"Done," I answer.

"Did she understand?" Tara asks.

"Yes. She's probably expecting a more detailed explanation from you tonight."

"I'll take care of it." She pauses. "Fearghus?"

"What?"

"Aren't you excited at all? Don't you get what this means?"

"It's hard for me to get excited about snipers shooting up my house in an attempt to murder the woman I love and my unborn child."

"I understand that. But you're looking at it wrong. She was saved. Things have already begun to change."

"I'll get excited when this is all over." When every person with Moore blood has been executed. I don't care who does it but I'd prefer it to be me. "Call me if Mamó sees anything else."

"I will. But you'll have to answer your phone."

I hang up.

"You *have* to be starving." Liv stands. "Can I heat up your lunch for you?"

I start to stand up with her, but she lays a hand on my chest. She heads into the kitchen.

"What are you going to do?" Christian asks as soon as she's out of earshot.

"Fuck if I know."

"You can't win against snipers. You got lucky this time, for whatever reason. Next time, you might not."

I close my eyes and exhale. He's voicing the thoughts already fighting inside me.

"They think she's been affected with some kind of protection?" he asks.

"They don't know anything. Where's the body?"

"By the river. Let me take a shower, and we can go down there." He goes to the front door and returns with a military sniper rifle.

"His weapon." He tosses it to me.

I catch it, and he heads down the hall to the bathroom.

A fifty caliber semiautomatic military-grade sniper rifle seems like overkill to take down an unarmed woman. Is there any defense for this besides fleeing? Why'd they never use this kind of offense on me? They've wasted so many resources for so many years. Why bring out the big guns now?

One answer. They're backed into a corner. They're desperate. And they aren't messing around anymore. Everything they've done to me up until now must have been for their own amusement.

Gentle hands settle on the gun and attempt to remove it from my grasp. I look up into Liv's carefully guarded eyes and release my grip. She sets it on the hearth and returns to sit on the edge of the couch and hand me a tray of lunch from the coffee table.

We need to pack and go. The Camaro's trunk will fit everything we need for months on the road. I feel a hand on my arm, and I focus on her face.

"Did you hear me?" she asks. "Are you going to eat?"

"Oh, yeah." I take a bite.

River and Trib will ride in the backseat—they'll take some convincing. If they want to stay here that's their call, but I've known River since she was a pup. It won't be the same if she stays.

"Trey, please stop obsessing. I want to talk to you."

"What?"

"I'm trying to talk to you, and you don't even hear me."

"Sorry."

She sighs and takes my empty plate from my lap.

We'll live in hotels until we find something permanent. We'll go wherever the road leads us and—

"Trey! My god, do you want me to just leave you alone so you can stew?"

"No, don't leave." I take her hand.

We can't stay in one place for long. A month, tops. Once I've killed every last Moore, we can settle somewhere, or return to Black River.

"He's in Trey Land," she says.

I look at her then follow her gaze to Christian standing in the doorway, looking like he wants to punch me in the face.

"Earth to Trey Land, do you copy?" He sits to pull on his socks. "Let's go. It's a quick walk."

"You're going to have to come with us," I say to Liv.

She looks from me to Christian. "Where?"

"To check out your friend."

"I suppose there's no way for me to talk you out of it?"

"No," Christian answers for me. "He won't drop it until we do it. Let's just go and get it over with."

"Are you sure you're okay to walk? It's kind of soon, don't you think?" she asks.

"I'm fine."

"One more night in bed and we can go tomorrow?" She bites her bottom lip and gives a hopeful grin.

I stand and pull her off the couch. She sighs in defeat and takes the dishes to the kitchen.

"I also want to go look for the SIG I lost the other night when those guys ambushed us."

Christian points at me. "You're insane. If your ribs snap, I'm not carrying you back again. Just so you know."

Liv returns and lifts my shirt to inspect my side. She walks her fingers up my ribcage. When I don't flinch, she goes back down using more pressure. She looks up at me for a reaction, but I keep my poker face.

"Fine." She throws her hands in the air. "You know best."

We head to the bedroom to bundle up, but I make a detour to the bathroom. It's been a long time since I've been so shocked by the disaster that is my face in the mirror. I'm unable to look away. This is after three days of immortal-grade healing. How am I not dead?

I check my teeth to make sure they're all still there. Now I understand why she was in such disbelief they didn't break my nose. It's bruised to hell, but still straight. Laughing to myself at my own strange luck, I open the door and walk straight into Liv.

"I was just about to knock," she says. "What's so funny?"

"My face."

"You should've seen it before."

"The fight wasn't that brutal," I say as we're layering on the clothes in the bedroom.

She pauses and turns to me. "Are you being sarcastic?"

"It wasn't much action. I'm surprised my injuries are this bad."

"You can't be serious. You're not remembering it all." She takes the amulet from the nightstand and strings it around her neck.

I free her hair from underneath the chain and slide one of my hooded sweatshirts over her head.

"There were ten, right? There was the guy who took out my knee, the guy with the knife…" I trail off when I see the torment in her eyes.

"I will not relive this," she whispers.

"I'll stop." It's her grief of my injury that I can't relive.

Her breath catches. "I thought you were going to die."

I take her against me to save myself from seeing her cry. She releases a shaky breath against my chest, and I hold her a few minutes until I know it's safe. She is not going to be happy about going back there tonight. Maybe we should skip it.

We join Christian in the living room, and we all put on our boots. I holster a gun under my shoulder and Christian does the same.

"What are you carrying?" I ask Liv.

Christian flashes an evil grin. "M16. On the back."

"I have a better idea." I go down the basement stairs for the small rifle she used for target practice in the back yard that day. "Since you were so good with the rifle." I help her into her coat then secure the rifle on her back.

Christian tosses us each a sock hat from the closet and we head outside. River and Trib greet us in the yard.

"We need some help tonight," I say to River, and she dashes away with Trib on her heels.

The sun hangs low behind the trees. We won't have much daylight left. Christian leads us along the bank of the river, whistling some song from our childhood I can't place. The water flows by in a slow babble, filling the otherwise still air. It's so good to be out of that bed. I need to remember not to get my ass beaten so badly the next time.

When the body comes into view, Liv jerks me to a stop and turns toward me. Her lips part like she wants to say something.

"This guy tried to *kill* you," I remind her.

She keeps her eyes on me. I can tell she's trying to avert them from the body. She's probably seen more dead bodies than me and now she's gone queasy about the corpse of the asshole who tried to murder her? I draw her sock hat down over her eyes, turn her forward, and wrap my arm around her shoulders to guide her.

When we get to the body, I turn her to face away from it and lift the hat off her eyes. She gives me a satisfied grin, so I join Christian at the body.

"I thought I blew more of his head off," Christian says.

I roll him over with my foot. His startled eyes stare up at us.

"Sick," Christian mutters. "The things I have to do for you."

"Don't get all sentimental on me now." I squat to check the corpse's pockets. They're still training them well. The only thing I find is extra ammunition. He must have stashed all his belongings in the woods, or left them in a parked car nearby.

I stand and wipe my hands on my pants. "Useless."

Christian walks around the body to the feet and removes the boots. "Nothing here either."

I unzip his jacket and pat him down. He's not even carrying a backup gun. We stand over the body, watching it like it's going to come alive and tell us everything we want to know.

"He looks familiar," Christian says.

"You think you saw him at the house?"

He doesn't answer right away. Maybe because he does recognize him. Not that it matters.

"*Sic semper tyrannis*," he says finally. Like we need to rationalize this. He's always had a weaker stomach than me.

I jab him in the arm, and we walk back to Liv.

"Should we take the body back for your garden?" Christian asks when we get near her.

"Right." I have heard this one so many times. But the shock on Liv's face is just the reaction he was hoping for. It's only going to encourage him.

"Don't you know? He fertilizes his garden with all the dead bodies."

I shake my head. She should know better than to believe anything he says. Her eyes move from his face to mine, relaxing once she sees my expression.

"You are perverted." She loses the harshness of her insult in her laughter.

"And you just thought he had a green thumb." Trying to salvage his story even after it's been blown.

She turns to walk back the way we came, and I catch her hand.

"I want to go back and get my SIG."

Without making the connection, she allows me to pull her in the correct direction. We make it a few paces before she stops. "Wait. Where's your SIG?"

"By the rock."

"You want to go back *there*?"

"It'll just take a minute. I know right where I dropped it."

"Come on!" Christian hollers from ahead.

"It's too far. You should be in bed!" Her eyes flash—a little angry, a little concerned.

"I'm fine. We'll be back at the house in an hour."

She allows me to pull her a few more paces and then she stops again. "All those bodies are going to be there."

"No, they won't. Trust me. Am I going to have to carry you?"

CHAPTER 20

LIV

Headstrong jerk. I'm not sure how I manage to put up with him. He must know when he smiles like that I can't help but go along with the most ridiculous of ideas. It's worked too many times already. The sex with broken ribs set a bad precedent.

Christian has stopped to let us catch up, and as soon as we're in earshot, he says, "I forgot to tell you Shawn McCalister says hi."

I yank my hand from Trey's sudden rude grip.

"To me or to her?" Trey says.

"To you. Jeez, don't kill the messenger. I had the impression he was a friend of yours."

"Is that what he said?"

Christian furrows his brow, sizing up Trey's reaction before moving on to me. He throws his head back and laughs. "Never mind."

I step away from Trey's rigid stance to follow Christian. Trey can stay there all night for all I care.

"Thanks a lot."

"So I guess Shawn McCalister is your boyfriend," he says just as Trey catches up behind us.

"You're not helping." I adjust my scarf. The wind has picked up, chilling my nose, making it run. The pine trees jiggle around us. The sun is lower now and the forest is losing contrast. It was stupid to come out here. They could send twenty more. Fifty. They could snipe us all right now.

"Did he come to the house?" Trey demands.

"Yep, came to the house and took Liv in the basement. I don't know what they were doing down there, but there was a lot of banging around and groan—"

I shove him hard in the back, and he falls to the ground and rolls, cackling madly. I drop to my knees in the pine needles next to him and seize his collar. Trey steps over him and keeps walking.

"You're not helping!"

He regains control of himself. "You're cute when you're angry."

We stand up together, and I brush the needles off his back before we rush to catch up to Trey.

"Where did you see him?" Trey's not going to stop until his quest for information has been satisfied.

"Just tell him so he can drop it." I poke Christian in the arm.

"And validate his behavior? I think psychologists would agree that we should not—"

"Tell him!" I upgrade my poke to a punch.

"God! Fine! He was there when I visited Kristen at work. He's a friend of hers."

"Of *course* he is." Trey hurls a stone into the trees ahead of us. I'm sure he aimed for Shawn's imaginary face. The speed would surely kill.

"What's that supposed to mean?" I ask.

He ignores me.

"I had a few drinks with him. Kristen told him I'm your brother and I'm staying with you, so Shawn told me to say hi. Big fucking deal."

"Damn small towns." Trey picks up a second rock. Maybe I should take it away from him. Christian's mouth could earn him a rock in the face.

"You've got a serious trust issue," Christian says. His tone conveys a joke, but he and I exchange a glance. We both know how true his statement is.

"Says the man who banged my wife," Trey jabs back.

"Can we please get past that? Water under the bridge, bro."

The terrain slopes down, and a gust of wind hits me and stays inside my coat as soon as I remember where we're going. Trey and Christian both seem unaffected. They continue their banter, a warm rhythm of voices and sporadic laughter. The sun has set now, casting a gray tinge all around. I realize I've fallen behind when they stop to wait for me. The land rises under my feet. Almost there.

Trey takes my gloved hand, and I see the rock formation looming in the distance.

"We're going to have some company up here." He says it without looking at me.

"Did you just now figure that out?" Christian says.

I jerk my hand away. "Then I'm staying here. I don't want to see it. You said they'd be gone."

"Not them." He takes my hand again. "Friendly company."

Ahead, and a little to the side, stands a coyote. Head lowered, eyes trained on us. As we pass he slinks behind us, circling to the other side.

We reach the base of the rock. Trey clicks his tongue and River's head appears at the top, right where I planted myself on that horrible night. I look at the ground under my feet, the spot where I thought Trey would die. Dried blood, all around. His blood. So much it looks like someone bled out.

"I want to go."

"Five minutes." He sprints up the side of the rock and into the trees. Needles rustle under his boots as he kicks through them in search of his gun. Christian follows him, and I turn around, facing out, taking in the view Trey had when those last three men attacked him. Shadowed figures lurk in the trees. We're surrounded by a whole pack of coyotes. The haunting presence of this site takes a new shape with a dozen sets of eyes watching my every breath.

Trib trots over, touches his nose to my leg. I notice more bloodstained ground. Streaks, splatters. Maybe it's not all his, but somehow that's worse. This is where Trey's back was on the ground. Where they were on top of him, beating the life out of his already broken body. The painted ground is evidence of their hate. Their power. That they'll stop at nothing to end us.

"Found it," he says, retracting the slide on the gun next to his triumphant grin. "Let's go home."

"Dude, there's blood everywhere. How much of this is yours? Did you see that huge stain up there?" Christian jerks his head toward the woods.

"I think that's where I blasted the stomach out of one of them." Just another day's work to Trey. He shrugs on another coat over the one he's already wearing. It's the one he wore that awful night.

"Awesome. I can't believe I missed it all."

Trey turns to follow Christian back the way we came, and I grab his arm. He looks at me. His smile falls. I remove my glove and touch the dark line of blood running from his nose.

He pulls off his own glove and wipes his nose, examining the smear left on the back of his hand.

"Just a nosebleed. No big deal." He wipes his hand on his pants and replaces his glove.

I catch the worry on Christian's face a split second before he covers it with a smirk. "Now you're in trouble," he says to Trey. He falls in line with my stride and leans down so his face is inches from mine. "Will you take your anger out on me again?"

I elbow him away, and Trey tacks on more force with his own shove, sending Christian further ahead of us.

"You're staying in bed for the rest of the night," I say to Trey.

He hangs his heavy arm around my shoulders. We catch up to Christian. "So I guess we're back at it tomorrow," he says to Trey.

"Yep. We've got to make up for lost time."

I hold my tongue. I'm not going to bother. If he thinks he can go straight back to building walls and carrying drywall in his condition, it's his business.

"Aw, crap." Trey stops to spit.

The trickle of blood has turned into a deluge from both nostrils. He spits again and removes his glove, using it to wipe his nose. The blood returns in full force, running over his lips and down his chin in a syrupy mess.

"Maybe we need a break." Christian makes no attempt to hide his stunned concern this time.

"No, keep going. This is only going to get worse until we get home." Trey spits again.

Christian and I share a tormented stare, then he turns around to lead the way home.

As we near the house, River and Trib dash ahead. The last fifty yards feels like an expedition. Inside the house, Trey goes straight to the kitchen, and Christian and I take off our coats and boots in a dismayed silence. I lean the rifle against the wall and follow Christian to the kitchen, where Trey is washing the blood off his face at the sink.

"Can I take your coat?"

He takes both coats off and hands them to me. His shirt is soaked with a wide half circle of blood. Noticing the stain, he removes his gun, pulls off his shirt, and hands it to me. I throw everything into the washing machine.

When I return, Christian's halfway through a beer, and Trey's leaning over the sink. The bleeding is still in full force.

"Maybe you should sit." I drag a chair away from the table. "Pinch the bridge of your nose."

He holds a kitchen towel against his face and goes past me, toward the living room. Christian and I share another helpless glance. We go into the living room together, but Trey isn't there. I find him in the bathroom vomiting in the toilet.

"I'm really paying for it now." He moves to the sink to rinse his mouth.

Anger and concern rage a violent battle inside me. When he's finished at the sink, I settle him on the couch with two pillows under his head to place him at a slight incline. I show him how to pinch the bridge of his nose. In the kitchen, Christian has emptied Trey's herb cabinet of all its jars, setting some aside and returning some to the cabinet. I shake off the grip those jars have on me.

Returning to Trey's side, I stick a few folded towels under his cheek to absorb the blood and sit on the edge of the couch next to him.

He closes his eyes. "I hate it when you're right."

"Me, too."

Christian joins us and hands Trey a small glass.

"Cayenne?" Trey asks and drinks it in one gulp.

Christian takes the empty glass. "I'm working on something else. Where's your goldenseal?"

"Downstairs."

"Do you have a humidifier?" I ask.

Trey closes his eyes, gives a slight shake of his head.

"What about ice? Ice sometimes helps."

"We could try that."

I go into the kitchen for some ice.

"He's got both of us working for him now." Christian levels off a spoonful of some powder and adds it to a glass.

"It makes me wonder how he survived this whole time without round-the-clock medical care."

"Was it ever this bad?"

"No, probably not. Their fight against him was casual up until now. I think it was more of a game than anything. They got serious, fast." He tramples down the stairs.

I follow him halfway down. "Where are all these men coming from? Who would volunteer for such a thing?"

"You'd be surprised. It's like any war. People volunteer their lives for the chance of glory." Jars clang together on Trey's basement shelves. I take a few steps down to help him, but he reappears with what he must have been looking for. "But it's a little different. Imagine what a powerful family like mine can offer to a war hero. And it's not all men. There have been some women."

"No way." I decide against using ice and go for the frozen peas.

"Yes way. Ask him."

I wrap the frozen peas in a towel and take them to the other room. The bleeding has decreased to a trickle.

"What else can I do?" I untie and ease off his boots. "Do you want a shirt?"

His answer is a reach for my hand. I sit next to him and bring his hand to my lips, holding onto it. All those other complications feel insignificant right now. I haven't known him long enough to love him like this.

Christian returns with another glass and a straw. Trey snuffs the liquid up both nostrils then settles back under the frozen peas. I dab his face clean so it will be easier to tell when the bleeding has stopped.

"God, why don't you have a TV?" Christian growls into his hands. He goes into the kitchen and returns with a deck of cards. "Time for some Gin Rummy." He drags the armchair to the coffee table and deals two hands.

We play three rounds before we realize Trey is sound asleep. The bleeding has stopped, so I remove the frozen peas. "He didn't eat dinner."

Christian gives me a pouty face. "Neither did we."

I throw together some pasta and vegetables and Christian and I eat in the kitchen.

"Darn it, I guess this means you and I have to share the bed." He tries his hardest to keep a straight face but fails.

"Is there anyone you won't flirt with?"

"Yes, there are a lot of people I won't flirt with."

"Who?"

"Men."

"You know what I mean. Are there any women you won't flirt with?"

"Yes, there are a lot of women I won't flirt with."

"Who?" I try not to laugh.

"Women under the age of eighteen." He loses it and laughs into his glass before he takes a drink.

"There's no maximum age?"

He pretends to think a moment to play it up. "No."

This is his public persona. He may be a flirt, but he's not a womanizer. He has too big of a heart. He uses this persona as a running joke, to lighten the load of loneliness. His life must have been as lonely as Trey's—they have more in common than I thought. For fifteen years he was under the control of the same woman who stole Trey's happiness. She has ruined two lives, with no apparent remorse whatsoever.

I clean our dishes. When I turn around Christian's still at the table, running his finger around the lip of his glass, lost in thought. It's a rare glimpse of him—slouched shoulders, hooded eyes. Palpable sadness. It hurts so much to see, it stings in my eyes. He's Trey's brother, and I love him like family. The feeling is unmistakable but I don't know how I'm capable of its recognition. I've never had family.

"Are you going to cry *again*?" he asks, and I realize he's looking at me with a rebuilt smile and an intact facade.

He goes for the refrigerator, and just when I'm about to complain he changes his mind, opens the freezer, and removes the vanilla ice cream. I take two spoons out of the drawer and we sit down at the table.

"Is there any way you can keep him from working tomorrow?" I ask.

"Do you have any handcuffs? Wait, don't answer that."

I roll my eyes.

"Don't worry. I think even *he* knows vomiting blood is a good reason to take it easy. It's going to take him a long time to get used to being mortal. He's just like everyone else now."

"I beg to differ."

"Oh god, here we go."

"Haven't you ever met anyone you couldn't live without?"

He winks. "You."

"Be serious."

"That word is not in my vocabulary." He leans back, stretching his legs out under the table. "Actually, there was one. We were together for three years. Until Kate put an end to it in her own special way."

I look up at him. I should've known.

"I know, I can't believe it either. I was monogamous for three whole years. Shocking."

"What was her name?"

He swallows hard and looks past me out the remaining pane of glass in the door. "Bethany." A long moment passes before he turns his hardened face to mine. "Your blue eyes can't even begin to compare to hers. Sorry." He crams the lid on the ice cream carton, shoves it in the freezer, and leaves the room.

Trey is right. Kate needs to die.

I get up and put our spoons in the sink. If his violence isn't rubbing off on me, then those bits that migrated over during the mind share have ignited in my head. I'm doomed to these thoughts from inside and out. The old me wasn't capable of wishing another human being dead. But have I known anyone else who's deserved it? Kate is the only purely evil person I've known. So far, at least. We'll see how her youngest son turns out. He may need to join her in hell.

What? Okay, this must be when I start to lose it. All this stress must finally be catching up to me. I need to put it away, focus on what's important: staying safe, helping Trey get well. I need a long bath, or a massage, or a slap in the face. I need to get out of this house—not for a walk in a forest full of snipers and dried puddles of blood. To see some real people. To experience normal, everyday life.

I shake out my limbs, take some deep breaths. Do a mountain pose, a forward bend, and a down dog. Then I wander into the living room to find Trey still asleep and Christian in a chair, lost in thought. Again.

I want to ask him if he wants to talk, but it doesn't seem appropriate. "Gin Rummy?" I ask instead.

He gives the thumbs up.

"Will you help me move him to the bed first?"

Christian groans. "Just wake his ass up and make him walk. You're spoiling him. Yo! Bevan!"

I shush him and lean toward Trey's ear. "Trey? Can we move you to the bed?"

He grunts. Tries to get up but falls back. Christian and I each take an arm and heave him to his feet. We put him in bed and I pull the covers over him.

"Come." The word stumbles out of half-asleep lips. His fingers grope across the mattress in search of me.

"Later. You need to rest." I kiss his cheek. He smells like the air outside, damp earth mixed with evergreen. Tempted to crawl into bed with him, I remember Christian and close myself out of the bedroom.

Christian is waiting on the couch in front of two dealt hands.

"Is it cold in here to you?" I ask.

He throws a blanket from his stack of bedding at me, and I wrap it around my shoulders and sit next to him.

After a few games, he clears his throat. "Think of something to talk about." There's a strange roughness to his voice that's new to me.

"Hmm…" I'm caught off guard and out of ideas. It seems like we're always talking about Trey. I need something safe. The weather? The news? Something that would interest him, take his mind off things. "Your car. What is it?"

"Infiniti G37."

"Is it fast?"

"Pretty fast. Not as fast as my other cars."

"It's a nice car." A pointless comment to fill in a conversation that's getting more awkward by the second. "How long have you had it?"

"A few years. It's probably time for a new daily driver."

"Would you get another one like it?"

He shrugs, lingering in that position. "Don't know. Haven't thought about it. I like the Nissan GT-R. It would give Trey's Camaro a run for its money." He beats me again and deals us each another hand. "But with a car like that, you get sick of all the attention."

"Sounds expensive."

He shrugs again. "Not really. A hundred grand."

"You don't like attention?"

"Not from men," he mutters.

"You're pulling a Trey," I blurt. It's out before I can stop it.

"What?" He looks up, surprised.

A blunt change of subject—I recognize I just pulled a Trey myself.

"Silently seething. Dwelling. I don't know." I wave my hand to dismiss my words. I don't know why I'm prying.

"Yeah, we all have our demons."

I hold his eye a moment then return my attention to our game. We play through the round in silence. He deals again.

He takes a deep breath and lets it out in a quick gust. "Kate found out I was going to marry Bethany. She didn't like it. It was none of her business. But she likes to play people against each other."

My skin flushes hot. I put my cards in my lap and shrug out of the blanket. I don't want to know what my blood pressure is. I need to get a grip on this stress or I won't need the Moores to do me in. A heart attack would fulfill their plan nicely.

He lays his cards down. "I hope she doesn't find a way in between the two of you. It seems impossible, I know. But she has her ways." He scrubs a hand through his hair. "And the worst part about it? Bethany never knew the truth. To this day, she believes Kate's game."

"You should call her. It's never too late."

He scoffs. "I stalked her for a while. She's married now. Why bother?"

"Closure."

"I don't need closure."

"You have nothing to lose." I wish I could do something. It isn't fair.

"She'd never believe me. She's a normal person, in the normal world, like you. She doesn't know anything about my family."

"You could try. I believed when Trey told me."

"Okay, let me rephrase that. *She* is a normal person, *unlike* you. You've got issues." He laughs, returning to the Christian I know for a brief moment.

"Why does Kate—" I stop because there's no answer to what I want to ask.

"Because she's evil. And power hungry. No other reason."

I gather my hair off my shoulders, twisting it around itself on the back of my head. The heat must have kicked on. I'm burning up. "But she isn't even a member of your family."

"I know, isn't that great? She married Trey to get in. And now, she's become one of us. Them. Whatever." He rubs both temples, visibly frustrated. He has the most difficult position in all of this. "Just don't ever let your guard down." He squeezes my knee hard—too hard. "That's why I'm telling you all this. Because when she strikes, you won't know until it's over. And you've lost everything."

CHAPTER 21

TREY

S HE'S TRYING NOT to make the floorboards creak but I already knew she was coming. It isn't easy to be sneaky in this little house. It was the silence that woke me, their missing voices. Now I hear her sock feet creeping around the bed and I turn down the cover on her side for her.

"I didn't mean to wake you up," she whispers.

When she's in bed I draw her tight against me. She feels so good, a prize I still don't deserve. I've cheated at something to get her. I'm just not sure what. "I'm glad you did. Take off your clothes."

She does, and I wrestle free of mine. Then she's fused to me, and I'm wondering again why I deserve her.

She's quiet on the drive to the clinic in the morning. All this time she's been spending with Christian and he's probably told her all kinds of shit she doesn't need to know.

She blows on her hands. "Is the heater warmed up yet? I'm freezing."

"Wait 'til it's twenty below." I turn on the heat, but it blows cold. "What'd you two do last night?"

"Played about a hundred games of Gin Rummy. And talked."

"Too bad I missed it."

She looks at me for a drawn-out moment before turning away. She must be working up the nerve to ask me something. Worried it's going to ruin my mood, I reach for the radio.

"Trey?"

Aw, crap. Here we go.

"Will you tell me what happened with Bethany?"

Relief seeps in. This sore memory holds no bearing on me. "That what you two talked about?"

"It was mentioned. Not in much detail. It didn't take a lot for me to realize how much it bothers him, though."

"You're his therapist now?"

She doesn't answer.

"They were together for years. He was going to ask her to marry him. Had this whole thing planned. Someone at the house didn't approve, and before Christian had his chance Bethany got shoved down the stairs. She had a miscarriage."

She gasps and covers her mouth. "Christian's baby?"

"Yeah, but it's even worse than that. They affected Bethany's mind so she thought Christian did it. She wouldn't listen to a thing he said. The effect was too good. He wasn't even able to visit her in the hospital. So she left him. Got a restraining order, the whole deal. My mother was going to help him cleanse her but they never got the opportunity."

With one hand still covering her mouth, she stares out the window until we stop in front of the clinic.

"Why didn't he…isn't there something he could've done? Kidnap her and cleanse her against her will?"

I shake my head. "It broke him. He just stopped caring."

"You couldn't do anything?"

"I wasn't living there. It was after I'd left, after I thought they'd killed Kate. He came to live with me in Arizona for a few months. All we did was drink and watch ESPN. It was pathetic."

"You never knew who did it?"

"Nope."

She turns away. I can't see what she's looking at but whatever it is should be glad she's not armed right now. There's a depth to that glare I've never seen in her. She unbuckles her seat belt. "I need to go in."

Confused by her reaction, I catch her hand. I feel like I'm missing something. Her eyes belong to someone else when they look up at me.

"What did I say?" How can she be mad at me?

"Nothing. Not you." She squeezes my hand.

"Then what?" She can't get out of the truck and leave me hanging like this.

"You don't want to know." She says this with such disgust I almost believe her.

"Liv—"

"It was Kate. He told me last night that Kate did some-thing to Bethany. He didn't tell me what, but you just did."

I drop her hand. How did I not put this together once I knew Kate was alive? It could only be Kate. It's just like her. Christian didn't tell me—he couldn't tell me. That effect had him gagged against all mention of Kate. I thought she was dead.

"I have to go in," she repeats, bringing me back to the present. "Please don't be mad at him for not telling you."

I thought this memory had no bearing on my revenge. I was dead wrong.

"I won't," I say, distracted by this new knowledge working itself around in my mind.

She opens her door. Pausing, she turns back to me. "I can't believe he carries this around with him. I would've never guessed."

"He's had a lot of practice. He's had so much abuse his whole life he's good at handling it."

She slides out of the truck and closes the door. I watch her walk into the clinic before I turn around and pull onto the road. As soon as I get home, I find Christian in the kitchen with a mug of coffee.

"Bethany," I say. "Was it Kate?"

He laughs without the slightest hint of humor in his voice. "Do you have to ask?"

"I thought it was your dad this whole time."

"He's capable, but no. Kate did it. She told me she was inspired by her favorite movie. *Gone with the Wind.*"

"I've never seen it." I don't need any inspiration for what I plan to do to her.

"Me neither." He refills his mug and steps over to the boarded up door panel.

"You know, I think your life sucks worse than mine."

He stills for a moment, his eyes lose focus. Then he chuckles into his mug. "So I assume we're going to replace this door today?"

"Yeah, it will be easy. Then it's over to Liv's to work on the basement."

After a few phone calls to locate a new sliding glass door, we slip into our coats and head to the truck.

"Why'd you tell her?" I ask as we're moving down the road.

"Liv needs to know what your darling wife is capable of, so when she comes after the two of you, Liv will be prepared."

"She can't touch us." I sense his skepticism without a glance in his direction. "If you'd just let me kill her, you'd have nothing to worry about."

He exhales and rips off his sock hat. "You can't kill my son's mother. I don't care if she's the embodiment of the devil himself."

"I think you have something there."

A few minutes pass, and I add, "He's better off without her."

He rubs his forehead. "I'll let you try to explain that to him after you slit her throat."

"How'd you know I wanted to slit her throat?"

After enduring several comments about the condition of my face to Christian's unashamed amusement, I help the sales guy load the door into the back of my truck and we head home.

The panel is easy to replace, and as we're finishing up, Christian's phone rings and he moves into the other room to take the call. I clean up the mess and transfer all the tools back to the garage.

"We're on for tonight," he says when I come back in the front door. "Double date."

"I hope you're joking."

"Kristen has the night off. It's perfect timing."

I look away, shaking my head. I don't know why he's always trying to make me into a socialite like him.

"Okay then. I guess Shawn McCalister will have to go in your place."

I snatch him by the collar. He shoves me backward, and I release him.

"Dude, you have a *serious* problem. You can't even take a fucking joke."

"It wasn't funny." I put on my coat and throw his coat to him.

"You were never this jealous when you were with Kate."

"Apparently, I should've been." I suppress the urge to hit him. He's the walking example of why I should've been.

"You know, you're lucky there are two people in this world capable of putting up with your bullshit. Otherwise you'd be a bored, lonely old bastard."

"Yeah, you and Liv are saints." He knows I'm mocking him. She may be a saint, but he's definitely not.

"Hey, have you noticed she's kind of…fidgety lately?"

"Fidgety?" If there's one thing Liv isn't, it's fidgety.

"Never mind."

We go into town for a quick lunch, and while we're there we make a beer run. It's been too long since I've had a drink. We pick up the Camaro from the shop and park it at my house then head to Liv's.

The smell of sawdust greets us inside Liv's front door, and Christian curses under his breath at the long afternoon ahead of us. He puts the beer in her fridge and we head downstairs. Our earlier talk of Bethany has put a damper on his mouth, and without all the unnecessary conversation, we get an impressive amount of work done. When it's time to pick Liv up from work, I leave him and drive to the clinic.

She comes out as soon as I pull up to the door. She takes her seat and looks at me, scrunching her nose. "You smell like a…man. What'd you do today?"

"We're still at it. Just wrapping up for the day at your house."

"Is he still depressed?"

I'll let her be the judge of that. Too caught up in our work, I honestly haven't noticed.

"I gave all of my hours for the rest of the week to Abby."

A savage thrill rises inside me at the idea of having her to myself all week. Good surprises are not a common theme in my life.

When we descend into the basement at her house, she gasps behind me. "The two of you did all of this?"

"Drinking without me?" I punch Christian in the arm as he takes a swig out of his beer. It spills down the front of his shirt, sprinkles the floor.

He shakes beer off his hand. "I'm not going to sit around and wait for you. You take way too fucking long."

Liv heads back up the stairs. "I'll see what we have upstairs for dinner."

"No," Christian calls after her. "We're going out."

Ignoring him, I pick up the drill and return to where I left off.

"Fun!"

Great. Now she's into it. Looks like I'm stuck going.

Thirty minutes later, we wrap it up. The fifty-caliber bullet hole in the door appears in my mind, and I glance at the stairs to find Liv missing from her spot.

Christian catches my eye and yells, "Hey, Liv! Call Shawn McCalister and tell him seven o'clock!"

I shove Christian against the wall, pinning his shoulders with one arm, the other arm free to punch him in the gut but I hold back. His knee jerks toward my ribs. I block and he pushes away from the wall and throws me into our new framing. Grabbing his shirt, I decide it's his turn to be thrown into the framing. He recovers and goes for my throat, so I duck and charge his waist but he knees me in the chin.

"You little shit!" I laugh and wipe the blood from my lip. "And I didn't say I wasn't going."

"Oh yeah?" He gasps for breath. "You should've said something sooner."

Both suddenly aware of a third presence, we turn simultaneously to Liv, standing at the foot of the stairs looking very irritated. "Are you finished?"

"Yes." Christian turns on the innocent face. "We're finished."

"You're going to build it and then knock it down?" she says.

I kick the framing with my foot. "We had to test it out."

"Held up well," Christian says, rubbing his chin.

"I don't know how I got stuck with two of the biggest idiots ever born." She stomps back upstairs.

"Now I've got to go in public with a bloody lip on top of everything else," I say to him.

He tilts his head back and cackles. When his head comes back down I fling my elbow into his mouth.

"Son of a—" He throws another punch but misses as I duck away.

"I had to even it out." I head up the stairs.

He sprints up behind me and I slam the door in his face just as he makes it to the top. His face is calm when he comes through the door, so I go to the sink and wash my hands. The freezer door opens, and I hear him take some ice. The freezer door slams, and he punches me in the neck.

"Stop it!" Liv yells, shoving him into a kitchen chair.

He snickers and holds the ice to his lip.

"You both have bloody lips? Am I the only adult here?" She looks from me to him.

"Wuss," I say to Christian, referring to his need for ice.

"I'm not into the whole brute image like you are. I try to look civilized when I go into public."

Liv throws her hands in the air. "I am in hell." She turns to leave the kitchen, and I follow her.

I find her in the smaller bedroom making up the bed with clean sheets. I reach for her, but she slips away from me.

"You're filthy. Do not come near me." She throws a quilt on the bed and leaves the room, flipping off the light with me still inside.

We file out the door. Christian and I throw our coats in the bed and we all get in the truck with Liv in the middle.

"Oh my god, gross. You are both so sweaty," she says. "Do not touch me."

Christian opens his arms for a hug and she gasps, unable to move away from him because she'd be forced to lean against me. Her struggle throws the truck out of gear, and when I jam it back in, the transmission grinds.

"Oh there you go. Breaking my truck again."

The unrestrained fury in her look throws me into painful, rib-cracking laughter, and the tires kick up gravel as we almost run off the road.

"There's got to be a story there." Christian laughs along with me at Liv's expense.

"I'll get you back. I'll tell Kristen about all your bad habits."

"I have none, so no worries." He clicks the corner of his mouth while giving the thumbs up.

River and Trib greet us on the driveway with two wagging tails, so I park the truck and we go into the house. Christian heads straight to the shower, Liv to the bedroom.

I go to the kitchen and take the bottle of scotch and a glass out of the cabinet. I stare at the empty glass. The pause itself is what throws me. Why the pause? This is what I do after a day of hard work. I open the bottle. Pour. Throw the whole drink back and swallow. Christian enters on his way to the laundry room with a shirt and pants to iron, so I take a shower then go into the bedroom.

"Up or down?" she asks, but I no longer know how to speak.

She's dressed in a pale pink dress over slim black pants and knee-high boots with heels. My amulet hangs against bare skin above the low neckline, and she's holding her hair up, waiting for an answer to a question I've already forgotten.

She drops her hair so it falls in gentle waves against her shoulders. "Down?"

"Yes." Yes to everything. Yes to the entire world.

"I thought so too. What are you going to wear? Do you have anything nice?"

It must be the color. I never see her in pink. Do I?

"Trey?"

I take a breath, go to the closet and open the door. This woman must carry some magic of her own. I can't think straight when I'm around her.

"Jeans are okay, but you have to wear a nice shirt. Do you have anything with a collar?" She browses through my clothes expecting me to help her, but all my attention is on her. I can't look away.

"Here." She pulls something out and holds it against me.

"I'm not wearing that," I say without looking at it.

"Please? For me? I'll iron it for you and everything."

"The iron is occupied."

"When he's done." She tosses the shirt on the bed.

I put on my nicest jeans, find a pair of socks, and sit on the bed. After fastening her white shell bracelet on her wrist, she leaves the room with my shirt, and I can breathe again. I need to take inventory of my herbs in the basement and dust my family's texts for prints. She must be experimenting in magic to have me so struck by a little dress and some heels.

CHAPTER 22

LIV

"HOLY CRAP, YOU clean up nice. Pink tunic and leggings? I love it," Christian says, pulling on a pair of stylish jeans. His crisp black button-up shirt hangs open, and a pair of Dolce&Gabbana alligator shoes await him on the floor. His hair has transformed from a just-out-of-the-shower mess to finger-combed perfection.

In the hall I walk straight into Trey's arms. He backs up until we're in the bedroom, picking me up in a long, deep kiss.

"You're taller." He takes his ironed shirt from me and puts it on over his undershirt without breaking my gaze.

The bright white of the shirt sets off his dark hair and turns the color of his eyes up to the max. If he didn't look like he's just gotten home from a violent bar fight, he'd pass for a hot date. But then, without the scars, he wouldn't be Trey.

"It's going to have to stay unbuttoned. It won't button with my gun underneath."

I follow him down the hall. Christian is standing in the living room with a gun he seems to be having trouble concealing on his body.

"Not going to happen." He drops the gun on the coffee table. "I tried."

"Untuck your shirt and put it on your belt." Trey might as well be talking to a child.

"And cover up *this* belt? You can suck my—" Christian's eyes flick to me.

Trey secures his gun under his arm. He turns to me. "What about you?"

"I'll be with you."

"Put your Ruger on your hip."

The emphasis in his voice curbs my argument. After the ambush in the woods, I do see his point, and I've certainly learned to pick my battles with him. Some things just aren't worth fighting over.

Unfortunately, the waistband of my leggings aren't right for holding a gun, and it leaves a bulge under my tunic. I look up to see Christian giving me a scolding shake of his head.

"In your purse," Christian says. He jerks his head toward the door.

I follow him and stash the gun in my purse. Not as accessible, but they'll never attack us in town. Trey's being paranoid. I suppose it's hard to blame him. He'd have left that fight in much better shape if he hadn't lost his SIG in the woods.

"I'll pick up Kristen and meet you there." Christian shrugs into a wool jacket and flips the collar up. "It's that pub on Fourth. The Scottish one."

"Matheson's," Trey and I say together.

"Sick," Christian says, slamming the door behind him.

"Do you have a blazer?" I ask Trey.

"You should be happy with what you got."

"Will one of Christian's jackets fit you?"

He crosses his arms and looks at me as if I should know the answer to that. I go to the coat closet and sift through all the rugged coats until I find a stylish black military-inspired jacket with front pockets and a heavy zipper that looks like it has never been worn.

"Is this yours?"

He exhales and shifts his weight.

It looks to be his size. I hand it to him, and to my surprise, he puts it on.

"Did he put you up to this?"

"Christian?" I ask.

"He bought me this for when we'd go out. I should've trashed it."

I brush him off. It's a little dusty from sitting but it looks great on him. "He has good taste."

He helps me into my coat. "He's a pain in my ass."

The cold air goes straight through my leggings outside. The heater doesn't have long to warm up before we're there.

Trey parks the Camaro on the street behind Christian's Infiniti and we go through the heavy wooden door adorned with a crest of two facing bears. They rear up with teeth and claws bared, one with a paw raised high, the other aiming for the guts. Between them is a small gold cross.

Inside under a Scottish flag, we find Christian with the tall, blonde, and classically beautiful Kristen on his arm. Her turquoise silk mini dress and black strappy heels would make her overdressed if she wasn't Christian's date. Christian finally has some competition for most fashionable. He introduces us out of politeness because as small-town life dictates, we all already know each other.

With the introductions over, Kristen looks back and forth between Christian and Trey. "Did the two of you get in a fight?"

"Yes," Trey answers quickly. He sets his gaze on Christian as if ready to shut him down.

"He started it." Christian jabs a thumb in Trey's direction. The swelling in Christian's lip has subsided, but the bloody split is impossible to miss.

"Why does he look so much worse than you?" Kristen asks Christian, grimacing at Trey's bruised face.

Christian chuckles. "You sound surprised."

"That was from something else," Trey says. He doesn't seem to want Christian to take credit.

I chime in before Trey has to struggle with his inability to lie about the specifics of that something else. "These two are magnets for trouble. Should we get a table?"

"He's a cage fighter," Christian stage-whispers to Kristen as we follow the hostess to our table.

The bar is packed elbow to elbow. On one end, a mob of guys spills into the dining area, easily the source of most of the noise in the room. Several of Black River's older residents have seats at the bar where they nurse tall glasses of dark beer. The hostess takes us to the secluded side to a booth spacious enough for six people, and we remove our coats and hang them on the hooks on the high wooden walls separating us from the adjacent booths.

"That's such a pretty necklace," Kristen coos across the table at me. "It looks like an antique. Is it a family heirloom?"

I instinctively reach for the cool metal hanging against my chest. "Yes." I keep my answer simple. Her curiosity sparks my own. I never did ask Trey where he got it.

Trey reaches for his water after it lands in front of him, and her attention drifts to his hands.

"And your rings. Are those antiques too?"

Trey takes a drink of water then looks down at the matching rings he wears on each hand. Those I know were handed down from his father and I don't think there's much secret about them. As far as I know they hold no magic. Our table's candle dances, throwing a glint onto the age-worn silver of the rings. The moment draws out to the point of discomfort. I feel myself holding my breath. He clears his throat. "Yes. Family heirlooms."

The waitress takes our drink order. A beer would be nice but not for our unborn daughter. I stick with water. Kristen orders red wine. Christian takes his time looking at the beer menu then orders something on tap. Trey orders a scotch and asks her to keep them coming. I try to catch his expression to gauge if he's drinking socially or feeding an addiction. He's really tapered off the drinking. I hope he doesn't return to business as usual because I have enough things to worry about. I'll take snipers or a ten-man ambush over alcoholism any day.

"So, Liv, how do you like it here?" Kristen asks.

"I love it." I'm more in love with the residents than the town itself. One particular resident, that is.

"Did you move into the new Joseph cabin or the old one? I always get them confused."

"I didn't know there were two," I say, surprised.

"You didn't?" She appears just as surprised as me.

"I live in the old one," Trey says. "Liv has the new one."

"You do?" I turn to him, searching his face. Why didn't he tell me? It's yet another coincidence that seems to matter in some way. I picked a house that was owned by the same family that owned his.

"I thought you already knew," he says in answer to my expression. "Didn't you wonder why the floor plans are so similar?"

"I didn't notice they were." But now I do. They're practically the same house except mine has a cathedral ceiling in the main room and an extra bedroom on the side.

"Mr. Joseph knew how to build a house, he just wasn't very creative." Trey scans the room, obviously impatient for his drink.

"Who the hell is Mr. Joseph?" Christian asks as our drinks arrive.

Trey takes a long drink. When the glass returns to the table his hand remains on it, his clasp more protective than casual.

When Trey doesn't answer, Kristen says, "He was an old recluse. But for some reason, everyone seemed to know him. Kind of like you, Trey, only you're not old." She cocks her head at him.

A loud, collective whoop goes up across the room. My eyes stay glued to her face. Was that a flirt? Trey looks up at her at the mention of his name, and she smiles. I can't tell if it's flirtatious or friendly. What if she *is* using Christian to get to Trey?

"Oh, he's older than you think," Christian says and aims a devious grin at Trey.

I need to get a hold of myself. I don't want to be this jealous, possessive, suspicious person. And no woman in her right mind would take a look at these two and pick Scowling Bar Fight Guy over Mr. Blond and Gorgeous.

I poke Trey in the arm. "Can I get out? I need to go to the ladies' room."

"I'll join you," Kristen says to my chagrin.

Trey and Christian stand to let us out. Another thunderclap of unified laughter has both of them looking toward the gang at the bar.

"Where do you shop for clothes?" she asks when we're washing our hands and checking ourselves in the mirror.

"I actually haven't been clothes shopping since I moved here."

"Oh." She frowns. "Your outfit's so cute, I thought maybe you knew of a store I didn't. There aren't many options around here."

"You seem to be doing fine. I'd never think you'd find a dress like that in a small town."

She smooths her dress. "I made this one."

"You *made* that?"

"Yeah. I thought I'd never wear it. It's hard to find an excuse to dress up around here."

"If you hang around Christian you'll have an excuse every day."

"I know! He's—" She stops preening to turn and face me. She's biting her bottom lip, wistful and sad and looking far too much in love with a guy who has no intention of staying here.

Shit. Why'd I have to mention him in the ladies room, where the shields between women are their weakest? "He's not staying, Kristen. I wish he would but—"

"I know, I know. Damn him. I wish I could just tell him to bug off." She reapplies her lip gloss and I'm a bit relieved. She's definitely got her eye on Mr. Blond and Gorgeous.

When we return to the table, we both take the outside spot and Trey and Christian slide toward the wall. From the smirk on Trey's face, it's apparent they were sharing a joke in our absence. His glass is full again.

The waitress returns for our order and as we take turns, Trey drains his glass. The waitress takes it with her, and I know she'll be heading back with another. He must be trying to make up for the last few days he was in bed without easy access to the liquor cabinet. I catch his eye. His glare proves he's reading my mind. I prepare to punch him in the arm. He flashes the most charming of smiles, detonating my worry and frustration on impact. I punch him anyway. He looks away, scratching his eyebrow, his smile turning smug. He saves those up like some secret weapon, ready to unleash when its surprise force will be most devastating.

Across the table, Kristen appears to be captivated by an animated story Christian is telling. He leans closer to her, lowering his voice, prompting her to draw near. Trey's not the only one with his game on. They do make a cute couple. It's such a shame Christian has to go home—he really appears to like her. He'll probably never get over Bethany, but companionship from someone new could sure dull that memory.

I elbow Trey and he chuckles under his breath. He bends toward my ear. "Bet you he gets laid tonight."

"God, I hope so. I'm ready for a break from all the attention."

He nods at the waitress for his replenished drink. His third. I need to stop counting.

Kristen bursts out laughing and shoves Christian away, shaking her head. As she reaches for her glass, she sucks in a quick breath. "Shawn's here! And Brady and…I can never remember his name." She raises an arm high. Waves. "Shawn!"

My stomach drops out of my body. I know it's my Shawn without having to look. I don't know if it's my bad luck or Trey's but every time we leave the house together we run into the one guy on Trey's enemy list he can't kill.

"Babe!" Shawn hollers from across the room. Yep, it's my Shawn all right. No sooner do I realize this than he's in front of us, flanked by two other guys.

I hope I'm the only one who notices the radioactive mass of aggression now sitting next to me. He hasn't moved a muscle, but maybe that's the problem. A predator is the stillest just before it attacks.

Christian chuckles. "This is going to be good." He turns outward on the bench, resting his arm along the back to take in the full view. Okay, hopefully he and I are the only ones who notice.

Shawn kisses Kristen's hand then turns to me. "*And* Liv? Wow, must be my lucky day."

Before I can respond, he's sliding into the seat next to me and Trey's fluid arm is wrapping around my shoulders in a possessive clasp. Against his body, I feel taut muscle poised for action. Another one of the guys slides into the seat next to Kristen. He must be Brady, because he's taking a drink out of Kristen's wine and she's not stopping him. The remaining guy stands at the head of the table.

Christian's fists settle on the table. Instantly up in arms, his amusement has left, now replaced by a shocked offense—he's been thrown into the same position he hoped to see Trey in.

"Two fancy cars outside. Should've known we had an easterner in town." The nameless man says in Christian's direction. His words are nothing more than a good-natured ribbing. It's what these guys do to each other. I witnessed plenty of it on my night out with Shawn.

Christian casually picks up his beer, takes a swig. Sets the beer down. Returns his arm to the back of the bench. "Thought I'd do some community service and bring a little class to a hick town. Your women tell me they're unfulfilled."

My toes curl in my boots. I want to scream. Doesn't he know when to keep his mouth shut?

Brady and the nameless guy share a look. A did-you-hear-what-I-just-heard look. Shawn throws his head back in a hearty laugh then offers his fist across the table to Christian. "He's an easterner, but he's cool. He's just giving you shit, guys."

The two other guys don't look convinced. Christian bumps Shawn's fist but remains focused on Brady. A measuring look. No smile, no hint of friendliness. Brady takes another long drink out of Kristen's glass, drops it on the table, turns his gaze on Christian like this is some silent battle of wills.

Shawn laughs at something the nameless man is saying, and Brady asks Kristen why she didn't call him. It's an obvious joke, but Christian doesn't look ready to take it that way.

Squinting at Trey, he mouths, "What the fuck?"

I can imagine their position. Ambushed and surrounded with their backs against the wall, this friendly encounter viewed as a bold invasion in their eyes. Affronted, their only instinct is to fight. And suddenly I feel like the gold cross between the snarling bears on the crest on the door.

Trey leans toward Christian. "For old time's sake?" There's a twisted, bloodthirsty element to his voice that chills my blood.

I place my hand on Trey's thigh and clench hard. It's a useless effort against his strength, but it's all I can do without bringing attention to what they're planning.

"So did everything work out?" Shawn asks in my ear, too close for friends. He smells like beer.

I'm surprised by the calmness of my voice. "Of course."

"Someday you'll have to tell me." He knows he's dancing on the line between spilling my secret and guarding it like a gentleman. His eyes dart to the amulet around my neck and linger there, analyzing it briefly before returning to my face.

"Of course," I repeat, with enough play in my voice so he's not tipped off to the tension of the storm on the other side of me.

"Does everyone know everyone?" Kristen seems oblivious to what's about to happen. "Shawn, I know you know Christian. Do you know Trey?"

Trey throws the rest of his drink down his throat, slams the empty glass on the table, and nods to Christian. I grasp a handful of Trey's shirt with my free hand. Another useless effort. If he stands up he's just going to take me with him like a barnacle hanging off some giant sea beast.

"Okay, everybody clear out," a voice calls from behind the wall of men to my right. "You guys need to go back to your seats and leave these poor people alone." Shawn and Brady hop out of the booth and the three of them back up to make way for two large trays of food.

"We'll catch you guys later." Shawn retreats toward the bar.

"Without a doubt," Trey calls after him. Another look at Christian.

Our table for six seems like a table for two as the waitress situates all the plates. It's a feast, and that's a good thing. If we take our time, maybe Shawn and his friends will find somewhere else to go and Trey and Christian will be too satiated to fight. After placing the last plate, the waitress takes Trey's empty glass and leaves us to our food.

"Don't eat too much," Christian says to Trey. "It will slow you down."

"Good point. But maybe I should. I don't want to make you look too bad."

Kristen catches my eye to see if I'm in on their joke, and I shrug and roll my eyes, as if they do this all the time.

"So Christian tells me you and Trey knew each other before you moved here," she says to me.

I glance at Christian. He should've told me if he made up a story. I don't want to contradict him.

"High school sweethearts," Christian says. "Isn't that so sweet you just want to barf?"

Trey snickers into his plate but otherwise remains silent. He must be used to going along with Christian.

"How'd you find him? Online?" Kristen seems to be in search of a romantic story. Our story might be considered romantic if the first half could be edited out.

"Through a mutual friend." It's partially the truth. The mutual friend just didn't know Trey lived here. It was more like fate, which I suppose is pretty damn romantic. If we hadn't been so abusive to one another in the beginning it would make a much better story.

"And he took you back?" Her voice becomes playful, careful not to pry but curious enough.

"Grudgingly," Trey answers into his plate. Another drink appears in front of him.

That's an understatement. Should I tell her we wanted to kill each other? It would be fun to tease him, but not tonight. I don't want anything else raising his blood pressure. I doubt he would find it funny anyway.

"Untrue," Christian says. "You two were right back at it. Didn't waste any time. In fact—"

Trey's head snaps up, throwing a warning with his eyes, and Christian jerks his head in the quick upward nod of a challenge.

I'm going to lose my mind. Do these two ever stop? Can't we have a simple conversation without every statement being pushed to the line?

Christian shifts in his seat to retrieve his phone from his pocket. He glances at the display and then answers. "Aaron? Hold on a sec." He takes a drink. "Sorry, I have to take this."

Kristen stands to let him out of the booth. I wonder if she knows he has a son. She and I make small talk until Christian returns. As she stands to let him back in, I notice an unmistakable change in him. He catches Trey's eye; an unspoken conversation passes between them.

"Is everything okay?" Kristen must sense the change as well.

Christian drains his glass. "Everything's fine." He pauses to look directly at me. "Aaron just wanted to tell me he has a new baby brother."

"Oh, how exciting!" she says.

My stomach goes tight. The threat of Trey starting a bar brawl and now this. There's no hope of keeping my dinner. I grope for Trey's leg under the table and find his hand. He squeezes so tight I'm sure my fingers will break. With his free hand, he finishes his entire full drink and slams it down on the table much too hard. All our dishes jump.

"Sorry," he grumbles, but Kristen barely notices.

"What's his name?" she asks.

"Rex," Christian says, still looking at me.

"Rex what?"

"I didn't ask."

"You didn't ask?" She chuckles under her breath.

The waitress walks by and takes Trey's empty glass. When she returns with a new one, he immediately reaches for it. I catch his arm.

"That's your fifth," I whisper.

"Who's counting?"

"I am. Please, Trey."

He exhales, frustrated and not able to hide it but he withdraws his hand. To cover the tension, Christian has Kristen engaged in another lively conversation. I nudge my plate away.

"You have to eat." Trey's voice is strangely gentle considering the circumstances.

"I know." I eye the food my stomach will surely revolt against. The plan is in motion, moving forward whether we're ready or not.

"I'm drinking that whole glass if you don't eat right now."

"A threat?"

"No, an agreement."

Sighing, I pick up my fork and bite, chew, and swallow repeatedly until most of the food is gone. Christian and Kristen are so engrossed in their own world together that I feel like they're not at our table anymore. He certainly has a knack for distraction. For turning blind when a gun's aimed in your face.

"Trey?"

He absentmindedly reaches for his glass, pauses, withdraws his hand.

"Please don't do anything stupid when we leave. I need you on my side tonight."

"I'm always on your side."

I don't answer. I wait for him to look at me.

When his eyes touch mine, I say, "I don't want to be mad at you tonight. Please don't do anything stupid."

He cants his head. "I'll be a lot easier to live with tonight if you indulge me."

"You have a punching bag in the basement."

"Not the same."

I bite my tongue. I want to tell him it's not the same as my friend's face, but I hold back knowing that simple word will only make him worse. He's not even fully healed. Does he not consider these things?

The waitress breezes by with the dessert menu and removes some of our dishes. Kristen picks something for her and Christian to share, and Trey picks something for us to share. When the desserts arrive, Trey picks up a spoon and crams a huge spoonful of brownie with ice cream into my mouth before I'm ready, sparking a spontaneous giggle from me that comes from nowhere. Trey watches as I try to manage chewing the giant mouthful, smiling the widest smile I've seen in days. Another one of his secret weapons I'm truly grateful for. We are going to get through this. Together.

When I can't take one more bite, I push the dish away. Trey finishes every last morsel. He then reaches for his still untouched drink, but I'm faster, and I take it from him and set it on my end of the table.

"Reflex." He sounds genuinely ashamed he almost broke our agreement.

I skim the room for any sign of Shawn and his buddies. The restaurant has cleared out, and I don't hear any boisterous conversation or laughter. It's been a while since I've heard a crowd outburst. Maybe they left.

I turn my attention back to Trey, who's squinting at Christian and looking a bit disgusted. Christian appears to have become very affectionate toward Kristen. Christian leans toward her laying on the works: bedroom eyes, sideways smile, soft words too quiet to hear over the ambient pub noise. When he reaches to stroke her cheek, Trey makes a choking sound.

"I think it's time for us to go." He tosses a couple one hundred dollar bills in the middle of the table and slides against me, popping me out of the booth.

Trance now broken, Christian and Kristen stand with us and we put on our coats. Christian drops a couple bills on the table as well, two more hundreds I know without looking. The waitress comes by with the check, and Trey hands her all four bills and tells her to keep the change. Her eyes widen. She gets a cocky two-finger wave from Christian. She wishes us a good night. Trey doesn't hear her; he's too busy scanning the room like some serial killer who needs to be institutionalized.

We stop just inside the door, and Kristen gives me a warm hug. "We definitely need to do this again. Or maybe we could go shopping sometime?"

"That would be fun." When she releases me, Trey drapes his arm around my shoulders. He probably doesn't want her to feel the need to hug him.

"We should go back to my house and watch a movie," she says to Christian. Her eyes carry the hint of a hidden agenda.

He takes her hand, playing it cool. But I know him well enough to notice the slight change in posture, the almost insignificant upturn of one eyebrow—signs of Christian Moore's extreme approval. I see it settle a tension, apply an ease to him that wasn't there before. When she looks down to smooth her skirt, his cool falters for a fraction of a second, just long enough to see a mixture of emotion so specific I'd recognize it anywhere. I witnessed it so often in the foster care system when I was older and more perceptive of these things. Kids desperate for acceptance from anyone. All they craved was someone to belong to.

Maybe I'd never have noticed it before, since he's so good at hiding these things with a smile and a witty remark. Or maybe it hasn't come up. I've seen enough sides of him to tell where each piece fits. Traumatic events bond people, whether you want them to or not.

CHAPTER 23

TREY

CHRISTIAN PUTS KRISTEN in his car and I put Liv in mine. As both doors slam, our eyes meet, and we come together on the sidewalk in between the cars. Christian blows on his hands. The steam from his breath rises in the air. I should have given Liv my coat for her legs.

"Is she freaking out?" he asks.

"She's okay."

"Are you freaking out?" His meaning is different for me.

"I'm cool."

"You're going to take it easy tonight?"

"Of course." I slap him on the back. "Be sure to wear a rubber."

"Shut the fuck up." He cackles, walking around the back of his car. "You would know!"

I start the engine and peel out around him. He whips behind me and rides my ass.

"Show-off," I say to the rearview mirror.

"You or him?" Liv says. "I know I should be used to this by now."

"It turns you on. Admit it."

"Is that why you do it? Spare me." She scoffs, reaching for my hand. Women and their mixed signals.

As soon as we hit the main road, I stomp the gas and leave him in my dust. I don't want to make him look bad in front of his girlfriend, but I just can't help myself.

"Which house?" I ask, aware that we have two now.

"Yours. I don't have the other house together yet." She takes a breath, turns to face me. "Why didn't you tell me both our houses were owned by the same family?"

"Thought you already knew."

"I didn't. Is there any significance to that?"

"Not that I know."

"So, they owned yours, and then they built mine?"

"Think so. The old man, he lived in mine and built yours in his spare time. Moved to yours when it was finished. Mine sat vacant for a while. Until I bought it."

"After you moved from Arizona? Why haven't you told me more about Arizona?"

"Didn't think it was important." My voice takes on an irritated tone, and I'm not sure why.

She catches it too. "Sorry for the interrogation. I just have some stored up questions—"

"That's okay." It'd be nice to keep my calm. I don't want her mad at me. I wouldn't mind getting laid myself tonight. "I went there when I first left the estate. Didn't stay long. It was too warm and sunny all the time."

She chuckles. "Usually, warm and sunny is a good thing."

"Overrated. I prefer it here." In a cabin in the mountains, there's less trouble to be found. Fewer jail cells to be locked in overnight to sober up. No sleazebags offering me money to fight. The money I could say no to. Saying no to the fights wasn't so easy.

"I don't think I could live in a warm climate. I'd miss the seasons."

I wonder if she's referring to my suggestion that we move to Mexico. I don't care if we move to Alaska. We need some kind of plan before they send twenty guys at once. Another sniper. An A-bomb. And I can't settle business with them and leave her somewhere they can find her. I don't know what the hell we're waiting for but I'm sure not bringing it up tonight. I've had too much to drink. I need her too badly. Then I need to get some sleep. Tomorrow, the three of us are going to sit down and figure this shit out and no one's leaving the house until we do.

She's silent until we get home. When she sheds her coat, her appearance stuns me again. I'm not used to seeing her dressed up. I follow her into the kitchen where she notices the new door for the first time.

"How did I not notice before? It's like it was never broken." Her words hang in the air, seeming to mean something much greater than what she intended.

She turns around to face me. "Rex."

I stand motionless, unable to come up with a response. It's another subject best avoided tonight.

"It's hard to believe a newborn baby can hold so much power over us."

"He holds no power." I flex my fingers to prevent my fists from tensing.

"That's not what I mean. I mean, how can a defenseless newborn baby hold any menace?"

"He won't be a newborn baby for long."

"How long do you think we have?" Her eyes cloud. Fear, sadness, I don't know what.

I take her against me. She comes up higher on my chest than what I expect because of the heels on her boots. "There's no deadline. There's no end if we win. And we will win."

She hugs me back with a burst of strength. "Of course we will."

"Are you trying to crack my ribs?"

"Yes. To keep you in bed, as my slave."

"I'll be your slave anytime." I already am her slave. A slave to her wishes, every day of my life.

"Do we really have the house to ourselves tonight?" Her voice sounds innocent but I know her thoughts are not.

"Yep."

She fingers the zipper on my pants. "What do you want to do?"

I shrug, feigning nonchalance. "Up to you."

She moves the bottom of my shirt aside. She unbuckles my belt and tugs, sliding it off my pants in slow motion. It practically undoes me.

"Let's change," she whispers. I watch her mouth, the flick of tongue. God.

She pulls me by the hand into the bedroom, and I watch her undress while I take my time removing my shirt and my gun. When only her underwear remain, she takes a tank top and flannel pants with her into the bathroom. I sit on the bed in my jeans. Still wound up from that fight I missed in the pub, I close my eyes and slow my breathing, slowing my heartbeat by consequence. She wanders into the hall in her tank top and flannel pants, brushing her teeth, so I get up and join her.

"Isn't it kind of early for bed?" I ask.

"Who said anything about bed? I have a sugar slick on my teeth from all the brownie and ice cream you made me eat."

"You can't blame that on me."

She spits and rinses her mouth. "Are you kidding me, Mister Cram-an-unexpected-monster-sized-portion-in-someone-else's-mouth?"

I nudge her aside and cup my hand for a drink from the faucet. She swats at me, but I catch her wrist before she makes contact. She kicks the back of my knee, buckling my leg, so I stand and spit a mouthful of water at her.

She gasps, frozen in place, her mouth open wide.

"Now you're going to have to take it off." I wipe my face on the towel and get a good look at her chest through wet fabric. An unplanned consequence I can really get behind.

"You are…primitive."

"Primitive?" I roll up the towel and prepare to snap her with it.

"Don't you dare." Her voice lowers with real intimidation, but all it does is make her more desirable. And me even hotter with need. I could pin her against the wall and kiss her, but I shouldn't—it'd be too predictable. From the look in her eyes I can tell she expects it.

I hang the towel on the rack, and she glides past me and closes the bedroom door. To not appear too desperate, I go into the living room, fall onto the couch, and prop my feet up. Maybe it would be good for her to have to pursue me for once.

Rex. Rex Moore. It sounds so arrogant. My Latin is rusty, but I know it means "king." They think they've already won. The comfort of their arrogance will be their weakness. Their downfall.

The bedroom door opens, and she comes from the hallway in a different top—a stretchy bra thing with skinny straps and a lacy front—and my flannel robe. Pants hanging loose on her waist, belly exposed.

"Comfortable?" she asks.

She lifts her leg over mine and sits down on my lap, straddling me on her knees. It takes all my self-control not to make a move.

"What's the history behind this?" She holds the amulet off her chest.

What I need is her beneath me. The moment draws out before my mind snaps into gear. I take the amulet from her, use it as an excuse to graze her bare skin with my hand. "Don't know. I've had it since I was a baby." I let it go against her chest, trace around it. Grasp her ribcage, slide my hands down to her hips. She shifts her weight. It doesn't appear to be a ploy to turn me on but damn, it does.

"Christian knows about it?"

"I used to lend it to him when we were kids. He knows its power firsthand."

"He'd wear it for protection?"

"Yeah. We used to have this asshole cousin who'd visit—" Recognition forms. Holy shit.

I release her hips and start to sit up, but she presses my shoulders against the couch.

"Don't get up. Tell me."

"Asshole cousin," I repeat. "Jared. Dillon's brother." Don't know how I didn't make that connection before now.

Her expression shifts into neutral. "Dillon does have an older brother named Jared. He used to visit us at home in Chicago."

I stare into her eyes. She's married to the brother of one of my worst enemies in that family. He's been to her house. How can she be so calm?

She leans in and kisses my bottom lip once, twice, three times. She knows exactly how to play me. How to turn it off.

When she pulls away, I keep my eyes closed. She needs to know and somehow, I have to explain it without being able to follow it up with jabbing a knife into his throat. Both brothers' throats. "I should've killed him. But he never went after me. It was always Christian. Never figured out why. When I started lending Christian my amulet, Jared couldn't touch him, so he gave up."

She runs a finger over my lips. I open my eyes. "You and that asshole's brother—" I don't know how it got out. It's not a good time.

"I don't think I love him anymore, remember? You removed it."

I'm caught by her strange use of words. Not *I don't love him anymore*. But, *I don't* think *I love him*—

"And there's this thing—I mean, I've been meaning to…" Her eyes glaze with this sudden trapped look. "Both times I've fallen in love were brought on by spells. One was removed. Do you think—" She places a hand on her chest like she might cry.

A stiff cold blows through me. Shame. I've said something wrong. I reverse the conversation, replay it in my head. She must not trust my work in removing Dillon's effect and I can't blame her for that. Spells to cover corpses and weapons I'm good at. Removing love? Shit, I should've taken her to my sister. "He's too far away to affect you. You can't worry about…"

She's biting her lip, shaking her head fast, and I know I've misunderstood something but it's too much to think about when Top Ten Ways To Kill Dillon Moore is playing like a movie montage in my head. I need to get him and Jared together somehow, do them both at the same time, make them watch each other die.

And now she's rubbing my hair with this sad smile, and I've surely lost track of the conversation. I've had too much to drink. She's sober. We're on different wavelengths. We need to do something other than talk but we've been steered too far away.

She sighs. Leans back, her weight on my knees. I give her a grin. She appears to be afraid to ask me something, but she does anyway. "Why didn't you use the amulet against your uncle?"

"It's cheating. Weak."

She inhales a sharp breath. "A child against an adult man will always be weak."

"Not always."

She shakes her head, lowering her eyes.

"I wanted to be strong myself. With no help."

Her eyes return to my face. "Jared would bully Christian?"

"Bully. Not quite the word. But yes." Can't think about her married to that asshole's brother. It's going to—can't think about it. Liv in bed with that asshole's brother. In the shower, like she said. I rub my face, hard, both hands. My pulse hits my ears. I breathe. I'll get my day. Not now.

"Poor Christian."

"I've saved his ass more times than I can count."

"You're a good brother."

"There are too many of them. Too many I don't remember, too many I don't know about. I killed some of the worst ones but there are so many…"

She remains silent, studying my face.

"We need to leave. Pick somewhere to go, somewhere you'll be happy where we can easily blend in. I'll make sure they never find us." So much for waiting until tomorrow. My mind fires rapid thoughts. Forming a plan. We can't name her Bevan. We'll all need new names. Once we're settled somewhere safe, somewhere they can't find us, I'll return to that fucking house and take my time killing every last one of them.

We sit in silence until she cuddles against me, burying her face against my neck. I don't know why I had to bring this up. I should've known any mention of the past would kill our evening. Just as I begin to settle into the couch, she sits up.

"Want to make out?"

"Okay." I wait for her to make the first move.

And she does. It's a kiss, just lips, nothing else. Her hands on my face. I take hold of her hips again, tighten her against me. I could die from the ecstasy of the unwind, the flood of calm, the loosening of muscle and limb. It flattens me under a steamroller and honestly, if she left it at this I'd be too stoned to complain.

Never would I have guessed how good it could feel to be conquered.

Jerking awake, I sit up and scan the room. Someone's here. I glance at the clock. Just past midnight. It could be Christian coming home, but something in the back of my mind says it's not. I'd have heard the car.

Liv turns over to face me. I clamp my hand over her mouth. She sucks in a quick breath. I hold a finger to my lips.

Everything's still. Whatever it was seems to be fading, or at least not closing in. Am I losing it? Have I become paranoid? I remove my hand from her mouth. She stays quiet, watches me for clues. The wind blows outside, creaking the roof, the window in its frame. Using the sound as cover, I reach over Liv for the gun on the nightstand and hop out of bed onto my bare feet.

River should've warned me but she could be off on her own somewhere too far to know someone's here. It's rare, but it's happened. I go into the hall, aware that I'm leaving Liv alone but for some reason I'm not worried, and not just because Liv can protect herself. Real threats tug at my subconscious like an invasion on the horizon. The more I ignore it, the closer it swarms, the deeper it tugs. The presence now is like a tick of a far off clock. Persistent, stable, unchanging. Only as annoying as I let it be and of course that's going to be a lot. It can't be a threat but it's something—if it was Christian it would make sense. I check the couch and the driveway, and neither he nor his car are here.

"I'm losing it," I whisper to Liv as I get under the covers with her.

"Mmm. You lost it a long time ago."

I wrap my arm around her and fall into deep sleep.

My body jerks awake. I sit up again and scan the room. What the fuck? The clock reads a quarter past two. Liv's hand slides up my arm.

"It's just bad dreams," she mumbles, half-asleep.

I creep back out to the hall and check the living room, the kitchen, the driveway, and the basement. Nothing out of the ordinary, Christian still not home. Is there any reason to be worried about him? I check my phone. No calls. I go back to bed.

The alarm clock screams so I reach over Liv and slam the snooze. She groans and rolls into me.

"I'm off work," she says. "I just realized that."

I pull her against me and just as I'm almost back in a doze it hits me like a sucker punch from a heavyweight. Throwing off the covers, I get out of bed and go into the kitchen for my phone.

"Was that you?" I say as soon as Tara answers.

"Could you hear me?" Her voice is broken. I barely recognize it.

"What's wrong?"

"I wanted to tell you in person."

"In person?"

"As in person as I could manage." Her voice is thick, like she's been crying. "I can't believe I finally found you. After so many years of trying." Her breath catches. She *is* crying.

"Are you going to tell me what's wrong?"

"She's gone. Mamó is gone."

Gone. It could only mean one thing. Our grandmother is dead?

"When?"

"Last night. I didn't want to tell you over the phone. I didn't want…I tried—" Her voice catches again. She takes a shaky breath.

Why am I so far away? She has no one with her right now.

"Does Máthair know?"

It takes a moment before she can gather her voice. "Yes."

I'm silent while I gather mine.

"She never got to see her one last time." She sighs, defeated. It's a dull blade through my chest.

"I'll be there as soon as I can catch a flight."

"No, Fearghus. There's no rush. Everything's fine."

"Is someone there with you?"

"Just Winnie and Will right now. They're still asleep."

"Then I'm coming. We're coming."

"No. Don't. Some people are already on their way."

"Who?"

"Bevans. I'm fine. Don't lose your head." She's starting to reclaim her demanding air. It's a step in the right direction. I'd feel a lot better if she told me off.

I exhale, looking around the kitchen. What can I do?

Liv appears in the doorway with wild hair, wrapped in a blanket. As soon as her eyes catch mine, worry creases her forehead.

"We can drive. We can leave right now and be there tomorrow morning," I say into the phone.

"Fearghus! I swear. *Please.* You have days. Just relax. Everything's fine." She pauses, then she says away from the phone, "Good morning, sleepyhead." Her voice lifts, and a part of me lifts along with her. "I have to go, the little ones are up. I'll call you later. Don't make any plans or do anything until I call you. Got it?"

"Got it."

She hangs up. I stare at the phone. There's nothing I can do. Liv takes the phone out of my hand, sets it on the table, and wraps her arms around me.

"Mamó," I say against the top of her head.

She hugs me tighter. It's all I need to say. She knows.

"It was Tara last night," I say, and she pushes away from me to look up at me. "Tara contacted me."

"She *did*?"

"What a bunch of freaks." I tighten her against me again. Christian is right.

I need to call Máthair to hear her voice, to know she's okay. Two calls so close together would be sure to tip them off, if they aren't already. I can't risk it.

"Are you okay?"

I don't think about the question. "Yes."

"You're stewing, I can tell."

"I'll be better once we're there."

"Driving?"

"We'll take the Camaro."

"What about Christian?"

"He's going to have to come with us. I doubt he'd want to stay here alone."

She releases me and wraps the blanket around herself again. "Do you think that will be okay? He's a Moore."

"Only in blood."

"Yes, but will Tara and the rest of your family understand that?"

She has a point. But it doesn't matter what they understand. He'll be with us. I dare any one of them to complain.

"He's one of us."

She starts the coffee. "Okay…" She doesn't sound convinced.

"He's my mother's son, just as much as I am."

"Will your mother be there?"

"Probably not. If they follow her, she'll lure them to all of us."

The front door opens and closes, and I can tell it's Christian by the sound of the shoes.

"Don't shoot. It's me," he calls.

"Just in time," I say. "We were just talking about you."

"I'm not surprised." He comes in and tosses me an orange. "Nice hair," he says to Liv. "What's under the blanket?"

"You're coming with us to Chicago."

"Thank *god*." He falls into a chair. "Get me out of this town."

Liv leaves the room.

"What's the occasion?" he asks. "Finally getting bored here?"

"Funeral."

He laughs. "I hope you're kidding."

"Nope. My grandmother."

That shuts him up. He straightens in his chair and spins to face me. I peel the orange.

Liv returns in my flannel robe with her hair in a ponytail. She pours three mugs of coffee and sets them on the table.

"So, you expect me to associate with a group of Bevans?"

I don't answer him. I give half the orange to Liv and sit down.

He takes a sip of coffee. "That's going to be interesting."

I look at him. "So?"

"So what?"

"You spent the night."

"Yeah?" He's playing stupid.

"And?"

"And it's personal." He can't even keep a straight face.

Liv scoffs. "My sex life is everyone's business, but yours is personal? Please."

"Details aside, I think the two of you sold me. So thanks for that." He raises both hands for a high five from each of us. We both ignore him.

"Had I known that's what it was about, I wouldn't have been on such good behavior."

"Asshole," he says, dropping both hands. "You get sex like twice a day, and you can't even help me out once."

"Your suffering is my specialty. I need you to call my mom."

He looks over at me.

"Two calls from me in such a short time period is going to tip them off. I need to know she's okay."

"She was her mother? Oh. Well, of course." He peers down into his coffee like it's just gone sour. The same pain I feel washes across his face. "Did you know her?"

"Liv and I met her once. She lives with my sister. Lived."

"What time is it there?" He turns around to look at the clock. He must be worried about her too. He digs his phone out of his pocket and dials. "Hi, it's Christian. Put me through to Sloane. Okay, thanks." He drums his fingers on the table. "Madam. It's your secret admirer. Are you alone? Is your husband around?" He pauses, his eyes flash to me. He wants to know if my stepfather knows. "Can I put you on speaker?" He sets the phone on the table.

"Christian, we miss you," she says.

"I've been sold into slavery. They won't let me leave. They have me doing hard manual labor."

"I'm not surprised." Her voice is guarded.

"So…how is everything? Are you doing okay?" There's a deeper meaning to the question I know she'll pick up on.

Her end is silent for a moment. "Yes."

Christian looks at me, raising his hand to ask if there's anything else I want him to say.

She speaks again. "Martin's taking me on a little trip. We're leaving today."

I start to speak, but Christian waves his hand to shut me up.

"Where?" Christian asks.

"Vancouver."

"Are you sure that's safe? You know those Canadians…"

"Don't be silly."

"Are you flying straight there?"

"No, we connect in the Midwest to spend the night. You know I can't handle all that flying in one day."

"She's coming," I say, to no one in particular.

"What?" she responds over the phone.

Christian waves his hand and glares at me. He directs his attention back to the phone. "I might take a trip myself. I'm getting sick of my current location."

Liv walks behind me and puts both her hands over my mouth. I drag her into my lap.

"Where are you going?" my mother asks.

"Somewhere with a beach."

She laughs. There's more to it than just a laugh. She understands. "Have you heard from Fearghus?"

"I talked to him the other day. He told me to tell you he loves you, that he's sorry he's such a bad son, and that he wishes he could be more like me."

"He's not a bad son. Tell him I love him with all my heart."

"*All* your heart? Then you have nothing left for me."

"I have a second heart just for you."

"Which one is bigger?"

"Yours. Don't tell him."

"So then Martin gets your liver?"

The laugh that comes through the phone is her real, unguarded laugh.

"I'm hanging up," my mother says.

"Goodbye." Christian hangs up.

"She'll beat us to Tara's."

"Martin will be with her. She'll be fine. *You* might not be able to take down a group of ten amateurs, but your dad surely can."

I get up and smack him on the back of the head.

"And so can your girlfriend." He ducks, expecting another blow.

"We're never going to get that basement done."

CHAPTER 24

LIV

As soon as I hear Trey turn the shower on, I refill my mug and sit next to Christian. "Why's he obsessed with finishing the basement at the other house?"

He stands to refill his own mug. "Because he has to have *something* to obsess over. I don't know. Don't you want it finished?"

"No, it's not that. It's just…he's determined that we need to move."

"Well that's why he wants to finish it. Duh." He returns to his chair and looks at me like I'm being stupid.

"No. Move away from Black River. Move to another country."

He raises his eyebrows then immediately furrows his brow.

"Yeah, see what I mean? So why spend time on the basement?"

Christian's laugh fills the room. "This is what he does. He knows the best thing for you would be to move far, far away, forget about all of this and live happily ever after. But it isn't in him. It's completely against his nature. He doesn't run. From anything."

I feel my eyes widen with an understanding I should have found myself.

"He's having a battle of wills, against himself." He stretches his legs out under the table. "One of them will win. Usually it's the meaner one. And why don't you ask him this stuff? You *can* talk, you know. You don't have to spend all your time together making googly eyes and going at it."

"So you're saying if I'd asked him this same question, I would've gotten the answer you gave me?"

He laughs, knowing my question is rhetorical.

"He's not even aware he's doing it," I continue.

"Talking to him about it would sure bring it to his attention."

"He doesn't need it brought to his attention. He has enough on his mind."

"You're too easy on him."

"Yeah, I guess I should just shove him against the wall and punch him in the mouth."

"Promise not to do it without me."

I stand to start on breakfast. To my surprise Christian gets up to help me.

"Don't look so shocked," he says, surveying the contents of the refrigerator. "I'm not completely useless all the time."

"Just some of the time?"

"You're catching on." He takes hold of my arm. "You can't change him. You know that, right?"

I look at him, unsure what he's referring to exactly.

"All of it." He must be reading my mind.

"I know. But I can make him happy."

"You've already done that." He looks down at my arm. "Hey, you're shaking again."

I jerk away. He's onto me. If he wants answers he's going to have to come up with some on his own. I have no idea what's wrong with me. My reaction must have spoken volumes, because he doesn't say a thing.

I do the cooking. He sets the table. We start eating without Trey and finish without him too, so I cover his food while we clean up. Christian heads to the shower. I wander into the bedroom and find Trey sitting on the bed in his boxers with his head bowed and his forearms resting on his knees. I settle next to him, and he looks at me.

"I'm so sorry," I say.

He hugs me against him with one arm, kissing my temple.

I wait for him to say something. We sit, him staring at the wall, me staring at him, until he goes for his jeans and yanks a T-shirt off a hanger. I'm half-dressed when I feel him behind me.

"What would I do without you?" His hands settle on my belly, pull me backward to the bed where he sits and turns me around. Still holding my hips, he looks up at me. "I was lost without you. So lost."

I don't know what to say. He sighs, relaxing his hold on me. I've never seen him look so worn. So tired.

I tuck my leg underneath me and sit next to him. "What are you thinking?"

"I have a bad feeling. Máthair shouldn't come. There's too much risk."

"You can't worry about things you can't control."

"I can't tell her to stay home for her mother's funeral."

"Everything will be fine." It sounds false in the air.

"I can't face them. Knowing we're going to leave. Destroy all they've worked so hard to set into motion."

I don't want to fight with him again. Not now. "We don't have to leave."

"Yes we *do*." His eyes flash, a strobe of temper through the melancholy.

"Remember what you said to me when Mamó told us we'd brought my Sloane back?" He doesn't answer. "You said, 'Forget all of that. It doesn't matter. Just think about this, right now.'"

"I said that?" He sounds surprised.

"Yes! And I'm saying it to you now. Stop thinking. Forget all of it, it doesn't matter."

He rubs the back of his head as if trying to accept this idea that was once his.

"Nothing matters but us. The two of us, soon to be three. Until we have a reason right in front of us, we don't need to worry."

"There is a reason in front of us."

"Where? You've created it yourself, and I don't see it."

"You don't see it?" He's getting agitated, but not at me. At the situation. I'm not sure I can blame him.

He shakes his head, his eyes closed. Disgusted. It's far too easy to absorb, to allow it to anger me, especially with that rich vein of temper he passed to me running straight through my active emotion. Anger won't help anything. It will only set us back when we need to gain some ground.

"All I see is you and me. A road trip to a place where you can meet all the relatives you've never met, and you can see your sister, your niece and nephew. Your mother." He straightens, meets my gaze. "And then we'll come back and protect our home and wait to be joined by our baby girl."

"How can you see it that way?"

"Because that's the way it is."

He watches me for a moment. As a smile spreads across his face I feel the earth shift, the vein of anger blown to rubble. All I have is one streak running through my head. He's buried in it. It's a wonder he can ever smile at all.

He rubs my arms. "You have goose bumps."

He stands and stretches—arms, shoulders, and back. "Let's get some work done at your house before Tara calls."

I stare at his back leaving the room. Five minutes ago he was talking about moving to another country, and now he's dedicated to finishing the basement. He really has no idea he's doing this.

One of Trey's hooded sweatshirts replaces my sweater. I change my nice jeans to my grubby ones and gather my hair into a ponytail on the way to the living room.

"You said we were going to Chicago," Christian grumbles, pulling on a pair of jeans.

"We can get a lot done in a few hours if you shut the hell up."

Trey gobbles breakfast while I'm downstairs selecting a few of his family's texts. He told me to study up, so that's what I plan to do. We load into his truck. Christian turns to me, inches away.

"Hi." He pumps his eyebrows a few times.

"You're riding back there on the way back." I jerk my head toward the bed of the truck.

"Better enjoy this while I can." He wraps his arm around me and kisses me hard on the cheek.

I elbow him in the chest. It only makes him tighten his arm. Trey snorts, but his eyes don't stray from the road. How can Christian get away with all the flirting, but Shawn can't even be near me without Trey wanting to rip his face off? Shawn's not the one who slept with Trey's wife.

When Trey makes the turn onto the gravel road that leads to my house, I feel a pang—the kind of pang that happens the moment you realize you forgot something, or made some awful mistake. Christian's arm weighs against me. Trey is too close. I swallow, wanting out of the truck. We ascend the hill. He's driving so slowly, and I need to get out, to get into the house.

Trey kills the engine and glances at me. "You okay?"

"Yeah." I get out of the truck on Christian's side.

Trey's line of stones still circle the house. They seem foreign somehow, like they've changed the air in a way I never agreed to. I should be grateful he's built that barrier around my house. Instead of demand I not come here alone, he made it so I could. It's all in my best interest. I shouldn't feel like there's something wrong.

I summon the image of my first day here. My Civic, packed with my belongings, parked next to my realtor's

SUV in front of a rustic cabin high on a bluff, the snow-topped Rocky Mountains far beyond. The fragrance of the damp earth and the fresh pine trees which surround the house. And my loneliness. My hopelessness. My lost world.

I'm here again, and everything's been found. So why does it feel like something's still missing?

Trey whistles. It cuts the air and goes through me. River and Trib burst from the woods and split up, galloping hard. He's sending them off to scour the property for any signs of an enemy. He squats to inspect his line of stones, looks abruptly at Christian. They each disappear around a side of the house and come back on opposite sides.

"What is it?" I ask Trey. I want to tell him something's wrong, but the wrongness I feel seems like something I should keep to myself until it's more explicit. Maybe I don't want to add to his long list of worries, but I think it's more complicated…

"No, we're good." He takes my hand, and we walk a few steps before he stops and spins around, tugging me behind him to scan the woods.

I'm blind behind his wall of a body. Not that it matters. A fifty-caliber bullet would penetrate us both, and I'd rather it be a surprise.

Christian walks closer. "Let's go inside and let the dogs do their job."

"What was it?" I ask once we're inside removing our coats.

"Nothing. Just a feeling."

This is the life he's known for the last fifteen years. Always on guard, never completely at ease. Hunted. Is it possible to get used to a life like this?

Christian stomps down the stairs. "Hurry the hell up."

"So anxious to get started? That's a first." Trey follows him.

Their voices fade, and I hear them tugging light chains. I should set a clock to determine the time interval before the first shoving match begins.

The air is chilled and stagnant like a deep freeze. I turn up the heat. The safety of the house has magnified that nagging feeling I've forgotten to do something here. The bedroom draws me, but that's silly—there's nothing to do in there. I go to the kitchen instead and open the refrigerator, expecting moldy cheese and rotten fruit. It's been mostly cleaned out. Trey did it on one of his trips here and we haven't brought any groceries since. I can scrape together lunch for today, but anything beyond that will be pushing it.

Warm air mixes with the chill which somehow makes me feel colder. I wander into the bedroom. The boxes I haven't yet unpacked cluster in the corner. I shouldn't start on that now. They might need my help downstairs, they'll need lunch…

I'm looking at the bottom of an empty box. I'm not sure where it came from. Its contents appear to have been unloaded onto the bed but I don't remember doing it. I'm holding a half-used book of stamps in one hand and a highlighter in another. If I wanted to unpack, I'd be putting things away not littering the bed with them. I start tossing everything back in. The wrongness that teased me in the driveway has grown bolder. But not any less vague.

After stacking the box with the others, I return to the kitchen and open the text with the faded indigo cover. It's handwritten Irish, and very old. With my limited knowl-edge of the language, I struggle through the indigo book, all the time ignoring the bedroom which still seems to be urging me inside. I find no mention of misuse of magic, or its repercussions.

I take a break to throw together a random lunch of the few things we have to eat. They inhale it, then Trey ushers Christian downstairs. Christian comes back up to take two beers out of the refrigerator and then clomps back down.

It's in the middle of the maroon text that I turn the page and see the word for "love." I flip pages. The rest of the book is dedicated to it, spell after spell. And as I read, I come to understand love spells require constant refreshing or they fade. A word, a charm, a tea, a scent—something must be used to revive the magic or it loses its hold.

I close the book. I stare at the worn bronze medallion. I don't know what's worse—that I'm right, that what Trey and I have won't hold, or that he withheld this from me.

There's a vibration in the table. The noise downstairs takes a pause, exposing a rumble coming from the front of the house. I go to the front door and look out the window to see a huge truck idling in the driveway.

I go downstairs. I can't say his name. There's a shadow hanging over me. A gag on my mouth. He flips off the drill and looks up.

"There's a big truck outside."

"Good." He jabs Christian in the back. "Drywall is here."

Christian announces, "Ladies and gentlemen, we have officially entered hell."

They go outside, Christian dragging his feet. An enor-mous pallet of drywall lowers from the truck. As they approach carrying the first sheets, I recognize the man who drove me to work that day in his shiny red truck. He's a perfectly-timed reminder. He was the middleman between Trey and me when we first met. If Trey and I weren't under a spell, our hate for each other would be as sharp as it was that day.

They struggle each time they hit the top of the stairs. It seems there is no easy way to make the turn no matter how many different angles they try. I've never heard so much cursing in my life.

"We should bring it through the back," Trey says on about the tenth trip.

"Why didn't you think of that sooner?" Christian drops the drywall to the floor and sucks his scraped knuckles.

When they're finished hauling, they gather in the kitchen to rest.

"Liv, you remember Wayne," Trey says before taking a drink of water.

Wayne laughs. "You're making this guy pay for what he did, huh?"

"Shit. I'm doing this out of the goodness of my heart."

"There is no goodness in your heart," Christian says. It's exactly what I used to think about Trey. What I should still be thinking about him.

Trey walks Wayne to the door.

I eye the maroon text. There isn't enough time to show it to Christian, to ask him to tell me it's all wrong.

"He's got a double major in biology and chemistry, and he's in rural Montana hauling drywall," Christians mutters.

More details about the father of my child. My destined mate. A man I barely know.

"You have a degree in biology and chemistry?" I ask Trey when he reenters the room.

He narrows his eyes at Christian. "Mister Ivy League needs to learn to keep his mouth shut." He wipes the sweat off his face with the bottom half of his shirt.

I turn to Christian. "What school?"

"He went to University of Richmond. I went to Yale."

Yale. I should've known. "For what?"

"Architecture and engineering, and lots of co-eds." Christian toasts the air with his beer bottle. "So if you ever need help reading some blueprints, I'm your man."

"You both did double majors?"

"Of course. Don't you know we always have to outdo one another?"

Trey's never been bothered by how little we know each other, so I shouldn't expect any change of heart now. His ways are usually stamped in concrete. "What else don't I know about you?"

"Do you know about his third nipple?"

Trey crosses his arms, leans against the wall. "What kind of doctor were you studying to be?"

I cross my arms, mimicking him. "Don't turn this around on me."

"Doctor, huh?" Christian raises an eyebrow. "Interesting."

"I'm just pointing out the fact that it doesn't matter," Trey says.

"That's a fact?" I suppose he's right. Why does any of this matter? We were united by some unnatural force. Our choices mean nothing.

"Uh, oh…" Christian says under his breath.

"Yep. A fact."

"I'm getting out of here." Christian disappears down the stairs.

"I read that text." I point to it. "Have you read it?"

He looks at it for a drawn out moment. "Not all of it." He won't meet my eyes.

"Liar." It's out before I can catch it.

His shoulders square, like he's bracing for a blow. I want to take it back. I want him to talk to me, but that damn word, it's just built a wall I didn't intend.

"You've read it. I know you have."

His eyes focus back on mine. He clears his throat. "Yes."

I see something in his face that makes me want to travel back in time and unread that text, to unlearn what I now know. His grief, it hits heavy inside me. Something about that word takes him to a bad place. Accidental or not—god, it still hurts me to hurt him. No spell can cause that kind of deep-seated emotion. It's a connection we've built. It has to be.

"Forget it," I say. "Can I just have a kiss?" Denial used to be my specialty. I can go right back to it. Easy. I back into the cabinets and grip the countertop.

"Okay." He puts his hands over mine on either side of me and leans down.

It's impossible to feel his lips and not reach for him, plaster myself against him. I smell his woodsy soap, his sweat wearing through it, sawdust. My hands are captive in his, as if all his desire to embrace me has transferred there, and the power of it, the tease, has my bones turning to pulp. Maybe he's my charm. He's the thing that revives our spell.

"I think that was more than one," I say around my rapid breath. An odd, uninvited thought stiffens my bones in a frightening way: *I'm going to miss this.*

"You didn't stop me." His lips are still an inch from mine.

"I didn't want to." His hands turn to shackles over my own and not in a good way. I struggle to smile, to mask the toxic mix of love, lust, confusion, loss. I've forgotten something. Overlooked it. I'm being pulled in too many directions. It's unwanted. It's not me. I'll figure it out and fix it and until then, I can't let him see it.

"Fearghus!" Christian yells from below us. "Any fucking day!"

Trey gives me a weak smile, like he's in trouble for something but knows I'll forgive him.

"None of this is your fault."

He tucks his hands in his pockets and watches me. "Some of it is."

CHAPTER 25

TREY

CHRISTIAN'S HUMMING IS on my last nerve, but it's the better alternative over his running mouth. At least he doesn't expect me to be paying attention.

"I'm going to get the other battery." Christian sets down his almost-dead drill.

My head jerks up. The amulet. If it can protect a person, it can protect a room. Probably a whole house. We did it when we were kids.

"*Hello*," Christian says. "Dude, you with me?"

"I know how to protect the house from snipers."

He scoffs. "Snipers? Please. What *I* want to know is—"

"I'll tap into my amulet. Tweak it a little. Like we did when we were kids. Remember?" We protected his room so he wouldn't have to wear the amulet. How he had to run for that room. It was priceless.

"You'll weaken its power."

"It won't need as much. Snipers already have distance as their disadvantage."

"Might work." He stares at nothing, mulling over my idea. "But snipers overcome distance. That's kind of the point of a sniper."

"But they have to be accurate. And precise. It takes nothing to alter a sniper's bullet."

"True."

"I'll have to change its center of focus. Expand it. Then reduce it when she's out of the house. She'll have its concentrated power when she's out."

"Man, your pea brain is working overtime today."

"It'll be easy to test. We'll know it works. I'll get started on it as soon as we get back from Chicago."

"What made you think of it?" He's glaring at the floor.

I start to remind him how we used it as kids, but this abrupt hate he now has for the floor has me thinking he's already remembered.

My phone buzzes in my pocket. I know it's Tara before I fish it out. "What's new?"

"Aunt Enid and Uncle Arthur are here. They—"

"Who?"

"Máthair's sister and brother. You don't know them."

Máthair has a sister and a brother?

"The funeral is Friday."

"We'll be there."

"Use the house key I gave you if you get in late. Same room as last time."

"Where should I put Christian?"

"Christian's coming?" The excitement in her voice proves she's never met him, doesn't know what a pain in the ass he is.

"You'll have to help me keep everyone from trying to crucify him."

"Everyone already loves him. I'll make up the room across from yours."

"We'll be there Thursday night." I say goodbye and pocket my phone. "I hope you're not cleaning up," I say to Christian.

"Hell yes, I am. Time to call it a day."

"Let's finish this wall."

"How about we not? I've got to pack all my crap, take a shower, drink some beer, and then get up early in the morning. Come on. Don't be a punk."

He has a point. I wouldn't mind a drink myself.

"I figure I'll just head back to Richmond afterward." He throws his hands in the air at the look I give him. "I'll be halfway there. You expect me to drive all the way back here, just to leave a few days later? I need to go home."

The risk involved with Máthair coming to Chicago seems insignificant when compared to the risk involved with Christian going home, inside enemy gates, full of new knowledge the Moores would love to get their hands on. And what if they find out he's against them now? My mother and stepfather are the only ones who'd protect him and they'd die trying. They wouldn't have a fighting chance against Dillon alone.

He slaps me hard on the back. "Come on, let's go."

I follow him up the stairs. Liv is on her hands and knees, wiping the floor.

"Ever heard of a mop?" Christian asks.

"I prefer this method."

He offers his hand and hauls her to her feet. She frowns as soon as she meets my eyes.

"Trash?" I pick up a full black bag by the fridge.

She nods. I carry it out to the truck and throw it in the bed before getting inside and starting the engine. After a few minutes, they come out together. Liv eyes me as she gets in next to me.

"What did you do to him?" she asks Christian when he's in and we're moving.

"Me?" he squeaks.

"Yeah, you. He was in a good mood when he left me, and now he's in a bad mood."

"I'm right here."

"I have no responsibility for that man's moods," he says.

She turns forward to stare out the windshield. "I need to unpack those boxes in the bedroom. There's something in there I need."

"Like what? If you haven't needed it by now—"

"I know, it's just…" She sounds confused.

"Aw, shit," I say when I see River and Trib waiting at the entrance to the driveway. This could only mean one thing. I stop the truck and get out. Two guys. We have just enough time to get Liv in the house. I get back in the truck and floor it up the driveway.

"Get her inside. There are two of them."

He tugs Liv out of the truck before she has a chance to speak. I sprint toward the woods behind the house to take one of them by surprise. He can't pull his gun in time. Asshole should've had it out. I twist his arm and knock his legs out from under him. When he hits the ground I snatch the gun, but he kicks it out of my hand and I don't see where it lands. Maybe I shouldn't kill this one. We could get information out of him. I'd like to know how many are left. Is he the last one? Christian wouldn't let me do much, but I could get started without him.

All this thinking has me on my back with several blows to the face. I catch his forearm, wind my leg around him, and we roll several times. His grapple tightens around me like a boa constrictor. This guy must be a wrestler. He's trying to keep me on the ground. Fuck this.

I get one arm free and dig my fingers into his throat, but his snakelike arm glides under mine, rotating my shoulder until I'm forced to release him. He draws his head back slightly to take a breath. I bash my forehead against his nose two times before he recovers and presses his elbow against my cheekbone to crush my face into the ground. If I could only get on my feet, this would be over quickly. He knows that, too. The smell of his blood and sweat fills my nose just before he rolls my face flat against the ground and I inhale dirt.

I throw all my strength into my legs, pressing against whatever part of his body is restricting them, and with a tiny portion of free space I thrust my knee toward him. He chokes and releases my face. My arms find freedom and I spin and pound him several times in the ribs then shove his body away and roll onto my hands and knees. He claws the ground, trying to get leverage to push himself up. I keep my eye on him and spit all the dirt out of my mouth.

Screw getting info out of him. I'll just break his legs. Pulverize his face until he can't speak. Watch him bleed.

"Trey!"

I roll back on my heels. Christian throws a gun. I catch it and aim.

"What are you waiting for?" Christian comes to stand next to me.

"We could use him for information."

"He's not going to talk. Remember? They never do."

I stand. Fire twice—chest, head. Look at Christian.

He asks, "Did you get the other one?"

"You didn't?"

We stare at each other for a split second before it hits us. She's alone. We simultaneously turn and sprint toward the house. He runs up the side of the house to the front so I take the stairs at the back and throw the door open. Water is running somewhere in the house. It sounds like the shower. I rush into the living room and stop at the wide-open front door. Christian comes through, laughing like a maniac.

"She got him." He gives the thumbs up and jerks his head toward the doorway.

I step outside. A body lies several yards from the porch, flat on its back with a knife through the eye. Christian follows me to the body. We stare down at it together.

"You two must have some crazy chemistry or something. For her to be able to use what you taught her in such a short amount of time..." He looks at me like I just grew a third eye. "For your brains to be that similar…it's a little fucked up. A lot fucked up."

I grasp the handle of the knife and jerk it out. It's dagger I gave her. I wipe it off on my pants. "I don't think she's ever practiced throwing a dagger."

"You're going to have another black eye."

We go inside, and I head straight for the bathroom and open the door to a cloud of steam. I push back the edge of the shower curtain. Liv's standing under the water with her arms wrapped around her.

"Nice throw."

"Thanks." She closes her eyes and backs up so the water runs down her face.

"Can I join you?"

She nods, her eyes still closed.

I lay the dagger on the sink and strip off my clothes. She opens her eyes when I step in with her.

She scrutinizes my bloody arms. "Not your blood?"

She steps aside, and I put my arms in the stream of water. We watch them rinse clean.

"Not mine." I give her a grin.

"Your face?"

I lean down to rinse my face in the water.

"Your eye." Her voice breaks.

I wrap my arms around her. "Will be healed tomorrow." I hold her for a few minutes until she pushes me away.

She looks different, and not just because her hair is flat and straight, bangs covering the tops of her eyes like a cap pulled low.

"Will you wash my dagger?" She eyes the dagger on the countertop.

"My pleasure." We get out of the shower. I wash it in the sink.

In the bedroom, she drops onto the bed with a heavy sigh. I put on a pair of sweatpants and a T-shirt. There's an unsettled element in the room. A hanging duty I'm not sure how to fulfill. If she'd say something, maybe it would lead me there. I'll admit sometimes I'm clueless. Sometimes I need help.

She looks up at me with those endlessly blue eyes. "Will you get me my lotion?"

I retrieve her lotion from the bathroom. She takes it, and I sit down next to her.

"This is going to take a while. You don't have to wait."

It feels like a dismissal. A failure. I open the door to leave.

"Trey?"

Here comes the question I already should've answered. The problem I should've known how to solve.

"Will they ever stop?"

"I wish I could tell you yes, but you know I can't." I sit next to her on the bed. I can see what's bothering her now, or I can at least guess. She's just killed another person. She's afraid she can't live like this. The dent in her confidence tears me in two. I should repeat the pep talk she gave me but I can't seem to remember the words. "Christian will be able to find out more when he goes back."

"I'm afraid for him to go back."

My unease about his return to Richmond hasn't fully hit me yet. But I don't want to tell her that. I take her hands in mine and bring them to my lips. Kiss them. Past her, the amulet lies on the bed. She catches my hand when I reach for it.

"I want to send it home with him. Please, Trey."

I fasten it around her neck without answering. She can't expect me to make this choice. If she doesn't offer to give it up, I won't have to decide which one of them should have it.

"It's done its job for me. He needs it now."

"Liv—" There's no person in the world more important to me than her. But asking me to decide between protecting her and protecting him isn't fair. I won't make that decision.

"Trey, think about it. You and I have each other. As long as we're together, nothing can happen to either one of us. He's going back there alone."

She reaches behind her neck to remove the amulet, and I watch her do it, unable to find the right words. I see what's different about her now. Her eyes are a little red. Wet. She turns away, picks up her lotion.

Christian is packing his bags when I pass through, and when he sees me he heads to the shower. Liv joins me in the kitchen, helps me with dinner. I feel a tension building inside me, and I know from past experience it's a tension that needs to be released before it turns into something I can't control.

"Hell no," Christian says, and I turn around.

Liv presses the amulet into his chest, and he backs away, arms raised in the air.

"Please," she says. I don't have to see her face to know she's unleashing the full force of her eyes on him. "You need this more than me."

"That belongs to you. And if you don't stop, you're going to piss him off." His eyes flick to me then back to her face.

"Okay, it looks like you've already pissed him off. So I'm going to save your skin." He takes the amulet from her, strings it around her neck and fastens the clasp.

She exhales in my direction. "Did you tip him off?"

"I didn't say a damn thing."

"I don't need to be tipped off to know better than to take that." Christian sits down to put on his socks.

"Why are you dressed up?" I ask.

"I'm going out to say goodbye to Kristen."

"She'll eat you up in that sweater," Liv says. "You look good in pink."

He gives her a cocky wink. "So do you."

CHAPTER 26

LIV

SIFTING THROUGH CLOTHES, I realize I have nothing to pack for a funeral. When I loaded my car for my move here, I envisioned a future of scrubs, jeans, and flannel.

A powerful blow rocks the house, followed by several rapid ones. I'm not sure why I look up since it's concentrated in the floor. Shit, a warning would have been nice. The house only feels like it's falling down because he's after that punching bag like it's his worst enemy.

The sound of fists pounding the bag grows sharper when I descend the basement stairs. From the looks of his chemistry lab slash herbalist's shop, he must have started packing but got sidetracked by the bag. His drink is waiting on the table for him. Would it be wrong of me to take it upstairs and dump it out? I sit on a stool and watch him, wondering what caused him to become distracted. Maybe the bag taunted him. Called him a name. Gave him a dirty look.

Silence takes over the room, a shock after all that pounding. At least he's wearing gloves this time. He places both gloves on the bag to steady its wild swinging and leans his forehead against it, breathing hard. Feeling like a voyeur, I slide off the stool. "I thought we were having an earthquake."

His head snaps up. "How long have you been down here?"

"Not long. Need any help?" I aim my thumb at the scattered jars, herbs, and handwritten texts.

"No. I've got it."

"I have nothing to wear to a funeral. I'm going to have to go shopping."

"You don't need to worry about that."

"I'm not going to show up in jeans and a flannel shirt to your grandmother's funeral."

"Our funerals aren't like funerals you're used to. You don't need to wear anything different than what you're wearing right now."

I look down at my oversized T-shirt, cotton drawstring pants, and red fuzzy socks. "Okay. I'll go shopping when we get to Chicago."

"You don't trust me? Then ask the prince of fashion when he gets home."

"I will." I poke him in the chest.

His expression turns thoughtful. He absentmindedly catches my finger. "I've never been to a Bevan funeral."

I'm jarred by a commonality in our backgrounds I never noticed before. He's lived his whole life isolated from his family. He did have his mother, but that's the only real difference. We're both orphans. It's a common thread I'm going to tangle myself in until I no longer need to hold on.

"We never unpacked the guns we brought last time. We don't have to repack." He smiles big, as if trying to express the greatness of this situation.

I give him the double thumbs up and an overdone mocking grin to cover the flutter in my heart. These are the things that please him, and I don't think he knows how painfully cute that is.

He tugs me against him, his lips to my ear. "Don't be a smartass."

I freeze when he tilts his head to kiss my neck. Some kind of strangled animal sound comes out of me. He leans away just enough to see my face.

"You are so gross and sweaty."

"You should know not to taunt me when I'm gross and sweaty."

He makes no attempt to release me, so I propel my knee into his groin and escape when he blocks the blow.

"That's the oldest trick in the book," I say.

He gives me a calculating look, and I dash for the stairs. I run all the way to the top with him right on my heels. When I reach the middle of the kitchen I spin to face him. He eases the door closed behind him.

"Are you done?" My voice cracks on the last word under a suppressed, hysterical laugh.

The look he gives tells me he is not.

"You are a caveman."

"That's weak, even for you."

"Okay then, the Paleolithic Era called. They need you back. They say no one can club a woman quite like you."

He keeps his poker face. "Where'd you put my club? I need it right now."

I dart past him and make it to the bedroom just in time to slam the door and lock it.

"Take a shower, you asshole!" Metal scrapes inside the doorknob, and I grab it, laughing out of control. "You wouldn't dare!"

"These metal hair pins of yours come in handy."

The lock clicks. The doorknob turns. My attempt to hold the door closed with my weight is a joke. He walks toward me, backing me into the bed. I sit down, roll back on my elbows, and plant both feet against his chest. It does nothing to block his advance. I slide backward on the bed under his force. He's not a caveman, he's an elephant. A tidal wave. Unstoppable. My legs buckle at the knee, his hands sink into the mattress on either side of me. I'm laughing, he's laughing. I'm not sure we've ever laughed this hard. It sounds good. So good.

All at once I get a yearning for that forgotten piece. That thing that's not here. I'm taken somewhere else for a moment, and I've curbed my laughter in a way that has him pushing away. Clearing his throat. Rubbing a hand over the back of his head, his eyes cast away from me.

An ill-timed moment for this confusion has detached me from him. I shouldn't even think it—it feels like a curse.

I'm so mixed up.

I reach for him but he's left the room. The thud of the bathroom door splits the silence. Then the shower.

I cover my face with my arms. This urge—this curse—is going to ruin us. If it's my old life, I need to come to terms with it. If it's his herb cabinet, I need time for the addiction to fade. If it's the possibility of our spell getting broken, I need to ask Christian how we can preserve it.

I need to ask Trey.

I'm still on my back when he returns. I'm stripped of my clothes before I can blink. He seems to have forgotten what just opened between us, or maybe he remembers and this is how he's chosen to deal with it. Ignore it and power through. He seems to do that with a lot of things.

"Trey," I say when his mouth releases mine. My hands find his hair, and he pulls back to look at me. When his eyes lock with mine, I forget what I was going to say.

"I love you," he says.

I forget how to form words altogether. The blissful weight of his body lowers against mine. He inhales against my neck and stays there like that's all he wants, or all he can handle. I wrap my legs around him and he's set back in motion, his lips hard on mine. I keep thinking it's simply lust but god, it's not. It's love so strong it both weakens and empowers. It steals those plaguing thoughts from my mind and thrusts in new ones. All doubt banished, trust reinstated.

Blind faith and pleasure and an overwhelming rightness fill the chasm between us. It doesn't matter what brought us together. We belong.

My eyes drift open. Heavy rain pounds the roof. I turn over to find Trey sitting up in the dark. I run my hand across his stomach. "Come back."

"She's in my head again." He stares straight ahead.

"Your sister?"

Lightning flashes, saturating the room with white light for a fraction of a second.

He collapses to his back. "If she wants to talk to me she needs to wait until the morning and pick up the fucking phone."

Thunder rolls through the valley, and I lift his arm to snuggle against his side. He runs his fingers down my back.

"She misses you."

"Should be used to it."

I close my eyes and settle in, waiting for the tension to release from his body. Lightning flashes like a strobe in the room, and I sit up to look at his face. His eyes are open, staring at the ceiling.

"Please go to sleep," I whisper.

"The storm. Keeps me up."

The pouring rain lulls me to sleep.

When the alarm clock goes off, I hit the snooze and roll over to find Trey missing from the bed. The rain has turned to a peaceful sprinkle, trickling through the gutters above my head. And I have the shakes again.

The darkness outside and the sound of the rain hold the house as if in night. It seems wrong to be up and about. I dress in jeans and a shirt.

The only sign of Christian is his rumpled blond hair sticking out from the edge of the blanket on the couch. I go into the kitchen and turn on the light above the stove.

I peek in the basement. It's dark. I peer outside, through raindrops clinging to cold glass. If he was any other man I wouldn't expect him to be out in this weather.

I start breakfast quietly so I don't wake Christian. I'm not sure how late he got in last night, and we all have a long drive ahead of us.

The back door slides open, and Trey comes in, shorn hair slick with rain, drops running down his face.

"Could you leave a note next time?"

"I thought I'd be back sooner."

"Where'd you go?"

"For a run."

"How was it?"

"Wet." He sits to untie his soggy running shoes. His black eye barely healed at all.

I'm not going to tell him how I worry about him. It won't change anything. It will just sour his mood. And mine.

I go into the laundry room and take two clean towels out of the dryer. He wipes his face and throws one towel over his head. I can tell by the set of his jaw how at ease he is now, after running around in the cold mountain rain while most humans were still asleep.

"You're making a puddle."

He strips off his clothes down to his boxers, throws the towel on the puddle.

Christian wanders into the room, stretching and yawning. "Somebody put some coffee on before my head explodes." His voice is like sandpaper.

When Trey goes to shower, Christian stands to look out the back door. "You'll call me if you need me. Anytime. Day or night. Agreed?"

The emotion in his voice puts a heat in my chest I'm not prepared for. He isn't leaving yet. I'm not ready to say goodbye.

"I can catch a flight and be out here the same day. Where's your phone? I'll put my number in it."

I dig my phone out of my purse and hand it to him. He enters his number and starts to give it back then changes his mind. "Let me call mine so I have your number." He scrolls through the list. His thumb freezes. "Do you know you still have Dillon in here?"

I nod.

"He'll go postal if he sees this, you know."

"I want a good warning if he calls."

He puts the phone to his ear. His phone rings from the living room, and he hangs up. "Be sure to explain that to Trey *before* he starts killing innocent bystanders. Do we have an agreement?"

I take his extended hand. He pulls me in for a hard hug.

"We still have a few days before you leave," I say as he releases me.

"I know. But it's going to be chaos once we get there. Funerals always are. I wasn't sure I'd get a moment alone with you."

"Trey told me to ask you what I should wear. I have nothing for a funeral."

He ponders a moment. "If it's anything like a Moore funeral, then you can wear that." He gestures at my jeans and light blue thermal shirt.

"Trey told me you'd tell me the truth."

"I am. You'll see when we get there. Come as you are."

I feel like I'm being pranked.

Christian showers, dresses, and Trey takes the duffle bags full of guns out to the car.

"Why is he bringing so many guns?" I ask Christian while putting on my coat.

"Why not?" Teasing. Always teasing.

Trey comes in the door and picks up our overnight bags. "It's still coming down."

I get my purse and we run out to the cars.

"Did you end up getting any sleep last night?" I ask once we're on the road with Christian following behind us.

"Yeah. Once the storm let up."

"You can't sleep through storms?"

"Not unless I'm really tired. Or really hung over."

"Why not?"

"The noise. I wouldn't hear them coming."

"You hear them coming in your sleep?"

"Of course. Otherwise I'd have been dead a long time ago."

I snuggle into the seat. Not long ago we took another road trip in this car on the same road, driving the opposite direction. "Wake me up at the first stop. I'm going to ride with Christian. It's not fair for him to be alone the whole trip."

I fall asleep to the rhythm of the windshield wipers and the rain splashing against the car.

When my eyes open, I'm blinded by the lights of a busy gas station. The sky is gray, with clouds even grayer, and everything's wet. Through the windshield Trey and Christian are walking toward me, both carrying a cup of coffee.

"You didn't wake me up," I say when Trey takes his seat.

"He wouldn't let me." He fastens his seat belt.

"Do you mind if I ride with him for a while?"

"Yes."

I kiss his cheek and get out of the car.

Opening the door of Christian's car breaks a protective seal that shields his pumping music from the rest of the world. Smiling the widest smile imaginable, he reaches for the volume as I take my seat.

"You're going to make him jealous. I love it."

Trey's tires spin when he turns back onto the road and Christian follows.

"See what I mean?"

"Oh, he's just showing off." I fasten my seat belt as we take the entrance ramp onto the highway.

He searches through his music list. "I have something you'll like in here. It's dark and brooding, just like your boyfriend. And sleeping is not allowed in this car. Just so you know."

I take a drink out of his coffee.

"That's yours now. You're infected with Trey germs."

"So are you. How soon you forget."

He looks at me like he's about to boot me out of the car.

I put the coffee cup back in his cup holder. He reaches for it and takes a drink himself.

Now's the time to ask him about that maroon text. We could discuss it at length and Trey would never know. I watch the Camaro's taillights ahead, the mist kicking up from the tires, fully aware I'm losing my chance but all my questions have caged themselves and tossed away the key.

TREY

Now that we're out of the rain, I bring the Camaro up to a faster cruising speed, leaving Christian and Liv far behind. He catches up and settles into a pace that matches mine.

How soon can I get away with making our next stop so I can have her back in my car with me? Watching the clock begins to wear me out, so I turn on the radio and flip the channels in search of something no one's playing. My thoughts swarm, and I bend, allowing them to overtake like an angry mob. My mother coming to Chicago. Christian returning home. Dillon Moore, and my need to dish out his death. With no feasible solutions to any of them, I turn my mind off and just drive.

It doesn't seem like much later when Christian passes me and leads me off the next exit ramp. I follow him to a gas station where he parks out front.

He rolls down his window in response to mine. "She has to pee."

I decide I do too, so I get out.

Christian gets out as well. "She drank all my coffee."

"That would explain it."

Inside the quick shop I wait outside the occupied unisex bathroom. When she comes out, her hair is down, loose curls clinging to her shoulders.

"Hi." She slips her hand into the front pocket of my hooded sweatshirt with my own hands.

It's a mingling more intimate than it means to be—her skin on mine, tucked between fabric. Her fingers explore, trying to situate themselves, to weave between mine.

I've never been loved by anyone like she loves me. I should tell her I'm not worthy. I can't go any longer without telling her all the things I've done, the things I want to do. Exactly what's inside me. If there's a way to screw this all up, to lose her, either I'll find it or the Moores will. They specialize in destruction, and I've been nurtured by it. One of us will sabotage this.

She puts her other hand in the pocket on the other side, gives me this shy smile. She's too sweet for my bitter world. It will dissolve her.

I pull my hand out, bringing hers with it. She heads toward the front of the store. When I come out of the bathroom, Christian hands me his coffee. I find Liv in the candy aisle.

"Are we getting lunch soon?" she asks.

"Whenever you want."

I get a coffee for myself and go up to the counter to pay for both. Liv follows me empty-handed.

"The blond guy already paid," the cashier says, ringing up only one of them. Apparently we're being watched.

Christian joins us, gives his two-fingered wave at the cashier, and leads us outside.

"I think she likes you," Liv says to Christian as soon as we're out the door.

"*Everybody* likes me."

I open the car door for Liv and then turn to Christian. "She's getting hungry. I'll turn off as soon as she picks something."

I slide behind the wheel. She leans to give me a kiss that has me planting my feet in the floorboard like I need to ground myself for a more humane death. Its current burns the sheathing off every nerve. I'm an exposed mass of sensation, yet deaf and blind, and I become aware of her pawing at me so I open my eyes. She's giggling, shoving my hands away, hands which have somehow gone up her shirt.

"I missed you," she says.

My tires screech when I pull onto the road. She's revived the kid in me—I'm an idiot in a 580-horsepower car again.

We pass several suitable restaurants by the time she finally picks one. I can sense Christian's hunger by the way he keeps riding up on my ass then falling back, over and over. I'm about to eat the steering wheel.

After lunch, she rides with Christian again, and I feel like we need to start doing this by the minute instead of by each stop. His intervals are longer than mine. Maybe it's time for me to claim an overactive bladder.

To both Christian's and my agony, we let her pick the restaurant again for dinner. Back on the road again only to hit another rainstorm as the sun sets behind us. When the amount of miles to Fargo starts looking like a possible goal, I decide I'm going to need some alcohol for the night, so I lead Christian to a liquor store on the outskirts of Fargo and we go in, leaving Liv in the car.

Christian and I split, him to the beer, me to the hard liquor. I pick a good whiskey then join him in the refrigerated aisle. "More Welsh beer?" I say when he makes his choice. "There's something wrong with you."

He gives me the finger. We head to the counter to pay, and we both turn to look outside as something catches our attention. Several men surround our cars. One of them goes for the handle on Liv's side and I'm shoving through the store's front door and throwing him against the Camaro. I didn't know I'd have an opportunity to kick some ass.

"Must be my lucky day," I think aloud, still gripping his collar. I slam him once more against the car before I release him.

"Nice car," one of them says behind me.

"Nice woman," another one says, and several of them snicker.

I step back to place them all in my field of vision. The guy I threw against the car spits at my feet. I've never seen a group of bigger rednecks in my life. Well, maybe I have. It's just been awhile. One of them leans against Christian's car.

"I wouldn't touch his car either."

He makes a belligerent display of removing himself from Christian's car. Christian comes out of the store, chuckling under his breath. He circles around the group, puts the bags in his trunk, and joins my side.

"Oh, these two are together. Must be a couple homos."

Christian slaps his knee. "You boys are creative. Never heard that one before."

The guy nearest me spits again. He's starting to get on my nerves.

"This is just comical," Christian says. "It's not even worth our time."

"It's always worth my time."

"And that's what's wrong with you. *Beidh muid in ann a dhul amú oraibh go héasca ar an mbóthar.*"

He's right—we could easily lose them on the road. But there's no fun in that. "*Níl spraoi ar bith ansin.*"

"*Feicfidh mé ar an mbóthar thú, a dhearthráir.*" He opens the passenger door of the Camaro. "It's my turn." He ushers Liv into his Infiniti then slaps me on the back. "Knock yourself out."

Liv eyes me as the Infiniti backs out. Two guys hop in a truck and follow them. They can't seriously think they'll be able to keep up with a G37 in their beat-up old pick-up.

"If you take turns, then you should let us take turns," the guy nearest me says.

I bury my fist in his mouth.

"I've called the cops!" a voice calls from the front of the store, alerting me of my timeframe and making me wonder if I should lower myself to the level of these inbred assholes.

Fights like these used to be fun. Maybe it's slow to kick in, but right now, it's doing nothing for me.

Another truck roars alive, backing up and positioning itself to follow me as soon as I decide to bail. One of the guys comes at me, so I shove him to the curb. I see an arm due for breaking, but I scratch my head instead. Maybe they've never seen an Infiniti. But do they think they have a chance against my car?

Christian's right. This is comical. And as it turns out, it's not even any fun. I'm giving them the trouble they came looking for, and why should I do that? I get in my car and back out, taking it easy on my way back onto the highway. Following the plan Christian and I have used since we were teenagers, I continue on the same road in the same direction, knowing I'll catch up to him sooner or later. The truck follows. I make no fast maneuvers so I don't lose them prematurely.

When I finally see the white G ahead, I lead the truck to him. I catch up to Christian and match his speed, and he looks over at me, obviously involved in a conversation with Liv. I stomp the gas. The truck makes no attempt to catch me. Its headlights disappear behind the Infiniti, pinned to his ass.

Several minutes later, I lower my speed and set my cruise control. We're miles past Fargo already, and it's going to take him a few more to catch up. Headlights peek over the horizon behind me. He gains on me, passes, whips in front and slams his brakes. I lay on the horn, laughing, but continue to follow him so he and Liv can pick a hotel for the night.

When he takes the exit ramp for Fergus Falls, I know he and Liv must be eating it up. I'm sure they already have some one-liners ready to go.

"Doesn't count. It's a different spelling," I say as soon as we get out of our cars at the hotel. "And a different pro-nunciation."

"Close enough," Christian says.

"We thought it was appropriate, since it's probably what happened back there at the liquor store." Liv bites down on her lip, trying to subdue a smile.

Christian nods, beaming with pride like he fed this to her beforehand. It's a little frightening to see her playing his partner in crime.

"No good. What else you got?"

"Umm…" She glances at Christian. "All the good ones were his. I can't take credit."

"That one was yours?"

"No, that was his too." She releases a belly laugh. "He said I could have that one."

Christian shrugs. "It was the crappiest one."

We head toward the entrance, and Christian hangs his arm around Liv. "So, two rooms. We only need one bed. Do you want one bed or two?" He keeps a straight face.

"Don't you ever get sick of yourself?"

Liv ducks under his arm and takes my hand. I wrap my arm around her instead, dragging my palm down the side of her body, imagining the things I'm going to do to her as soon as we're alone.

We check in then drive around the building, park, and unload our luggage. Christian brings his beer into our room. "Don't start going at it yet. I want to have a few beers with you first," he says before going back to his room.

Liv props our door open and turns to face me, hand on hip. "I hope you didn't kill anyone."

"I didn't." I pull off my sweatshirt and sit on the bed to untie my boots.

"I could've handled it. You don't always have to start a fight. There are other ways—"

"Don't be mad."

"I'm not. Well, I was, until your very rational brother talked me out of it."

Christian comes in behind her, brandishing a deck of cards and a bucket of ice. He buries two beers in the bucket and opens another. After taking a big drink, he holds it out to Liv. She waves him away.

"So fill us in." He drags the table out so we can all sit comfortably. He deals three hands and looks at us, sighing with overdone impatience.

I drop into a chair. "Nothing to fill in. I knocked out some teeth. That's about it."

Christian fakes shock. "They had teeth?"

Liv sits on the edge of her chair. I open my bottle of whiskey and take a long drink. Hell yes.

"Do you want a soda or something?" I ask her. "Orange juice? Water?"

"No, I'm still full from dinner." She walks over to the heater and turns it on full blast.

"I don't think so," Christian and I say together.

"Just for a minute then I'll turn it off." She sits back down.

"I will die," Christian says. "Give her a sweatshirt or something."

"You have your own room," she snaps.

"Whoa." That's a surprise. It's a tone I know too well, but I've never heard her use it on Christian, especially unprovoked. He needs to apologize. I don't want her mad when we go to bed. Or would that make things more interesting?

Christian frowns deeply, drawing it out.

"I'm sorry. I don't know what's wrong with me." She rests a hand on his arm, looking as shocked as I feel. She turns off the heat.

We play through a few rounds until Christian gets bored. It doesn't take long. Or, he's cutting me some slack. He's been known to do that. I should give him more credit.

"Okay kids, it's been fun. I'm going to retire to my room and watch some...*television*." He chokes up with fake emotion. He picks up his bucket of ice and Liv catches his arm.

"I really am sorry for snapping at you. I feel so bad." She stands on her toes to kiss his cheek. I can't take my eyes off her ass.

"What? I don't even remember that. You can kiss me again though."

If he doesn't get the fuck out of here I'm going to tear out his throat. She opens the door and nudges him out. When she turns to face me, I can tell she's up to something. I screw the cap on my whiskey.

"We need to get rid of your black eye so your family doesn't think you're uncivilized," she says.

"Good idea." I try not to show any emotion.

"But I think I'm going to play hard to get."

"Is that right?"

She nods and pulls the rubber band out of her hair. "I'm too easy."

"You *are* easy. But so am I." She has no idea how easily I could overpower her. Or maybe she does, and that's the game.

She turns off the light, and we slide under the covers together. She moves in and gives my bottom lip a soft nip. It almost sends me over the edge.

"This is hard to get?"

I didn't think it was possible to take eternity and draw it out to an even more impossible length of time. But by the time she gives in to me, I've lived a million immortal lives, none of them ending, each overlapping the other, stretching time to the point of rupture.

The beating rain in the back of my mind becomes a reality when I wake in the morning. This rain is going to slow us down. I allow us to sleep until half past seven anyway. With Liv showing no sign of waking, it's a challenge to want to get up myself.

Another full day of driving mirrors yesterday's, minus the gang of inbred rednecks, plus an endless onslaught of rain, and we eat a late dinner a few hours outside of Chicago.

When we park in front of Tara's red brick row house, every window is dark. The rain has stopped, but large drops fall out of the canopy of the oak trees along the sidewalk. A haze surrounds each street light. The block is calm, but like most city neighborhoods, never quite asleep. Activity hangs all around, a presence more felt than heard or seen. It's a nag on my senses I can never ignore.

We carry our luggage up the steps to the porch, and I unlock the door. We lug our bags up the narrow staircase, and I show Christian his room. Inside our room, Liv and I strip down to our underwear and meet under the covers. She tangles her legs around mine and folds into me.

Sunlight wakes me, hot on my face. The rain has made its exit. Liv is frowning in her sleep, so I stroke her cheek. She stirs, opens her eyes.

"I had a nightmare." Her voice is still thick with sleep. "We hated each other again."

I chuckle, remembering it too well.

"It's not funny." She winds her arms around me. "It felt so true to life. Just like it felt before."

I sit up and throw the covers aside. I don't want to think about this. My head is too full of everything else. She watches me put on my clothes from yesterday then takes my offered hand. She gets dressed in clean clothes and twists up her hair. In the hall, we run into Christian coming out of the bathroom with a towel around his waist.

Looking at me, he nods toward Liv. "You need to fire her. You still have that black eye." He closes himself inside his room as Liv drags me into the bathroom.

She makes me sit on the toilet so she can examine my eye in the bright light. "It does look a little better. It's healing, just not—"

"It's fine."

She tilts my head, but her eyes have gone from analytical to thoughtful, almost sad. She presses two cool fingers against my childhood scar. An intake of breath through parted lips—she's about to ask me something I have no answer for, not while my head is so burdened by everything else.

I take her fingers away. "Liv, it's fine."

Something in my tone prompts her to step away. When we emerge, Christian appears in his doorway. Scruffy, road-trip Christian has been transformed into clean-cut, pretty-boy Christian.

He points both index fingers at me in unison. "I'm sorry you can never look this good."

Voices carry from the stairwell, so I lead Liv and Christian down the stairs and into the living room.

"There they are!" Tara's voice doesn't match her tired expression. She ambushes me with a forceful hug, and I return it by picking her up and squeezing her until she laughs. She wiggles away and I study her face. Something's different, and it's not just her grief.

She turns to hug Liv, and Christian goes straight to Máthair who's pinned under both her grandchildren on the couch and kisses her cheek. He steps aside, and he and Tara lock eyes.

Máthair reaches both hands to me. "How lucky I am to see you again so soon." I sit next to her, and she reaches out for Liv in the same way. Liv takes a seat on her other side. I look into Máthair's face and can see no sign of pain. My mother has always been so strong.

"What's wrong with you?" I say to Christian and Tara. They're having some kind of awkward face-off.

"It's weirder than I thought it would be," Tara says.

"Yeah," Christian says. "Trey in female form. It's frightening to say the least."

"How do you think I feel?" Tara asks. "You're like a make-believe person I know all about, appearing to me in the flesh."

"You know all about me? How?"

"From Máthair's mind," Tara and I answer together.

Christian takes a step back. "In stereo? Now *that* is just wrong."

I should let her do the speaking from now on. I never liked talking anyway. No need to further prove what freaks we are. The visual is enough.

"And I've resented you for most of my life," Tara continues to Christian.

"What'd I do to you?"

"Fearghus was supposed to be *my* brother, not yours."

Christian's obnoxious laughter booms through the room. "You can have him!"

I turn to Máthair. "I need to talk to you."

"I know, Fearghus. And I need to talk to you. But can it wait? This is the first time I've had you all together."

Her smile tames me, but I fight against it. "Where's my father?"

She lays a hand on my knee and gives me a look with which I can't argue. "We have a big day ahead of us."

"Come help me make breakfast," Tara says, poking me hard in the arm. She drags me into the kitchen where I spin her to face me.

"What's different about you?"

She shrugs out of my grip. "I lost someone very dear to me. Get the eggs."

I get the eggs out of the fridge and start on a family-sized portion of scrambled eggs. She remains silent, so I change my strategy, hoping to extract something from her.

"Is this the first time you've seen Máthair in person?"

"No, she used to visit a lot. Whenever she and Martin would travel, they'd always stop here."

"You've got to be kidding me."

"This is the first time she's seen the twins in person. She wanted to come when they were born, but she was afraid it was too risky."

"And now it's not?"

She cocks her head and exhales. "Please don't ruin this for her. I know exactly what you're thinking, so just keep it to yourself. It's too late anyway."

"You're god damned right it's too late."

"So get over it." She stares me down.

"Christian and I need your help. We've been working on an effect for his protection. He's going back to Richmond from here."

"Fun," she says, overtaken by a grin. "I'd love to help. I feel like I've been excluded for forty-five years."

"You have."

She pauses her chopping. Holds a breath. It wasn't meant to be a jab at her, but I see now it is. It's not my fault the truth sucks. It *is* my fault for confronting her with it. I should say something else but all I've got is more jabs meant for them that will instead strike her. She wipes her eyes on her sleeve, throws some chopped peppers and mushrooms into my skillet of eggs.

Change the fucking subject, idiot. "The kids are okay?"

"Yes. They don't know what's going on. Winnie was sleeping with her when she passed."

I turn to look at her.

"She insisted on sleeping with her that night. They went to bed early. When I went to check on Winnie before I went to bed, she was curled up next to her. And she was gone."

"She knew."

Tara nods. Tears well into her eyes.

I dump the eggs into the bowl she hands me, and she throws a towel over it to keep them warm.

"I wasn't sure when to give you this, so I'm just going to give it to you now." She pulls an envelope out of the pocket of her robe and hands it to me. "It was left on her dresser."

Fearghus is written on the outside of the envelope in the careful writing of an elderly hand.

"You don't have to share it with me." She takes the food into the dining room.

I open the envelope and unfold the paper.

A Fhearghuis, a leanbh na páirte,

Bí láidir; ná tarraing céim siar. Is treascairt na tragóide é an crann greamaithe.

Tá grá agam duit,
Mamó

I fold the paper and tuck it back inside the envelope. The message repeats itself in my head. In Irish, then English, driving itself home in every way possible.

Be strong; do not retreat. A destiny embraced is a tragedy overcome.

And now I know. The decision of where Liv and I move is made: we stay in Black River. We won't flee. We'll face this war head on. And we will win.

CHAPTER 28

LIV

Tara places winnie and Will's plates on their little table in the corner, and Trey brings an extra dining room chair from the basement. The food circulates; everyone digs in without needing an invitation. It's too natural. Too easy. A normal family eating a meal as if it's a daily occurrence. I fit here like I belong, like they were made for me. Or I was made for them.

It makes the unwelcome thought that I can't seem to subdue feel like even more of a betrayal. Dillon could be at our house right now, and I'm so close. I could confront him. Tell him I know what he did. Tell him it's over. Slam that door that seems to keep inching open on its own and never look back.

"When you want to talk to me, pick up a damn phone." Trey is stabbing his finger in Tara's direction.

"I wanted to tell you in person."

"Not that. The night before we left. You did it again."

"No, I didn't." She twists in her chair to look at Winnie. "I told her you were coming that day. She and Will were both so excited you were visiting again—"

"She can do it too? Ninety-nine point nine percent of my thoughts are not for little girls."

Christian snorts a laugh. "No amount of therapy would undo that kind of damage."

"You don't need to worry," Sloane says. "She can't see anything you don't show her."

"She can come in without my permission," Trey says.

"Yes, but that's it. She's approaching you, nothing more. It's similar to walking up to someone on the street. You can say hello, but you can't make them say hello back, and you can't make them tell you their secrets. Just ignore her. She'll lose interest soon."

"You think she's capable?" Tara asks Sloane.

"Of course," Sloane says, smiling at Trey. "And you're the first person she sought out. You should be honored."

"What a family of freaks," Christian says.

"Look who's talking," Tara snaps, leaning briskly forward on her elbow like she's about to reach across the table for him.

Christian's gone wide-eyed again. He glances at Trey then back to Tara. He's probably going to need some time before he can get used to their resemblance.

After breakfast, I help Tara clean up the table. I want to ask her where she got the bruise on her eye she's carefully concealed under heavy makeup, but I figure Trey already gave her a hard time when they were in here alone together, and I don't want to bring it up again.

"I have nothing to wear to the funeral," I say while drying dishes.

"I already have it covered. No pun intended." Her somber face brightens. "Fearghus and Christian too."

I stare at her, trying to prepare a response. Am I supposed to know what she's talking about?

She cocks her ear toward the ceiling. "That's my cue. I'm taking a bath before all the water runs out." Before I can speak, she's out the door and heading up the stairs.

Glancing through the doorway to the living room, I catch sight of everyone but Trey, so I go upstairs to our room to find him fresh out of the shower and clean-shaven for the first time in a long time.

"What happened to Tara's face?" I say.

"What about her face?" He furrows his brow.

I bite my tongue. I can't believe he didn't notice.

"What?" He's growing more impatient by each fraction of a second.

"Oh, nothing." I try to sound casual as I see a sequence of events transpire in my mind. What happened to Tara's face is the only thing that could have happened to her face to make her want to cover it up. It would have remained her secret, if I hadn't brought it up.

"Liv." He's taken hold of my shoulders, and I know the only way to make this situation worse is to lie to him.

"She's wearing all that makeup."

"Yes. Makeup." He stares into space as if he's just found the answer to a puzzle. He releases his grip.

"She's covering a bruise." I give it all up. Why draw it out?

"A bruise." It clicks. He practically rips the door off the hinge, and I hear him stomping down the stairs, then back up, followed by heavy banging on the bedroom door at the end of the hall.

The click of the doorknob, the sound of it opening. "What?!"

Even though I can't see them, I know he's grabbing her face to examine it. Feet shuffle and clothes rustle, and she most likely shoves him away.

"Yeah, get over it," she says.

"Get over it?!" he yells. "So it was him?"

"I don't have to tell you anything."

Clothes rustle again, and she gasps, "Stop it!"

"If you're not going to tell me, I need to make sure that's what I think it is before I kill him." His voice has gone quiet in that way it does when a line's been crossed, when someone's just bought a death sentence.

"Don't you dare. This is none of your business."

"It's none of *your* business. Now it's my business, with him. You're out of it."

I sit on the bed. Silence draws out, and I know they're staring each other down. With a sharp intake of breath, her voice comes again, only this time it has lost all of its confidence, all of its threat. It has broken.

"Fearghus, please don't. I can't take it. It's all too much." Her voice fills with tears. Her crying is muffled by what must be his embrace.

The door closes with a soft click. No matter how much pleading she does, he won't be swayed. Christian will have to talk to him. I know Trey would think he was doing her a favor by killing her abusive ex-husband, but it'd only serve in multiplying Tara's grief right now.

I pass their soft conversation and go down the stairs to the living room. Will has Christian on the floor with him building a tall tower of blocks, and Sloane is braiding little Winifred's hair.

"Uncle Fearghus is mad," Winnie points out as soon as she sees me.

I suppress a laugh at this simple statement. My first response is to tell her he's always mad, and that we should only start to worry when he's not.

"He's okay," I say instead. "He was confused about something. He's better now."

"Doubt it," Christian mutters.

"I told her it was futile to hide it from him," Sloane says without looking up from her braiding.

"Christian, you have to talk to him."

He groans and casts his gaze to the ceiling. "Why does it always have to be me?"

"Because you can sell anything."

"I might be on his side for this one."

"Oh, no you're not."

"Afraid I am. Ever since I missed out on the rednecks, I've been pining for some action." The block tower falls, and he and Will cry out with exaggerated disappointment and start on a new one.

"What happened?" I ask Sloane.

"Tara came home from an errand yesterday and he caught her on the street. She said some things she probably shouldn't have said. She's under a lot of stress."

Christian turns toward her. "*I don't care what she said*—"

Sloane raises her eyes to him. "She knows she shouldn't be speaking to him. Sometimes, the strong thing to do is walk away. Some fights don't need to be won."

"It doesn't make it right."

"Of course not. But it could've been avoided." Sloane fastens the end of Winnie's braid and sets her down on her feet. "There. You look like a princess. Play nicely so you don't ruin them."

Winnie selects a book and climbs into my lap, her blonde hair braided around the crown of her head like a tiara of golden strands. She must be the spitting image of Sloane when she was a little girl, only with caramel swirls in the trademark Bevan green of her eyes.

"So when is this shindig?" Christian leaves Will to his tower building to join Sloane on the couch.

"We'll leave after lunch." She takes Christian's hand in her lap. "When are you coming home?"

"From here."

"Aaron could use you right now."

"I know."

Heavy footsteps descend the stairs, and I open Winnie's book to the first page and start to read. Trey goes out the front door in his coat without a word, and as I turn the page I give Christian a pointed look. Christian beams and shrugs. It's a lost cause. I should be glad he isn't going with him. We don't need both of them in trouble.

Tires squeal outside, and I don't have to look to know the sound is coming from a black Camaro peeling away from the curb. His intentions seep from his every action. Not that he would ever try to hide them.

When I finish Winnie's book, I slip out from under her to go upstairs and check on Tara. I tap her bathroom door. "Tara?"

"Come in."

She's standing in front of the bathroom mirror with her face washed clear of all the makeup and a purple bruise around her eye.

"Fearghus and I match. What an absolute joke." Her eyes are still red from crying. "My makeup ran. I have to redo it all."

"Want me to do it?"

"Don't you ever get tired of taking care of people?"

"Never. Do you have a stool?"

She leaves the room and comes back a few minutes later with a stool. I move aside so she can sit on the toilet.

"You spend all your time taking care of other people. You'd help other people before you'd help yourself."

"I enjoy it."

"And I wonder how my brother survived so long without you."

"He didn't need me. He was immortal."

"Yes, physically. Mentally? He was a mess."

Taking note of her use of the past tense, I remain silent. I have nothing to compare to his current mental state except the short amount of time I knew him before he woke up from the coma. During that time, I was in a bad place myself, and anything I witnessed would've been skewed by my own depression.

"He still has his faults. He just stormed out of the house." I leave it at that. I don't want to open the wound again.

"He promised me he wouldn't kill him."

"He promised?"

"I don't know why I care." She must not understand the magnitude of one of Trey's promises.

A comfortable silence forms, and I embrace it with the relief gained from that promise. One less death on his hands may seem insignificant when compared to all of them combined, but somehow, it matters. It may not matter to him, but it matters to me.

"There." I stand up and step back. "I can make it darker if you want."

She examines my work in the mirror. "It's perfect. There's no way to erase it completely." She takes her hair down and brushes it out. "The person I didn't want to see it already knows. If anyone else notices, I'll just tell them someone insulted Fearghus and I had to stick up for him."

"Good plan. I need to stick up for him all the time. He just can't throw a punch like he used to."

She smiles at me in the mirror and I pick up the stool.

"Do you know a good divorce lawyer here?" I ask.

She takes the stool out of my hands and walks it into her bedroom. "The one I used was pretty good." She sets the stool down and crosses her arms, facing me. "You know you'll probably have to take him to court. You'll have to face him. Are you okay with that?"

"Yes."

"Did you talk to Fearghus about this?"

"No."

She raises her eyebrows. "Do you think maybe you should?"

"He's already said it's too much paperwork. He doesn't care we're both still married to other people. And he's not going to want me to have any interaction with Dillon."

"Then why bother? It's really messy, believe me."

I look away. Explaining it to her will get me the same result as explaining it to him. They think too much alike. It's a waste of words on either of them.

"I just want a clean break," I say, for lack of anything better. "I want my old life behind me."

"Okay, I'll give you his name, but I'm not involved in this. Fearghus is already after me. I don't need to give him any more reasons." She takes a notepad off her nightstand, writes a name and phone number, and hands me the paper. "Be glad you don't have kids with your ex."

Where would I be right now, at this very moment, if I did share a child with Dillon? If our baby had lived? The likely answer is our own red brick Chicago house, not far from here, with its cute urban garden out back and a fireplace in every spacious room. His wedding gift to me, my name wasn't even on the mortgage. I'd be back to working part-time at the hospital like I'd planned, leaving the baby with the nanny he'd planned to hire. I'd be at the ballet studio three times a week. I'd be working on my doctorate. And Dillon would be taking his regular business trips to cheat on me with Kate.

"Liv?" Tara reaches for my arm.

"I want a clean break," I repeat.

"I know you do. Let's go downstairs. There's no use in dwelling on this now."

As soon as Tara and I settle in downstairs, the front door opens and Trey enters. All eyes shift to him. Oblivious to all of us, he takes off his coat, throws it over the banister of the stairs, and walks into the kitchen. Christian, Tara, and I all look back and forth between one another, silently deciding who's more suited to confronting him.

"God, fine!" Christian gets up. "Yo!" he says as he goes into the kitchen. "Give it up. Damage report."

Trey's answer is too quiet for us to hear, so I get up and go to the doorway to eavesdrop. Christian walks into me.

"He went there. No one was home." Sensing my relief, he adds, "Don't get your hopes up. He won't give up that easily."

"What am I going to do without her?" Tara asks suddenly.

Sloane puts her arm around her. "Things will fall into place. Don't worry."

Tara lowers her head onto Sloane's shoulder and lets out a long sigh. "What about the kids? Who's going to watch them when I'm working?"

"Quit," Trey says, returning to the room. "You don't need to work."

She raises her head. "Neither do you."

He drops to the couch next to me. "I work because I get bored. You won't get bored with two kids to watch. You can't stay here anyway. You won't survive without Mamó's foresight."

"I'm pretty sure I can stay—"

"That phone call you made to the house. They'll trace it, and they'll find you. And now you'll have no warning."

"There's no reason for them to trace one random phone call," Christian says. "You're so paranoid."

"Paranoid? Says the guy who was affected for how many years?"

I cringe. Those words apply to me, too.

"You're coming with us," Trey says to Tara. "You're moving to Black River."

"No I'm not."

Trey leans forward. "You don't have a *choice*."

"Fearghus," Sloane says. "Please."

"Where's my father?" Trey asks Sloane for the second time today.

"He's staying with some friends downtown."

"The address. I need to see him."

"I'll give you the address tomorrow. You need to focus on other things today."

Tara leaves the room. She returns, carrying a pile of heavy brown fabric.

"It's going to take me a minute to figure out whose is whose," she says, dropping the fabric on the arm of the couch next to me.

"This one I know is mine." She sets one piece aside. "Máthair." She hands one to Sloane. She holds another one up and looks at me. "This one was Mamó's. It's yours now."

I take it, lay it across my lap. Unsure what it is exactly, I don't know if I should take something of Mamó's.

"Fearghus, this was our father's." She hands one to Trey, who is now staring at Sloane. "It's yours now." Tara lays it on his lap when he makes no effort to take it from her.

"And this last one should fit you, Christian. Aunt Enid brought it. It's an extra of Gareth's. He's about your height."

Christian stands so Tara can hold it up to him. As the length of fabric falls to the floor, I recognize the shape of a long cloak. A simple lace on the chest, like on a shoe. Long, wide sleeves and a hood.

"Perfect," Christian says. "But brown? My god, couldn't you people have picked a better color?"

"We Bevans like to blend in, not stand out like the Moores." Tara keeps it to a careful tease.

So this is why it doesn't matter what I wear. We'll all be covered head to toe.

Trey finds his voice. "Enid and Gareth. What's with the Welsh names?"

"Bevan is Welsh," Sloane says.

Christian bursts out laughing.

Trey doesn't seem to hear him. "But we're Irish."

"We are. Our ancestors fled from Ireland to Wales and took a Welsh name to cover their identity."

"So much for making fun of my taste in beer," Christian says.

Trey withdraws. I know the signs too well now. I grope for his hand and hold on, wishing I could pass a thought through skin. This wasn't deliberately kept from him. Sloane must have a reason she couldn't tell him.

"The Moores are Irish," Trey says, more to himself than anyone else.

"They are." Sloane pauses, studying his expression. "*A chroí*, these are things I couldn't disclose, for my safety and yours. Please understand how it pained me to keep these things from you."

"I understand." He clears his throat as if to purge the roughness from his voice. "It's not your fault. It's *their* fault."

"It's no one's fault. It's how it had to be."

"*Their* fault." The roughness hasn't left, and he makes no effort to subdue it this time.

Sloane doesn't reply. She must know anything else she says will only provoke him. Tara folds the two remaining robes which must be Will and Winnie's due to their size. Winnie breaks the silence. "Mama, who is the pretty lady who came here?"

Tara squats in front of her. "I don't know, sweetie. What did she look like?"

"She had a long white dress. Can I have a long white dress like hers?"

Tara appears to be at a loss for words. She looks to Sloane for help.

"When was she here, Winnie?" Sloane asks.

Winnie furrows her brow and tightens her lips, looking up at her mother.

A loud crash jars the room, and Will giggles so hard he falls into a sitting position with his tower of blocks scattered around him.

Forgetting her question, Winnie joins her brother to start the construction of a new tower.

"I'm trying to remember the last few people who came over," Tara says. "There have been so many."

"How long before we leave?" Trey asks.

Sloane glances at the clock. "A couple hours."

"Then we have time to work on Christian's protection." Trey holds a hand out to Sloane. "*A Mh*áthair, we need your help."

Everyone stands but me. "I'll watch the kids. Tara, show me what you have planned for lunch, and I'll get that started."

Tara takes me into the kitchen and Trey, Christian, and Sloane disappear through a door leading to steps into the basement. When Tara joins them downstairs, Christian's voice rises from the stairwell. "Dude, is this sick or what? She has the exact same setup as you. What a bunch of freaks!"

CHAPTER 29

TREY

Máthair and Tara make Christian and me look like a couple of amateurs.

"I think I'm just getting in the way," Christian says, stepping back. He must be feeling as incompetent as I am.

Tara and Máthair make eye contact and something unspoken passes between them. They probably have some high-level psychic thing going that Christian and I could only dream of mastering.

"How are you going to wear this?" Tara hands Christian the tiny packet. "I'll see if there's something you can use in Mamó's room."

She climbs the stairs and we all follow her.

The charm Tara finds clicks in Christian's fingers, opening to reveal a hidden inside compartment. "Anyone who sees this is going to know exactly where I got it." Christian closes the spell packet inside the charm and hands it to me.

"That's why we added Discretion," Máthair says.

The charm is marked with the symbol from my amulet. I apply pressure to the sides, and it clicks open. Liv stretches to see over my arm. I close it and pass it to her.

"How do you open it?"

I take it from her, show her, hand it back. She tries again.

"You won't be able to open it, Liv," Máthair says. "Only a Bevan can open it."

Liv does a silent *Oh* and hands it back to me.

I nod toward Christian. "He can open it."

"He can open it?" Tara asks. "I was wondering about that."

"I'm not taking it," Christian says.

"Don't be ridiculous. If you're Bevan enough to open it, you're Bevan enough to have it. Here." Tara holds a heavy silver chain to Christian. He shakes his head.

I hand her the charm and she hangs it on the chain and fastens it on him. He ignores the whole thing.

"I'm giving it back," he says without looking up.

"You can give it back," Tara says. "When you're done with it."

I remove the page of notes from my back pocket.

"Fearghus, wait," Máthair says. "Let's wait until we have more people. The more who join, the stronger it will be."

Shit, I am stupid. And getting stupider by the minute. We're about to be surrounded by the largest group of

Bevans that's ever gathered, as far as I know, and I'm not thinking to take advantage of it. I start to put the page back in my pocket but Tara holds out her hand.

"I can make copies upstairs."

I find Liv in our room later, rummaging through her bag.

"What should I bring?" she asks without looking up from her search.

"Nothing. You're only supposed to bring yourself."

"Is my Chapstick allowed?"

Her innocence draws an unwilling smile out of me. "I think I can get them to bend the rules for you."

"Good. But you're going to have to carry it. I have no pockets." She hands me her Chapstick, and I stick it in my pocket. "You're not bringing anything?"

"Nope."

"Not even a gun? I don't believe it."

I chuckle. "They'd crucify me if I brought a gun there."

And there are two SIGs stashed in my car because of course I'm bringing a gun there.

She opens her mouth to say something but decides against it.

"What?"

"It's really none of my business."

"I'll be the judge of that."

She sits on the bed. "Why don't you and Tara need to work?"

I sit next to her. I'm surprised she doesn't know this already. "My mother's been secretly funneling money into bank accounts in our names since we were kids."

"Their money?"

I nod.

"Why?"

"Never asked."

She takes a few moments to think this over. "Because they killed your father?"

"Christian just said that the other day. But he thinks my stepfather is behind it, that my mother couldn't do it on her own."

"*Could* your mother do it on her own?"

I shrug. Why question it? Yes, it's their money, but that's why I only use it for guns and motorcycles and Camaros. I don't live off it, even though they do owe it to me for killing my father. But can my father's death be measured with money? It's not the kind of payback I'd ever accept.

"Anything else?" I ask, elbowing her to catch her attention.

"Nope. Mystery solved." She leads us to the hall and down the stairs.

"Christian rides with me," Tara announces, putting a coat on an impatient Will.

I get my robe and Liv's robe off the couch. "*A Mh*áthair, you're with us." I open the door for her.

I help Liv into the back seat and Máthair into the passenger seat then walk around the back of the Camaro.

"Lead the way," I say to Tara as she and Christian buckle Winnie and Will into the back of her Honda CR-V. I get in the Camaro and reach under both front seats to confirm the two stashed SIGs are fully loaded.

"*A Fhearghuis…*" Máthair scolds, turning away to look out the window.

Tara escorts us out of the city, deep into rural Illinois on a two-lane highway crossing through farmland until we make a turn and thick forest sweeps in on both sides, tight against the road. When she signals to turn off, I can't see the dirt road until we're right on it.

"Have you been here before?" I ask Máthair.

"Yes."

She leaves it at that. There's something in me that won't allow me to ask more.

A solemn air has overtaken the car. After thirty minutes of uneventful driving on the dirt road through the trees, we round a turn to an unexpected clearing that's serving as a parking lot for at least a hundred cars.

"Wow," Liv breathes, giving voice to my thoughts.

Tara adds her CR-V to the mess, and I pull in beside her. We share a glance through the window, and the pain in her face becomes a rooted pain of my own.

Out of the cars, we all shed our coats and put on our robes. I free Liv's hair from under the heavy fabric, and she looks up at me like an angel.

"How does it feel to have crossed over to the dark side?" I ask.

"You should've asked me that a long time ago." She holds my gaze until I break under the need to kiss her.

Everyone's dressed except Will, who's more interested in picking up every rock he sees. Christian and Tara wrestle him into his robe then Christian lifts Will to his shoulders, letting him keep a rock for each hand.

Tara and Máthair step out of their shoes, and I squat to remove mine. Liv is looking very confused.

"We go barefoot," I say, standing up.

"My feet will freeze," she whispers from behind her hand.

"No, they won't. I wouldn't ask you to do it if that were true."

"I'm not magic like all of you."

"That doesn't matter."

She holds onto me for balance and removes her shoes and socks. Máthair takes Winnie's hand to lead the way. Tara falls in step with Liv and me.

"Did you explain any of this to her?" she asks.

"I'm as much in the dark as she is. I only know Moore funerals."

"Well, I only know Catholic funerals," Liv says, as if to prove I'm more in the know than I'm admitting.

"Are you freaked out?" Tara asks Liv.

"Not yet. Should I be?"

"Not at all. This is an ancient tradition, and it's actually become very tame over the centuries. We wear robes to disguise ourselves from the spirits, so when the spirit world opens, we blend together, and the spirits don't notice us. There's only one person they should notice today."

Liv nods slowly, a bit unsure. She must think we're about to sacrifice a goat.

"That's the story, whether you believe in spirits or not."

"Why are we barefoot?"

"To ground us. To connect us to the earth."

I take Liv's hand. Our path narrows, forcing us single file. I pull her behind me through the old forest, holding limbs back for her to pass. We round a bend and come upon a massive oak tree conquering its space, at least one hundred feet tall and fifty wide, the lowest limbs too high to even think of climbing. Around it, bare dirt, like no living thing dares take residence so near. As we walk under its fiery-leaved canopy my palms tingle, power transferred through earth into flesh like a backwards lightning rod. Whether I want it or not. My vision flexes, clears, a lens shifted into place to brighten shadow, deepen color, heighten detail.

"Cool, huh?" Tara says.

Christian's rubbing his hands together and grinning like a madman.

And Liv—she's taken two quick steps away from me. I should take her hand for reassurance, but damn, I'm afraid I'll electrocute her. The power's so strong and steady there's an ebb and flow to it. Feeding me, drawing away, synching to my bloodstream, my heartbeat. Making me a part of it. I'm both god and pawn at the same time.

Liv looks about ready to bolt.

"It's nothing you haven't seen before," I tell her.

"Yes it is. I've never seen you look like that."

Although I feel the magic coursing through me it shouldn't be visible from the outside. So I'm not sure what she means.

Tara hands me a wreath of woven oak leaves. After passing another to Liv, she points to the one on her own head she's now wearing as a crown.

"What the—" Christian says.

I turn the wreath over in my hands. This is new to me.

"Oak leaves are sacred," Tara says to Liv. "You have to wear it. You'll feel out of place once we join everyone else if you don't."

Christian and I look at each other. Liv places hers on her head and looks up at me.

"Come on, boys." Her eyes move from me to him. "This is your tradition, not mine, and I'm willing."

Through an unspoken agreement, Christian and I put ours on at the same time.

"It suits you," Liv says from her wary distance from me.

I go to her. "You look like a Druid priestess." I trace her bottom lip. If she can feel the might of the elements inside me she makes no indication.

Still eyeing me, she takes my hand. We continue down the path and step onto warm earth. Liv's head jerks up to look up at me. She stops walking.

"I told you," I say.

"How did the ground get warm?"

"They affected it. Special occasion."

She looks at her feet. Then back up at me with the same awestruck expression.

"Kid, you are heavy," Christian says when we catch up to them. He sets Will on his feet, and Máthair pauses for Christian to join her. She takes his arm.

"Doing okay?" he asks.

Our path is guiding us toward a hum that I soon recognize as human conversation, voices becoming sharper the closer we get. When the path dumps us into a clearing, I'm not prepared for the assembly of people who all grow quiet and gawk at us as we approach. There must be hundreds. Many more than the amount of cars predicted.

"Holy crap," Christian says under his breath.

"Too tight," Liv whispers, and I ease my deadly grip on her hand.

With this amount of people, there could be countless enemies among us. Any one of them could've been followed, including us. My SIGs are in the car. I could conceal them under my robe. But there's no fucking point. I don't know any of these people. Any one of them could ambush me, and I wouldn't have time to wrestle a weapon free. I'm better off with bare hands.

We stop several yards from the edge of the first line of people. It's impossible to blend with a crowd when every set of eyes is focused on you. They seem to expect one of us to say something but it sure as hell isn't going to be me.

A white-haired older man steps forward, kisses Tara's cheek, and takes Winnie out of her arms. He turns toward the crowd. "Carry on, everyone, you'll all get a chance to meet them."

Muffled voices sound around the crowd.

"Oh my god, I'm fucked," Christian whispers, turning to look at me.

Before I can answer, Máthair drags him into the crowd which parts for us like we're royalty. My feet carry me forward on their own. Bodies press in behind us, erasing our wake. The only escape is up. Without Liv's touch, I'd be shoving through the opposite way and disappearing into the trees. Faces pass, and I analyze every one of them. The few that eye Christian get carefully dedicated to memory.

Now's not the time. I can always find them later and explain the situation the easy way.

The hum of conversation returns, and we stop in the middle of the clearing. The white cloth draped over Mamó's body draws our attention as it should. The only bright object in a sea of brown-clad people in the woods. Tara makes a little gasp and I reach for her, spinning her against me without dropping Liv's hand. Máthair's strong stance tells me this vision won't break her. Christian remains at her side, speaking too softly for me to hear. From the motion of his lips, I know it's our language.

"Fearghus," Tara says, wiping her eyes. "Where are my babies?"

Will and Winnie seem captivated by the old man who greeted us. Tara pushes away from me toward them, and several people from the crowd come forward to seize her in their comfort.

"Not you, too." I wipe Liv's tears with my thumb.

"Sorry. It just happens."

Christian comes to stand next to us and I see Máthair become engulfed by the crowd.

"Now I know what it feels like to be the prey," Christian says. "These people are going to eat me alive."

"Let them try."

"Who *are* all these people?" His eyes dart from face to face.

"Hell if I know."

As if to answer our exchange, a woman steps toward us.

"Fearghus," she says. She sounds just like Máthair. "I'm your mother's sister. Your Aunt Enid. I've waited so long to see you again. You've changed quite a bit since the last time I saw you."

She grasps my hand, studying me for a long moment as I remain silent.

"And Christian." She moves her hands to his. "I never knew a Moore could be so handsome. Sloane continues to brag about the good man you've become to this day."

He answers her with his token lady-killer smile.

"Liv," she continues, "we're honored to finally have you. You and Fearghus are people of legend. Stories of you will pass down to children and grandchildren until the end of time." She places her hand on Liv's belly. "*Mo bheannacht ar do leanbh.*"

Liv raises her eyes to me as Aunt Enid hugs her and says, "I'll give you up. There are a lot of people here who want to meet you."

The crowd has thinned. People have spread throughout the clearing and finally I can breathe. Having a decent amount of air around me is a welcome change. Tara comes up, her expression lifted.

"Relax." She clutches both my arms. "I can sense your tension from all the way over there. This is the one place in the world you can lower your guard."

"That's not a concept he understands," Christian says. "But that's okay. I'll need him when all these people stop being polite and decide to skin me alive."

A loud voice bellows from behind Tara. "Who invited the Moore?"

The owner of the voice is broader and heavier than me, but when I grab his collar I know I could have him on the ground in the blink of an eye. I'm in his face, daring him to make a move and give me the pleasure of shutting him down.

As he lifts his arms in surrender, I hear Tara's voice in my ear. "Fearghus, stop! Let him go!"

Christian yanks me off him and shoves me back. "Dude, it was a joke. Get a grip."

"It was a bad joke."

The man chuckles. "Well at least you live up to your reputation. I'm Gareth." He offers a handshake, and my reflex is to take it.

Christian shakes his hand after me. "Gareth. Thanks for the loaner."

"No prob. I figured you wouldn't want to show up in Moore red."

"Good call." Christian gives him a high five.

Well, it looks like Christian made a friend. I search the nearby faces for Liv. If she gets away from me in all these people, I just might lose my mind. I spot her about a hundred feet away and surrounded by a group of admirers. A pulse rushes down me, to my bare feet then into earth. Our eyes meet across the field. She says something to the woman nearest her, something else to another, and she's walking toward me. She places a hand on my chest. The worry in her face chills my blood. The only thing that could be bothering her here is me. I think I need a breather.

"Hey." Christian elbows me. "Who are they?"

I turn back to him and follow his gaze to two blonde women standing nearby.

"Our cousins," Tara says. "Shannon and Alis. We have a lot of twins in the family."

"Twins." Christian drums his fingers against his chin. He turns to me. "So, I'm not blood related to any of these people, right?"

The question is rhetorical. I don't answer him.

"Shannon!" Tara hollers, and one of the women turns. They both head toward us.

"God, don't encourage him," I say.

"He needs to get acquainted with everyone," Tara says.

Both women take turns placing their hands on Liv's belly and saying, *"Mo bheannacht ar do leanbh."* I hope Liv doesn't mind because this will go on all day.

"Shannon and Alis," Tara says. "This is Liv, Fearghus, and Christian."

"We already know your names, but it's nice to meet you," one of them says.

"So, who is who?" Christian looks from one to the other.

"I'm Shannon."

"I'm Alis."

"And how do I tell you apart?" Christian asks.

Oh, here we go. I look sideways at Liv. She bites her bottom lip, trying not to laugh.

"I have a scar on my hand." One of them extends her hand toward Christian to have a look.

"Ah." He takes her hand and holds it. Gets a long look. His eyes narrow then dart back to her face. She laughs and pulls away.

"So you're Christian," the other one says. "Is that your middle name too? Like Fearghus?"

"It's my first name."

"What's your middle name?" one of them asks.

"Maximillian," I answer for him before he can come up with a lie.

"Christian Maximillian Moore?" the women chant together with identical raised eyebrows.

"Yes," he grumbles, giving me a look that says I'm going to pay for this.

"So you really are a Moore?" one of them says as if she already knows the answer. She just wants him to confirm it.

"Yes. I am a Moore."

"Moores are *bad*," she teases.

"Yes." The lady-killer smile reemerges. "Moores are very bad."

"You've created a monster," I say to Tara and tow Liv away before I throw up.

When I get Liv away from the crowd, she stops and turns to me. "What is *bheannacht*? What do they keep saying?"

"Blessing."

"My blessing on your child?"

"Yep. And get used to it. You're going to hear that five hundred times today."

CHAPTER 30

LIV

"ARE YOU OKAY?" I know he's not. He's so ramped up it will take an elephant sedative to get him to calm down. "Do you want to go sit somewhere quiet?"

"Let's find the food first."

He takes my hand and leads me through the crowd, ignoring all the mesmerized stares that would impede a normal person's progress. We stop in front of the largest assortment of food and drink I have ever seen in my life. At least ten long folding tables with brown tablecloths. Fruit, bread, and cheese on the nearest. Down the line I see casserole dishes, cookies, cakes.

Noticing my amazement, he says, "It will all be gone by noon tomorrow."

"Tomorrow?"

"We spend the night here."

"Spend the night where?" I search around us for a tent, a cabin, any evidence of overnight shelter.

"On the ground." He grins, waiting for my reaction.

"What if it rains?"

"It won't rain."

"Everyone sleeps on the ground?"

"Yep."

"Communal sleeping. All these people. You can't even sleep during a rainstorm."

"We can find a quiet spot."

"Why didn't you warn me?"

"You didn't ask."

I punch him in the arm and pick up a plate. He gets one for himself and follows me down the tables. "Who brought all this food?"

Trey spins around, lightning fast. And just when I thought he was calming down.

"Everyone but the most closely bereaved," says a man behind me. "Fearghus." It's the man who first greeted us when we arrived. He reaches out to shake Trey's hand. "I'm your Uncle Arthur. The last time I saw you, you were tucked inside your mother's arm. What did those people feed you?"

Trey says nothing. I wish he'd put away the cold glare. These people are his family. His *real* family. But I'm afraid that word—family—has a different feeling for Trey than it does for me. Family is something I've always longed for. Family is something he's spent his whole life trying to escape.

But it doesn't change the fact that right now, he's being a complete pain in the ass.

Uncle Arthur kisses my hand. "Liv. An honor."

He returns his attention to Trey. "Your father was a good man. We all loved him like a brother." He pauses to look down at the ground, take a long breath. "I know your mother doesn't talk about him. It's easier for her that way. But if there's anything you'd like to know, I'll do my best to answer."

"I don't need to know anything," Trey mumbles, looking past him to the sea of cloaked people.

"I understand. Just remember, in case you decide you do." He squeezes Trey's shoulder until Trey returns his eyes to him. They share a look. For a second, I see Trey soften like he's going to take Arthur up on his offer and ask one of the many questions he must have. His jaw sets, his eyes go hard and cold again. He has an opportunity to learn any-thing he wants about his real father. Instead, he's going to be stubborn about it.

Arthur squeezes my arm and returns to the crowd.

Trey's eyes are far away, so I tug his arm until he snaps out of it and leads me into the woods behind the tables. Low-growing plants tug at the hem of my cloak as I try to avoid rocks and branches. Walking barefoot in the woods isn't the easiest task, especially when carrying a plate mounded with food. The hum of the crowd grows fainter with each step, and just when I begin to wonder if he's ever going to stop he wades through some underbrush to a clear spot on the ground.

I follow him and sit, crossing my legs under my heavy robe. The warmth in the ground radiates under the material, giving the effect of sitting in a heated bubble. He sits the same way, facing me, and we set our plates on our laps. A large limb hangs over us like a roof. The sun is low; one side of the sky has started to grow dark.

"Should we be this anti-social?" I take a bite.

"Yes." He opens his water and drinks half the bottle. "I'm considering staying out here for the rest of the day."

"You'll be awfully lonesome."

"Are you cold?"

"Not at all. Why is the ground warm all the way out here?"

"It stops right there." He points about twenty feet beyond us.

"How do you know?"

"I can see it."

"You can? No you can't!" He's playing with me.

His sudden smile gives him away, and I throw a carrot at him.

He picks up the carrot from the ground and pops it into his mouth.

"Nice. You just lost all kissing privileges for the rest of the day."

"As if you have the power to control yourself."

I want to tell him he's one to talk, but the thought falls into the hole where that sickening doubt lives. Neither one of us has had the power of control ever since the night the stars aligned. That spell is what's at work here. Attraction this strong isn't human. Without that spell we'd have nothing, we'd be nothing but strangers who hate each other.

Whatever he sees on my face has faded his smile, made him go still, put that brooding look in his eyes. I can't bring this up here at Mamó's funeral. The pressure to keep it locked up is even stronger now that I see I'm some kind of celebrity. My chance has slipped far away, like when you wait too long to ask someone to remind you of their name. There's a point when questioning something just isn't right anymore even if the question burns brighter with each day. So I bow my head and eat. I feel his eyes on me but I can't look at him. He goes back to eating, silently watching me while I pretend not to notice.

"We need to go back," I say as soon as we're done.

I stand. He stands next to me and takes me by the shoulders. Of course I look at him. It's what that move provokes. But if he thinks I'm going to offer anything he's wrong. He'll have to draw it out of me, something we both know isn't going to happen. Words aren't his specialty, and it shames me to use that weakness against him.

"Wrong way," he says when I take a step in the wrong direction.

But I continue until my bare feet settle on frigid ground and my lungs fill with the chilly air. It surprises me how quickly my whole body turns cold. I step back onto the warmth. "You're right. It stops right here."

"Say that first part again. You need to get used to saying that."

Spoken so dryly, it's humor with a bitter edge. Words straight from the mouth of the Trey I first met, the one who could piss me off like no person ever has. Cocky, arrogant, rude and unapologetic. Total asshole. I see a glimpse of that man—I remember him. He's eclipsed by the man

I love. That's something I need to hold on to. I know him now, inside and out.

I return to his side. "How'd you know? For real, this time."

"I can sense it. It's…"

He leaves the sentence to hang and I don't press him. We walk back to the big clearing. He doesn't hold my hand this time. He tosses our trash then heads to the large coolers at the far end of the food tables. If I wasn't familiar with his drinking routine, I'd feel like I was the one driving him to drink. Hell, maybe I am. I'm just not sure how to fix it.

"*Mo bheannacht ar do leanbh.*"

I focus on the face in front of me. What follows is an endless stream of people, all so pleased to meet me, so kind, so warm, I think I might have their warm-the-earth spell figured out. It seeps from them, into the ground, such high compression of power it radiates right back. Like Tara said, they do blend in—cloaked in brown from shoulders to toes, heads topped with orange autumn leaves. They're smaller, mobile versions of the trees that surround us. The event starts to feel more like a wedding than a funeral, and I'm the bride, receiving an unending line of guests. My groom stays by my side, occasionally stepping away for another beer or being pulled away by people taking him to meet others.

When Sloane's familiar face advances toward me, I reach for her in reflex, driven by my relief.

"Holding up all right?" She takes both my hands in hers.

"Yes. Are you?"

"Of course." She turns away from me to look at the people around us.

"It's unlike any funeral I've ever attended."

"That's a good thing, I hope? This is how it's always been."

"And we spend the night here?" The darkening sky has bled to the opposite horizon. Stars twinkle in the east. Torches flicker around the perimeter of our gathering space, filling the air with the scent of burning oil.

"We spend her last night on earth with her, and then we release her to the spirit world."

A firm hand slips around me to cover my belly, and a voice whispers in my ear. "*Mo bheannacht ar do leanbh.*"

I raise an eyebrow as Christian steps around me.

"What?" He fakes surprise. "You'll take everyone else's blessing but you won't take mine?"

"Be serious, *a chroí.*" Sloane hugs his arm, pulling him next to her in submission. "Can't you ever be serious?"

He straightens his face, only to lose it in an abrupt smile. More people approach, offering their blessings and their greetings, shaking Christian's hand and hugging Sloane. When Trey rejoins us, the line of people has another hand to shake. Remembering names and faces became impossible a long time ago, especially with everyone dressed in the same brown cloak. Some have raised their hoods, their oak leaf crown holding it tight above their eyes. It's beautiful. Magical. I believe in these people.

Tara distributes sheets of paper through the crowd. She comes to take Christian by the arm, pulls the charm from under his robe and has him make a fist around it. As if on cue, every voice in the clearing chants the words to seal Christian's protection. The intensity of the joined voices chokes me, stings in my eyes. Yes, I believe in them. Maybe they can make me believe in me and Trey.

When the chant ends, Christian curses and drops the charm. He flaps his hand, stops to blow on it. I see the concave triangle inside circle motif burned cherry-red on his palm.

Tara raises his hand to the crowd over his head and my eardrums throb with everyone's applause, hoots, and whistles. Gareth steps forward to grab the back of Christian's neck. He says something to Christian I can't hear, and Christian laughs, taking his hand in a rough handshake.

"I'm going to leave you," Sloane says when Christian returns to our group. "I'll see you all in the morning." She gets a kiss on the cheek from both Trey and Christian before disappearing into the crowd.

"Man, I *cannot* figure out where I've seen Alis. She's so familiar to me," Christian says to Trey.

Trey shrugs. "She's not familiar to me."

Christian makes a fist and brings it hard against his lips. "It's driving me nuts."

"Why just her? They're identical."

"The scar."

I yawn, and Trey catches it. "Ready to call it a night?"

"Ready when you are."

"Where are you sleeping?" Trey asks Christian.

"Hopefully between two blondes." He slaps Trey on the back and saunters off.

"Glad to know you're having no trouble fitting in," Trey hollers to his back, and Christian raises his hand behind him and flips his middle finger. Trey looks at me. "You saw that, right? So I'm not going to feel bad if they kill him in his sleep."

Trey and I wander through the clearing, catching a few hugs and handshakes while we look for a quiet spot to call our own for the night.

"I think we're going to have to go back into the woods," he says.

I groan. I'm not thrilled by the thought of sleeping without cover in the woods.

Trey takes a candle from one of the tables. We end up in a little clearing similar to our lunch retreat except there's nothing blocking our view above. There's a perfect tunnel through the tree limbs, a skylight opening to midnight blue sky.

"I don't think I can have sex with you in the woods, if that's your plan." I sit on the ground next to a fallen log.

"Oh yeah?" He doesn't sound convinced. He sits facing me, sets the candle beside us. "You had sex with me in the woods in Virginia."

"No, *you* had sex with *me*. I wasn't conscious, remember?"

"You were conscious," he says as if there's no argument against that whatsoever. "You heard me talking."

Flashes of that day jolt my brain. I close my eyes. The smell of the rain and wet earth. The warmth of his skin. The sound of his voice, far away yet so clear, like a beacon aimed straight for me. The feeling of leaving my body, rising, feeling lost, until he brought me back.

His gentle lips on mine return me to the present, and I lift to my knees, my hands on his rough cheeks, meeting his kiss and lingering there.

I open my eyes and break the kiss, lean away. He gazes up at me for a drawn-out moment and I get the sensation of a jab in my gut. That brooding look from earlier has returned. He's going to ask me what's wrong, and I can't lie to him now. I want to sink down and back away. I'm not worthy of any of this—of the attention from his family, of my responsibility to them, of how much he cares about me even if it is the result of a spell. But I'm frozen on my knees above him, shackled by a question I don't want him to ask, an answer I must give but don't want voiced in this place.

He raises his eyes to the sky above us. "Look," he whispers.

I let my head drop back. Layers of stars framed by darkness of foliage in deepest shadow. Without a frame, a perspective, we'd be swimming in them. They'd be twinkling around us, close enough to touch. A balmy breeze jiggles the branches above, stirs my hair. Carried on the wind is the burning oil from the clearing and the moist fragrance of the woods. I look down at Trey. He's chosen to spare me. To leave things be. To sanctify this moment, this perfect snapshot of time. Kindness seeps from him when it truly matters. He's my hero.

He slides his hands around the backs of my thighs and tugs me onto his lap, my knees still folded against the ground. He removes my crown of oak leaves then removes his. The breeze touches us again, snuffing out the candle. He pinches the wick and it relights. The flame dances, threatening to go out again. He passes a hand over it. The flame stills.

"I was a little afraid of you earlier, when we came upon that tree and you—"

"You don't need to be afraid of me."

"It just caught me off guard. You looked so different. So…feral."

"Feral is different? That's a good thing, I guess."

"Well, a different kind of feral. I'm used to the rip-some-body's-throat-out feral. I'm just not used to you lighting candles with your fingers and…"

"And what?"

I shrug. He's aware of how little I know about what he can do. There's no use in proving it. I lift his hood. It casts a shadow on his eyes but leaves his mouth lit by candle-light. He must be watching me watch him, as I imagine what he can do with that mouth.

"You can't resist," he says.

"Do you like that?"

"You have no idea." He draws me against him.

When he rises to his knees against me and lays me back against the ground, I know we have set something in motion neither of us can stop, and I forget everything but him and the unrivaled brilliance of the stars above.

The rising sun wakes me. I turn over to find Trey lying on his back, hands behind his head, eyes open to the pink and orange sky. I sit up and stretch my arms above me. "Strangely comfortable."

"I love it."

"You would." I finger-comb the leaves and pine needles out of my hair.

"The moon is still out." He sits up with me and points to the moon in the darker part of the western sky. "We need to go back. They'll need my help."

As he pulls me up, something slips down my chest and drops against my feet. I kick the bottom of the cloak aside. My amulet and its chain lie on the ground. Trey picks it up, and I turn around and hold up my hair so he can fasten it in place.

"The clasp is broken." He hands it back to me. "Must have broken last night. Tara will have another chain you can borrow until we can get this fixed."

"I have no pockets, remember?"

He pockets it and takes my hand. We return to the clearing where half the bodies are up and moving around while the other half still clutter the ground. Trey takes a handful of green leaves from one of the food tables and puts them in his mouth. He offers me a handful. "Mint leaves?"

He pours two cups of coffee and makes a plate of assorted breakfast foods. We find a place to sit and share breakfast off the same plate. When we're finishing up, Christian whistles at him across the clearing.

"Okay," Trey says, standing up. "You'll be on your own for a while."

"Are you coming?" Trey asks Christian when he nears us.

"Yeah. It's me, you, Gareth, Adam, Tommy, and Brock." He casts a look around us then jabs Trey in the arm. "Hey. Get this. Alis, right? She lures me into the woods last night and has her way with me. At least I think it was Alis..." Christian rubs his chin then shakes his head like it doesn't matter.

"Only you would use a funeral as an excuse to get lucky," Trey says.

"It wasn't my fault! It was her! And all this holy-oak-be-damned Welsh beer!"

"I thought you liked Welsh beer."

"I do." Christian nods happily.

Trey touches my arm. "We'll be back."

"Where are you going?"

"Burial plot. Not exactly sure where. Deeper into the woods. Can you survive without me?"

In their absence, I lend my help to pack up food, gather trash, and break down tables. People keep taking things from my hands, eliminating my tasks like I'm a princess trying to work among villagers. Or maybe they're all hopped up on tree magic, and they feel sorry for the only non-magic person here.

When Trey and Christian return, they're carrying their cloaks. Dried mud cakes their feet up to their ankles, lines of sweat streak through the dirt on their faces. They clean up, scarf lunch, and we all head back to the cars after a million goodbyes to all the people who still remain. When we get to the end of the footpath, half the cars are missing from the makeshift parking lot.

"Wait." Trey drops my hand and pushes ahead of Tara and Sloane. "It's that fucking car."

Tara gasps, covering Will's ears. "Fearghus! Watch your mouth!"

Christian slides past to stand next to Trey. They seem to be watching the parking lot for any sign of life and I get an awful thought: sniper. Start shooting now and we'll all be dead in seconds. We'd never see it coming.

"Everybody stay here," Trey says.

Tara catches his arm. "Wait. There's nothing here that could be a threat. Calm down."

"That car has been stalking me for fifteen years."

"That's the car?" she asks, looking toward the gray car that Trey has followed again and again only to lose it every time. The car that found me at work one day, but left before Trey had a chance to get there. The car that Trey was chasing the day he ran his truck into me, the day we first met.

"Whose car is that?" He grabs her shoulders.

"I don't know." She makes a visible effort to stay calm.

Footsteps and voices sound on the path behind us, and Trey pushes past me to the end of our line. Gareth and one of the blonde twins appear from around a bend. I catch Christian's eye. I mouth her name, *Alis*? He sizes her up. Nods.

"Gareth," Trey says when they're close enough to hear. "Who drives the gray Acura?"

Gareth and Alis look at each other for a long moment, then Gareth nods to Alis and she nods back. He turns back to Trey. "I do."

Trey's fists clench, and Christian elbows past everyone to join his side.

"Mind telling me why you've been stalking me for fifteen years?"

"We had to know when Liv found you."

"Who's we?"

"All of us." Gareth looks at Alis again for some kind of confirmation. She takes a measured look at Christian. "Something had to be done when she found you, and we didn't know when that would happen. So I had to keep watch."

Trey's chest fills. He's taking in air, trying to calm himself down. He glances sideways at Christian.

"I'm sorry," Alis says to Christian. She reaches, changes her mind, withdraws her hand.

"Sorry?" Christian deepens his frown.

"I thought you were like *them*. I thought it would be easy. But you weren't like them. You were such a nice guy. So…" She eyes our entire group and seems to decide to hold back the details. "I feel so bad we had to trick you."

"Trick who?" Trey's attempt to calm down doesn't seem to be working. His agitation is about to reach a dangerous level. "Somebody better explain something really fucking fast."

When Gareth and Alis don't jump in, Trey spins to face Tara as if he just realized she must hold some blame in this puzzle.

"Tara knows nothing about this," Gareth says. "Neither does Aunt Sloane. You only have us to blame. Or thank." He grins at Trey but gets nothing friendly back. "Okay. What we knew was this: when Liv found you, someone's loyalty would be in question. Not hers but the person closest to you. And if that loyalty wasn't restored, the prophecy would fail. It's all built on this complicated series of events, things relating to other things… It needed him. You know?"

Trey says nothing. Neither do I. I'm too overwhelmed by the truth of it. These past few weeks would have been very different without Christian. And going back further, Christian's visit to bring news of Kate being alive set a series of events in motion: Trey's decision to go to Richmond, my almost-death, his act to save me.

Gareth's nodding at us, like he can hear our thoughts. "So when we were sure Liv had found you, Alis and I went to Richmond for Christian, baited him to a hotel room, and used an effect that would restore his loyalty."

"I'm so sorry," Alis says again to Christian.

"I knew it." Christian takes a step toward her and points a finger in her face. "I *have* met you before. I remember you."

"There's no way you can remember me."

"You screwed up." Christian hugs her hard. "But it doesn't matter. I'm just glad I finally figured it out. The Glass Beacon. About a month ago."

"Yes," she gasps, shocked.

Christian looks at Trey. "I woke up the next morning in a hotel room. I just thought I had a rough night. But I knew I had to tell you about Kate and Aaron, so I went back home, packed a bag, and took a cab to the airport."

"That's the day you came to visit Trey? When you and I first met?" I ask.

"Yes," Christian says, still looking at Trey.

Trey turns to Gareth. "So I don't have to kill you?"

Gareth laughs. "You can if you want, but you'd have no reason."

"I don't usually need a reason." And just like that, all hostility has vanished. "But I've seen you since then. Since Christian came clean."

"I had to make sure we were successful," Gareth says.

"Why you?"

Gareth shrugs. "I thought it'd be fun."

"And you?" Trey asks Alis.

"I thought I'd be sticking it to a Moore. But like I said, he wasn't what I expected. He's nothing like a Moore."

She and Christian share a long look. "I guess that's a compliment," he says.

"I apologize for the games. And deception." Gareth chuckles. "You're a good driver. Just not as good as me. I knew to avoid you at all costs when you were riding that sport bike."

"You should come for a real visit sometime."

"I will."

"Family of freaks," Christian says. "Let's get on the road."

We pile in as we did before—Sloane up front, me in back, Christian riding with Tara. Trey follows Tara down the long dirt road, to the highway, toward Chicago.

Sloane breaks the silence. "Gareth is a good kid. Alis, too."

"You knew nothing about this?" Trey asks.

"Nothing."

"Whose kids are they?"

"Gareth is Enid's son. Alis and Shannon are Arthur's."

"My father is buried out there," Trey says abruptly. "His name was Fearghus Donnelly?"

In the pinched quiet, I'm afraid to move. Sloane stares out her window. The pain in her stillness is hard to miss.

Trey drops back into contemplative silence and remains that way until we hit the Chicago city limits.

"We're going to have to leave soon to get you back in time for work on Monday," he says to me in the rear-view mirror.

"I called Abby yesterday. She said she'd take my hours through Wednesday."

"You're not going to have a job to go back to."

I look away from his eyes in the mirror. He may be joking, but I know he's right. I can't take off any more time. If things don't settle down, I'll lose the one normal thing I have: my job. I look ahead and notice Tara's CR-V is missing from my view through the windshield, so I look out the back window to find them behind us. From Christian's gestures I can tell he's telling one of his stories, and Tara leans forward, laughing against the steering wheel.

We turn onto Tara's street, which seems abnormally full of cars. Trey pulls to the curb a few houses down from Tara's and kills the engine, but makes no move for his door and neither does Sloane. When Trey takes a sharp breath in, I look at his face to find his jaw clenched and his eyes narrowed at something in front of us.

On the street ahead is an idling black limo, double-parked in front of Tara's house. A woman in a long white coat open in the front stands on the sidewalk. Tall, dark-haired, and as beautiful as a fairytale queen, she assesses the house as if she's planning to burn it down. Kate.

Sloane places her hand on Trey's arm. "Wait. She could be leaving."

"I don't wait." He shoves through the door, slams it behind him.

A few long strides take him to the limo where he yanks open the rear door to check inside. Kate turns on the sidewalk to face him. He checks the front of the limo then steps right up to Kate, into her face. His mouth does not move. Words are not necessary. His expression and body language speak volumes.

Kate's back is to us, but it's obvious she's speaking. I imagine her southern drawl wrapping around Trey's name in that disturbing way it does. She takes one step forward. The cold glare I wished he'd put away at the funeral has been shot up with steroids. And I realize what had been missing from it earlier: intent. So far he's made no move, but I know that expression. It's the look of a man about to strike.

Seconds tick by—him frozen in full rage, her talking away. She takes another step forward, white-gloved hands rising toward Trey's face but he's still frozen. Just when I think she has him in a powerful trance, that she's wielding some sort of power over him, he jerks her forward by the arm, drags her up the porch stairs and inside the front door.

"What do we do?" I say.

Sloane remains quiet, watching the closed front door. I twist in my seat to look at Christian and Tara behind us who are both staring after them in the same manner as Sloane. With the gun Trey stashed under his seat in my hand, I fold the driver's seat forward and open the door. I make it around the car before Christian has my arm.

"I'm going in!" I jerk my arm away.

"If you're going in, we're all going in." It's a shock to see so much of Trey in his expression. "Don't move." His face, his voice, shackle me to the ground.

Sloane joins my side while Tara and Christian unbuckle the kids.

"I'll take them upstairs." Sloane takes Winnie and Will by the hand.

Christian, Tara, and I look at one another for a moment frozen in time and then storm the house like the front line of soldiers going into battle.

CHAPTER 31

TREY

WEAPONS AREN'T NECESSARY. I'll kill her with my bare hands. Her death is so close I can taste it.

"Oh, how perfect. You're all here," she says, turning away from me.

They shouldn't have come in. I don't want Liv and Tara to see this. It won't be self-defense. "Go upstairs."

"I was just telling Trey that I wanted to have a chance to talk to Tara before they dispatched the two men here. It was hard to get here so—"

I grab her shoulders. "Do not speak to them. It's you and me."

The baby tucked in a sling on her chest stirs, but I keep my hold.

She sighs. Tilts her head. "Get control of yourself, Trey. I'm just here to talk. They don't even know I'm here."

"I'm not here to talk." I push her away from me and take a step back. I need a new strategy now. I have witnesses.

She looks at me like she used to when she's about to twist things. "It doesn't have to be this way."

"You need to leave," Liv says from the other end of the room.

"Everyone needs to go upstairs now," I say to them, my attention still on Kate.

"I'll walk her out." Christian takes Kate by the arm.

I'll let him get her outside before I follow her. He moves her halfway to the door when she stops in front of Liv. Then I'm next to them but Christian shoves me back with more force than I'm used to from him. I raise my palms, give him a look to cool it. A fight with him will only get in the way of what I need to do. He needs to step off.

"Calm down," he says, and we both look to Kate as she speaks again.

"Dillon tells me you were an orphan. You know nothing about your family." She pauses, but Liv doesn't respond. "I didn't want to be the one to tell you this, but it's very possible you and Trey are closely related. Perhaps you should look into it while there's still time. For a termination."

The motion is so quick I barely catch it—Liv slapping Kate across the face with the back of her hand. Tara seizes Liv by the arms and my back slams into the wall at the far end of the room.

"Get her out of here!" Christian yells, turning away from me. He shoves me against the wall again as I try to break free.

Kate places her hand against her reddened cheek. "I wish you could know how easy you just made this for me." She takes a few steps toward the front door before turning back to Liv. "He only wants you for the child. He'll never love you like he loves me."

A growl escapes me. I struggle against Christian. He rams me harder against the wall but loses his grasp, and I make it to the door just as it closes behind her. The doorknob comes clear off in my hand. I didn't expect to tear apart a door, but that's what I do. The damn thing won't budge.

A gentle hand settles on my arm and I look down into the eyes that hold my serenity.

"Don't let her do this to you," she says.

Tara closes the shade on the front window. "She's already gone."

"Shit!" Christian punches the wall.

"Everybody needs to come in here and sit down. Before you destroy my whole house." Tara pushes Christian into the living room out of our sight.

I back into the staircase, drop to the landing, pull Liv toward me by her hips, and bury my head against her belly. My mind shifts to a different wavelength where time stands still.

"God, Trey. Your knuckles." She tries to pry my hands loose but I keep my hold on her. Right now it's all I have.

"Let's go to the living room where it's more comfortable." Her body slides against my face, and I open my eyes to find her kneeling on the step below me. She places her hands on my cheeks, her eyes darting between mine, inches away. I have no idea how long we've been here.

She stands, and I allow her to pull me up and into the living room where I drop onto the couch. She sets a gun on the mantel and sits next to me. I focus on the coffee table, where the glass bevel meets the wood. I should've punched through that glass, thrust a sliver through Kate's heart.

Máthair comes into the room. "They're watching cartoons. They're both about to fall asleep."

"Did you hear all of that?" Tara asks her.

I feel Máthair's eyes on me, but I don't look at her.

"I never should've come. Fearghus and Liv's joining has given us so much hope it's made us careless."

"It's not that," Tara says. "You didn't bring them here. It was my phone call to you, to the estate. It's my fault."

"Who cares whose fault it is?" Christian says. "As soon as we leave, you and your kids are dead. We need to get the three of you out of here." He looks like he needs to punch the wall again.

"She's coming to Black River," I say. We already decided this.

"I cannot move to Montana!"

"You can, and you will." I stare her down. This isn't open for discussion. It never was.

She stands and picks up the phone. I get up and snatch it out of her hand. "Who are you calling?"

"I'm calling the guy who just fixed my doorknob. Apparently he didn't fix it the first time."

"I'll fix your *fucking* doorknob. Sit down." I slam the phone back onto the table.

"I won't listen to you speak that way again," Máthair warns in my direction. "We're all under a lot of stress. We must be careful not to take it out on one another."

"Winnie saw her coming," Liv says.

Everyone looks at her, and I sit next to her. It seems to be the only fixed position in the room. She's stable, stationary, while everything around her spins and collides.

"Remember? She asked about the pretty lady in the long white dress who came here. It had to be a vision. She didn't understand it hadn't happened yet."

Christian raises a finger. "Her white coat."

"Did she say anything else?" Tara says. "I can't remember."

"That was it," Christian says. "She got distracted." He looks at Máthair. "Did Kate see you here?"

"No. But we can't assume she doesn't know I'm here."

"Does Kate know something we don't?" Liv blurts. All eyes go to her, but no one answers. "About me."

She's sitting rigidly now, on the edge of the seat. The chaos swarming around her seems to have knocked her off balance. I take hold of her shoulders and turn her toward me. "Forget every word she said. They're all lies."

"How do you know that?" It breaks on the last word.

I lean down so my face is level with hers. "Because I do."

"Should we check into it?"

"No."

She looks down. "But even you said our minds are similar. That the mind share is never that easy." She blots her eyes with her shirt. "I don't know why I'm crying. I think I'm overwhelmed."

"Our minds are not similar for any reason Kate would understand." I clench my jaw to keep from screaming. Kate's running free, coming to Tara's house, spewing lies. I should have dealt with her by now. I need to get my shit together and finish this.

"What if it's true?"

"It's *not* true," Máthair says. "Our prophecy wouldn't bring you together under the circumstances Kate insinuated. It's a blatant lie, designed to shake you, to make you question your purpose and drive a wedge of uncertainty between you and Fearghus. You must trust in each other, as you always have."

I get up to walk off some energy. Liv was my only vulnerability before today. Now I have Tara and the kids to stash somewhere for a few days while I take down everyone in Virginia. And Máthair. I have no idea what to do with her. "I'll rent a truck. Christian and I can have you packed up in a day."

"Fearghus…" She covers her face with her hands.

"Tara, you aren't safe here anymore," Máthair says gently.

"That doesn't mean I have to move to Montana!"

"Move to Richmond." Christian gives a sly smile. "They'd never expect that. And I could protect you."

"Not unless you're with her twenty-four seven," I say. "And it'd make it too easy for them if they did find her."

"I could hire someone to watch the house. Or a bodyguard," Tara says.

"Unless that person is me, they wouldn't be good enough."

"Well, aren't you cocky."

Christian squeezes her shoulder. "Yes he's cocky, but he's right. If you hire someone you're just setting up another innocent person to be killed."

Liv leans forward. "What if you just come to Black River for a visit? Just for a few weeks. No commitment."

Yes—a visit. Why didn't I think of that? It will just be a very long visit. I'm not going to let her leave.

"It'd be good for you to have some time off right now," Liv continues. "We have an extra house. You can have a whole house to yourself."

I keep my eyes on Liv even though it's Tara's turn to speak. She's come up with an indisputable argument. She knows Tara needs a vacation, and she's used this as our solution. Always recognizing what other people need before they recognize it themselves.

"Settled," I say before Tara can speak. I drop to the couch next to Liv.

Tara rolls her eyes. Stubborn, but she knows we've won. It's going to take her some time to admit it. By then we'll have her house packed into a rental truck.

Liv suddenly grips my knee and leans forward.

"What?" I ask.

She has a strange look in her eyes. She said I looked feral before. Now it must be her turn. She glances around the room, hesitating on Christian. His eyes widen. He clutches Tara's armchair, fingers buckling fabric. He and I both must need to release some energy.

"I…don't feel right," Liv says.

"Do you want to lie down?" I stand to offer the rest of the couch.

Christian brings a pillow for her head and hovers over her, watching her like she's about to do something. When I catch his eye, he runs a hand through his hair.

"I'll get her some water."

Liv's gaze follows him out of the room. When I sit on the edge next to her, she startles.

"Are you hungry?"

"I don't know." She stares at me, frowning a little. Confused. Like she doesn't know me.

"It's probably your pregnancy," Tara says. "Did you have any nausea the first time?"

"I was sick for months."

"There you go." Tara heads toward the kitchen. "I'll whip something up."

Christian returns with a glass of water, which he hands to me then goes up the stairs without a word.

As she drinks the entire glass, I remember I wasn't supposed to kill Kate. If they hadn't come inside when they did, Christian would be pretty upset with me right now. Maybe I should write it on my palm. A cheat sheet: *Don't kill Kate.*

Tara hands Liv a mug.

"I think I'm okay now." She takes the mug.

"Drink it anyway."

She takes a sip, then another. She folds her legs under her on the couch and pats my arm. "Don't look so worried."

After a good look at my face, she laughs. I wonder if Tara has any liquor in the house.

We'll need to leave soon. I have two matters of business here and my time is running out. I run a hand down Liv's arm. "Will you be okay if I'm gone for a few hours?"

She nods over her mug.

"Máthair, I need that address."

Like the flash of inspiration, I have it. Guns still stashed in the car. I wouldn't mind a drink, but it will have to wait.

"Don't do anything stupid," Tara says to my back as I head to the front door.

The doorknob's missing. I pick it up off the floor. The screws must be stripped. I tore the whole thing, screws included, straight out of the door. The mechanism inside the door is stuck, so I give it a calculated slam but it still won't budge.

"How do I get out of here?" I call. "Front window?"

"I completely forgot," Tara says. "Those windows don't open. You'll have to go out the back and through the gangway. Your key will also work the back door."

I check my pocket for keys and find Liv's amulet on its broken chain. "Do you have a chain Liv can borrow until I can fix this?" I hand her the amulet.

"I can find something."

"Get it on her right away."

There's freedom in the air outside. Kate's visit left a residue in the house I'm glad to be away from. I need to know her hidden agenda. There's no reason for her to precede their first attack of Tara's house. To warn us of their knowledge of Tara. Even though it looks like she saved Tara and the children's lives, things don't happen that way with Kate, not even by coincidence.

I lower the window in the Camaro and revel in the calming wind, trying to keep my foot easy on the gas. I need to find out how long they've known about Tara. How they found her. Why they didn't kill her sooner, and why they're ready to kill her now.

The address jumps out at me, and I reverse down the street and into a parking spot at the curb. I reach under my seat for the stashed SIG but find nothing. I take off my seat belt and lean further into it. Liv must've taken it. A good instinct for her, but it doesn't help me out now. I reach under the passenger seat and find the other one, relieved to have the backup on this shitty day that might be about to get worse.

I stick the gun in the back of my pants and get out of the car. The doorman greets me. "Can I help you, sir?"

"I'm here to see a guest of a resident in the penthouse. Martin Moore."

"May I tell him who's visiting?"

"His son."

He leads me to a reception desk and picks up a phone. I analyze the lobby while he calls upstairs for me, not happy they'll be warned but there's no easy way around it. "Elevators are around the corner to your left, sir."

"Next time you see me you'll forget I was here." I slide a fifty on the counter. He thinks it's simply a bribe, but it's more than that. A token we both believe in, a medium to carry a spell. Money's convenient like that. If I leave the building a different way it's not going to work but it's the best I can do right now.

When the elevator opens on the top floor, I go to the only door and knock. A smiling older woman answers. "You must be Trey. We've heard so much about you. Come in." She steps aside to allow me inside. "I'm Regina, one of your father's oldest friends." She doesn't offer a handshake and neither do I.

"Can I get you something to drink?" Her complexion's too dark to be family unless she married in. Italian blood, maybe. I'll need to see her husband to be sure they're not Moores.

"No, thanks." We're not near the kitchen or the bar, and I'm not trusting anything she pours while out of my sight.

"Your father's in his room. We're so thrilled you could visit." She takes me down a hall. So far, so good. They may not be a threat after all. But I can't let my guard down until I'm out of this building.

She stops in a doorway and taps on the open door. My father appears.

"Be sure to come out and visit us before you go." She's just about laid a hand on my arm when I look sideways at her. She changes her mind.

I wait until she's out of earshot then turn to my father. Only a few weeks have passed since I last saw him but he seems to have aged several years.

"Trey, I'm glad you came. Come sit."

His walk is slow and careful, like he's nursing a sore muscle. I follow him to a sitting room and we take seats facing one another.

"We were worried when you left that day," he begins.

I glance away, hoping to cut off what could come next. I'm not here to talk about that day. "You don't need to worry about me."

"I know we don't, but we do. It's our job." He turns away to look out the wall of windows beside us. "How's your mother?"

"Fine." It comes out angry. I owe him more than this. "She's happy, considering..."

He faces me and smiles. "I knew she would be. Tell her to take as much time as she needs. We can cancel Vancouver, if she wants. Maybe if she hears it from both of us she'll give in to her needs for once."

"I can't convince her to do anything she doesn't want to do."

He laughs, jerking me back to the time when I heard his laugh on a daily basis. "I think you have something there."

"You've met my sister?"

His guard goes up. "Yes."

Looking away, I shake my head, unable to hide the disgust. My stepfather, a born and bred Moore, a direct relation to the same people who are killing my family members one by one, knew about my sister before I did. Spent time with my sister before I knew she existed. I take a deep breath and look back at him.

"Every time we went, I knew it was a bad idea. But I couldn't deny your mother. She asks so little for herself. When I have an opportunity to indulge her I can't resist."

"Why?"

"Because I love her."

That answer leaves me with more confusion. "Why?"

He turns back toward the window. "I loved her the first day I laid eyes on her."

"She was an enemy. Taken prisoner."

"As were you. And when I saw her that first day, with you, I knew I had to help her. I went blindly along with everything they did until that day." He nods at the window. "And that day, my eyes were wide open. I was only twenty-five years old." He leans back against the chair and folds his arms across his chest. "It wasn't without their resistance. It was a complicated game, Trey. To my surprise, they didn't throw me out on the street. But it's been a struggle the entire time."

"They didn't care you married their enemy? Their prisoner?" I struggle for better words, but nothing fits.

"They cared. Most of them got over it with time. Many of them figured it was better that way, that it would make it an easier transition for you to become one of us."

I lean forward, put my arms on my knees, and stare at the floor. "Did you train me, knowing I'd revolt? Knowing I'd someday be against them?" I look up for his answer.

He studies me for a few seconds before looking away. "I did what I thought was right at the time. I had no agenda." He turns to me and leans forward. "You have always been a son to me, and you always will. I raised you as I would have raised my own. And that's all I have to say about that."

He stands, pours two glasses of liquor, and hands one to me as he sits back down with his. We drink together in silence, both staring out the window at the city below us. Metal and glass jutting from the ground, sun reflecting, blue sky beyond.

When I finish my drink, I set the empty glass on the coffee table. "I can no longer hold you accountable for anything they've done."

He hears me but remains staring out the window.

I continue without needing his reaction. "Thank you for taking care of my mother, even though she was who she was." I pause, raising my eyes to the ceiling to gather the evasive words. "And I respect you, and thank you, for raising me as your son."

He makes no response. I stand. He sets his drink down and stands with me.

"I'm glad you came." He offers his hand, which I take without hesitation. He walks me to the door. "I'll tell them you had to go," he says, saving me from an agonizing conversation with his friends.

"I owe you."

He smiles. I don't remember him looking so old.

The same doorman's at his post. I raise a hand to prompt a look into my eyes. He waves back, blinks hard. Done. His memory now a non-memory, but I suppose it doesn't matter since I didn't leave any bodies.

On my way back to the Camaro I stop on the sidewalk. Pennies in the shape of a peace symbol are concreted into the slab under my feet. It's a hand shoving into my brain, ripping a memory out of a box. I was a little kid, not sure what age. Much closer to the ground. My father at my side—just me and him. Days outside the estate were rare then. I look up and there's that music store we'd spend hours in, hunting for something perfect for my mother. Not in the racks. In the crates they'd drag from the back just for him. It's a power my father has over people. So normal to me, I never recognized it for what it was. I see it now. I wonder if he's wielded it over my mother. Or tried to—I doubt she'd let him.

I turn around and go in. A kid with a backward baseball cap and a lip piercing nods at me from behind the counter. I nod back. Posters cover the walls; the carpet is well-worn. Either it's changed too much or I remember too little. The store is narrow and long, and from where I stand all I can see for sale is vinyl. Not much good to me right now.

"Can I help you, man?"

"CDs?"

He jerks a thumb over his shoulder. I go through a doorway next to the counter into another room. It's newer, shinier, with modern-looking racks broken up by genre. I locate ROCK, walk down the alphabet to T and flip to Tool. There are a few albums I don't recognize so I pick the one I know.

There's another doorway at the far end of the room. I go through it, back to the older side of the store, and find the carpeted step I'd sit on while my dad went through those crates. He'd buy me baseball cards and ice cream. Hush money—a concept I understood but couldn't name. Everything about those trips was our secret. The places we'd go, the things we'd do, my absent mother. I'd always wonder where she was, but even my child's mind knew there were some things I didn't ask my father.

Now I understand why she cried every time we left this city. Why she ignored my father for days afterward. Why he allowed it.

And why they stopped bringing me here.

"Killer choice," the kid says, ringing me up. "A bit before my time but their newer stuff—"

"I don't think this will play in my car."

His head juts backward on his neck, like a chicken. He tongues his lip piercing, staring at me.

"I don't have a CD player in my car."

He's frozen in that position—neck back, tongue stuck solidly under his bottom lip pressing that metal stud outward. "Dude, we don't install—"

"I need you to put this on something that can play in my car."

He takes a step back, gives me a good look-over. "That isn't really part of the deal…"

I take five twenties out of my wallet and drop it on the counter between us. "Does that make it part of the deal?"

His eyes get big. He slides the cash over, pockets it with a sideways glance like he's just sold me drugs. "How old's your car?"

"Brand new."

"What kind of phone you got?"

I dig it out, show it to him.

He snickers. "That's not gonna help us." He collects a couple things off the wall behind him and I get out more cash. He rings it up. "You been living under a rock or something?"

"Haven't listened to music in a while."

"How long's awhile?" He cuts the thing I just bought out of the plastic packaging.

"Fifteen years."

He pauses to look me over again. "Don't they let people listen to music in prison?"

I don't answer him. It's a good enough excuse.

He pulls a laptop out of a backpack on the floor behind him. "Dude, you're gonna have way more space than just one CD worth." He opens the Tool CD and pops it in his laptop. "You've missed a lot in fifteen years. You like metalcore?"

I shrug. He takes a CD off a STAFF PICKS display on the end of the counter and sets it in front of me. The cover has a black and white image of the earth as a waning crescent, a fancy script below it. "These guys are Australian. And I've already got the MP3s on here so we don't have to rip it."

"Okay," I say. "What else?"

"Want me to hook you up?"

I end up paying for five more CDs, then I make him come out to my car to show me how to use the thing I just bought. The sight of my car has him convinced I was doing time for auto theft. Me stashing my gun under the seat has him upgrading it to murder. Then he won't get in the passenger side until I give him two more twenties. When I finally pull away from the curb, he's standing on the sidewalk like he just witnessed an alien encounter and no one's ever going to believe him.

The music's good. The hardest shit I've ever heard and it breaks something loose in me I haven't felt in years. The drums hit heavy and fast, and the speed limit isn't enough. I need to get home to Liv but she's in good hands, better hands than my own. There's something else I need to do.

I turn the Camaro onto the highway in the direction of his house. I may get lucky this time and find him home. He'll be wishing he was home the first time, when Kate's words weren't so fresh and this music wasn't so hot in my head.

CHAPTER 32

LIV

CHRISTIAN'S BAD MOOD radiates off him like an entity all its own. He takes the furthest seat from me, crosses his arms, and puts his feet up.

"It's not contagious," I tease. I peer into my empty mug. I'm not sure what I drank but it sure made me feel better. I set it on the coffee table.

"Yes it is," he mutters without looking at me.

"What's gotten you all bent out of shape?" He's too far away. I want him to come sit by me.

The muffled voices of Sloane and Tara's conversation seep in from the kitchen.

He leans forward in his seat. "What are they doing in there?"

"Come sit by me." I pat the couch.

He stares at me for a long moment then flashes an unexpected smile. "Why not?" And then he's next to me.

I rest my elbow on the back of the couch and turn my body toward him. He's glaring into the room like he's having a hard time with something.

"I need to get out of this house," he grumbles. When I don't reply, he looks at me.

I've never noticed the gray in his eyes. Brilliant blue lined with gray. Maybe I've never looked closely.

"You can't leave until Trey comes back." I smile at him in a way I'm not used to smiling at him.

He watches my face, and my heart skips a beat. Shocked, I turn away.

"What are you doing?" he says.

"Me? I'm not doing anything."

"Then what's wrong with you?"

"Nothing. What's wrong with you?"

"Nothing," he grumbles, turning to stare forward again. "I just need some fresh air."

"I need your help with something."

He groans. "This can't be something good."

"I need you to help me get Trey to agree to stay until Monday. Tuesday, actually."

His laughter bursts through his grouchiness. "Right."

"Come on. For me." The flirt in my voice seems inappropriate somehow, but I don't seem to care.

"Why?" He lowers his eyes down my body before he catches himself and looks abruptly away.

"I have an important appointment."

He closes his eyes and sighs a deep, extended sigh, dropping his chin to his chest. "Please tell me he knows about this important appointment."

"It's a lot easier if he doesn't."

"No," he snaps. "I'm not helping you. Sorry," he adds as if he just caught the coarseness of his voice.

I roll my eyes, and he watches me intently. I return my attention to him and cannot look away. He's running a knuckle between slightly parted lips, a gesture that's usually subconscious. Absentminded. But not this time.

"Liv." Tara startles me from the doorway. Christian leans back against the couch, and I sit up straight.

"What?" I must have missed her question.

"Are you done with your mug?" It comes out slowly, like she's repeating it, or thinking something else entirely. "I'm about to start the dishes."

I reach for it. "I'm done."

She crosses the room, holding Christian's eye the whole time.

"What?" He throws his hands in the air.

She gives him a thorough inspection before turning toward the doorway.

He sits up straight. "Wait—what did you give her in the mug?" He seems more than simply curious. He sounds like he's onto something.

She rattles off a few ingredients I don't catch, and he leans back against the couch, a finger to his lips.

"Is that okay with you?" Her tone is off. Hostility? Accusation?

"I'm not questioning you. I'm just curious. Shit." He waits for her to leave. "Total Trey moment," he says once she's out of hearing range. "Now we have two of them to deal with."

I put my elbow back where it was on the top of the couch. "So what did she give me?"

"You don't know?"

I shake my head.

"So, you just accept any strange drink anyone puts in front of you?" His eyelids lower, zoning in on me in a playful way.

"I think I can trust Tara." I give him a soft punch on the arm.

He catches my fist and holds it. I try to pull away, but he tightens his clasp. Footsteps travel down the hall toward the stairs, and he releases me, presses his body back into the couch, and props his feet up. "God, where'd he go? If he doesn't get back soon, I'm leaving anyway. I've got to get out of here."

"What's the big deal?"

"I don't know." He sounds genuinely confused. He rubs his face with both hands and moans.

A second set of footsteps follows the first up the stairs, leaving Christian and me alone together. As if someone flipped a switch, the air in the room closes in, crushes me, sweltering but without heat. A connection forms in my brain. The walls cave in.

I'm attracted to him. He was a brother to me once, but not anymore.

"God, why do they keep it a hundred degrees in here?" Christian tugs his shirttails out of his pants and starts to unbutton his shirt.

He can't do this to me right now. I twist away from him and stare straight ahead, frozen and afraid to breathe.

Will appears in front of us like magic, holding out his hand as if he has the most special present of all.

"For Uncle Christian. To put on Liv. Mama says." He drops the amulet on a new chain in Christian's palm and runs away, back up the stairs.

Christian studies the amulet. Sets it on the coffee table. "I can't put this on you right now."

"Why not?" I ask without looking at him.

The question hovers, and I wish I could take it back. I don't want to know the answer. I'm playing with fire.

"Because," he finally answers. "There's something wrong with me, and I need to get out of this house before I do something really, really stupid."

"There's nothing wrong with you." I turn toward him. Defined chest muscles under a tight white undershirt. I've seen him shirtless so many times, and it never affected me.

"Liv."

I raise my eyes to his. He releases a breath.

"You need to stop," he whispers.

There are no words for a reply.

"Because if you don't stop, I'm going to kiss you, and it would be the biggest mistake of my life."

"Do it."

His jaw clenches. My heart pounds in my ears. He shoves off the couch and walks across the room, stopping with his back to me. I imagine following him, stopping behind him, wrapping my arms around him and running them up his chest.

"What's going on?!" he says finally, spinning around.

When I don't answer, he comes toward me and sits on the coffee table, facing me. He puts his palms on his knees and leans into my face. "This ends, right now. Agreed?"

I nod, knowing it's the correct answer.

"Swear to me," he says.

I watch his face, his blue eyes with the gray outline, his perfect nose, the curve of his lips. Everything about his face is perfectly symmetrical. He should be a model.

"Liv…"

"Just once," I hear myself say. "Once, and it will mean nothing, and we can put this behind us."

"Are you insane?"

"An experiment." I need to know if my feelings are real, or if they're just a symptom of stress. More importantly, I need to know how his lips feel against mine. I can almost imagine it.

"When did—why is this happening? Have you felt this way about me the whole time?"

I have to think about that one. I don't think I have, but he's gorgeous. That's a fact. His charm only adds to the draw, and I've always loved him. Just not like this. Not in this specific way. Or have I?

"You've always flirted with me," I say instead of answering his question. "From day one."

He leans away from me to sit up straight. Taken aback, like a witness on the stand just caught in a lie. "I have but it was always a joke. It meant nothing. You knew that, and so did he." He looks away and rubs his fingers against his lips. "Don't put this on me."

With an icy jolt, I remember Trey. The most violent and jealous man in the world was never jealous when his cousin—the man who slept with his wife—flirted with me. He had no reason to be. The invading guilt tells me now he has a reason. My feelings have changed for Christian. Have they changed for Trey? Can I love them both? Now that Trey's isolated himself from the Moores, maybe it's not so bad. Why am I trying to rationalize this?

"You've been Trey's Liv. Nothing more." He rubs the back of his head. "Until today. We're both stressed out. We need to get some sleep, and everything will be back to normal."

I nod. But I don't want things back to normal. How can I have them both? Could we keep it a secret?

He drops back down on the couch next to me.

"Will you put my amulet on me?" The seduction comes out on its own. I am powerless against it. It feels so right, yet so, so wrong.

He faces me. His lips part, and the tip of his tongue touches his upper lip. "I don't just want to kiss you." He watches me closely, looking anxious—almost excited— for my reaction.

I become aware of myself leaning toward him, but I don't pull back. I love Trey. I can't do this with Trey's cousin. His *brother.* How can this be happening?

He takes my face in his hands.

"This is so wrong. But I can't help myself," he says.

"We can't do this to him." My blood pounds so hard in my head with every rapid beat of my heart that it seems to be emanating from me, vibrating the air around me.

"Stop me," he begs, his lips inches from mine.

"I don't want to stop you." The words trickle out on their own. I won't be able to stop at one kiss. I don't want to stop at one kiss.

The back door in the kitchen creaks open and closes, and Christian and I do the worst thing possible. We freeze.

Footsteps close in and stop. Christian lowers his hands from my cheeks and stands up to face Trey.

My words erupt. "I made an appointment with a divorce lawyer on Monday." Anything to distract him. Even that.

"You—what?" Trey says.

"We need to stay here until Monday. I'm going through with a divorce."

He takes off his jacket. I struggle to breathe. He comes to us, stops at the end of the couch.

"It's your watch." Christian steps toward Trey in the narrow space between the couch and the coffee table. "I'm out of here."

Trey moves aside too late, and Christian's shoulder catches Trey's with a force strong enough to knock someone my size down. Trey half turns, watching Christian's back with narrowed eyes. Christian snatches his coat and leaves without putting it on first.

Trey sits next to me. "I shouldn't have left you."

"Everything's fine."

"You don't look fine." He notices the amulet still on the coffee table and picks it up.

I hold up my hair. He fastens it around my neck.

"No divorce," he says. "You're not getting involved with him."

"I'm already involved with him. I want to end my involvement with him."

"No." He's trying to end the discussion.

Not if I can help it. "Do you want Dillon Moore to be our daughter's legal father?"

His head jerks up. I described him as feral before. It fits now more than ever. Just as I suspected, this idea had not occurred to him.

"He would not be."

"He would. I'm still married to him. When I have a baby, he'll be the legal father. At the very least, he'll be the step-father." Although I don't know the law specifically, I know this is a messy situation. I don't even know which state laws bind us. Montana, Illinois, or Virginia?

"But it's backward. A stepfather…" He loses the words to his thoughts.

"Is it worth arguing? Isn't it better to get divorced and not have any reason to worry at all?"

He knows he's at a loss. He remains quiet.

"The baby Kate had with her earlier today? You're his stepfather right now. You're probably his legal father. And I'm his stepmother. We're stepfather and stepmother to the same child."

"No you're not!" he yells into the room.

I take note of his use of words. He's only concerned about me. He doesn't care he himself is involved.

I remain calm despite his raised voice. "In a way, I am. The baby is Dillon's son. I'm still Dillon's wife. So…" I pause as he seethes. "I'm getting divorced. And you should too. I know being married to them means nothing to you, but it has legal consequences."

"He could never claim our daughter." His voice has gone dark.

"Is it worth the risk? The worry? I don't want her born into this mess. We need to make it right."

He doesn't answer. He must be digesting this new information. Should I bring up the worst part?

"If something happens to us," I begin, "Dillon will be her legal guardian. They could take her, and raise her, just like they did to you."

Still glaring into the room, he inhales through his teeth and then releases the breath so slowly I fear he's stopped breathing altogether. "Never."

I know my argument has been made. Any further discussion will only push him to the point at which he loses control. If he's not on my side now, he'll never be.

"What was going on when I came home?" It's a startling change of subject.

My heart pounds. I thought I'd gotten him past what he saw. "He wanted me to tell you about my appointment with the divorce lawyer." It's not an answer to his question, but it is the truth.

"So now you're talking about things with him instead of me?"

Shocked by the truth of his words, I look away. Christian was right to be mad at me. I should never use him to go around Trey. And I should never, ever go around Trey.

"I didn't want to upset you." My voice wanes under an overwhelming sickness. I've made so many mistakes. Betrayed him in so many ways. In the worst way. With Christian, of all people. If he finds out, he'll be so broken I doubt he will have the strength to kill us.

"I don't like thinking you can't talk to me."

"I don't like to upset you." It may be repetitive, but I have nothing else to say.

"Then stop talking to people behind my back." He turns to me, and his eyes soften when he sees the pain in my face I cannot hide. He wraps his arm around my shoulders and squeezes me against him. "Fine. Go to your appointment and get your divorce. But when it goes to court, I'm coming with you."

"It may not go to court."

"I'm done talking about this." He stands. "Where is everybody?"

"Upstairs."

He goes up the stairs but I remain glued in my seat, trying hard to absorb the tragic change that's transformed my entire world.

Kate's words resonate in my ears. *He only wants you for the child.* If it's true, my attraction to Christian could be my own desperate move. The reaction to being wronged. When did he first tell me he loved me—before or after we found out I was pregnant? As I search my memory Sloane's words emerge, beating Kate's words into submission. Kate is trying to drive a wedge between us, and as much as I hate to admit, it might be working.

Exhausted and confused, I lie down on the couch and fold my knees against my chest. It doesn't matter how I look at it—to validate my desire to cheat on Trey with his own brother is beyond wrong. I'm mixed up. Overwhelmed. So much, my mind is tricking me. I need to drive it out and away. All of it. Like an exorcism.

I open my eyes and find Trey beside me. He grips the back of the couch, his thick arm stretching over me as he leans down. "You missed dinner."

I sit up. "Where'd you go earlier?"

"To see my father." He sets a plate of food on my lap and leaves the room.

I stare at the food like it's poison. My stomach is a void, but I have no desire to eat. I go upstairs and lock myself in the bathroom. Stare into the mirror at my bloodshot eyes. I run a bath and submerge. Under the water, everything's too loud in my head. I'm made of concrete, and I'm sinking.

When the bath water cools, I know I should get out but I can't seem to muster the strength. I remain in the chilly water until my teeth start to chatter. Commotion in the hall conveys children going to bed, and when I finally leave the bathroom, the house is quiet. I put on the robe from the back of the door and go downstairs for Trey.

Every light is off downstairs, Trey nowhere to be found. When I return to my room, Christian's door opens.

"I thought you drowned in there." His grin washes away all evidence of his foul mood from earlier, but it also proves my attraction to him is still very real.

"Where's Trey?" I push it away. It feels so good but it's toxic. Foul. I wonder if the Bevans know how to exorcise a demon but there's no one I can safely ask.

"He left again on another mission."

My heart crumbles. The floor falls out from under me. I need him here. I can't trust myself without him. I go into my bedroom and sit on the bed. As if in a dare, Christian follows and sits next to me.

"I'm over it," he says.

"Good," I reply, knowing I'm not.

"Get dressed. I want to take you clubbing. You'd look hot on my arm. Can you dance?"

A thrill rises inside me. Like I'm sixteen, conspiring to sneak out of the house with a cute boy and stay out all night. Of course I can dance. He must not know this about me, or how much I miss it—to be lost in it, music around me like falling rain, the vibration of bass notes in the floor beneath my feet. It's too easy to imagine. No doubt he'd get us into some elite club. Bodies packing the dance floor lit by strobes timed to thumping electro. And Christian and me, moving to the music's pulse in the air, sweating, much too close.

"I have nothing to wear." Why didn't I say no? This is dangerous, especially since I can't tell if he's flirting like he used to, or flirting…for real.

He glances at the clock. "I'll take you shopping first. We have just enough time."

I watch his face. The two of us, out of this house, and no one would know. Is that his plan? I hope it is, because I don't want to admit it's mine. He said he wouldn't lie to Trey ever again. If we go out together, things are going to happen that Trey can't know about. And I can't ask him to lie to Trey. I already did, and it was wrong. "I'm sorry I tried to use you before. To help me get Trey to stay so I didn't have to tell him about the appointment. I won't do it again."

"I don't mind helping you. For most things."

"I know." I refuse to look at him. How could we have spent all that time together when Trey was sick, and nothing like this happened? Not even a hint whatsoever, and with all that harmless flirting. Maybe it's built up, surrounded us, too much closing in too fast and we can't get away.

Sensing his eyes on me, I look up.

He looks quickly away. "Just don't use me to avoid—"

"I know." I can't stand to hear him say it. "Too many people have already used you."

He laughs. "It's pathetic how easy I am, isn't it?"

I stare at my hands in my lap. "Not pathetic. It's just… you've had a lot of pain in your life, and you never get any acknowledgement. It all goes to Trey for what he's been through. But you've had just as much as him, if not more."

I've been thinking this for a long time, but I never expected to tell him. When he doesn't answer, I look at him. He's biting his bottom lip, staring at me with the same lustful expression he was hours ago.

"I don't know what's wrong with me. I was over this." He looks away and rubs his hands on his jeans.

"Well I'm not." It's a shockingly intentional flirt. I lean toward him to a closeness that could tempt him into only one thing.

"Stop," he says.

To my bittersweet satisfaction, he doesn't withdraw. He doesn't stand up. He doesn't leave.

"I have a very active imagination, and you are not helping," he says.

My crazed mind accepts his words as a come-on. I slide my hand onto his thigh. His eyes lock with mine then move to my lips that are inflamed with desire for his. Just like before, this is not going to end with one simple kiss.

"Liv, can I sleep with you and baby Sloane?" asks an angelic voice beneath me.

Winnie climbs into my lap without an invitation.

"That's the best idea I've heard in my life," Christian says. "And a great reminder. Baby Sloane." He's up off the bed now, shuddering, shaking himself off.

Tara appears in the doorway. "What are you doing out of bed?" The viciousness of her voice seems overdone for her innocent three-year-old, and as her eyes tear into me and Christian, I understand the real focus of her anger.

"Can I sleep with Liv and baby Sloane?" Winnie asks.

"If that's okay with Liv."

"I'd love for you to sleep with me." I doubt anyone's told her about baby Sloane, but I'm learning not to question these things.

Winnie climbs to the pillows and crawls under the covers. I wonder if she knows the tragedy she just prevented.

"*Christian*?" A Trey-grade warning, coming from Tara.

Christian follows her out without a look in my direction.

I turn out the light and get in bed. Winnie falls asleep in minutes. She must've woken from a deep sleep to come in my room. I lie in bed, listening to her sweet breathing, wishing I could fall asleep myself. My mind is running a marathon without my consent. I can't relate this to my struggle with insomnia—just can't do it. Once that connection is made, I'll be right back in its clutches. That mental connection, that surrender to it, is what feeds it.

After two useless hours of waiting, I admit sleep is not going to come. What I should admit is it's just like old times. Insomnia in a big old house. At least this one's not empty. I'm not alone. I get up, put on a robe, and head down the stairs. I sure didn't have any trouble crashing on the couch earlier today. Maybe that's all I need.

The streetlights from outside shine through the windows with enough brightness for me to see, so I go into the living room without turning on any lights. When I spot his blond hair, I turn around. Maybe I can make it back upstairs without him hearing me.

"You too?" he asks before I have a chance to get away.

"I can't sleep."

"Me neither. Come join me. It will be better if you're here."

"Not a good idea." I can't help but chuckle at his fortitude.

"No, I don't mean that. I'm waiting for him to come home. I'm going to tell him. We need him to know so he can keep us honest."

"What are you going to tell him?" My blood flushes with adrenaline. I walk around the couch so I can easily face him.

"That I'm hot for you, and you seem to be hot for me. And that all I can think about is…"

"What?"

"I can't finish without use of the F word in its literal meaning."

"Please tell me you're not going to say it that way."

"I'm saying it."

"It's going to kill him." Tears collect in my voice. I'm surprised they're more angry than sad. "There has to be a better way."

"He's a big boy. He can handle it. We'll all figure this out together."

We both turn toward the stairs as a light flips on.

"I'm getting tired of finding the two of you alone together." Tara looks even more unhappy than she did before.

"Man, I can't get away with anything in this house with all these psychics lurking around." Christian's smirk seems very out of place next to me, fighting tears.

"That supposed to be funny?"

"Yes, *Trey*, it is. I'm trying to bring some humor into a very distressing situation. You don't know how much you sound like him, do you?"

"What the hell does that have to do with anything?" Her tone unintentionally proves his point.

Christian exhales. "We're down here waiting for him to come home so we can all discuss a major problem that has surfaced." He puts his feet up and crosses his arms behind his head. "Unfortunately, you may have a few more broken doorknobs in the morning. And maybe a double homicide if we get off easy."

CHAPTER 33

TREY

Looks like my waiting has paid off. My man has finally shown. I check the clock for the millionth time, this time knowing the countdown has begun to being in bed next to Liv.

He parks the car I memorized from our first encounter, and I wait for him to get halfway to his front door before I get out of my car. I don't want him to think I'm a carjacker. It's much worse than that.

I follow behind him up the steps to the porch. When he senses me, he starts, and spins around. The alcohol on his breath reminds me of too many sleazy fuckers I've crossed paths with in my life. To my satisfaction, he recognizes me immediately.

"Tara's new boyfriend," he slurs.

I take his keys away from him and hurl them into the street. Is he going to make it this easy? Where's the fun in that?

"Hey." He reaches for the keys that are long gone.

"Brother," I correct before clocking him in the eye. When he straightens up, I realize my mistake and fix it with a second blow. It was the other side. "Is that about right?"

"Fuck you," he mumbles, grabbing the iron railing for support.

"You can if you want, but I guarantee you won't like it." I wait for him to regain his balance. "You're not even going to fight back?"

Please, give me something.

"You done?" he asks. No intention of fighting at all.

"Only a coward hits a woman." I shove him into his front door.

"Some women deserve it."

I twist his arm until it snaps. He screams and falls to his knees. I didn't want to make a scene like this, but with a comment like that, all bets are off.

He slumps against the house and slides down to a squat. "You don't even live here." He pants and holds the arm. "I'll just wait until you leave town. You can't protect her if you're not here." He manages a snicker through the pain of a broken arm.

Scanning the street, I catch too many signs of life. The bad thing about big cities is there are too many witnesses. And I promised her I wouldn't kill him. I pick him up by the throat and slam him against the house. The crack of his skull against the brick is more satisfying than I should admit. He grasps my arm with his good arm in a useless attempt to free himself.

"The beauty of it is, at any given moment you won't know *where* I am."

A door creaks open a few houses down, and I know that's my cue to leave. Someone's probably already called the police. I drop him like a sack of shit and get back in my car. What a letdown.

On the drive back that asshole's words find me again. He's right—I can't protect Tara when I'm not here. He'll have it out for her now. I just bought her more abuse. He's going to use her to get to me.

None of this matters, though. Her new home is in Black River. I can never let her return to Chicago without me.

I don't expect to see the light on in Tara's house in the middle of the night. I grab my paper bag from the music store and glance at my phone as I get out of the car. Surely they'd have called if something happened. The gangway seems like it's a mile long on my way behind the house. I need to fix her doorknob. It's not safe to have only one exit.

Three expectant faces greet me when I enter the living room. I wait, but no one wants to speak. Whatever this is, it better be good if it's keeping me out of bed with Liv. I look from face to face, and on the second round I notice the tears in Liv's eyes.

"What," I demand.

"We all need to talk," Christian says.

"Sit over here." Tara forces me into the chair furthest from everyone.

Sudden heat, a rush of sweat. I take off my jacket.

Christian looks between Tara and Liv. Exhales. "If neither of you are going to say anything then I'm doing it." Liv opens her mouth, but Christian waves his hand to silence her. "Trey, there's something going on between me and Liv."

The words stumble on their way from my ears to my brain. Something going on. Usually, when someone says that phrase, they mean only one thing. I look at Liv.

"Trey, it's not our fault."

"What did you do?" My jaw is so rigid I can barely speak.

"Nothing! We did nothing!" She stands.

"Sit," Tara says.

Liv sits.

"We wanted to do something. Several times. And I still do, right now." Christian's aloofness has me standing fast.

"Wait, wait, wait." Tara presses a hand against my chest. "Hear us out."

"You." I point around Tara at Christian. This is where the words dissolve. Where action takes over when words have failed. I've got Christian's collar. I jerk him up from the couch.

"Calm down!" He shoves me away. My foot catches something on the floor that crinkles upon contact. CDs spill across the floor.

I go for him again but Liv's slid into my way. She's defending him. They've both betrayed me, and now they're ganging up against me.

"Tara, tell him!" Liv says.

I'm crippled just hearing her voice. I look back and forth between the two of them. Tara's talking behind me but I can't hear what she's saying.

"Why?" I ask them. They stand side by side.

"Kate," Christian answers. His mouth moves again but I'm not listening.

This is history repeating itself. He did this with Kate, and now he's done it with Liv.

"Kate did this." Liv has hold of my arm. "Please, Trey. Listen."

My hands rise to my temples, pressing bone. My head is going to explode. I have to get out of here. I shake Liv off and take a few steps back. The hurt in her eyes brands my soul. I force it away. This is her fault. She has done this.

Tara sinks her fingernails into my shoulder, and the words she's been speaking land fast and hard.

"Kate affected them."

"Impossible."

"It's the only explanation."

I stare at her face. Is my twin sister capable of lying to me?

"And it gives her a reason to have come here. Think, Fearghus. The amulet was broken. Liv wasn't wearing it when Kate was here. Liv slapped her. Made contact. The effect passed to her. It makes sense, right? They wouldn't betray you of their own will. They wouldn't."

I spin to face them. Christian nods rapidly in agreement with Tara's explanation, his eyebrows raised, expecting my acceptance. Both Liv's hands cover her mouth under her wide, tear-filled eyes.

"You do agree it's a possibility?" Tara asks beside me, but I remain staring at Liv.

She couldn't do this to me on her own. It's not in her. I've been in her head. I've saved her life; she's saved mine.

Taking my extended gaze as an invitation, Liv rushes forward, throws her arms around me, hugs me so hard I feel the rib fractures like they're new again. I catch Christian's shoulders slump in relief just before I close my eyes and press my lips against her hair.

Only one person is capable of this nightmare. And she was here today. For no other apparent reason.

"She didn't touch Christian. And he's protected."

"It had to have been a dormant effect," Tara says.

"I cleansed him. It would've been cleansed."

"Did you target dormant spells? Didn't think so."

She's right. What I used wouldn't have had any effect on dormant spells. It never occurred to me he could've had one.

"Kate affected Liv today, it triggered Christian's dormant one, done deal," Tara says.

If this is the case, they would've had no control over themselves. I pull Liv away from me to look at her. I wipe her eyes.

"What did you do?" I know I shouldn't ask. I don't want to know the details. I was gone so much. They've had all day. All night.

"Nothing. I swear to you, Trey."

I raise my head to Christian.

"Nothing," he repeats. "You saved us the first time, Winnie the second."

"You almost—?" I can't finish it.

Christian holds up his index finger and thumb with a millimeter of air in between. "This close."

"Nothing?" I ask, unsure how close to what specific act he's referring.

"Nothing. Well, I think she touched my leg. Does that count?"

"Yes." I could punch through his face.

"Okay then, she touched my leg. Other than that, nothing."

"When I came home earlier, that's what was going on?"

"Yes. But due to your excellent timing, we were saved."

I turn back to Liv, holding her away from me. "You lied to me."

Her eyes fill with tears. "I couldn't help it."

"Give her a break, Fearghus. You know how it is." Tara steps forward to take Liv away from me, but I refuse to give her up.

"Did you remove it?" I ask Tara then turn to include Christian.

"Haven't had a chance," Christian replies.

"So it's still in effect?"

"Afraid so." He's picking my scattered CDs off the floor, putting them back in the paper bag.

My stomach turns over with a sickness so intense I feel I need to be cleansed myself. I drop to the couch, bringing Liv down next to me.

"And get this," Tara says, sitting on the arm. "He," she points to Christian, "thought it was real, and he was going to tell you anyway. It took us awhile to figure out they were affected."

Christian raises his fist in the air. "Loyalty."

"Will you let me kill her now?" I ask him.

"No, but I'll let you torture her all you want. And this is a one-time offer. Take it or leave it."

I look down into Liv's eyes. I knew she wasn't herself earlier, but I didn't question it because I had other things on my mind. I left her two times to take care of business for myself. This isn't her fault. It's mine.

"What are we waiting for?" I push to the edge of the seat.

"Tomorrow," Tara says.

"And let this go on overnight? No."

"Tomorrow." The aggression in Tara's voice rises to match mine. "It's tricky with Liv being pregnant, and none of us are in any state to do anything right now. Máthair can help us tomorrow. We shouldn't attempt anything without her."

I stare at her. She's out of her mind. This has to end now.

"You can tie me to my bed," Christian says. "Well, maybe that's a bad idea." He laughs.

"Not funny."

A strange look washes over Liv's face as she understands his joke, and I recognize it as soon as I realize how out of context it is. This look only surfaces when she and I are alone. It belongs to me. I'm not going to make it. This is going to do me in.

"Trey, if you let this get to you, you'll be letting her win," Christian says.

"Don't talk. Anymore."

"Everything will be fine tonight," Tara says. "Just keep her with you. I'm going back to bed. Christian, you should come upstairs with me."

Christian blows a kiss to Liv as he walks by, and it takes every ounce of strength to stop myself from ripping his arm off.

"This is not happening," Liv says after they're both gone. "I'm going to wake up and find out it was all a nightmare."

"It is a nightmare, but it's not going to go away when you wake up." I go into the kitchen and search the cabinets. All I find is one bottle of champagne. Not even any beer in the fridge. This woman is not my sister.

Liv joins me, leans against the door jamb. "How can Kate do this? She's not one of you."

I return the champagne to the cabinet. It's hard to explain Kate's power without taking some of the blame myself. I'm the one who brought her into the family, who taught her enough to make her dangerous. Since then, they've had fifteen years to groom her. And now she's in league with Dillon Moore. "You're right—she's not of our bloodline."

"Then how can she do it? How'd she do what she did to Christian for all those years?"

"She's working with someone. She works with all of them. She's a carrier."

She doesn't answer. Doesn't ask. But I have to tell her.

"A carrier is a normal person who's learned to carry dormant effects and apply them to a third party. Once applied, they become active."

"She learned to do that?"

"Yes."

"How?"

"Once someone makes you a carrier, it's easy to learn."

"Who made her a carrier?" The innocence in her face twists the knife that is my guilt.

"I did."

I am responsible for everything she's done to Christian, everything she's done to Liv. I enabled her, created who she's become. If only I could make it right and end her. I should've done it before she created that baby—that's my slipup, too. From my inaction. My lethargy.

"It's not your fault." She lays a hand on my chest, right over my heart. "How could you have known?"

"It is my fault. I didn't see her for what she was. Let's go to bed."

She doesn't move. "Winnie's in our bed. She wanted to sleep with me. She saved us, just like Christian said."

"He was in our room with you?" This would've never been a problem for me before today.

"Yes, but we were just—" She stops there. She knows not to lie.

I look toward the stairs. He's up there now, and I'm going to have to kill him. I have no choice.

"We were talking, and Winnie came in."

"I'll sleep on the floor." I can't think about this anymore.

Our bed is empty when we enter the bedroom.

"Tara must have taken her back to bed," she says, closing the door and turning on the light.

She gets in bed and sits against the headboard, waiting for me.

"I'm not so much as touching you while you're thinking about him." Somehow, I manage to speak the words.

"I'm not thinking about him. I'm thinking about you."

"Impossible." Even though I know it's not his fault, I fall asleep envisioning colorful ways I could kill him.

In the morning, I wake up on fire with her body woven into mine. Pressing against her out of reflex, I savor her reaction as she moans and nuzzles into my neck. Floodgates open, spilling last night's events, and I push her away. Her wide eyes stare into mine.

"Sorry." I drop eye contact.

"Don't stop," she whispers.

I sit up and get out of bed without looking at her again. I know if I do, the hurt in her eyes will break me. She follows me into the bathroom where I lock the door and get in the shower. I don't need to tell her she's my captive. She sits on the toilet to wait.

When we go into the hall, she stops to look at Christian's open door. I grab the back of her neck, steer her into our bedroom, and slam the door.

"You don't have to be so mean," she says, narrowing her eyes.

"It's for your own good." I put on a T-shirt and jeans then study the floor while she gets dressed. On our way out the door, she steps in front of me.

"One kiss?" She's attached herself to my waist, a belt loop in each hand.

I pry off her fingers. "No."

"Hug?"

"Later."

"Can I hold your hand?"

I don't answer. She takes it as a yes. It's hard to go down the steep stairs holding her hand, but she refuses to let go, and I don't have it in me to reject her again.

Christian's wild smile greets us. I poke him hard in the chest. "Don't give me a reason."

"I'm a *victim* in this," he whines. "Have some sympathy." The facade is broken by an unrestrained grin.

"Everything has to be a joke."

He catches my arm. "Can't you understand how relieved I am that this is reversible?"

I give him a hard look. Decide it's best not to disclose how many different ways I killed him in my dreams.

In the kitchen, Tara and Máthair are funneling a mixture of ingredients into capsules.

"You already did it?" I ask.

"Yes." Máthair squeezes my arm.

"It's similar to the one you used on her for Dillon, but we fixed it to account for the baby this time. And made it *very precisely* targeted to Mr. Christian Moore. Don't have any room for mess-ups here," Tara says. "Liv, you can expect the same process as last time, without the memory loss. This is hers." She hands Liv's capsules to me. "Christian's is different. You hold onto hers and we won't get them mixed up."

I pocket Liv's capsules. "I hope you put something real nasty in his. Are you packed?"

She gives me a long look.

"He's got it out for you now."

"What did you do?" she asks.

"Broke his arm."

"*A Fhearghuis!*" Máthair and Tara say together.

"That's it?" Christian hollers from the other room.

"Two black eyes. I couldn't remember which one. Had to do 'em both."

Tara's a little too close to the kitchen knives to be giving me a look like she is.

"How could you marry a creep like that?" I ask.

"You're one to talk," she snaps.

"We leave tomorrow," I say.

"After my appointment," Liv reminds me.

After breakfast, Tara and I take Liv and Christian upstairs. I sit on the bed next to Liv and watch her take the capsules. When she lowers the glass of water, she smiles sweetly at me. "Can I have a kiss now?"

I can't help but chuckle. This will all be over soon. I recite the words off the page Tara gave me, lay her down on the bed, and leave the room. Tara's closing Christian's door as I'm closing Liv's. I sit on the floor. She stares down at me.

"You can't stay here the whole time."

"Watch me."

"Do you want a book or something?"

"Nope."

She steps over my feet and goes downstairs. Hours pass. I stretch my legs out and study the ceiling. The natural light in the hallway darkens with the setting sun, and I try to remember how long it took Liv to wake up the first time we did this. It didn't seem this long, but I know it doesn't matter. Both the situation and the recipe are different.

Will brings me his trucks for company, one at a time, lining them up in a miniature parking lot against the wall. He then goes up the stairs to the third floor where his room must be. I listen to the muffled sounds of his play through the ceiling while trying to fix a broken wheel on one of his trucks.

An alarm shrieks in my head similar to River's warning call. A breach. I'm on my feet rushing down the stairs before I can think.

"Mama, there's a man outside," Winnie says, clutching the seam of Tara's jeans in her tiny hand.

Tara looks up at me as I burst through the kitchen and out the back door just in time to see a man shouldering through the basement door below me. I leap over the railing and land at his back. Before he can turn, I push him through the open door and close it behind me.

We trade a few punches before I'm able to knock him down. As he flips onto his back on the floor, he pulls a gun and aims it at my forehead.

"Where is she?" he says.

I wipe the blood off my lip with the back of my hand and take a few seconds to catch my breath. They seem to be getting younger. Maybe it's because I'm finally aging.

"Last chance. Where is she?" His teeth are red with blood.

I kick the gun out of his hands. Drop to my knees on top of him. Grasp his head with both hands and slam it against the concrete floor. His eyes roll back into his head. I slam his head a few more times. This is going to make a mess.

I take the stairs two at a time to the second level where both bedroom doors hang open. In Liv's room Christian is running his finger along her neck, another body lying facedown on the floor at their feet.

"She's fine," Christian says, seeing me and stepping aside.

I take her by the shoulders. Analyze her face.

"He tried to cut my throat." Her pupils are huge.

I tilt her head back and examine her neck. She doesn't have a scratch on her.

"And?"

"And I kicked him in the face and then strangled him with your belt." She hands me my belt.

"That's when I got in here," Christian says. "She had him down on his knees. Bastard couldn't get a hold of her."

"Is he dead?" I turn to look at the body.

"I don't think so," she says slowly.

I kneel on his back and twist his head until his neck snaps. When I stand, Liv has buried her face in Christian's chest.

"Chill," he says to me, dropping his arms from around her. "We're both back to normal. See?" He grabs her jaw with both hands and kisses her hard on the lips. He pulls away. "Nothing."

I shove him so hard he slams into the wall behind him.

"You ass!" She wipes her mouth on the back of her hand.

"Don't *ever* do that again," I say in his face.

"Lighten up." He elbows me away, steps over to the window. "This is how he got in?"

"When?" I ask Liv.

"I heard him coming through the window as I was waking up."

"Just now?"

"A few minutes ago, I guess."

There were two. There could be more.

"I guess Kate wasn't lying about that," Christian says.

"Let's get this body in the basement."

"I'll tell Tara to take the kids somewhere first," Liv says.

I watch her leave then return my attention to Christian.

"What?" He laughs hard. He may as well be asking outright for a punch in the mouth. He returns the armchair to its feet then faces me with a sick smile. Like this is all some goddamn joke.

When we hear a stampede ascend the stairs to the third floor, we drag the body to the basement and lay it next to the other one.

"You're going to have to take both of them back to Richmond with you," I say as we head back upstairs.

"Hell no. I'm not putting two bodies in my trunk."

"What do you expect me to do with them?"

"Take them back with you!"

I exhale and give him a look.

"They probably won't even fit in my trunk," he says.

"Are you certain you're back to normal?" I step in front of him.

"I swear on the elements. Every stone. Every tree. That giant oak near the Bevan graveyard. I swear on that fucking thing."

I study his face. Would he lie? He stares me down. I go to the foot of the stairs and call everyone back down. Liv comes first; I study her face as well.

"Don't worry," she says. "It's like it never happened."

The strange look she had in her eyes yesterday is gone. What I assumed was tiredness was actually something unimaginable. I need to pay closer attention to these things.

"I'll arm wrestle you for it," I say to Christian when we join him in the living room.

"Winner takes both bodies?" Little shit. He knows I'd never intentionally lose.

After dinner, I take Liv directly upstairs with me before she has a chance to get comfortable anywhere else. When

I lock the bedroom door and turn around, she's eyeing me with that special look. *My* look.

"Do you want to cuddle?" she says.

"Later." I cup the back of her head and kiss her hard.

She pushes me away. "Trey, wait. I have to ask you something. I've put it off and I shouldn't have. I need to know—don't look at me like that. It's important to me. To us."

I scrub my hands against my hair. More shit to deal with. Nothing to say to stop it.

"That spell—The Alignment—it's what made us fall in love. It wasn't…our choice. How can we trust in that? How do we know it's real?"

That's it? Can't be it. I'm missing something. I need a drink to clear my head.

She looks afraid, like she needs to keep talking to stall my answer. "How do we know it's permanent? Can a love spell—"

"It is permanent."

"You can't just say that. I need to know why. I need proof."

"It's not a love spell. It was an alignment. The spell turned us to face each other. That's all. It didn't change what was in us."

"Then we could unalign. Another spell could do that."

I'm shaking my head. She's shaking hers, parroting me, desperate to believe me.

"It would take a hundred years. That spell was built by generations of my family, piece by piece and put into the night sky to be invoked by one specific arrangement of stars. By the time a new one was created, we'd be long dead."

"Not a love spell."

"Nope. More like we were in the dark, and the spell flipped on the light."

I start nodding. She parrots me again, serious at first. When I grin, so does she. I close in, kiss her again.

She squirms away and ducks under my arm. When I turn around to face her in her new position, the playful look in her eye has me wanting her even more. I reach for her, but she slips away again, this time twisting my arm to spin me away. Two can play at this game.

Laughing and dropping my eyes to throw her off, I wait a moment then seize her around the waist and throw her on the bed. She uses my momentum to pull me down with her, rolling out of the way at the last minute. Before I can react, she twists my arm behind me and takes a seat on my back.

I laugh again into the bed. I taught her too well, and it's coming back to haunt me. Strength is my advantage, but it's completely useless against a natural contortionist.

"Give up?" she whispers in my ear.

"Yes." I turn over and hold onto her so she remains on top of me.

She slides down my body, settling her weight on my hips, her elbows on my shoulders. "I'm so sorry."

"It's not your fault."

"I wish…I wish we could've fixed it sooner. So you didn't have to know."

"It's better that I know."

She sighs and closes her eyes. "Yeah, but I wish we could've spared you. I didn't want to hurt you. Hurting you is like…" She shakes her head and opens her eyes.

"It hurts you more than it hurts me." I take her face in my hands.

"It will haunt me forever." A tear runs down her cheek and drops onto my chest. "I'll never love anyone but you."

"No more secrets. Ever."

"No secrets."

"It's the two of us, against it all."

"The two of us."

"And if you start acting strange again, I'm going to assume it's another spell and bring on the nastiest cleansing effect I can find. Deal?"

"Deal."

She touches her lips to mine. My need for her surges over me like a tsunami, carrying my body for miles before it finally deposits me, drowned and helpless, on a new continent where anger and vengeance do not grow.

I sit up in the dark. I'm still in Tara's house, but I swear I just heard River. The phone rings downstairs. The landline. In the middle of the night? Liv props herself up beside me.

Another ring. And then a high-pitched shriek upstairs.

Liv goes to the duffle bag and I go to the door, catching the gun she tosses on my way out. Tara's rushing up the stairs so I go down and pick up the phone in the kitchen. "Who is it?"

"Trey." My father's voice. "Get everyone out of the house now." He hangs up.

I run up two flights of stairs.

"Scary people in our house! Mama! Too many people!" Winnie has two fists full of Tara's shirt, hanging on while Tara strokes her hair. It's not a nightmare—it's a vision. Those two guys were scouts. Cannon fodder. We're about to be ambushed by the army.

"Tara, get the kids in the car now."

Winnie screams again, scrambles backward on the bed. Her eyes dart all around, seeing the attackers who aren't here but soon will be.

I go to the window and look down at the street. A black utility van cruises by. Too slowly. Stops at the end of the street, turns right.

"Is there an alley behind this house?"

Tara stands with Winnie in her arms. "Yes."

"Out the front. Now!"

Tara thrusts Winnie against me. "I have to get Will!" And she's gone.

I run down a flight and hand Winnie off to Liv. I tug on my jeans and shirt. Jam feet into boots. Grab my keys. I'm heading down the hall when a heavy blow jars the house. I aim my gun down the stairs to the main level, hugging the wall on my way. Another blow. Halfway down I see it's Christian, trying to kick the doorknob out of the front door. That's when I remember it's broken.

On a count of three, we go at it together—him at the knob, me below it, trying to jar it loose. We're kicking from the wrong side. It doesn't budge.

We're out of time. That van's unloading now, men surrounding the house. Máthair comes down the stairs. Tara and Will. Liv and Winnie. We stand in a cluster. Christian braces a hand against the wall, bows his head to breathe, to think. I squat to tie my boots.

Winnie says, "Mama—"

I hold a finger to my lips. My pulse beats fast and heavy in my head. There's a slow creak somewhere below us. Then a shuffling. I'm at a disadvantage here. Unfamiliar territory. No home advantage. If it was just me, I'd have this. There are too many of us.

Christian picks up a lamp and smashes it through the front window.

Will covers his ears and Winnie screams, fighting Liv's arms until her feet settle on the floor. She runs to the back of the house, Liv on her heels. Christian's helping Máthair through the window frame and I push Tara and Will toward him. The window on the side of the house blows out.

I swivel and aim my gun at the side window but glance down the hall at Liv. She's caught Winnie—she has her on her hip. But she's not coming forward because two men just entered that side window and they're in between us.

They can't see her, but they can see me. "Hands in the air," I say.

In the corner of my eye, I see Liv zip Winnie's lips closed with her fingers. I see her look quickly at the basement door. I see her backing up. Just before she's out of my sight, she gives me a composed nod. Holds up one hand and presses it downward. *Steady. I've got this.*

I turn to my left and start shooting foreheads. More bodies pour through the window. They're crawling and falling and I'm almost out of ammo. Christian whistles— he's gotten everyone out.

Except Liv. Except Winnie.

That's when the second team bursts through the basement door. It's a frenzy of insects, a charging mass. There's no choice but to turn around, away from Liv, severing the possibility of helping her and Winnie. The action fills me with a white-hot pain, a hundred bullet holes. I jump through the front window frame. Tara's CR-V peels away from the curb.

Christian's at my car. "Let's go!"

I toss him my keys. I run around the side of the house. It swarms with men. I run to the other side. More men.

The Camaro's engine starts up. Revs. They're coming at me, too many at once. I scale the porch. The gutter breaks off the house with my weight, but I get a last-second grab and haul myself onto the roof. Two guys follow me up, one on each end. I wait in the middle. They try to take me at once. I duck two fists, jab one guy in the nose and use the other to knock him off the roof. Two bodies hit the ground. I kick out Tara's bedroom window and climb through jagged glass.

Inside, I wipe bloody hands on my jeans. Footsteps thunder up the stairs. I need to get to the duffle bag of guns in my room. I'll need that advantage. They won't be armed; they don't want the noise of gunshots bringing the police, leaving a big mess to clean up. But it's too late for that. I already unloaded my gun downstairs.

I meet the first guy in the doorway. He goes straight for the ribs, almost like he knows. I take it hard, fall into the wall. Two guys enter behind him. I lure them over to Tara's nightstand and smash her alarm clock over a head. When he's down, I stomp his neck. A mistake—I take a hard hit to the jaw and see stars. I take another to the temple. Another to the ribs and I'm eating floor.

A foot comes at me but I grab it and twist before it makes contact. He goes down. I roll to the nightstand, tear out a drawer. Bash it over the next guy. He deflects it with his shoulder. I take a blow from behind that I didn't see coming and I'm down again. Instead of getting up, I charge knees. The first goes down. The second gets me in a waist lock. I haven't even made it out of one room. Screw the guns. I need to get downstairs, to Liv. To follow her, through the only escape she had—the back kitchen door. Just about the furthest point in the house from here.

But I've been hauled to my feet, arms pinned behind me, and the biggest guy in the room is stepping forward. They've spotted my weakness. If I take any more hits to the ribs I won't be around to find Liv. If they've caught her, I won't be alive to save her. If they've killed her, I won't be able to hunt every one of them down and make them bleed.

I slam my head back into a nose. Head butt the big guy who just lost his chance of breaking my ribs. He recovers, so I head butt him again, hook my arm around his neck and slam his face into my knee. I go into the hall. A second wave is pounding up the stairs. My legs give and I stumble, bracing against the wall to stay on my feet. There's a fuzzy hum in my head. I shake it hard, see blood splatter the wall. I take a step back but end up on my knees. There's no way to win here. Liv had it handled. I have to trust she'd get the hell out and run. I can't get myself killed going after a woman and child who are long gone.

I retreat, back to the bedroom, out through the window I entered. With no easy way down, I jump, roll upon landing.

The Camaro's heading up the street. It screeches to a halt. I'm halfway in the car when Christian pulls away. I should've stayed back there, let them break all my bones, stomp my face, rip out my heart. It would feel better than this.

We catch up to Tara's CR-V and drive the surrounding neighborhood for two hours. No sign of Liv and Winnie. No one has a phone and we're sure Liv doesn't either. Three times I've gotten out of the car to go back there. Three times they've talked me out of it. Christian remains optimistic. Máthair's showing her usual quiet calm. Tara's about to crack. When we pull into a gas station so he can take over the wheel of Tara's CR-V, I tell them this time, I *am* going back. Alone.

That's when Tara has one last idea. "Liv's old house. It's a long walk, but she could do it in the time we've been looking. She knows I know where it is."

My heart's in my throat the whole way there. When my headlights sweep over a figure cradling a child on the front stoop, I know it can't be Liv. My life doesn't work that way.

Tara bursts out of the CR-V ahead of me. Bare feet running across pavement then grass and she's scooping up that child from that woman's arms and hugging the child so tightly I'm propelled from my car. The woman on the stoop stands. The motion sparks a recognition so deep, I have to brace myself against the car to offset a sudden weakness in my knees.

She comes toward me. Then she's in my arms. And again, I wish myself back to that house. Being beaten to death by a mob seems a more humane way to go than being pummeled by relief this profound.

My life works this way now, because of her. She's healed a lifetime of atrophy. She's my antidote to the Moores; she lifts the weight they load on me. She gives me power to fight them.

LIV

Months have passed since Tara and her children moved permanently into my house on the bluff. With so few attacks from the Moores to mark the passing days, the time blurs together into a shorter length in my mind. The only evidence of passing time is my expanding belly, enlarged to a size beyond belief.

We decided to stay in Trey's house and give mine to Tara. That house never felt like mine, and she'll make immediate use of the extra bedroom and finished basement. We won't need another bedroom for a while if we do at all. This baby isn't going to leave my arms. Once she's here, I'm never going to let her go.

Every day I wake up thinking this will be the day they finally send the army. My fears worsen with each approaching night until I'm out of bed, alone in the kitchen, as sleepless as I used to be. Only this time, it's not only insomnia. The night shakes have become more regular. If Trey knows, he hasn't let on.

To pass the time when I can't sleep, I've started unpacking the boxes from my Chicago house. Trey moved them to the basement where he expected I'd forget about them. I agree with him—I shouldn't mix my old life with my new, but there's something in there I'm missing, and I won't know until I find it.

Trey's confidence in Winnie's visions has relaxed his obsession with our safety, although it doesn't hinder the occasional phone calls in the middle of the night to check on Tara and the kids just because he has a bad feeling. All it took was Winnie's prediction of one sniper, and his trust in her was sealed. Being Trey, he can't rely on one safeguard alone. River and Trib have run a permanent path between the houses from the number of scouting missions he demands of them. And I've learned to listen to the animals, especially the birds. If they're screeching across the forest, I run to get Trey so he can translate. Every creature in these woods has his back.

As an answer to the lack of action, Trey has begun training Will and Winnie with simple survival skills like navigation and plant identification, and low impact martial arts. The children, especially Will, have taken to it with enthusiasm. Trey's patience surprised me at first, until I realized it's not patience that drives him. It's determination. He's training them like he was trained. But instead of becoming Moore-trained killers, they'll be Bevan-trained defenders. Just like him.

My hope they'll never need that training is boxed up inside me. I want to unpack it, to let it breathe in the air we've been breathing now that people don't seem to want to kill us every other day. I can't assume something is building just because it feels that way.

"You are enormous," Trey says, helping me out of his truck in Tara's driveway.

Unfortunately, I have nothing to stab him with.

"And beautiful."

"Nice save."

"It's no save. Both are true."

"I'd stop talking if I were you."

Winnie runs into my legs, chattering about the new sprouts from whatever plant she and Will are growing. The kids' fascination with nature in these mountains was the single reason Tara decided to move here for good. She couldn't tear the kids away.

I follow Winnie; Trey goes in the house. Summer in Montana is supposed to be mild, but my overheated body has skewed that idea. Before long I'm sweating, so I untangle myself from the kids and go inside.

Shawn's boisterous voice greets me before I enter the room. I'm not proud to admit I introduced Shawn to Tara out of spite against Trey, but had I known the connection they'd make I would've done it sooner. To Trey's continued disgust, Shawn doesn't appear to be going anywhere soon. Sometimes I wonder if Tara likes Shawn so much because she knows Trey doesn't.

"My first love," Shawn says as soon as he sees me. He wraps his arm around my shoulders and kisses my temple.

Trey's empty water glass settles too hard onto the counter, and Tara gives him a strained look.

I'm not sure how much longer we can keep our secrets from Shawn. I'm surprised he hasn't noticed he's dating a witch. Whose daughter sees visions of the future. Whose brother leaves enemy corpses in the woods for his coyote friends to dispose of. Maybe he has, and he's just keeping it to himself. It's just like him to respect our privacy even though he's becoming one of us more each day.

"I've got to run." Shawn gives Tara a peck on the lips.

Trey's already hard face transforms to a nasty glare.

"Gorgeous," Shawn says before he kisses my cheek. "Oh, you smell so good."

Tara meets my eye and tries hard not smile as the front door shuts behind Shawn on his way out.

"You really need to lighten up," Tara says to Trey.

"Hey, if you're okay with your boyfriend flirting with another woman, it's your business."

"He does that all for you. You make it so easy for him to taunt you."

Trey cracks his knuckles. "As soon as you're ready to get rid of him, just say the words."

"I plan on marrying him and having at least five of his babies. And I'll be sure to tell him you liked his donuts."

Trey stops chewing.

Winnie and Will burst through the back door, ruddy-faced and breathless.

Winnie tugs Tara's shirt. "Mama, can I sleep with Seanmháthair when she comes?"

"Seanmháthair won't be able to visit for a while," Tara says.

Winnie focuses far away for a moment then returns her eyes to her mother. "Is the bad man going to hurt Seanmháthair?"

"Who, sweetheart?"

Winnie wrings the hem of her dress. "A bad man."

"What does he look like?" Tara squats down to Winnie's level.

"He looks like Uncle Christian. But Uncle Christian is nice."

"Uncle Christian," Tara repeats, looking up at Trey. "Could they have gotten to him again?"

Before Trey can answer, Winnie speaks again. "He has a line right here." She points to her eyebrow.

"Dillon has a scar in his eyebrow," I think aloud. "And he looks a lot like Christian."

Things are much easier now that I've learned to be direct and honest with Trey, no matter what. I've given up trying to control his temper with carefully chosen words and roundabout truths. My purpose before was to protect him, but I learned a tough lesson that my attempts to protect him can so easily cross over the line to betrayal—and a threat to our safety.

"He does," Trey agrees. Trey must know the placement of every hair on Dillon's head after how closely he studied him in divorce court. He goes for his phone but pauses mid-dial. "Christian just left for Vegas. And my dad's still in Europe."

"I don't like that man at all." Winnie gives one desperate look at Trey before burying her face against Tara's leg to cry.

Trey watches Tara comfort Winnie, but then there's a shift, like he's detached from the room, and instead of watching them he's staring through them. His breath deepens, slows. He gets all too still. The calm before the storm.

"I can be back in four days."

He can't go back to that house. What is he thinking?

"Liv, you'll stay in this house with Tara until I'm back. They could be baiting me there to get you alone."

"They could be baiting you there to kill you. You can't go."

"I have to go. I shouldn't have waited for a reason. This is long overdue."

Tara raises her palms to him. "Fearghus, wait. Christian, he can—"

"This isn't Christian's fight. Liv, let's go." He heads toward the front door.

"He's crazy," I say to Tara.

"There's nothing we can do," she mumbles in a voice so helpless it doesn't sound like her. "He's already made up his mind."

I know she's right. My fear, night after night of it, assembles into a hard knot in my chest. This is what's been building. We've been spared for months to give them time to collect an army to take him down. Unable to speak on the drive back to our house, I gaze out the window in a trance. He'll be walking into a trap. They'll finally have him, then they'll come after me. They won't stop at me. Tara and her kids will be next.

"Pack a bag," he says when we arrive at the house.

I numbly pack a bag for four days at Tara's. There has to be a way to make him stay, but I doubt I'll have time to find it. This could be my last day with him. Should I really spend it trying to come up with a plan that doesn't exist?

I drop my bag at the front door and find him coming in through the back door.

"River and Trib are on high alert. Listen to Winnie. Keep a weapon with you at all times. Call me if you see anything suspicious. If it gets bad, put everyone in the car and leave town."

"This is reckless and stupid. You can't go."

"Four days. Everything will be fine."

"Give it a day. We can come up with something."

"Do not worry and stress yourself out. Do you hear me?"

I shake my head. What he's asking is impossible.

"Damn it, Liv. You're making something out of nothing. This is an easy job. They won't even know I'm there. Once he's dead, I'll come straight home."

"I can't live without you."

"You'll only have to live without me for four days."

He rushes into the basement. He has no idea what he'll be walking into. He is only one man, and there are so many of them. I'd demand to go with him so we could die together, but not with Sloane inside me. I'm stuck.

"I'll come with you and stay in a hotel," I say when he comes back upstairs with a heavy duffle bag.

He doesn't even look at me. "Tara needs you here to protect them. Keep a loaded rifle on hand. Don't let anyone get too close to the house."

"Trey—"

"Let's go." He heads for the door.

He throws my bag over his shoulder, picks up his two bags, and walks out to the car. I stand frozen in the open front door. This can't be happening. He knows this is a blatant trap. And he's going to storm in there anyway.

"Liv!" he hollers from the car. He raises his hand to shield his eyes from the light.

When I don't move, he crosses the yard to get me himself. We're back at Tara's in a heartbeat. Our daughter will never know her father. Just like he never knew his. Just like I never knew mine. There are so many tragedies at play here, and he doesn't see any of them.

He opens my door, unbuckles my seatbelt, and pulls me out of the car. Tara opens her front door, and he pushes me inside and drops my bag at our feet.

"Call us every hour," Tara says.

So we know when you're dead, I finish for her in my mind.

He nods to her and turns away.

"Trey." I grab his shirt.

He hugs me against him. "Don't worry."

"Don't leave me," I manage to choke against his chest.

He holds me out to see my face. "I would never leave you. I'll be right back. I promise."

Gravel sprays as he peels away, and I stand immobilized in the doorway with the heat of the summer on my front and the cool, still air of the house on my back until the sound of his screeching tires hitting the main road travels up the driveway and into my waiting ears.

In the silence that follows, I remember exactly what's missing. What I've forgotten. And I know right where to find it.

ACKNOWLEDGMENTS

My thanks go to—

Robyn, for her unconditional support of my book even before she read it.

Karen, for reading (again!) and helping me when my confidence in this book was at its lowest.

Clay, someone I should have thanked in the first book. Praise from a stranger means so much.

Pam Schuster, for sharing your knowledge (again!) to help me make this fantasy world sound and believable.

My team: editor Jennifer Wingard, photographer Keith Lee, and the artists at DamonZa.com, for all your talent and patience.

All my family and friends, for the help and support that ease my overloaded days so this imaginary world has room to remain alive in my head. And for your confidence in me, which keeps me writing and publishing.

My readers, for spending your valuable time with my books. I used to write for myself. Now I write for you.

the
ALIGNMENT SERIES

The Alignment

The Two

The Oak and the Moon

The Catalyst

The Warrior

VISIT KAYCAMDEN.COM FOR MORE